ORGANIZED CRIMES

ORGANIZED
CRIMES

Nicholas von Hoffman

HARPER & ROW, PUBLISHERS, *New York*
Cambridge, Philadelphia, San Francisco, London
Mexico City, São Paulo, Singapore, Sydney

1817

Grateful acknowledgment is made for permission to reprint the following:

Lyrics from "Big Bad Bill (Is Sweet William Now)" by Milton Ager and Jack Yellen, ©
1924 (renewed) Warner Bros. Inc. Lyrics from "Let's Do It (Let's Fall in Love)" by Cole
Porter, © 1928 (renewed) Warner Bros. Inc. Lyrics from "Night and Day" by Cole Porter,
© 1932 (renewed) Warner Bros. Inc. Lyrics from "You're the Top" by Cole Porter, © 1934
(renewed) Warner Bros. Inc. All rights reserved. Used by permission.

Lines from "In a Coffee Pot" by Alfred Hayes from *The Big Time* by Alfred Hayes
(Howell/Soskin, 1944). Reprinted by permission of the author.

FIRST EDITION

Designer: Sidney Feinberg

Library of Congress Cataloging in Publication Data
Von Hoffman, Nicholas.
  Organized crimes.
  I. Title.
PS3572.O46O7   1984   813'.54   84-47605
ISBN 0-06-015049-1

84 85 86 87 88 10 9 8 7 6 5 4 3 2 1

To Virginia Barber,
Susan Dooley,
and
Ted Solotaroff

Every poet has his hell. Dante had
Florence and I have Chicago.

EDGAR LEE MASTERS

ORGANIZED CRIMES

Chapter 1

Allan saw a crowd down the alley behind the McVickers Theatre on Madison, near State Street. Not a big gathering, fifteen or twenty men looking up at an old man on a platform of the theater fire escape. As Allan's curiosity brought him down the alley, he could see that the old man had a sea chest or footlocker up there with him. Next to the footlocker were several large sheets of corrugated cardboard, which he had been using as a mattress.

"Look, buddy," a man in a Chicago fire marshal's uniform called up to the platform, "if it was up to me, you could live there the rest of your life, but you're a fire hazard. I mean you're creating one. I mean if there was a fire in the theater you'd block the exit. You're an obstacle."

"I don't want to be an obstacle, but where am I gonna go? I got no place. I got no money. If you throw me outa here, I gotta go over to Skid Row and the jackrollers'll get my chest."

Allan had never met a homeless man. He knew there were more such people than there used to be since Black Friday last year when the Market crashed. But Allan had not been aware of the silence that had taken over the Loop. The hammering had stopped. A year ago new skyscrapers were under construction all over town; now they could be seen, half finished, abandoned as though a plague had taken off the high-iron men and the cement trucks.

"They'll get my chest," the old man said. "It's got my recipes and my menus. I been a hotel chef for forty years. A first-class chef in a first-class place, he's gotta have his recipes and his menus. I worked the Bismarck and the Sherman House. I worked the best."

"You have to get off there, buddy," the fire marshal repeated.

"If there was jobs, which there ain't, I'm too old to get one," the

1

ex-chef said, moving around the platform. It was his stage and this was the only audience he would have. Allan went through his pockets for pencil and paper to take notes. In the process he dropped his copy of Ernst Troeltsch's *The Social Teachings of the Christian Church.*

"They tell me now I'm even too old for dishwashing—that's the whole story of it. I got no friends and my money's gone. Will you help me get the sea chest down? Maybe there's a place I could keep it?"

Allan began to write down all the ex-chef cared to say. He was trying to sharpen his perspicacity. His favorite professor at the University of Chicago, Robert Park, had told Allan that he was an intelligent young man with closed eyes. Allan was working at getting them open, but it was hard to satisfy Mr. Park. Around the seminar table, whenever Allan or some of the other graduate students ventured an opinion, they risked having Mr. Park look at them owl-eyed and inquire, "Vas you dere, Cholly?" a tag line made famous by a vaudeville comedian on the Keith Orpheum circuit in Mr. Park's youth.

"The past is a turned-over page," the old man on the fire escape unaccountably declaimed. Allan recorded the words. The unemployed were a big thing: "significant," "important"—words like that were used to describe them. You read about them every day. They were reported to be sheltering themselves on the underground level of Wacker Drive, the doubledecker roadway that the Mayor, William Hale ("Big Bill the Builder") Thompson, had constructed along the banks of the Chicago River.

The fire marshal helped the old man down the stairs with his sea chest and Allan went on his way toward the Illinois Central Station, where he took the train down to the university on the days he did not feel like driving. The unemployed were soon displaced in Allan's head by what the *Chicago Tribune* was calling "the bridge battle of the century, the 150-rubber series pitting Mr. and Mrs. Ely Culbertson and their systems of approach against long-time leader of the bridge world Mr. Sidney Lenz and his partner, the exciting young player Oswald Jacoby."

A man came out of a cigar store in front of Allan and walked in the same direction on Randolph Street toward the public library and the entrance to the Illinois Central Station. A homburg in a sea of fedoras. Later Allan would try to remember when he first cut the man out of the crowd and saw him as a person apart. It might have been as they came abreast of the public library. Allan would never be able to reconstruct these details to his satisfaction.

2

"I got him" or "I got it" or "You get him" or "Did you get him?" The man had shouted something like that to two men in a roadster idling by the stairs at the corner of Michigan and Randolph, stairs leading to the underpass. Afterward, he could not decide if he'd heard the words from the man or heard the words later from people who had heard the man. He was sure, though, he had seen the man stop at the newspaper stand at the top of the stairs and buy a racing form. He remembered noticing the racing form's masthead, so different from regular newspapers. That would fit in with the words the man may have spoken to the occupants of the roadster. If they had shouted something like, "Ya got Big Nose in the fifth?" it would have been logical for him to answer, "I got him."

The underpass was almost empty so Allan could see that two other men, one on each side, were now walking next to Mr. Racing Form. They hadn't been there and then they were there. What registered on Allan was how close the three were to each other. Almost as though Mr. Racing Form had been stricken and they were propping him up.

Then the man on Mr. Racing Form's right side veered away and vanished. As he was doing so the gun's *pop* reverberated in the tunnel. Try as Allan would in the coming months, he could never work it out, whether he had seen the weapon or not. The murder, though, had a surgical quality about it that was unusual in that era of carmine-splotched men found and photographed in the trunks of cars. The killer, using a small-caliber gun, put it to the base of his victim's skull. Not in keeping with Chicago's reputation as a big-caliber town. Thick steaks and big round revolvers. The gesture of bringing the little gun to the neck was done in a way that made it look as though the murderer was throwing an arm around a pal. Mr. Racing Form fell forward on his face and looked as dead as he was.

In the instant that it took Allan to accept what he saw, the murderer took off in a broken-field run through the people in the tunnel going toward the trains and the ticket booths. Allan had seen dead bodies before, but he had never seen a body become dead, and certainly not that way. It slows the reflexes. No one gave chase; no one understood what had happened soon enough, but, as suddenly as the *pop* had popped, there came the murderer again, gun still in hand, running with violent exertion back past Allan and the body. This time Allan, without thinking he was pursuing an armed man, started after him when—*smack!*

"Hey, sorry, fella," a voice said, a runt-stump of a man, a chunk of a human being, fat but hard. Allan moved to go around him and the man, apparently trying to get out of Allan's way, moved in the same direction so that they bumped again. Allan could see the murderer on the first step back up to Randolph Street. Taking the man by the shoulders, he was in the act of shoving him aside, but the runt-stump man, who gave off a reek of odoriferous sweat and alcohol, did not shove. A third time they tangled in a confusion of "sorry fella"'s and "beg pardon"'s before Allan successfully got around the man's side.

As he ran down the tunnel after the now disappeared murderer, Allan's memory recorded fragments of the runt-stump man. A vile red complexion and a Roman collar. Had the man been dressed in black? Was he a priest or somebody dressed like one?

The killer had gone. A pair of gray gloves he probably wore were found in the alley behind the public library; the gun, dropped in a sidewalk waste container, was reported to the authorities by a garbage man a day later. Its provenance was never established. Allan got up to street level, saw no one to chase, and asked the newsstand man from whom Mr. Racing Form had bought his tout sheet if he had seen anyone. The man replied he saw at least twenty anyones every minute, so Allan went back down the stairs.

The Social Teachings of the Christian Church was on the pavement where Allan had dropped it. Allan picked up his book and got out his pencil and notebook again. More practice, more training in the science of seeing what is happening around one. Mr. Park liked to say a good field observer made sure he knew what he knew.

The authorities were now coming down the underpass to the corpse, some running, some ambling, some with a smiling, officious swagger. The varieties and gradations of functionaries were unknown to Allan. Until the talkies, American young people, with no more reliable sources of information than Nick Carter detective stories, did not have a close understanding of how police departments were run. The great gangster movies were still being lived; they had not yet begun to be made. Even the cops did not know how cops behaved. They hadn't been to the movies either, so they did not know the correct behavior for a plainclothesman on a crowded murder site.

Milling around, they boomed out unheeded, contradictory orders to each other; and the public, pressing to see, was pushed aside by a hierarchy of ever more important persons grunting, "Lemme through.

4

Lemme through, goddammit." Once the lemme's did get through, they stood looking at the dead person, doing nothing.

Allan held his position in the front row. This was better than an unemployed cook on a fire escape. The circle was now being pushed back to accommodate the men with stretchers, medical bags, yardsticks, chalks, and cameras. The cameras were big, noisy machines, Speed Graphics, into which their operators slammed metal-framed glass plates. When detonated, the cameras exploded light. To Allan, watching the photographers aim their instruments, fire them off, and litter the area with spent flashbulbs and film plate wrappings, it seemed like more noise was made taking the dead man's picture than shooting him. "Hey! Hey! Hey!" a voice shouted. "Don't move the body until we get a picture of McNamara pointing at it. . . . Mac, come on over and stand here." Mac was a full captain of uniformed police with more gold on his blue uniform than an admiral has on his.

A sergeant with a brogue was shouting, "Is there anyone here who might've seen the crime?" Allan and one or two others called out, but the sergeant was distracted by his superiors, all of whom were simultaneously in charge and all of whom agreed it was time to turn the body and look at the face of the deceased. Allan now had to crane over shoulders, but he did see the small irregular red circle where skull and neck meet and then, as they rolled the dead man over, he saw his cigar, wet-ended and chewed, adhering to his cheek. But what Allan was staring at was the man's belt. It was studded in diamonds in a double-diamond pattern. Fancy, indeed.

"Holy shit!" rang out. "It's Jake! . . . Jesus, Jake Lingle . . . from the *Tribune!*"

Allan knew the names of the city's prominent people. Hack Wilson, the home-run hitter on the Cubs; Cardinal Mundelein; Al Capone; Isham Randolph, the owner of the title of "civic leader"; Col. Robert R. McCormick, editor and publisher of the aforesaid *Chicago Tribune,* the brass trumpet of Republican orthodoxy, which styled itself The World's Greatest Newspaper. If one of them had been shot Allan would have cried out too, but who was Jake Lingle?

Allan learned who Jake Lingle was as he held his position in the shoving, questioning, and shouting crowd clogging the passageway. Jake Lingle was a reporter for The World's Greatest Newspaper. Now the shooting was truly a crime. You do not shoot reporters any more than you shoot ministers. Reporters were the protectors of the people; they were special protectors whom you could go to for justice when

5

police and law courts failed. That's why newspapers were called *Tribunes*, *Heralds*, *Vindicators*, *Examiners*, and *Inquirers*.

The last Allan saw of Jake Lingle was a white buckskin and brown leather sport shoe, the one visible part of the people's tribune coming out from the cloth laid over his body.

They shoot everybody, he thought. They shoot people on the streets, they shoot horses in the park. Allan remembered the execution of Blue Boy in Lincoln Park. It had happened when he was in prep school, the years when the daily civic life of Chicago was limned by gunfire. For him, though, Blue Boy's death was more memorable and more moving than the St. Valentine's Day Massacre.

Oh, unhappy Blue Boy fated to be rented by the stable to carry the notable nonequestrian Nails Morton for a morning canter so that the celebrated gangster could draw the fresh air of Lake Michigan into his cigar-corroded lungs. Nails was the brute, Blue Boy the civilized spirit who grunted and arched and whinnied and stared out of pained and panic-globed eyes as his rider beat him and beat him. The riding crop rose and fell, rose and fell while the animal took small backward steps in a confused and tortured circle that made Nails whip him the more.

Five thousand people went to Nails's funeral, but in the northern suburbs and on the Gold Coast where the rich Anglo-Saxons lived, Blue Boy was recognized as a public benefactor, more efficacious in justice than the police or the State's Attorney's office or the courts. Bloodied Blue Boy, who rose up and threw his rider the way bloodied Chicago couldn't and stamped him to death. Goodbye, Nails, you bullying bastard. But five thousand people turned out to say so long, pal.

In the pressroom of City Hall there was speculation that Blue Boy's name would be tacked up on Dead Man's Tree, that large, stinky, female ginkgo grown up between the sidewalk cracks at Taylor and Loomis where the Moustachios from Sicily used to post the name of the soon-to-be-departed. Afterward, a serious Two-Gun Louis Alterie had told inquirers, "We don't put the names of no fuckin' horses on the tree. You pricks wouldn't ast the question if ya had respect for human dignity."

That did not make the account in the *Tribune* with the picture of Blue Boy which the fourteen-year-old Allan read and grieved over. The article told how Louis had called the stables, arranged to rent Blue Boy, walked him into Lincoln Park with a crowd of Nails's other friends, all Deeny O'Banion's people—not one of them dared ride the horse—and when they reached the place where Morton had been killed, each took out his revolver and fired a big bullet into Blue Boy's head.

"We learned that goddamned horse of yours a lesson," Louis is supposed to have said on the phone to the stable. "If you want your saddle, go get it." Al Capone, interviewed at his Metropole Hotel offices in his boardroom under the portraits of Washington, Lincoln, and Big Bill Thompson, pronounced it a "cheap shot" and then broke up laughing. "Ya get it? Cheap shot, ya get it?"

All shots were cheap, which was why so many were fired and so many people were killed. Too many for young Allan to focus on. Within two years most of Blue Boy's executioners were dead. They blew the abdomen out of Deeny in the flower shop he operated as a front, hard by Holy Name Cathedral; that one was so good it was used in a lot of the gangster movies. But most of the murdered, hundreds of them, were found in drab locations. Allan, the boy, focused on their killing of animals. After Blue Boy, the State Police stopped Dingbat O'Berta, who was really a Guinea with an inexplicable shine to put an Irish O' at the start of his name, and when they checked out the back of his eight-cylinder Duesenberg for what they thought would be whiskey, they found three hundred or so doves, shotgunned to earth and dumped, bloody feathered, on the leather upholstery and in the trunk.

Allan, the young man, was now focusing on the killing of a reporter. He had to talk to somebody about it and the closest person was his father, a few blocks away in "the counting house," as the family called the Great Lakes National Bank, over which Elting Archibald presided in one of the most splendid of the cast brass and marble skyscrapers. La Salle Street held the palaces of commerce— Adler and Sullivan's Stock Exchange, Burnham and Root's office building, the Rookery—structures of lushly exciting and fluid design. Chicago had the nation's worst gangsters and best architecture.

On the city's North Shore, where Allan's family lived, they said of his parents, "She's a Fenwick; they have the money and he has the looks." Elting Archibald's wife and his brother-in-law had the kind of money it was impossible to make as president of a bank, even a big bank like Great Lakes National. Mr. Archibald had come to settle for being very social and civic and very Presbyterian. He had worked at his job and at keeping his figure, but he could eat anything and not gain weight; at the bank, too, it wouldn't have mattered; he was one of those brothers-in-law who become president whatever they do.

On some Sundays he went to church in Winnetka and afterward had the chauffeur drive him downtown to the Loop so that he could attend the Sunday Evening Club, where hundreds of the city's most pious Protestant businessmen and their families would come together for fellowship and to hear a sermon by one of the country's outstanding preachers. In those pre-airplane days, freighting in a minister from Los Angeles or Mobile, Alabama, was a sign of the most affluent devotion.

On other days he would go to meetings of the board of the Art Institute and the Field Museum. He liked being on boards, liked the feeling that he was a figure to be reckoned with. He contrasted himself to his brother-in-law, who refused to take a role in the city's life, though he had been shamed onto the board of trustees at the University of Chicago. Fenwick was not a figure to be reckoned with; he wasn't social, he wasn't civic. What Fenwick was was two bulging eyes, floating on the green seas of commerce, enormous scaly body concealed, waiting unnoticed for what he wanted. When he saw what he wanted, there would be a quick and terrible movement of whitened water and then the two bulgy eyes would be quietly floating once more.

"Dad, I think I could recognize the murderer if I saw him again," Allan told his father. "I'm sure I could."

"They never solve these crimes. I think President Hoover should send the Marines to Chicago. Clean this city up. Forceful measures."

"I could go over to police headquarters and give them my name in case they do catch someone, Dad."

"Give them your name? Well, that's an idea, isn't it? Give them your name so it might be in the papers. Allan, it's going to take more than that. It's going to take a full-scale mobilization of the community. Like 1917."

Allan had noted that whenever there was a big problem—whether gangsters or this incredible drop in business—his father and his father's friends would talk about mobilizing like 1917. It seemed to be the all-purpose answer. Allan himself was too young to remember anything about 1917 but the parades and the songs.

"I could ask them to keep my name out of the papers, Dad."

"We need a full-scale committee to stamp out crime. Something full-scale. Representing all segments: meat packing, steel, light manufacturing, something across the board. You might want to talk to the people on the Chicago Crime Commission. I'm on the board, Allan.''

"That one too?"

"I have to go, Allan. I have an appointment with Sam Insull.''

"I thought you didn't like him, Dad.''

"This is business. Don't repeat this, Allan, but I think he wants to—I should say needs to borrow a lot of money. From what I hear he is being squeezed . . . by the East, by Wall Street . . . by Morgan.''

Sam Insull was a major annoyance to Elting Archibald. Sam had as much money as Elting's brother-in-law but *he* was social and civic. He was the biggest figure in the city, the power behind the symphony and the opera. Not only on every important board, committee, and commission but always the chairman. He was a national figure, which irked Allan's father, who took time and care trying to make remarks that would cut the pretentious little Englishman down to size. But Sam Insull was not an easy target, and Chicago was a city of first-time winners. The fanciest names in town, the Potter Palmers, the McCormicks, the Armours, hardly went back more than sixty years. As for Insull's pretensions, they were modest alongside those of someone like Mrs. Potter Palmer, who was said to have built her French chateau on Michigan Avenue without a doorknob in any of the fifty rooms so that her footmen would see to people getting in and out. As a boy, Allan had wondered how Mrs. Palmer's footmen were able to open the doors.

Gladys, Sam's wife, had made something of a jerk of herself by leasing an entire theater and staging a play in which her fifty-six-year-old self starred as an eighteen-year-old ingenue. It went on every night for two weeks. That it was for the benefit of St. Luke's Hospital made it all right, and the newspapers loved it. But the publicity added to the sneers and disdain of people like Elting, who thought of himself as old money, though his father still plowed the land behind two horses on a farm outside of Galena, Illinois.

Elting's brother-in-law may have been as rich as Sam Insull but he was secretive about it. Sam made money by the hundred-gallon barrel and let everyone know. If you had asked anyone in Chicago how much Sam Insull made last year, they would have been able to tell you that it was $150 million. "My God!" he was supposed to have said, in astonishment at his own riches and in departure from his strict Methodist principles about the use of the name of that denomination's divinity. "You know what I am goin' to do? I'm goin' to buy us an

9

ocean liner!" He was supposed to have said this in a cockney accent, but Sam was more American than those native Chicagoans with aristocratic ambitions. Sam courted the popularity of the masses. If the opera, with its blue-blood associations, was his favorite charity, he found a way to democratize it. He made the succession of great-voiced divas popular heroines at the same time that he cut many an ordinary Chicagoan in on the money. Tens of thousands of people got—not rich, but less poor buying stock in Samuel Insull's utility companies. These were the people who would never have gone into a stockbroker's office with their pittance, but you could buy stock in Sam's Commonwealth Edison where you paid your light bill. He made it easy for working people to get in on the Market, merchandising stocks to the masses. Last year the price of Commonwealth Edison's stock had doubled and the masses responded by taking their savings out of their mattresses and sugar bowls and out of banks like Great Lakes to buy into Insull's utility empire, which controlled the power in half the forty-eight states of the union.

The investment banks like J. P. Morgan's and the brokerage houses had not been cut in. Excluded from what they deemed their fair share, they had, as the times got tougher and the business depression hung on, organized a great bear raid on Insull. Morgan and Cyrus Eaton, his conspirator in Cleveland, knew how to make money and take power by pushing down the price of Sam's stock. The attempt had to be carried out fast, before business got better, so the financial centers—Wall Street, La Salle Street, Montgomery Street—listened to the ursine herd snuffling and padding through the woods to pounce on the great utilities tycoon while Insull was out in the country at his Libertyville farm occupied with the breeding and care of his Suffolk workhorses.

"Insull may be having some problems *this* time," Allan's father told him, "but I'm not sure we can accommodate him. He may not be as good a bet as he used to be." There was malice in the voice.

Father and son went their separate ways, with son shaking his head about the father's going on and on about Insull when his son had just seen a reporter shot down in front of him. Allan would take Mr. Park's Cholly down to the seminar, where he would, for once in his life, be able to say, "Cholly und me, ve vas dere."

Allan was late for the seminar. He was also disruptive, since his story of Jake Lingle's death, albeit an interesting one for the department lounge, had nothing to do with the topic: Race, Class, and Social Mobility in Northern Cities. However, Allan was new, a first-year graduate student, and the seven or eight people around the oval table were indulgently polite. Mr. Park, wearing his favorite suit, a black and green plaid, listened with sympathy to this big-shouldered tale of the suddenly dead. The story had an excitement to it, you had to admit, but it died in the seminar room of golden oak trim whose leaded windows overlooked the Gothic campus that Mr. Rockefeller had built at such cost for youths of Allan's background.

Education had not taught Allan to hear himself as others heard him. He had spent too many Sunday afternoons listening to Uncle Fenwick roar and imprecate about the gangsters, about Chicago turned into another Battle of Belleau Wood. "Italo-Americans, Celto-Americans, Polo-Americans, Coono-Americans, Krauto-Americans, Kiko-Americans," Uncle Fenwick trumpeted in his loud, not unimaginative style of invective. Stop the wop. President Coolidge should have sent the Marines to Chicago, not Nicaragua. And though Allan's account of the murder contained none of Uncle Fenwick's insulting pejoratives, its implication was that crime and corruption resulted from the good people's being inundated by Europe's masses.

Without raising his voice, Allan had used several "It's high time that"s and recommended that Mr. Hoover ought to think about sending in the Marines and/or that there should be a local civic mobilization similar to 1917. "When they start shooting journalists down on the streets," he concluded, "even people at the university, scholars, should understand this thing touches everyone."

A chair shuffled. Everyone looked at Mr. Park except Irena Giron, the only woman at the seminar or in the sociology department. "The beauty" or, variously, "our beauty" or "the Polack Pickford" were some of the ways the men in the department referred to her. Being blond and tall, Irena did not look like Mary Pickford, but, though her time had passed, the movie star's name was still a synonym for beauty. Irena looked at Allan, who had inherited the Archibald looks along with the Fenwick arrogance; she was hoping he would not make more of a fool of himself. He did, though. He looked at Mr. Park, whose taste in suits was attributed around the department to an allegedly gamey youth spent as a newspaper reporter.

"And what does your famous Cholly have to say about that, sir?" Allan asked, with the air of someone who had just brought his tribe the secret of fire-making.

"I think we're about at the bell. Cholly will reserve judgment on this till next we meet," said Mr. Park, who was not the sort who enjoyed humiliating students, even those who might deserve it.

By the next day, Chicago's newspapers had erupted. Together they offered a sum of $65,000 in rewards for the capture of Jake's killer. "If, as we suspect, this is indeed an underworld attack on the press," the *Evening Post* told its readers, "it may well prove to be the biggest tactical blunder gangland has made. Chicago's newspapers are not to be deterred from doing their full duty in behalf of the public by any show of gangster terrorism."

Allan had clipped out that editorial and others for the seminar, which, being about the construction of studies of social and ethnic groups, had nothing to do with assassinations. Nevertheless Chicago was full of people talking about putting the foot down, calling a halt, and drawing the line. Several of the other young men in the seminar had also become indignant, though not to the extent Allan had. He saw this as the biggest chance to volunteer since 1917, when he'd had to stay home on account of being eight years old. It rankled. Allan belonged to those who are haunted by the idea that they were born too late, that they came along after all the good claims had been staked, all the great adventures past, all noble wars waged. Here, however, was a once-in-a-lifetime exception.

Not for Mr. Park. "We're here, gentlemen, and you too, Miss Giron, to learn to be social scientists, to practice the craft if possible. We're not policemen." He was quiet for a minute, and then he continued in the avuncular way of a man explaining the practical consequences of original sin to a group of candidates for the ministry. "Someday sociology may have something to say about this kind of crime. It will never be able to tell the policemen whom to arrest, but it may make people see the struggle between good and bad as less Zoroastrian. . . . Allan, the murder of Jake Lingle is not what you think it is. I can tell that from your description of what you saw the other day."

"You can?"

"You said that when they turned Lingle's body over he had on a belt which was decorated with a double-diamond pattern. Didn't you say that?"

"Yes, sir."

"Well, all right. I'll make a bet with you. I will bet you that your martyred journalist is a gangster himself. I'll bet you that the free press has not been threatened, that this man was involved with the people who killed him in some way or other. If I'm right about this, Allan, I want you to let me choose your thesis topic and that topic will be gangsters, organized crime. If you lose, Allan, it means you'll have to take yourself out of Harper Library. You'll have to start being with people instead of reading about them. Life on the hoof, Allan. Do you want to make that bet with me?"

Allan believed that Mr. Park was a brilliant man, a leader in his field, but he *was* a professor and in this situation he was out of his depth. Both Allan's father and uncle had called the crime an outrage, and next to them what could Mr. Park know?

"Yes, sir, I'll accept your bet, Mr. Park."

The following days the great backdown began. The newspapers, Col. McCormick's world's greatest *Tribune* included, descended from bellowing to whistling a tiptoeing ditty, for the dope oozing out on Jake, the $65-a-week legman, the reporter who had never had a byline in his eighteen years on the paper, blotted out the description of him as a paladin of truth.

It came out that he did not live in a modest flat on the mid-North Side convenient to the El stop, but in a $115-a-week suite at the Congress Hotel on Michigan Avenue. In short order Chicagoans were told that there was a beach house in Michigan City, Indiana, after which a $2,000 chauffeured Hupmobile drove into the picture; a stockbroker's account jointly held by Jake and a deputy police chief, once worth several hundred thousand dollars but now much diminished thanks to the crash; and a safe deposit box, although there was a dispute over whether its contents were trash or a maharajah's jewels. Since it also came out that Jake was sick with the gambler's disease, the box more than likely held trash, but by the end of the second week after his death, the papers were estimating that the *Tribune*'s most anonymous reporter—the Colonel had not even known the man's name—was making $75,000 a year from someone for doing something.

When the seminar met again, Mr. Park did not immediately bring up the bet with Allan. He was in a mood to tell stories and rhapsodize about the city he was teaching a new generation of scholars to go out and study firsthand. He was the first sociologist who said that theory was nothing, library work less, that what must be done is to venture forth and see how people live. He was given to moderate venturing forth himself, which, he told the seminar, he had done the previous evening by dining at Schlogl's on North Wells Street, a restaurant much patronized by the hyenas of the press, as he called his former stablemates.

"It's the food I go for. The Königsberger chops with anchovy sauce." He winked at them.

The men from the *Daily News,* the more literary reporters, liked Schlogl's, and like all the other insiders they threw back their heads in laughter at Police Commissioner Russell's hypothesis that Jake Lingle had been done in by the brother of "a woman of good family whom he had an immoral relationship with." Big Bill Thompson said, "I'm giving the crooks twenty-four hours to get out of town." The deadlines on Big Bill's ultimatums fluctuated. The previous February he had given them forty-eight hours to leave Chicago, but this was a much, much more important case.

The Commissioner of Police did not abandon his hypothesis easily. He followed up by saying his department had "proof positive there is one of those 'other woman' angles to this case."

"Sure, purely personal, yeah, I'll bet," was the judgment rendered at Schlogl's as waiters pounded down the dishes on planked tables. "It's an established fact that, among all peoples, be they Swedes or Bohunks, the brothers of a dishonored sister always hire out-of-town gunsels to avenge the clan's virtue."

Chicagoans had become connoisseurs of murder. They knew by reading the descriptions that the reason for the men on either side of Jake in the I.C. underpass was that an out-of-town gunner must have a "spaniel," a pointer to show the target. Only a *paesano* can look an associate full in the face and kill him. The city loved its reputation and hated it; its inhabitants doted on their proficiency in technically correct information about the most awful things and retched when they happened. The most entertaining were the gangsters' invented nicknames, the least were finding real dead bodies.

It was at Schlogl's that one Diego Amatuna was given the nickname Smoots. Then, because they liked the way it sounded, they kept putting the bugger's name in their stories: "Police Looking to Question Smoots" and "Gang Warfare All Smoots Out on South Side." The litterateur from the *News,* who had given Smoots the name which made the other gangsters think he was a bigger Amatuna than he was, had the luck to be with the State's Attorney's squad that found Smoots—on the basis of a telephoned tip—after four nights and five days of August weather in the back of a Hudson sedan. Good God!

Allan was ready to let the Jake Lingle thing slide, but Irena pushed him. They were not close but Allan had concluded she was a pusher, a person who meant well but who would make your business her business. "Mr. Park will think you have welshed on a bet, Allan. You have to go through with it . . . at least give it a try."

She succeeded in pushing him inside the door to Mr. Park's office. "I don't expect you to be a detective, Allan," the professor said. "Nobody is ever going to solve Jake Lingle's murder, although I wouldn't be surprised if some unlucky soul went to the penitentiary for it. I don't want you to solve the crime. I want you to study it. I want you to study organized crime. It's never been done. You'd be the first."

"I don't think I can do it, sir. It's so far . . . I mean, couldn't I do something like Wirth's doing? He's studying his own background. You know, the Jewish ghetto."

"And you want to study the Gold Coast, is that it, Allan? Well, I've thought of encouraging you to do that. It hasn't been done either, but I don't think you can do it yet. You can't study your own background until you've been away from it, and—please don't take this amiss—I don't think you have."

"Come again, sir?" said Allan, now nonplussed as well as vexed at not being able to slip out of this nightmarish master's thesis topic.

"To understand a society you must be able to see it with two sets of eyes: you must see it as the people who live in it see it and as it might be seen by someone from a different background. That's how you get perspective . . . by comparing differences. Otherwise you have no way of knowing what you are looking at."

"But gangsters—"

"Look, a man like Louis Wirth came into a different world from the West Side ghetto by coming here to the university. That's how he acquired *his* second set of eyes. That's why I could suggest he go back to the ghetto and study it. But you've never been away, you haven't learned to look, and I doubt, with your lack of experience, Allan—and I'm not saying this to hurt your feelings, you're young—with that lack of experience, a project to study the Protestant upper crust wouldn't come to much. You'd be afraid you were snitching, telling gossip on your parents' friends; you would pass over really important things. I don't think you can do it yet. I say yet. I'm not saying never."

"But gangsters, Mr. Park. . . . I've never even met a . . ." Allan

15

almost used his uncle's favorite word and said wop. "I've never even met an Italian."

"Try it. Your parents have taken you to Europe. You've met Italians galore, I'll bet. What you've never met is an Italo-American, and there are three hundred thousand in this city where you live."

"I don't know, sir."

"Allan, travel, motion across geographic space, isn't always broadening; sometimes you need to move across social space. I tell you not only as your teacher but as an older friend, someone who knows your parents and who thinks you are going to have a lot to give some day if you push yourself."

"Yes, sir."

"You take my vaudeville friend, Cholly, and see if you can't get there. I think you can."

Chapter 2

Allan was alone in the graduate students' lounge, his well-dressed body in a sprawl on the sofa. He was lying in wait, hoping to jump the next three people who wandered in. It was bridge he had on his mind. The championship match in New York had whetted his desire.

His somewhat damaged copy of *The Social Teachings of the Christian Church* sat on the coffee table on top of his volume of Tönnies, both demanding to be read before the social theory seminar would meet again. "Mr. Archibald," Allan could hear old man Burgess asking him, "how would you apply the *Gemeinschaft–Gesellschaft* dichotomy to a new and basically nontraditional society like ours?" Nobody had told Allan, he complained to himself, that sociology would be reading long German books printed in Gothic type and slinging big Teutonic terms around. Why hadn't he applied for law school? Then he could sling big Latin words around.

Sociology was to have been his way of learning about people without people learning about him; it was to have given him a cloak of invisibility which let him get to see the center of things—but safely, without risk. Instead he spent his days reading fat books; or there was the preposterous thesis topic. That would put him in the center of things. Or he could go over to the gym and find someone to play tennis. Or he could read the *Chicago Herald & Examiner,* a copy of which was staring up at him from the floor. Over the masthead a streamer shouted:

**DON'T PATRONIZE FOREIGN PAUPER LABOR—
BUY AMERICAN**

Allan too was proud that American working people had the highest standard of living in the world, although there had been some recent signs of slippage.

He was reading a story about President Hoover's younger son, who was also named Allan, and his two pet alligators when he became aware that Irena Giron was standing next to him. Viewed from his slumped position on the sofa, she looked even taller as she studied him from the pinnacle of her blondness.

Brundage called her the "Thing of Beauty," in a disparaging tone, as though someone with such good looks antagonized him—as though she did not belong among them. The other men treated her as a colleague in the formal sense. They made sure to invite her to the departmental get-togethers, but she was not included in the bull sessions. Irena herself was unable to see how she affected others. Her forward ways did not endear her to the men and her offsetting, ingenuous charm was lost on them; Irena was first to put up her hand at the seminar table, first to make note of a book reference casually dropped by an instructor, first over to Harper Memorial to get the book in question. She was good-natured but, for a woman, too positive about too much and oblivious to men's sensibilities. "A thing of beauty is not always a joy forever," Brundage quipped.

"The male ego would not survive a date with La Blonde," an older graduate student had said of Irena. "She even corrected Park the other day when he was quoting a line from Schiller. I'll take my blondes dumb, thank you."

"What has got you?" she was smiling and demanding to know. Irena spoke with a grating stiffness of diction which made her sound as if she had learned English from a Polish grammar.

Allan glared up at the happy smile coming out around the white, symmetrical teeth. "Do you play bridge?" he asked.

"No."

"I guess you don't play tennis either," he said, arching his back and giving a stretch but thinking, Well, she *is* a thing of beauty. Her beauty was the more intriguing for him because it was the perfection of a face and body type not seen on the North Shore. She was a different kind of blonde; Allan liked to look at her in seminar and note her features.

Brundage had warned him about her at lunch the other day. "Archibald, you are being stalked by the Thing of Beauty. Are you man enough? Do you feel flattered to have been singled out by our *Übermädchen?* The Thing will grab you by the hair and take you off to her aerie. God help you, Archibald. When she's finished with you, you'll be a depulped grapefruit rind."

Brundage was always talking about Irena, how she was too smart, or how she was not as smart as she seemed, or how she could not be smart because she was Polish, how her name was actually Gironovski. "That woman is hiding her 'ovski,' mark my words, Archibald," he liked to say.

Allan looked up into Irena's face as long as he dared without embarrassing either of them. She did not look as if she was stalking; she looked as if she was being friendly.

"What has got you, Allan?" she repeated.

"I was thinking, Irena, I might go to law school this fall. Sociology isn't my ticket."

"Come on," she said, reaching down and hauling him up to his feet. "The judge would overrule you and you would sulk." The idea of Allan, the too-sensitive lawyer, being knocked about by the brutes in black gowns who presided over Chicago's courts had Irena laughing her full-shouldered Slavic laugh as she pushed him out of the room and into the sunshine of a mild summer's morning to walk him down the Midway Plaisance, the fanciful name officially given the strip of parkland and boulevard along which the university had been built.

Some people in the department thought of Allan as aloof and arrogant, but not Irena; she saw him as shy. He struck some people as lacking depth; for Irena he seemed to have breadth, the most accomplished young man she had met. Last fall at the departmental mixer at Mr. Park's, he had spent the evening at the piano, a cigarette hanging out of his handsome face, offhandedly playing "Tea for Two."

Irena had never met anyone like Allan, but her experience was circumscribed; she had never been on a date. Her little sister, Steffy, acned cheeks and all, had been on the facsimile of a date; boys did show up sometimes to ask her out for a Coke. For Irena, there had been no boys, no men in her busy life, and she had not missed them. The accidental encounters she had had with men had been alarming and frightening in the hints of aggression they directed toward her. Until Irena met Allan, males were not men to her, but non-female persons with whom the conventions prescribed a different kind of behavior. The first six months of their acquaintance Irena only knew she liked to look at Allan. Being near him sometimes made her fluttery, but she avoided thinking about that.

She did not act fluttery. As they walked together Irena tugged at him, then slipped her arm under his while yanking at his sleeve with her free hand. Occasionally she would step away from him to get better leverage for delivering an encouraging whack on the back.

"You cannot know unless you try researching the thesis," Irena lectured him, taking Allan's sulks head on. "If it cannot be done, you can return to Mr. Park and tell him, 'I tried, I cannot do it.' He will not understand if you quit before you try."

They were standing near Lorado Taft's Fountain of Time. He looked at the sculpture and then at the living blonde. What if Brundage was right, what if she was hiding her "ovski." When he had been an undergraduate there had been a scandal when somebody found that a colored girl had hidden her antecedents and managed to get pledged to a sorority. The nigger in the Alpha Nu woodpile. The fraternity men had teased those girls for weeks. Of course, Poles are blond—or are they? Irena was the first person of Polish extraction Allan had met. There were tons of them in Chicago, he knew, and most of them worked in the stockyards or the steel mills, but he could not have said what they looked like. In newspaper pictures they had on bib overalls and goggles as they stood holding long rods in front of open-hearth furnaces. The Pole he did know, however, seemed as pretty as this summer forenoon, standing with her feet planted apart as if to make her words emphatic, smiling at him as she glistened in the green and gold of a still, cool day.

Irena kept coaxing and bucking him up until Allan conceded that he owed it to all concerned to give it a try. "But how am I supposed to do it? I suppose I should look up Alphonse Capone in the phone book, dial his number, and say, 'Hi! I'm Allan Archibald, a sociology student at the University of Chicago. I want an appointment to come over to see you. I want you to tell me everything so I can write my master's thesis and, just incidentally, put you in the electric chair.' And he'll say, 'Ya mean, kid, you're de famous well-known nobody, *de* Allan Archibald, de kid what's gonna be de famous social scientist? Hey, come right over, fella.'"

They were both laughing. He was coming out of his crankiness, but in a way, he did think he ought to be able to call up people and get them to talk to him by identifying himself as a student of society. The university had given him a license to pry, and there was so much he wanted to see. "Of course, Mr. Park did say that I was to learn about them, not try to put them in jail," he said meditatively. "I have to remind myself I'm not going to find out who killed Jake Lingle. That's not my job. Organized crime, that's my job."

20

"Sure!" Irena boomed at him.

Allan looked at her, his focus flicking down her body. Brundage said that Polack women "like it done to them." Brundage was an odd one himself, the only person in the department to talk that way. Allan could not have talked that way, but he liked to listen to Brundage. Brundage probably knew a lot. Brundage was probably very experienced, but you could not ask without making it obvious that you were probably not. Allan looked into Irena's face, trying to judge if she was a handsome specimen, trying to guess what she would look like with her clothes off, whether, fine specimen that she was, she would resemble the white marble ladies brought from Mediterranean lands to stand in the Art Institute forever. Or there was Minsky's burlesque on South State Street where the MC would introduce tall girls like Irena with the word "statuesque." For the last year or so Allan had been going to Minsky's at night, by himself, his collar up, his hat down, at the box office, telling himself each time would be the last time, that it was disgusting, that he was there as a social observer. He had rehearsed that speech often and held it in readiness against, God forbid, running into somebody he knew. The women he saw on the stage at Minsky's pursued him through his imagination, even though those shows were a cheat. They did not take their clothes off really; it was hardly more than you could see at the beach.

"When you are not frowning, Allan, you are a pretty handsome fellow," Irena, who had been doing her own thinking, said. "We'd make a good-looking couple." As she said that, she made a whoop, bent over laughing, put the tips of her fingers to her mouth, and told him, "I am not to talk that way. Oh, well!" she added, pulling him down a path as she demanded to know, "So, how are you going to begin? How are you going to try it?"

"Try what?" Allan asked.

"The gangsters! You will be an urban Margaret Mead! Instead of sailing away ten thousand miles to live among primitives, you, Allan Archibald, will dwell among the criminal anthropophagi of Chicago and describe the daily life of savages who inhabit an area only seven miles away. Think of it!"

"Irena, did anybody ever tell you that you were a little bit nutty?"

"Allan, did anybody ever tell you that you were a little bit serious?" she replied, again laughing. "But you know, Mead is not even thirty years old and she has two books out already! Both sensations. You might do the same. You could. The subject is as exotic. Imagine, publishers lining up for permission to print your thesis: 'On the Spot: A Monograph Describing Patterns of Organized Crime in Chicago' by Allan Archibald, M.A.''

"You can buy a steamship ticket to Samoa, Irena, but you can't buy a ticket of admission to the underworld. You and Park both skate over that detail. I'd need a regular Virgil to take me there," said Allan. Everybody who went to college then studied Latin and had some glancing knowledge of the major poets.

"So, Allan, you will have to find your own Virgil. Like Margaret Mead. She had to find people to tell her what was going on, and she did not even speak Polynesian when she got there."

"The heck with La Mead, Irena! A Virgil in Samoa is a stool pigeon in Chicago, for God's sake," he said, raising his voice. She swung away from him and looked eastward into the sun, in the direction of Lake Michigan, where the day's first bathers, mothers with toddlers, for the most part, were coming onto the municipal beaches.

"Irena, I'm sorry."

"I want to help you, assist you, Allan. I—"

"I'm sorry. I truly am," Allan said and touched her arm, whereupon she swung back on her heel to face him. She was smiling again, the sun coming through the halo of blond hair. Truly beautiful, he thought, and asked her, "Was it your feelings I hurt or were you standing up for La Mead?"

Irena laughed her square-shouldered laugh, got him by the arm, and had him marching again, this time back the way they had come, a tall blond young woman towing a tall blond young man along the paths and through the greenery, telling him in the most positive tones, "This is how I would go about it, Allan. I would get on the El and I . . ."

A few days later Allan did get on the El to ride to 22nd Street, there to descend to walk the half block to Michigan Avenue and enter the Hotel Metropole, on the upper floors of which, as any reader of Chicago newspapers knew, the Big Fellow kept his headquarters. Allan had no plan, no trick idea, no cunning stratagem for getting to Scarface Al. He was there, he grumbled to himself, because he had allowed Irena to goad him, to tell him he might as well stew down at the Metropole as in the students' lounge, where he surely would not get a clue as to how he might get his study under way.

The lobby was an unremarkable place of spittoons and heavy,

carved wood chairs, but now that he had gotten himself to it, Allan felt conspicuous. He might be taken for a detective. For sure, people were looking at him. He walked quickly to the coffee shop. He ordered a cup of coffee, took out his copy of the *Chicago Daily News,* and got on with the business of looking invisible.

SOCIAL FUROR OVER
MRS. OSCAR DE PRIEST WORSENS

Washington society, notably the Southern contingent, was still agog today over the news that Mrs. Hoover had had a colored woman to tea at the White House. The center of the scandal is Mrs. Oscar De Priest, wife of the well-known colored Chicago Congressman, the first of his race in almost 30 years to serve in the House.

The matter reached the floor of the Senate today when Sen. Coleman T. Blease (D, S.C.) read a poem entitled "Niggers in the White House." After several of his colleagues requested, Sen. Blease agreed to have it struck from the *Congressional Record,* not, as he said, "because I am ashamed of my verse or consider myself an inferior poetaster, but out of deference to the misconceived feelings of some of the other members of this chamber."

In Tallahassee the Florida State House of Representatives passed a resolution condemning "White House social policies and questionable standards of taste."

Allan put the paper down, savoring the grand feeling of coming from a Republican family: he, his father and his uncle, Herbert Hoover and the Great Emancipator. In the coffee shop, overhead fans turned. He looked at the scattering of seated men. Which were the gangsters and which the traveling shirt salesmen?

"Hey, fella, if you're gonna sit there all day, buy somethin' once in a while, will ya? This isn't a park bench, ya know," Allan was told by the waiter, a young man wearing a white duck outfit with a slightly soiled towel around his waist. Allan ponied up another nickel, whereupon the waiter, whose name was Andy, turned friendly and asked, "From outa town, huh? . . . We get lots of tourists in here. Ya go to Hollywood to see the movie stars; you go to Chi Town to see the gangsters, right? Sometimes we got so many tourists in here, there's no room for the hoodlums. Ain't that a laugh? . . . You look like you're from back East somewheres. . . . If you got an extra quarter on ya, I'll hip you to the real glamour guys."

"You will?"

"Would I shit you, pal?" Andy asked as Allan pushed a coin across the table top. "See that guy? That's Patsy O'Dea. He's a slugger for the Cleaners and Dyers Union."

"He is? What's a slugger?"

"What's it sound like? He slugs people."

"Thank you," Allan replied with hauteur. Slipping out from the booth, he walked over to this representative of organized labor, who was dunking a doughnut into a cup of well creamed coffee. "Mr. O'Dea?" Allan ventured, thereby distracting the slugger long enough so that the dunked part of the doughnut began to disintegrate. "I'm Allan Archibald from the University of Chicago." Mr. O'Dea raised the doughnut and, seeing the precariousness of its condition, rushed it mouthward but not soon enough. The wet part broke off in passage, splashing back into the coffee and making a mess on the table.

"Die!" ordered Mr. O'Dea.

"What?" Allan asked.

"Die. Stop living."

"I said I was from the University of Chicago. We're doing a study about—"

"I'm not buying any!"

"I *said* I am from the University of Chicago and I am doing a study about . . ."

Allan realized that the next words out of his mouth would have to be "organized crime." He stopped in mid-sentence, not that Mr. O'Dea was paying attention. He was rising to his feet, saying as Allan was talking, "And *I* said scram, lunkhead." A genuinely threatening tone had come into Mr. O'Dea's voice.

"Mr. O'Dea, you don't have to cooperate with the University of Chicago if you don't want to, but you do have to be polite."

Mr. O'Dea was readying himself to do something bad when Andy got between them. "Hey, Patsy, don't pay no attention. The guy's a nut. Lemme clean ya up here, get ya another doughnut," he said to O'Dea, who was subsiding back into the chair as Andy, both hands on Allan's arms, maneuvered the student back into the booth. When he got him there, he looked at him and said, "You're a real muff diver, you are."

Vas you dere, Cholly? he thought as he watched Patsy O'Dea drop some coins on the table and walk out without looking toward Allan. Seeing the man leave made Allan angry again. What kind of people were these?

"That mick stiffed me 'cause of you," Andy said with deep pecuniary meaning, his thumb rubbing against the tips of the front two fingers on his right hand. Allan pushed another quarter toward his guide. La Mead must have found a better one in Polynesia.

For Andy, Allan was a quandary. He was worth catering to because he had money, but the guy lived in some other place, as though he did not know what was going on. "I'll point 'em out to you, OK? But you just look at 'em, don't talk to 'em. . . . See that guy with the schnoz? That's Eddie the Eagle. Baldelli's his last name. He's a heavy hitter; even the tourists never heard of him, so I'm giving you information you wouldn't get on your own. An' the guy he's having coffee with is a big shot on the Near West Side. That's a lotta pounds, that guy, a real heavyweight. Frankie Yale. None other but. . . . Your lucky day, boy."

Still smarting from the humiliation by Mr. O'Dea, Allan steeled himself for a new try at Eddie the Eagle and his friend Frankie Yale. But the indignation in him died down and was followed by a hopelessness about the undertaking. He thought an unkind thought about Mr. Park, yet it was difficult for Allan to criticize older men of his own class, so he put the blame for his public embarrassment on Irena. He had told her, dammit, that you could not go sailing up to these guys like that. Well, he had tried, precisely as she had been nagging him to do, and now he was going to tell that bossy Polack that she might speak five languages and get A's, but she was just as dumb and stubborn as the rest of them out there in the Back of the Yards. He was rehearsing his speech for the second time when he got a fresh cup of coffee he had not ordered slammed down in front of him and he heard Andy, in a breathy low voice and with a rueful shake of the head, tell him, "You're a fuckin' muff diver, ya know that? A goddamn muff diver."

Allan felt as if he had been staved in. How could he learn the ways of these people? He was fighting off a blush. He was sure he was blushing, his face felt so hot, but he made himself look up at Andy, who had his hands on his hips in a stance of almost parental disapproval.

"What's a muff diver?"

"Jesus."

"The trip across social space—yes, not an easily negotiated passage," Mr. Park had concurred, although that was not how Allan thought he had presented his problem to the professor. He wanted to know if Mr. Park had some practical ideas for cracking this thing or, alternatively, if he had changed his mind, decided that Allan could not, that maybe no one could, collect the material for this thesis topic. "Fieldwork methods, Allan, an area almost no work has been done in. Keep good notes. Everyone is learning that the data are not stacked in packing crates out there waiting to be shipped over here to the university. . . . We're going to have a fieldwork methods seminar in the fall. I've asked Irena to head it up." Then he split off from Allan, going in the general direction of the Faculty Club.

Irena was senior to him, she had her master's, had passed her Ph.D. orals, and was gathering data for her thesis about Polish Chicago without the trouble Allan was having. Despite these rich grounds for resentment, Allan confided in her. He did not tell her; he let her read his notes, his fieldwork diary. At the Chicago Latin School he had suffered public put-downs of the same order of painfulness as that administered to him by Mr. O'Dea. But everyone got destroyed by the third-year English teacher; you knew it going in, and when it happened it stiffened junior-year solidarity. It bore no resemblance to being dressed down by a person whom Mr. Archibald would not have hired to be the gardener's assistant. The completeness of his demolition by such a person was why he could not tell Irena about it, why he delayed showing her his notes, and why he watched her as she read them. If she had laughed or sympathized, they might never have become close. Whether or not Irena intuited the strength of Allan's feeling about his run-in with the labor goon, she said the right thing. She put the sheets of paper down to commence discussing who were the legitimate, recognized question askers in society, the people who could come up to strangers and get their questions answered. Census takers, policemen, newspaper reporters, but not many others, they decided. Not graduate sociology students, that was for sure. She took him seriously.

In the mornings before going off to do his stint at the Metropole, Allan would drop by the department to have coffee with Irena and tell her what had happened or, usually, what had not happened. Days and days went by with Irena pouring coffee in the morning and Andy in the long afternoons, when the coffee shop had few customers and Allan's senses were taken over by the sleepy murmur of the overhead ceiling fans and the banging of the bell as one of the Chicago Surface Transportation Company's red trolleys clanged along 22nd Street in the summer torpor.

Having failed with the direct approach, Allan could think of nothing to do but hang out in the coffee shop until some idea presented itself. "I'm going to hold this line if it takes all summer," his grandfather was always quoting General Grant as having said, when he was urging Allan to keep at one job or another. He would lay siege to these gangsters the way Grant had laid siege to Richmond.

A muggy heat had taken possession of Chicago. The Lingle murder was dying off the front pages for lack of movement of any kind and, seated in the coffee shop, Allan was absorbed in reading about the onward march of the Chicago Cubs toward perhaps another National League pennant. Of a sudden, on the other side of the glass doors separating the shop from the lobby, Allan caught sight of what he took to be the face of the runt-stump man from the murder.

The small lobby had no one in it as Allan circled around. Back through the glass door, he saw Andy, with a what-the-hell-was-that-about expression, pick up a knocked-over chair. The runt-stump man was nowhere, although his red and ugly face hung on in Allan's imagination.

The next morning, on his way to share the first tidbit he had had in days with Irena, he fell in with Brundage, who told him he too was going to the Social Science building, where Irena had been given a small office next to Mr. Park's. "I am going to lower myself," Brundage told Allan in his loud and lordly manner. "I am going to take the Polack beauty out and do such things to her as good taste forbids me to describe, even to you, young Archibald, who, I can tell from your overall deportment, knows how tall wenches like to be treated. Can you imagine the delectably abominable practices those huge Polack boys teach their women?"

Allan nodded, but he was so far from such imaginings he barely understood the implications of Brundage's question. He understood enough, though, to be nettled at hearing Irena discussed in those terms, even by Brundage, whom he admired for his audacity. Such speech applied to Irena made him bridle, Allan discovered, but at the same time the hints contained in Brundage's language titillated him against his will. They made him tingle. Could Irena be a wench? For a young man who had not yet seen what was behind the pasties on the girls at Minsky's, Allan was an easy mark for Brundage to tease and befuddle. He would save his account of the runt-stump man for tomorrow morning's coffee with Irena.

The wench in question was surprised to look up and see Brundage's head looking around the door to her cubicle, with a friendly may-I-come-in expression on it. "Miss Jeeron or should I pronounce it Gearon?" Brundage said. "I hope I am not intruding." Brundage was supercilious, but he was also the departmental darling, his doctorate written and all but approved by his thesis committee, Harvard-bound and brilliant.

"I have come to tell you, Irena, that others may take you seriously, but I know you are, *au fond,* a girl, an embodiment of the female principle."

Irena stared at him. She knew she was being assaulted, but she had not had the opportunity to learn to defend herself from men who used words as weapons. Where Irena grew up, men with Brundage's motives did not talk; they grabbed the woman. "A magnificent exemplar of the female principle, I should say," Brundage continued, examining her with such a frankness that Irena unconsciously crossed her arms. "You will be the cynosure of all eyes in a party frock, which is what I propose that you wear this Friday when I take you out to dinner. That is what you have been waiting for, what you want."

"What *I* want?" Irena said, getting angry.

"I know what you want, Irena, and it's more fun than sociology, huh?"

"I do not think you should be talking to a colleague like this. It is not professional."

"You're going out Friday night with me . . . in something low-cut, whatever it is you wear with your . . . well, with whoever it is you go out with."

Irena listened to Brundage, letting the insulting implications go past her, as she considered that she owned nothing low-cut, nothing the gifted Mr. Brundage would consider a party dress. The major part of Irena's wardrobe came from what she, her mother, and her grandmother could sew from the patterns the family bought at F. W. Woolworth's Five and Ten Cent Store.

"I am not going out with you Friday or any other day of the week ending with a *y,*" Irena said after allowing five or six seconds of silence. Jejune but serviceable, her wisecrack came from one of the brush-off formulas the girls at Our Lady of Victory Academy would teach each other for use in repelling the world's oncharging Brundages. Then she remembered "Slow, Moe, you gotta l-o-o-o-ong way to go" and "Hit the road . . . Toad." The memory of high school sillinesses made her want to giggle. Irena's composure returned.

To Brundage it was a novel expression of scorn, but the kind of thing, he recognized, a counter girl might say to an importuning drugstore cowboy. Its triteness goaded him. "You may have the other men cowed, Irena," he persisted, "they may think you have an I.Q. of two hundred. I know you're a smart girl, but not that smart. You have a photographic memory . . . that intimidates them, but not me . . . makes them think you're too intelligent to take on. Well, I'm not afraid of you, Irena."

"Oh, Brundage!" Irena said in her practiced oldest-sister voice, the one that said you were acting like a baby.

"Then we shall have an interesting evening Friday night, now that we know where we stand."

Irena had no sense of why this man was acting this way, but she could see that if she stood her ground, he would back off. Verbal assaults were a step up from physical ones, she decided, as she showed him a face with her death-mask expression on it. "No, thank you, Brundage." On this go-round she spoke the words to suggest not patience but fatigue.

"Well, if you get tired of your Back of the Yards types, let me know. If you'd ever wear something other than those drab rags, you just *might* be a knockout," he told her, and his face was gone.

Irena stiffened at that parting dart, but then she gave herself a little downward inspection, made an expression almost pert, and whispered to no one, "I bet I would."

The *American* had a story that could not be serious:

WCTU CELEBRATES DRY BIRTHDAY

The Women's Christian Temperance Union held a party at the Auditorium Hotel this afternoon to celebrate the 10th anniversary of the Noble Experiment. The city's soberest revelers were directed in a triumphal chant by the Rev. Mr. Herbert Sweetbread Whiting, a pastor of the North Shore Baptist Church. The clergyman led an estimated 400 ladies and 50 gentlemen to shout in unison:
"Strawberry shortcake, huckleberry pie!
"V-I-C-T-O-R-Y!!!
"Are we in it? Well, I guess!
"VICTORY! VICTORY!
"Yes. Yes! YES!"

Allan put down his paper in time to see a thickset man drop into a chair at Frankie Yale's table. "Jack McGurn," Andy whispered. "Machine Gun McGurn . . . he did St. Valentine's Day, he's the one that did the massacre . . . mean, mean bastard."

Allan noted a roll of flesh on the neck coming over McGurn's shirt collar. Irregular swatches of hair were growing on it.

The *Evening Post* was carrying details on what they called a break in the Lingle case. To Allan, though, the headline was misleading; there was no break in the case but more proof, as if it were needed, that his father and his uncle were right: Chicago was crying out for law and order.

The police had brought in a man for questioning named Moe Rosten, "a Russian-born nationalized citizen"—the *Post's* way of saying he was Jewish. After twenty-four hours of unrewarding interrogation they let Mr. Rosten go free, but he refused to leave the premises. The paper quoted the terrified gangster as saying, "I don't want to go outside. I'll never get back alive. You took me from a safe spot. You owe me to get me back to a safe spot." Conceding Mr. Rosten might have a point, the police loaded him in the back of one of their green touring cars and took off up State Street intending to deposit him somewhere north of Wilson Avenue, but as they got to Harrison Street, right in the middle of the Loop, somebody or bodies fired a great many bullets at them. Mr. Rosten vaporized into the night "and is believed to be safe, but Elbert Lusander, 41, a streetcar motorman, was killed and Henry Sullivan, 26, a janitor at the Standard Club, was wounded."

"Don't start in on those lousy jokes of yours, Jack," Mr. Yale admonished Mr. McGurn.

"Aw, for chrissake, you ain't ever heard this one yet," answered Jack. "It's funny. I swear to God it is."

"Shit!" Allan heard Frankie Yale reply.

"Aw, give it a listen, will ya?" McGurn half ordered, half pleaded. "OK, ya ready? . . . OK, tell me what's a polygon? . . . Ya know, what's a polygon? Tell me what it is. Ya give up?"

"I give up, Jack. What's a polygon?"

"A dead parrot!" Deep silence. "A dead parrot. Doncha get it? Polly gone. Like Polly wants a cracker."

"*I* gotta be gone," Yale said, looking at McGurn with flat eyes. He picked up the check and tossed it at him. "You gonna tell jokes like that, Jack, *you* pay the check." And Mr. Frankie Yale was out of the coffee shop.

Allan had looked down at one of his newspapers when McGurn said the punch line. A front-page box informed him:

NEWS TO RUN FREE WANT ADS

Because of the growing seriousness of the unemployment situation, the *Daily News* will no longer charge for classified ads by people with positions to fill. This policy will continue in effect until prosperity returns, which Secretary of the Treasury Andrew Mellon predicts will occur in late summer or early fall.

A shiver of anger vibrated in Allan. It fixed on Irena. She was the one who kept him here in this coffee shop, being patronized by Andy, listening to these morons. She with her Margaret Mead and her homilies. "Allan, this is good for you, this is going to make a man out of you, having to do for yourself this way." Who was she to know what would make a man out of him? Was she going to go out with Brundage? He was so sophisticated and charming and he could make her do whatever he had in mind, that Minsky's stuff. She's just a girl from the Back of the Yards, she all but smells of sausage, telling him he would have to find ways of ingratiating himself if he wanted people to open up to him.

It was as surprising as it was demeaning, this wanting to know if she was going to go out with Brundage. He remembered their sharing sandwiches on the Midway, her high cheekbones, the almost white blondness of her cloched hair in the sun. Why did Brundage call her a wench? If Irena was one, why wouldn't she give him her telephone number? Why did she tell him the ringing bothered her grandmother? And talk to him as if he didn't know he had to ingratiate himself with these idiots if he was to get anywhere with them. She must have a high opinion of herself.

Allan lit another cigarette and watched McGurn on the prowl for his next joke victim. As McGurn told another clunker, Allan gave off a little laugh, which the Machine Gunner did not hear because one of the men at his table was telling him, "McGurn, you're a crazy palooka. You've killed more guys with your jokes than with your chopper."

Whatever was said next at McGurn's table Allan could not hear, though he tried. He was jumpy, he was on to something. He put out a cigarette and lit another, trying to hear McGurn.

"You smoke too much, pal," Andy interrupted. He leaned over

toward Allan to whisper, "An' if you'll take my advice you are not gonna try to get tangled with McGurn. You don't know. I do. The guy's dangerous. You owe me four bits for the information."

For his advice Andy got an arrogant upper-class look from Allan, who drew heavily on his Old Gold cigarette ("Not a Cough in a Carload," the billboard ads said) and then, instead of exhaling, let the smoke meander out of his open mouth as he stared at Andy, who shrugged, called him a muff diver, and went off to attend to Mr. McGurn's pleasure. Allan picked up one of his papers to read about a man who attached a hose to the exhaust of his Essex automobile, taped the other end into his mouth, and then turned on the key, activating one of the Essex's newest features, its highly reliable electric ignition. Not a cough in a carload of that, either.

Ingratiate yourself, Irena said. Lower yourself, Allan was thinking. It would be the first time he had acted this way, but he was not going to spend the rest of the summer pushing quarters at a Greek waiter in a coffee shop for the honor of being patronized.

The Gunner began to pop another gag on his squirming victims.

"Hey, give us a break, will ya, Jack?"

Jack was not to be stopped. The punch line died in the summer afternoon air. A fly buzzed. The overhead fans moved. Allan, however, put his head back and filled the shop with three peals of forced laughter.

"Funny, huh?" McGurn said. "I got a lot more where that came from." He got up and, coming over to Allan's booth, plopped down next to him, his sleeve brushing up against *The Social Teachings of the Christian Church*. Allan wanted to back away from contact, but he made himself stay where he was, noting the pomaded hair on top of McGurn's head and the unpomaded hair growing out of his nostrils. The mixture of last night's alcohol and this morning's eau de cologne was nauseating, yet Allan kept his position. They, Mr. Park and Irena, both were going to know and acknowledge he could break into the inside, and he was going to get to the center, where he would find out how the world was run.

"I'm a funny guy," the gangster informed him.

Past McGurn's ear Allan could see Andy behind the counter. He had his lips pursed.

McGurn's teeth impressed Allan. They were wide, flat, filed-off stones. Allan saw them close up and often, for the Gunner started to come into the shop looking for this new audience. Then he began inviting, though it was more like ordering, Allan to come along in the evening to the Gunner's favorite speakeasies, where they would sit at a small table and the gangster would move in until his mouth was six inches away from Allan, not to confide but to dominate. When he got up close he did not lower his voice but talked loud enough to rattle Allan's eyeballs, which had a choice of looking at the Gunner's pearly whites or fastening themselves on the heavy eyebrow which seemed to march unbroken across McGurn's face. The guy was hairy.

Sociable too. He took Allan to a speakeasy and ordered the bartender to "Give my buddy here a beer. Put it in my personal stein."

When the personal stein arrived, Allan lifted it, toasted the Gunner, and, putting it to his lips, experienced the beer dribbling down his chin onto his tie, his shirt, and his waistcoat. Wiping himself off, he tried a second time, with the same results, as the gangster laughed. "What did I tell ya, Al. I got a great sense of humor." He took his fist and laid it against Allan's cheek, the flesh of which he jiggled.

"So what are ya, Al?" McGurn wanted to know after Allan had mopped himself up and the laughter of everyone in the room had subsided. Allan had laughed too. Humiliating. "What are ya?"

"A sociologist."

"A social worker, huh? Not as good as a Catholic priest, but Protestants are OK, leastways the ones that mean it. . . . Al, are you a sincere guy? That's what it takes." Henceforth for McGurn, Allan became "the social worker," a misunderstanding which rendered him innocuous but respectable, and possibly useful should some special need arise.

After the evening of the personal beer stein Allan got himself a joke book, intending to establish himself in his own right by repayment in kind, but it was made clear to him that Jack liked to tell jokes, not listen to them. The man's lack of interest in Allan, except as audience and occasional foil, irritated him like wet wool on naked skin.

"He doesn't want to know anything about me," Allan complained to Andy. "I could be from a rival gang. I could be a detective. I could be anyone."

That struck Andy as funnier than the Gunner's jokes. "First off, pal, they know who all the detectives are 'cause they're on their payroll, and, second off, there isn't a detective in the world that looks like you, talks like you, or acts goofy like you, Allan. But you watch your step with McGurn. Nobody's friends with that guy. He's too fuckin' dangerous. You're gonna get squashed. You are."

"Well, why does Capone have him around?"

"Why does Snorky have him around? Because he kills people for Snorky on the days when Snorky doesn't have time to do it himself."

"Snorky?"

"Snorky's what his close personal friends call the Big Fella."

"Who calls him Scarface Al, his close impersonal friends?"

To which Andy responded, "You can be a real muff diver when ya want, ya know that?"

That was one exchange Allan did not put in his fieldwork diary, but when he let Irena read his notes on his first visit upstairs at the Metropole, she told him she thought he had made a breakthrough.

It had come without warning. Allan and the Gunner were in the coffee shop when he said there was somebody upstairs he wanted Allan to meet. On the way up Allan had wondered if it might be Snorky. It wasn't, but it was Snorky's cousin and second in command, Frank Nitti, whom the papers called the Enforcer.

Nitti was curious about Allan. "Where did you go to school?" and a jeweled and manicured hand took silver-rimmed glasses off to get a better close-in peek. "What did you say your father does?" and the glasses went back on with the right hand as the palm of the left grazed the greased contours of the hair. "You have an uncle, name of Fenwick?" as the thumb and forefinger of the right hand came close to touching the knot on the tie and the other three fingers fanned apart in tension. "But you already got your college degree and you're takin' more, goin' on to be a professor?" and he checked out the buffed nails on the right hand and then the left hand. "An' you're studyin' us for your school, huh?" and the right hand went to shoulder level, the wrist gave a little shake so the coat sleeve dropped an inch to show the cuff links preparatory to the hand traveling out to pick up the glass with the white stuff in it.

Chapter 3

Nadja Pringle, Mr. Archibald's secretary, moved from her desk to the door of his office. She opened it a crack and inserted herself into the room whose mahogany and leather appointments gave the place the feel of a men's club library.

For what she had to say, Nadja Pringle could not use the newly installed intercom system. "There is a colored man in the outer office, sir. He says he has an appointment." She was nearly whispering, moving her lips with exaggerated precision.

"His name is Moncrief Borders. I wrote it in the appointment book. I should have warned you a colored man would be coming in, Miss Pringle."

Never having received a colored businessman in his office before, Mr. Archibald was uncertain of the etiquette. Should he stand? Should he sit? If he stood, should he also shake hands? There were no rules for such a situation, and Mr. Archibald liked it best when the standards and guides were prescribed. In the end he half rose from his desk, extending a hand over its top to the strong, willful-looking person who had come into his office and now made bold to sit in the visitor's chair without being bidden.

"What can I do for you, Moncrief? . . . That is, I'm glad you came in, Borders. I've wanted to meet you," the banker said with complete untruth. He was rattled. How do you address a colored person under these circumstances? First name is not exactly fitting. The man was in the banking business, if among the colored. Mister conferred equality. Even the *Chicago Daily News,* which recently had begun to call colored people Negroes with a capital N, did not refer to them as Mister. Borders began to explain his trouble.

Mr. Archibald already knew something about Borders. Years

ago, back in 1916, there had been an article in the *News* about Mr. Archibald's unusual visitor: "Moncrief Borders has a bank at 2024 South Wabash. It is the only bank in Chicago headed by a colored man, of which all the employees and most of the patrons are colored persons."

The city's bankers, in accordance with Republican Party tradition, had smiled on this effort and, although they gave it no material support, they kept vaguely abreast of Mr. Borders and his bank, as though his progress redounded to their credit. They did not fret when it came out that Mr. Borders's father-in-law was Washboard Jones, the gambler. A colored banker was such an anomaly that he could be indulged because, as Mr. Borders had said in the article he had framed and hung on his office wall, "Most of the colored businessmen in Chicago have started with nothing, for the race is young as a free people in the nation and still younger in the North."

After that, no particular news of Mr. Borders other than an occasional joint venture with a white bank on a loan too big for the black one to handle by itself. Piddling stuff. No one wanted colored business. Mr. Borders and his bank were not where the money was rolling in as Chicago and its commerce roared through the twenties.

Borders was saying that the only bank in Chicago headed by a colored man was going broke. "An' I'm gonna go to jail for embezzlement," Borders added, explaining what he had done. For several years he had been taking large amounts of his depositors' money and using it as margin to buy Insull stock. His idea was to expand his bank's base, make it a bigger bank by putting the profits from the stock speculation back into the bank to "help the race," as he assured his white counterpart. "I didn't use none of it for myself. I did it for my people. I wanted them to get in on some of that money Mr. Insull was making for everybody."

The embezzlement would have worked had Borders taken his early winnings and cashed in on the stock of the electric utility holding companies. Instead, he had used the paper profits as down payment to buy more stock on margin. He then had done the same thing several times more, each time adding to his paper profit and his real debt, until the unimaginable had happened. Insull stock, which only went up, went down. The real debt remained but the paper profits were gone.

"Every respectable colored family in Chicago has their savings in the Borders State Bank, Mr. Archibald. It's the race bank here," the black man said, looking straight at the white banker. "Just about every merchant, every professional man, every Pullman-car porter. If my bank goes down, there won't be no difference between the respectable and the nonrespectable colored people in this city. No, sir, they both be wiped out."

"And you want me, my bank, Moncrief, to lend you the money to pay for that stock, money for which you have no collateral, is that right? You are asking to borrow money to pay for stock bought at four hundred dollars a share that is now selling for two hundred, is that right?"

"It would only be till the stock went back up. I mean this is Mr. Samuel Insull stock, Mr. Archibald. You know it's going to come back up. It's the very best stock there is. Everybody knows that. Blue-chip, gilt-edge, Mr. Archibald. You can keep it in the vault in this very bank here. Sell it as soon as it rises. Make your profit."

"I'm to buy it from you, then, Moncrief . . . for how much?"

"Three hundred thousand dollars, Mr. Archibald, sir."

"That is a stupendous figure."

"Do I get it?" Borders pressed and fell quiet. Both men were thinking that if one little black bank had that much Insull stock in its safe, there must be a lot of white banks that had plunged on those holding companies. If it got out that the little black bank had been taken under by its Insull holdings, why not the white ones, why not a bank panic? Elting Archibald had been through the one in 1907.

"I don't know if you get it, Moncrief," Mr. Archibald answered testily, looking into Borders's eyes and seeing little red squiggles of bloodshot. "I'll need some time," said the banker, who prided himself on his deliberation. His brother in-law Fenwick would jeer about Elting's decisions to his sister. "He doesn't like to make his mistakes quickly, he likes to think about them first."

"I don't have much time, Mr. Archibald."

"I said I would let you know, Moncrief. Goodness! That's a lot of money. I said I would let you know, and I will."

"Yessir, yes*sir*, Mr. Archibald," the black banker replied, and for a trice the white one thought he had picked up a slight tint of the nasty in his tone.

That Friday Allan and Irena had their first date, stuffing themselves for a dollar fifty at Thompson's Cafeteria, where Irena had guided them, and then sitting through a cowboy movie at the Mc-

Vickers, where Allan let his hand touch Irena's, then move away, then touch again and move away again through the first third of the film. "There!" Irena breathed in the darkness as she put her hand into his. For Allan, the rest of the movie was ruined while he thought about putting his arm around the back of her chair.

Outside afterward, Irena put her arm under his, smiled and laughed, and told him she liked him and that she had had a good time, but she would not let him drive her home. Something about her grandmother again, something Allan could not understand as Irena bade him good night before walking up the steps to the El stop at Wabash Avenue.

Their second date caused their first fight. The fault was Brundage's. He was in one of his moods when he and Allan had lunch at a speakeasy near Lake Park and 55th. An uncomplimentary critique of the Sociology of Sociology chapter of his dissertation was circulating around the department and was giving his thesis committee pause. He might have to do some rewriting, which would mean he would graduate later than he planned, and that could change his chances for Harvard.

"Been seeing the Thing of Beauty?" Brundage wanted to know.

"We're going out tonight," Allan said and was immediately sorry he had.

"She's gorgeous. That cowlick she has at the top of her pubic hair is cute. Quite blond between the legs too, don't you think? I was surprised. Most of them—when they're as blond as the Thing—owe more to peroxide than nature. Agree?"

Allan put down his beer and excused himself as Brundage, the smallest grin on his face, watched Allan leave the speakeasy to walk back to the university in search of Irena.

He did not believe Brundage, whose peers knew he was an academic Iago, but even so, Brundage had gotten to him, confused him and left him in an irritable quandary.

Working it off, he complained to Irena about the inconvenience of not being able to telephone her; he called it eccentric and thoughtless and ended by saying, "Call up the phone company and tell them to move the phone to a part of the house where it won't disturb your grandmother. That's all you have to do."

Then Irena lost her temper and her bashfulness to say, "I can't call up the phone company because we don't have a phone."

"Well, get one."

"We can't afford one!" Irena shouted, stung by Allan's ignorance of how people lived.

Irena's father had worked for a lumberyard, unloading the cars that were backed into the company siding, until he'd had an accident. One of the freight cars cut off his leg two inches above the ankle. For a long time afterward the stump remained infected and he spent his time sitting in the living room, lamenting his ill luck at having worked for the lumberyard instead of the railroad, which would have paid him workman's compensation benefits. As it was, he got nothing but the trouble of a lawsuit being conducted by an attorney named Walleck with offices over on Ashland Avenue. Mr. Giron knew that a neighborhood lawyer could not win against the lumberyard's Loop lawyer, and, even if Walleck could, he would sell out his case. So Mr. Giron was convinced that he could not win and that nothing would ever heal the stump. The infection refused to clear up—never critical but always painful. "We can't talk about a prosthesis yet," said the doctor, who also had offices on Ashland Avenue. "What does *he* know?" Mr. Giron would ask, any time the subject of an artificial limb came up. "I know that guy. He's from St. Hedvig's. He grew up around Paulina and Forty-seventh. What does *he* know?"

Then one day, a year or so after the accident, he was gone, having left on his crutches, without the artificial foot he despaired of ever getting. Run away, the family said; Irena came to think it must have been suicide. Although that was a sin, she believed allowances would be made for such a terrible-looking stump. Attorney Walleck, who had been giving the family a little money to encourage them to pursue the suit, wrote to say that with Mr. Giron's disappearance the family should take what it could get, so Irena's mother walked over to the office on Ashland Avenue, signed some papers, and was given $172.

It was decided that Irena, as the oldest, would have to get a job. She left Our Lady of Victory Academy and went to work at Swift's in the bacon packaging room. Soon the foreman was coming along twice a day to feel her ass. Her beauty was a misery to her. One day the foreman brought a clerk from the timekeeper's office around to her machine and she heard him say, "If you think it looks good, cop a feel. Grade A bacon." He did, putting his hand on Irena's buttock and moving it toward the crack. Irena spun around and almost lost a finger in the packaging machine. She gave the man a murderous look that turned him as limp as spinach. Later the foreman stepped in to tell her, "Tend to your work. No fooling around."

The foreman was forever after her. His object was to get Irena alone. He coaxed her, credited her with packaging more bacon than she had, told her she could leave early. He cajoled and terrified her. One time he told her to go and wait for him. "That's an order," he said. But this was before the Crash, when people did not have to do almost anything to keep their jobs. Another time he managed to jump Irena from behind the packing cases. He started to manhandle her when her friend, Alma Jakucki, intervened. "Hey, Rudy, she's just a kid. Come on back here with a woman," and the two of them went off while Irena fled to the washroom to hide or do she didn't know what.

A few minutes later Alma came in, lips tight, brushing the hair out of her face with the back of her hand. She went to the basin and washed, saying as she did, "I gave him a hand job. That calms 'em down every time. Like a balloon shriveling."

"A hand job?"

Alma explained. It sounded like the men's thing was a single, right-side-up cow's udder which got very hard and had to be milked to get it soft again. "It takes the animal out of them," Alma observed, "but when they come, they get the jizz on ya, which you should wash off as quick as you can. It'll give you a rash if it stays on your skin. Hand jobs are OK, they don't take long."

"Is it a sin?" asked Irena, who thought Alma was brave to do something like that for just another girl in the bacon packaging department.

"Mortal for them and venial for you if you don't enjoy it. Father Imiorski gives me three Hail Marys." Alma Jakucki taught Irena as much as she knew and, if some of it was not accurate, much of it was useful for a beautiful young girl who was frightened by the men she attracted without meaning to. Alma tried to show Irena how to have fun with boys safely. It was she who took Irena along with the older girls on the Halsted Street streetcar Saturday nights to dances at St. Leo's. "Don't tell 'em you're Polish. Irish boys think Polish girls are fast. Don't tell the guys you're workin' in the yards either. They'll think you smell and all. Tell 'em you're a secretary for an insurance company in the Loop." Several of the girls worked in "wet casing," where they prepared animal guts for sausage coverings; the brine used in the process ruined the girls' hands and cracked their fingernails. No Loop secretary lie for them; besides, Irena thought, they were heavy. They looked Polish.

40

But no matter what she told the boys, Saturday nights at St. Leo's were not happy times for Irena. Her beauty intimidated the shyer boys whom she might have gotten to like; the other boys, and men too, reacted to her graceful tall looks by wanting to hurt her, to humiliate her. She had always had a quality that seemed to provoke sadism in males. As a ninth-grader she had been jumped by three boys, two of whom held her down while the leader kissed her. God knows what else they might have had on their little minds when Irena heard a crack and an "Off-f-f!"— Monsignor Szymczak, the pastor of Our Lady of Victory.

Two of the boys escaped, but the monsignor seized the last one and forced the names of the others out of him. Irena he picked up and dusted off. When he got her calmed down—she was in a fury—he told her about Blessed Dorothea of Rimini, "a young girl only a little older than you," who was set upon by sinful and lustful men demanding that she "submit." Each time she refused, they stabbed her until, when the knife entered her innocent flesh for the seventeenth time, she died. "The Holy Father has put her up for canonization as a saint and martyr. He has asked us to pray for her because she needs three certified and attested miracles to make it all the way to sainthood," Monsignor Szymczak said. He then told her to "offer it up." "Pray to Blessed Dorothea of Rimini, pray to her, Irena, when men do bad things." Good girl that Irena was, she said, "Yes, Monsignor." But later, in the stockyards, after she had met Alma Jakucki, practical girl that Irena was, she decided if that happened to her again she would try the hand job, disgusting as it was. Blessed Irena of Chicago did not suit her, even in the daydreams in which she cast herself as every kind of heroine. The roles Irena never cast herself in were those of bride or lover. She withdrew from thoughts of boys and men, of love and romance. Irena did not think about them.

Work days in the bacon packaging department and Saturday nights being manhandled by the young Irish thugs at St. Leo's was a short period in Irena's life. It ended because Monsignor had had a fight with the nuns who taught at Our Lady of Victory Academy.

What the feud was about was to be the subject of gossip and speculation around the parish for years. Right reverend monsignors did not disclose church business to their flock, least of all in "the Polish League." That was what the Irish canon lawyers down in the Chancery Office behind Holy Name Cathedral called the clergymen charged with responsibility for the spiritual well-being of the three quarters of a million Polish Catholics in Chicago. One version circulating around the Women's Sodality had it that Monsignor had accused the nuns of hiding several ancient sisters in the school convent, nuns too old to teach or perform housekeeping services, so that Our Lady of Victory was paying for their retirement. Others were that the nuns had complained that Monsignor was too stingy on the food allowance, that when one of the sisters had to go to the doctor's or run some other errand he would not arrange for them (they traveled in pairs) to be driven in his automobile.

Monsignor Szymczak retaliated by threatening to expel the Polish nuns and bring in sisters from an Irish order. The threat made Sister Superior waver, but then the monsignor blundered; he made good on the threat and kicked the sisters out.

From the start, the Irish sisters were a failure. They could not talk Polish so they could not communicate with half the parents. In the parish office, without so much as a by-your-leave, they dismantled the heavy frosted-glass partition with cashiers' wickets in it, which they said made the office look like a savings and loan association, though such partitions were much favored in Polish parishes as a means of protecting the sacred from the profane. The Irish sisters did everything different, meaning they did everything wrong. They, too, wanted the use of a car and driver when one of them had to go to the dentist's. They prayed to Celtic saints, they did not eat sauce, and they ran up the grocery bills. Also they singled out the brighter children. It was during their tenure that Irena had been noticed.

Irena's ability in languages, a skill greatly prized by Catholic schools, enabled her to stand out. Her Latin was better than her Latin teacher's, better, much better, than Monsignor Szymczak's. She repeated as an all-city champion in the Latin contest sponsored by the Archdiocesan School Board, beating out the boys, including those from Loyola, the Jesuit preparatory school on the North Side where the sons of the successful Irish were sent. Irena was started in French and she excelled at it too. So when she dropped out of school, the sisters went looking for her. A girl who could read and understand Livy could not be lost to Swift's.

Kind, upright, and given to command, Sister Mary William appeared in the starched linens and rough cloth habit of her order, rosary beads dangling from her cinch, to tell Irena's mother that her daughter was too gifted to devote herself to the packaging of bacon. She must go back to school; after-school work of a suitable nature—not in the stockyards—would be found for her.

Who would have thought it—a language genius out of Our Lady of Victory? Occasionally Irena would overhear the nuns speaking of her in wonder as "our Polish prodigy." The washed-out ladies in dark blue fustian, their faces pinched white by coiffing linen, loved and mothered this pretty blond girl of extraordinary talent and moved her along to Mount St. Mary's, a college of no distinction but with great strength in the faith. Irena became the only member of her family to finish high school and then the only graduate of Our Lady of Victory Academy (for girls) to finish college. At length she added another only to her list. She became the only graduate of Mount St. Mary's to go on to a higher degree and, *mirabile dictu,* to do so at a secular university, the pagan Gothic pile erected by the heretic Baptist John D. Rockefeller.

The university was as hostile to the One, Holy, Roman, and Apostolic Church as vice versa. It even encouraged students to read books on the Index Librorum, the list of titles forbidden to Catholics without permission of the Chancery Office. Yet the sisters, though worried about the dangers to Irena's faith, knew that no Catholic institution in America could offer their Irena instruction worthy of her ability, not only to pick up languages but to understand their structure. For some weeks the nuns weighed exposing Irena to the rabid secularism of such a place against the advantages of its redoubtable scholarship.

Through the persistent ingenuity of Sister Mary William, Irena was admittted to the Department of Philology at Chicago where, thanks to a small scholarship, waiting on tables, and doing translations, she maintained herself. After Sister Mary William's visit to the packing plant, Irena had depended on the nuns to guide her to places whose existence she had barely known about. Mount St. Mary's had not been a real place, because it was mainly for rich girls, and the university was but a name until she came there. The sisters' admonitions about the dangers to her faith made her timorous, and for a time she clung to the ark of religious practice. Irena was not devout. She was, in fact, bored and perfunctory, but her religion gave her a place to put her feet while being in the midst of strangers. By the end of her first year at the university, however, she began to get a feel for the different branches of the social sciences and, instead of simply excelling in course work selected by others, she began to get her first sense of what *she* might like to study.

It was her translating that first put Irena in touch with Mr. Park and sociology; deep down, she would have liked to take up anthropology and follow Margaret Mead to the South Seas or Africa or China, or any place that bore no resemblance to Chicago. She was sure she could pick up Polynesian or Chinese with the same facility that she had mastered a language like German. But the anthropology department at Chicago already had its fur up in reaction to Mead's fame and was not of a mind to rear a glamour girl of its own. They knew what their colleagues at Columbia thought about Mead.

Allan and Irena's third date was Jack McGurn's doing. "We're goin' out tonight, pal," he said. "You social workers gotta have a good time too. Paint the town red tonight, you and me and Mona an'—you got a girl? I can get ya a broad." Allan drew back. "Nah, a clean one. I swear to God, I wouldn't get ya no dirty girl."

For this big event Allan wanted a girl he could talk to. He had met some of the Gunner's girls, and the young women he knew and grew up with in Winnetka would also be unsuitable. It had to be Irena. He got back to campus to walk in on her cubicle, where she was working hard and looking virginal. "Yes!" Irena said with immediate enthusiasm. "I'll remember everything and give you my notes."

They met at the College Inn in the Sherman House on Randolph Street, a place, according to Andy, where the Gunner and the other gunsels could circulate without peril since the Loop was neutral, truce territory. According to Andy also—how did he know these things?—a new agreement had been struck a few days ago extending the neutral area into the North Side of the city, but Allan was skeptical. Why were the papers full of accounts of dead bodies found in Loop ashcans if Andy was right? Andy always had to make it sound as if he were in the know.

In Chicago, nice people met under the clock at Marshall Field & Company; notorious people met in the lobby of the Sherman House. The hotel had become so well known for its underworld clientele that the newspapers were complaining, but with vacancy rates dropping down toward the disaster line even in the swankiest places like the Drake or the Edgewater Beach, the management of the Sherman still had 80 percent of the rooms booked and its restaurants jammed with crooks, politicians, and tourists.

Allan arrived to see the three of them across the lobby, McGurn, Mona Jupiter, the woman the papers called his scandalous child bride, and Irena, who, recognizing McGurn from his pictures in the public prints, had introduced herself. Allan marveled at Irena, thinking how long it had taken him to strike up an acquaintance with a criminal.

Ben Bernie, "The Old Maestro," and his orchestra were playing to a College Inn full of table-hopping men who would stand up and talk into each other's ears as their women looked at the art deco ceiling and spun the swizzle sticks in their highballs. On every table there were whiskey bottles in brown paper sacks. The hotel made its money on the setups and the bellhops made theirs fetching the booze from the bootlegger on the third floor, who had the hotel concession. Only the smallest of fries and the tightest of wads arrived with their own hooch. The table-hopping went on every night, but this night, man and boy, the guys had something to hop about. Klondike O'Donnell, ally and business partner of the Capone group and monopolist beer distributor in the Pilsen neighborhood on the Near Southwest Side, had been arrested for vagrancy.

"Like he was a bum," said a hairy fat man, pushing a finger into the Gunner's chest, "a man with ten grand in his pocket, they treat him like a hobo, like a bindlestiff out in the Santa Fe freight yards." The speaker was Jake Guzik, the man who handled the books for the same Capone group. His friends called him the Thumb and the newspapers Greasy Thumb because of the stories that he kept an ashtray full of automobile grease on his desk. According to one version, he would skim the grease with his thumb when he was counting the receipts the beer drivers would bring in to make sure two bills did not get stuck together. The better version was that when he counted out the payoffs he would smudge each greenback, so that he could say as he handed the money over to the officer, "Sergeant, tell your captain there ain't no such thing as clean money."

"I don't get it, Thumb," said McGurn. "What kinda beef is vagrancy? Ain't that sixty days in the Bridewell an' you're back out on the street?"

"Asshole, ya can do ten years sixty days at a time. Didja think of that?"

The big news at the College Inn was on the front pages, the switch in strategy signaled by a major bootlegger's arrest on a trifling misdemeanor charge. The Lingle killing, a decade of street warfare, the deaths of hundreds, including noncombatants like the car motorman the other night in the Rosten shootout, had pushed the ministers, the old-line money, and normally indifferent officials into an awareness that something must be done. Law-and-order declarations from the Mayor's office would not suffice.

This time President Hoover had been reached. Washington was promising a true crackdown, and, locally, the unbribed officials, plus those who could be repurchased at reasonable prices by the forces of reform, were beginning a harassing action. The Chicago Crime Commission, a semi-official body of businessmen and ministers, had come up with a new phrase and a new idea. Public Enemy. A monthly Public Enemies list was to be published and men like Judge Lyle, who was responsible for Klondike O'Donnell's jugging, had promised to issue bench warrants for the arrest of every man on the list for vagrancy. The arrests would be followed by quick bench trials, with the gangster being immediately rearrested after serving his sixty days.

On the dance floor Irena happily clutched Allan and did a hippity-hop step which she understood to be a fox trot. Allan felt edgy and out of place as she shouted at him, "I saw you looking down in between. I guess you like her better than me." Irena was laughing, but Allan was flustered that she'd noticed his glances at Mona Jupiter's spectacular décolletage, which contrasted with Irena's dress, the collar of which ended with a modest bit of lace frill where her neck began. "Would you like to see me wear a frock like that? How do you think I would look, Allan?"

Allan, who was as graceful a dancer as Irena was not, smiled at the herky jerky of her movements, looked at the plainness of her dress, and thought about Irena's enthusiasm, her willingness to try. "I'm not a good dancer, am I, Allan?" Irena asked. She had gone to a few dances in high school, but since then her only turns around the floor occurred in the kitchen in time to radio music with her sister, Steffy. "You could teach me," she said.

"Relax!" he shouted at her over the Old Maestro's loudest notes. "You're not doing a polka." By dint of forceful leading Allan smoothed the hippity-hop out of her dance step and, drawing her to him, edged Irena into a graceful, gliding partnership. Something of the flutters inside Irena were communicated to Allan, who became aware of a tender feeling spreading out in him.

Over Irena's shoulder Allan could see Mona. Her dress was cut so low that at any moment you might see a nipple. Oh, the nipple problem, the female nipple, the full breast bared, which Allan had never seen. At Minsky's they wore pasties which did not fall off, though a few streets farther south on State Street, in the Levee, Andy had told him there were girls who stripped for you in private rooms and . . . you could get killed down there, Andy said.

Back at the table, Irena sailed into conversation with the Gunner. "Don't you have to carry a gat?" she wanted to know of the gangster. Allan could not believe Irena could come out with questions like that. "A man in your business. You must carry a gat at all times. How can you get at your gat in your double-breasted suit? Wouldn't it snag if you needed to draw your gun quickly?" They were questions Allan had been wondering about since he had met the Gunner and had considered two dozen ways of broaching. He decided manners might be an impediment. A girl from the slums could be more direct. Did Irena live in the slums? She had no phone. Are slum girls good girls or do slum girls let you see their nipples?

Craftsmen in any line of work are pleased to explain how they do what they do. "We don't call it a gat," McGurn corrected Irena. "We used to call it a gat but don't no more. Your correct name is a heater, or just plain heat, an' you don't carry a heater, you pack it."

Mona Jupiter leaned over toward Allan, asked for a light for her cigarette, and gave him the opportunity to glance down the décolletage. She watched Allan's eyes. He didn't look down. He was cute and he was safe. She could play with him. She was not going to spend the evening watching the Gunner drool over that enormous blonde with the fifteen-dollar dress that must have come from a dump like the Boston Store. God, the rag could be homemade, but, admit it, that big broad could wear anything and look all right.

Irena was learning about Meyer Newfield from the Gunner as Allan strained to hear what he was saying. Meyer Newfield had held on for two generations as *the* tailor to Chicago's flashier politicians and more successful criminals. A Newfield ensemble was particularly in demand because you could pack heat and there was no bulge. He also had designed easy-access pockets, each different depending on caliber and shape, so that the most constricting buttoned double-breasted did not leave the fashionable gunman groping for his weapon among the inner folds of his raiment when the need for speed was pressing. The Gunner, with a sly dexterity of finger, demonstrated a remarkably unnoticeable opening near the lapel of his soup-and-fish, a vulgarism that Dorothy Dix and other newspaper etiquette writers admonished their readers against using.

The Gunner was wearing his soup-and-fish because his plan was that after dinner the four would go on to the First Ward Ball. That

47

was why Mona Jupiter—nobody called her or thought of her as Mrs. McGurn—was in her scanty spangles. Allan protested he wasn't suitably dressed; Irena did not protest because, having looked at Mona, she knew she could never be suitably dressed.

Everybody in Chicago knew about the First Ward Ball, but only the wicked and the daring attended. It was deemed so great a threat to public morals that the *Chicago Tribune* printed the name of every person its reporters could identify there, not always an easy task since slumming socialites and businessmen who came for a variety of reasons, political, economic, and lustful, often wore dominoes. At the hour of the grand parade everybody was supposed to take off his or her mask, but not everybody did, which did not inhibit the city from poring over such names as were printed the next morning. Not that this was a problem for Irena and Allan. They could not be identified. She had never seen a newspaper reporter, and the only one Allan had ever looked at had been dead at the time.

Through dinner Allan said little. He had fallen into a state of self-astonishment, asking himself how he had lost his placid pleasures, bridge, golf, tennis, a good book, to take on this humiliation and strain. He was beginning to talk like these people! And the strain of being on the alert, watching what was going on around him, never relaxing. It was easier in Winnetka, but in Winnetka he did not stand out in his crowd, except by playing a better than average hand of bridge or sitting down at the piano. He wanted to bring back incredible tales to the suburbs, to astonish and bedazzle, to be pointed out as someone who had gone somewhere and seen some things. It wasn't polar caps he wanted to investigate, it was smoke-filled rooms, places where decisions were made; he wanted to discover how the world works and take the news of it home to the North Shore. No book he had read in college had spoken more personally to him than *The Education of Henry Adams*. There was a man who also had the need to be near the power, the social generator.

The First Ward Ball was the antithesis of the inner room of power, for it was unguarded, welcoming; a "regular lalapalooza" is what Bathhouse John Coughlin, the First Ward's alderman, called it. They had had it every year for almost forty years, this grand promenade of Chicago vice and criminality where every madam, every burlesque operator, every gangster, every dope den proprietor, every speakeasy owner, every dip, every prowler, every yegg who worked the First Ward or used it to hide out in came, bought tickets and tables, advertised in the program, or operated bars and concessions for the glory, profit, and advancement of the regular Democratic organization of the First Ward, the alma mater which protected against occasional honest judges, aberrantly incorruptible policemen, and other impediments to commerce.

Or that is how it had once been. By the time Allan and Irena followed McGurn and Mona Jupiter into the old Coliseum where William Jennings Bryan had made his Cross of Gold speech, Bathhouse John and his partner in politics, Hinky Dink Kenna, had lost their power to levy tolls against the vice industry in their ward, which covered the Loop and all of downtown including the neighborhood of the Metropole. These two made their money on the small stuff, the droppings from the barbecue—selling permits, extorting some insurance business, petty kickbacks; because they went way back with the Capone people, they had not been eclipsed. There were sentimental ties, and if they lacked the clout they had had in the days when Carter H. Harrison II was Mayor and men wore black silk plug hats, they could still be of service, this pair, the Laurel and Hardy of Chicago politics, with Bathhouse over six feet and 250 pounds and Hinky Dink no bigger than a small jockey.

"Where the hell is everybody?" McGurn wanted to know. The huge hall, decorated in pinks and yellows, contained fifteen hundred people or less. Nothing approaching the twenty thousand who, by legend, used to come. "Ah, it's early yet," the Gunner explained to himself as music from the band made empty echoes off the iron beams of the rafters. "Ya got money?" McGurn asked in a patronizing tone that irritated Allan. "OK, circulate. We'll catch yas after."

Allan and Irena drifted over to where Bathhouse John was speaking to a semicircle of splendidly costumed riffraff. Without conscious deliberation, Allan had reached for Irena's hand and held it—two youngsters at the county fair—while they listened and looked. The alderman of the First Ward had on a black velvet suit with purple silk lapels and slippers of the same color, a Prussian-blue floppy cravat, and over his pink-trimmed ruffled shirt was a fine wide red ribbon. "To show I was a knight, doncha know? It's the order of disorder," said the man who had gotten his nickname and his start as a rubber in the ornate and luxurious bathhouses at the turn of the century where rich businessmen came to be massaged and manicured. "Oh, but there's too much decorum in this place tonight. What's wrong? I never seen it like this. This ain't a real lalapalooza. No indeed."

It was true. There were more potted palms placed along the sides of the dance floor than there were people on it. "It'll be a miserable grand finale tonight. When they have the parade of the pimps and the pricks, the line won't stretch across the floor," said a morose man with an eye for female flesh to Irena.

"There are ladies present," Allan interjected.

"Oh, Jaysus, why do you swells from Lake Shore Drive come down here? Stay in your churches and your nursery schools. If you don't want to hear bad words, stay the fuck where ya belong." The man belligerently put his nose three inches from Allan, who reacted by letting go of Irena's hand and getting ready to fight. Irena suddenly shouted and tugged at Allan. "Look, Allan, champagne." Nearby was a booth selling generous glassfuls.

He had protected her, Irena thought, feeling the *pop* of the champagne bubbles as she put the glass to her lips. She was close to telling Allan that this would be her first sip of this storied white wine, but she shied away. He was so accomplished, had done so many things.

He had protected her, Allan thought, watching Irena's lips—the girl had such full lips—touch her wineglass. It made him feel good. Irena looked at him, her face expressionless. Allan wondered what she could be thinking, this girl who was so unlike any girl he had ever known.

As they clinked glasses and looked at each other's faces, the music began again and an older man wished them good health and volunteered he had been a precinct captain in the First Ward since the year Allan was born. "Nuthin's the way it was. It's the motorcar and the Prohibition which did it. The Prohibition turned the honest people into crooks and the crooks into monsters. Twenty years ago when I was comin' up, they had a higher type o' crook. A crook wasn't a murderin' fiend like now. Anybody who knows anything'll tell you that. I'll buy you two a drink, if you'll listen to my stories."

He told them about the saloon Hinky Dink had had for years at Clark and Van Buren. It was called the Working Man's Exchange and the bar was one inch shy of being a hundred feet long, with its enormous mirror on which were cut the words *In vino veritas,* which Hinky Dink said "means when you get your snoot full you'll tell your right name." The old precinct captain swayed and moaned. "My Gawd, what a saloon. He had a sign in front that said 'Free Lunch and Five-Cent Beer—The Largest and Coolest in Chicago.' It was the largest. I never seen beer schooners like that anywheres else. When the Volstead Act closed the Working Man's Exchange—that was a bad day, let me tell you—there was people from all over which wanted them beer schooners. They got one in the museum that tells the history of this city, and Hinky Dink sent another to the lady what runs the Women's Christian Temperance outfit, if ya can call a woman engaged in such a disreputable occupation a lady. They say she keeps it on her desk, filled with pencils, would you believe? Ah, them schooners. Every morning he had five or six bums—he slept upstairs, ya know— he had them bums polishing them schooners. I tell ya, if the country does go back wet like they say, it ain't gonna be the same."

Allan and Irena moved off to stand around uncertainly, looking at transvestites and other specimens drawn out of dusky corners of the city that neither of them could imagine. The swish and the cocked chin of rouged male faces was so out of their experience they could only blink and guess at what their eyes beheld.

"Homosexuals," Allan whispered in Irena's ear, as if he would explain at a more suitable time. That time would not come soon, for beyond saying the word, Allan knew nothing. He had had one grazing sexual contact with a male in his life, an ambiguous touching by an upperclassman in the gym shower several years ago. A back washing. It had first excited, then alarmed and frightened him so that Allan had made himself forget it, and in no way could he connect what he might have felt in the shower with these seeming males who had the hip movements of women and the wrist movement of no mammal Allan had ever observed.

The queens mixed with the ruddy types, who appeared to bear with them as a normal part of life, allowing these flaming personalities to get their two cents in about Klondike O'Donnell's arrest. There was speculation that it was the arrest that had cut the attendance so badly. They said people were afraid that even though it was Bathhouse and Hinky Dink's show, the special prosecutors from the State's Attorney's office, a powerful position in the hands of the reformers, would be raiding the Coliseum.

"Bullshit!" Allan and Irena overheard one ruddy type tell another. "There's nobody here 'cause there's no goddamn money in this town. There's no goddamn money in America. There's no goddamn money left on the face of the earth, that's the God honest truth. There's no fuckin' money left so there's no money left for fuckin', and that's why this joint is empty."

The tradition at the First Ward Ball was that around one or two in the morning the more flamboyant partygoers would line up behind Bathhouse John, who led this assemblage of the panderers and the pandered-to in a majestic procession around the hall, after which the Bathhouse would make a drunken and orotund benediction and there would be the playing of "Auld Lang Syne." Masks were then torn off and the modest went home as the more indecent part of the revels began. From then till dawn the night belonged to Dionysus. Tonight, however, the arched and caved hollowness of the old structure made the fifteen hundred present feel like a few huddled persons taking shelter. The empty hippodrome, high-ceilinged and girdered, worked against the spirit of lewd games. Nevertheless, Bathhouse would not hear of abandoning the promenade. "Be it short or be it long, it'll be. I must have it," Alan heard him say as he watched a man with a domino standing close to Bathhouse. He looked like the runt-stump man.

The band lit up with "When the Saints Go Marching In" as Bathhouse, followed by a thin retinue of dancing, jingling, cakewalking zippies, made his promenade wearing a plug hat and a cape to complete his dress. When he got to the raised stand where the band was playing, the music died out and there were handclaps here and there and a cry for "Poem! Poem!" The Bathhouse was famous for his verses; they printed them in the newspapers. The people in the crowd began shouting the names of their favorites: "Two Thirsts with But One Drink," "She Sleeps at the Side of the Drainage Canal," "They're Tearin' Up Clark Street Again."

"I'll give ya a stanza of 'The Silver Moon Shines Over Smiley Corbett's,' but I wanta say, I wanta talk to ya first. I wanta tell yas, I think it's over for us. I dunno why, but there's—well, ya can see it ain't the way it was when we started. They don't party the way they used to, no, not no more. They don't and that's a fact, which leads me to make an official declaration here. That is the— Ay, Lord, I'm gettin' woozy. I'm thinkin' the bootleggers have been holdin' back on the good stuff. So as I was gonna tell yas, this here, this is the last o' the lalapaloozas. . . . No more after this year, an' tonight for the first, last, and on'y time drinks are free till sunrise, gratis and on the house, considerin' we're not gonna make nuthin' anyhow. . . . 'Should auld acquaintance be forgot . . .'"

The tears came down Bathhouse's cheeks and there was other weeping in the half-moon of people surrounding the alderman. The pumpkin-round head topped by a gray crew-cut tilted backward, howling the last, the final, the sad, sweet notes until choked off by a spasm of mucus and self-pity.

The band changed the mood of the party to erotic hilarity. A hot, short-noted Italian jazz trumpet with much brass and little sweetness erupted into "Mariootch, She Dansa the Hootcha Ma Cootch, Down on Coney Island." *Rat-tat-tat-taah,* and Allan and Irena were part of a circle of shouting people surrounding two young women who were stripping. Nothing on. Backsides facing the group, they dropped their panties and smacked their buttocks together each time the drum hit the heavy beat—the *ootch* in the Mariootch. "You shouldn't be watching this," Allan shouted at Irena, taking her and turning her away from those women who were now dancing profile to Allan, nipples and curly hair visible, the whole, all of it, bumping and grinding, the screwing motion, mons venera out and up each time the stick hit the big drum: ootch, *ootch,* OOTCH, squeeze my cootch. "Don't look," Allan instructed her as he looked.

"My God, Allan, why not?" Irena said, irritated and swinging around back in the direction of the dancers, whom she saw fully for the first time. "My God, Allan, I won't look!" Irena shouted, swinging her head away again from the bawdy ladies. "And you shouldn't either!" she exclaimed, swinging back and getting him by a sleeve.

"Irena! It's part of my job. I'm a social scientist," he bellowed over the noise at her. One of the women had very wide areolas, her paps standing straight out. Nipples, nipples at last.

"Not to watch dirty girls, that's not your job," Irena shouted over the music and the clapping and the lascivious shouting.

"I have a professional interest," he bellowed into her ear, having turned away from the naked women as he realized his penis was erect and almost brushing against Irena. *Oh, God, help me.*

"You do not have a profes—oh!" Irena interrupted herself to let go a shriek. A man had just hit her on the rear end and was screaming at her. "Take it off, honey. I want to see your tittie-e-e-es!" The word was elongated by the force of McGurn's blow as he decked the guy. Other men were beginning to rip the clothes off women everywhere on the dance floor.

"We're getting the hell outa here," McGurn shouted, pushing, guiding, directing, and protecting Mona, Irena, and Allan off the floor toward an exit. "What a bunch of nuthin's, and this broad wrecks a seventy-five-dollar pair of shoes an' my goddamn foot. I oughta kill ya, Mona." The four of them walked out of the Coliseum, McGurn limping from a spiked heel wound Mona had inflicted.

"I seen ya trying to cop a feel."

McGurn replied that he had not touched anyone.

"Then you were gonna. Ya wanted to. You can cop a feel with your eyes, ya know."

Mona had an array of tricks for controlling the Gunner. One was to attack first, which she did sitting next to him in the front seat of the LaSalle. The back was so roomy Allan and Irena could talk without being heard as the automobile slipped along cobblestones and trolley car tracks through a misting Chicago out to the Southwest Side, locked-up Capone territory, to a roadhouse in Blue Island.

At the beginning of the ride both were drawn in on themselves, listening in fuzzy fashion to Mona bicker at the unresponsive Gunner, who had shut his ears down and was taken up with the joy of conducting this powerful automobile full speed through the streets. Irena could not get over being surprised at herself, at how she had acted toward Allan. Not even with her baby brother, Robert, was she as bossy as she had been with Allan at the Coliseum—but Allan telling her he was looking at those women as a sociologist! She saw how he was looking, and that was not a sociological look. That was a look-look. Maybe they are the kind of women he likes.

"Margaret Mead had to look at women dancing in grass skirts and no tops," Allan said, as though he knew what Irena was thinking.

"Those were girls, adolescent girls. She didn't watch any men without clothes on," Irena replied.

"She would have if there had been . . . as an anthropologist," he persisted.

"I guess so," Irena conceded, falling silent for a short spell, before asking, "You don't want a woman to do things like that, do you?"

"If she was wearing a grass skirt on the beach, I might."

"You know what I mean. You wouldn't want a someone, a girl . . . you know. . . . Do you like girls like that? Do you, Allan?"

"No, I do not like girls like that. I don't know any girls who act like that, Irena," and then added to himself he wished he did. Turning to see her profile in the dark comfort of the backseat cushions of the LaSalle, Allan could see she looked proper—proper and beautiful. And Irena, she stole a look at him, this handsome boy, horny but with good manners, charming and brave. She liked him so much, Irena realized, thinking too, after the Coliseum, the nuns who taught her were right—men *are* bulls; even this one with his soft ways has that particular animal in him. Like the guys in the yards, the meat-packing plants. She knew about them.

The man behind the bar at the roadhouse greeted the Gunner with a dirty limerick Allan could not shield Irena from; but, after the Margaret Mead discussion, she was not in a mood to be shielded:

> There was a young man from Kilbryde
> Who fell in a shithouse and died.
> > His heartbroken brother
> > Fell into another,
> And now they're buried side by side.

That got the Gunner going. Seating himself next to Allan, he gave him a painful shot in the arm before saying, "Knock, knock. . . . So say 'Who's there?' Come on, for chrissake, don't ya like a joke?"

"Who's there?" But it was difficult for Allan to smile.

"Socket."

Allan was smiling without saying anything.

"Well, come on, goddamn it, come on," McGurn bellowed, swallowing a third of a water glass of whiskey which he did not need. "Say it, say it, say it."

"Socket who?"

"Socket to me," McGurn roared and then socked it to Allan, a brutal blow on the upper arm, one that would leave a bad bruise. "OK, now do it right on this one. . . . Knock, knock," the Gunner continued.

"Who's there?" Allan asked wanly.

"Come on, goddamn, louder, so the people can hear the joke. Mona, can you hear the joke?"

"I can hear the joke, Gunner."

"Well, I'm gonna start again and you say it loud, Al. . . . *Knock, knock.*"

"Who's there." Allan said it loud.

"Radio."

"Radio who?"

"Radio not, here I come!" and with that the Gunner leaned over slowly to Allan and took him by the ears, twisting them as he shouted, "'S funny. Ready or not, here I come. Get it, Al?" Still holding Allan's ears, the Gunner pulled Allan off the chair onto his knees.

"'S funny!" he repeated as loud as he could, looking down at Allan, who had tears in his eyes and the remnant of the smile distorting his mouth. Allan put his hands on top of McGurn's, not trying to pry McGurn's hands off his ears, merely keeping them there as though the touch would moderate the Gunner's twisting force. Cholly, Cholly, I'm here, where are you? Help me, Cholly.

Mona was up screaming at McGurn as Irena grabbed the collar of his coat, but the gangster let go of his own volition and, rising to his feet, told the company, "I'm shit-faced. Goin' to bed." Pulling his shoulders up and swelling his chest out as proof of sobriety and self-command, he walked away, nearly toppled into a party at the next table, and then was assisted to a room upstairs by three stout waiters.

"Let's go, Allan. Let's get out of here," Irena said, leaning to help him. He was still on his knees, tenderly touching his ears, but when she extended herself toward him, Allan twisted his shoulders away from her. He did not want to be touched. In a few seconds he got up from his knees, dusted his pants, and went to the men's room, where he could inspect himself. His ears were still hurting; they were red and somewhat bruised. A little more torque, Allan realized, and the flesh and cartilage would have begun to tear. He thought of putting water on them but the men's room was a sewer, urine and cigarette butts. He looked at himself, the dust on his trousers, his bruised ears. This could not have happened to him; it could not.

Outside, Irena had gone to arrange for a taxicab, and while she was gone Allan sat on a bench in an alcove where Mona had ice cubes wrapped in napkins.

"Don't move. This'll make it feel better," she told Allan, leaning over to apply the ice. As she did so his face felt the skin and contours of her breasts; sexual excitement took command of Allan, overriding the pain of his ears. "Here, you hold the ice," Mona ordered him, as he made an idle gesture toward straightening his hair with a hand. "You're not hurt too bad. Your big blond friend can take care of you an' . . ." Mona paused. "I'm sorry about tonight, but I guess that's how it goes, huh?"

In the cab, Irena was importunate. "Allan, you have to stay away from that man. . . . That man is the most dangerous, the most frightening man I've ever seen. You have to stay away. Promise me."

"I don't want to talk about it," he answered.

"I was wrong. Mr. Park was wrong. This *is* too dangerous, Allan. It is."

"Nothing is going to happen to me. He didn't hurt me."

"He did too. I saw it."

"He did *not* hurt me. He cannot hurt me. I cannot be injured by such a person."

"Oh, Allan . . ." Irena said, thinking that she wanted to kiss him, that she might have kissed any person she'd lived through this night with, any other person but Allan. She would not bend to kiss him because she liked him too much.

Irena's block on Marshfield was like most blocks in the Back of the Yards, which is why she did not care to have Allan see it. She could guess what kind of a house he must live in. But at four o'clock in the morning they were in front of the old wooden house, its paint peeling and its high ungainly wooden steps rising from the sidewalk up to the second floor.

She got out and made her mouth into an O for blowing him a kiss, and although he was too shocked or self-absorbed to show it, Allan too was feeling strong emotions for her. "I'll call you in the morning," he said.

"Remember, I don't have a telephone."

"You should get one."

"I will call you," Irena told him.

It was dawn when Allan got to bed. His ears throbbed weakly, yet he still trembled with sex and with hatred for that man. Mariootch, she got my cootcha, *boom-ba-da, boom-ba-da . . . baaa.* He thought of Mona. Squeeze her nipples, watch her wiggles. Mariootch . . . down, way down on Coney Island, and he came without touching himself. Irena would be disgusted. She was not a wench. Bad boys should stay away from good girls, he thought, going into a dreamless sleep. Stick with Mariootch, cootch, cootch.

Chapter 4

The news Elting Archibald was getting from his friend in New York would distress any banker. He was being told the details of the collapse of the Bank of the United States. Mr. Archibald could not remember anything like it, not even in 1907. Fifty-seven branches, four hundred thousand depositors, hundreds of millions, and now there were armored trucks racing through the Bronx and Brooklyn trying to get cash to the branches and hold off the thousands of panicky depositors. Immigrants. Jews mostly, Archibald's informant emphasized. "The pants pressers' bank is what we called it here, Elting." The depositors had trusted their own, put their money in a non-Wasp financial institution.

"I didn't know so many Jews had bank accounts," Mr. Archibald wondered.

"Small ones, Elting. I think the average account was probably not more than five hundred dollars. It was the Communists who started the rumors. They got the Jews stirred up. A lot of them are reds. Lenin was a Jew, you know. Trotsky too. *They're* behind it."

Mr. Archibald was not exactly sure who "they" were. Nor was it clear whether the Bank of the United States had really gone bust or whether—and that's what it smelled like—the New York Clearing House, the financial cooperative dominated by the old-line big banks, had let the immigrant bank sink. "Yeah, they could have saved it," the New York end of the telephone wire was saying, "but it was a Jew bank. Would a Jew bank help a Gentile bank? The idea of a bank going down makes me nervous, but it's down now, and I may do some bargain hunting among the assets. I tell you, Elting, you'll never see prices like these again. Not in your lifetime, not in this century. You can buy a skyscraper for half of what it would have cost a year ago.

"Pounce, Elting, pounce. What you get now you'll be able to sell for five times the price next spring," the voice from New York, the voice of confident and aggressive business acumen, told the Chicago banker. "And you can thank God or President Hoover or whoever it is you thank for life's smaller blessings for this little crunch in the market. It's picking up the sissies and the Jews and the suckers and the fainthearted and it's turning 'em upside down . . . shaking out their assets into our laps. You can make more money in one good market crash than in all the last ten years of market boom."

After he hung up, the prospect of profit continued to agitate Mr. Archibald. He tried to distract himself by reading and rereading a report from the Kelly-Springfield Tire Company telling him that their Miss Lotta Miles, "the winsome lass who represented us and our tires on two thousand billboards between 1903 and 1910, is coming back in the modern garb of 1930 to carry the American motorist down the road to prosperity." But other thoughts pushed their way in. If the New York Clearing House would not help Jews, who were, after all, white men, the Chicago Clearing House, where Mr. Archibald would shortly be going to plead Moncrief Borders's case, was not likely to save a colored man.

"A nigger bank?" snorted Ralph Van Derveter, the unpopular president of Inter-Ocean National, after Mr. Archibald had explained the problem to the men in the Chicago Clearing House's boardroom. "For Christ's sake, Archibald, that's not a bank, that's a pawnshop. You got us over here for that?"

Archibald persisted, but the more he talked about Borders, the more raillery there was around the boardroom table.

"Land of my fathers!" Van Derveter called out. Washboard Jones's son-in-law! Elting, you're a crazy sonofabitch. The New York Clearing House won't save the Hebe bank, worth four hundred million, and you want the Chicago Clearing House to rescue a nigger pawnshop."

"A bank is a bank." Archibald tried again. "And when a bank goes down—I don't care if it *is* a colored bank—you have an erosion of public trust. The news will get out to the whites, Van Derveter, that the only colored bank has closed, and it'll make people ask questions about their own bank."

"Elting, you're a damned hypocrite. I can see through you." Van Derveter attacked. "You're as bad as the Hebes in your own way. You're trying to save the Insull stock that nigger's got in his vault. Erosion of public trust, my ass!"

60

Mr. Archibald winced, as did several of the other men around the table. It was said that Van Derveter had not scraped the stable off his shoes.

Ben Croaker, president of the Illinois Corn Bank, chimed in. "Our friend Van Derveter here has got you. I know you, Elting. You like to pick up the small change, the low-risk, sure-thing side bets. You do, Elting, I've played cards with you. But I'll tell you this—the banks aren't going down. This isn't 1907." The men in the room understood Croaker's reference to the great panic of twenty-three years before. Lines of depositors in banks in the small country towns and the big cities waiting to get their cash out of the banks before the tellers put up the out-of-money signs. "It can't happen again. Not with the Federal Reserve System. But if the other fellows here want to come in on it, I'll put up twenty-five thousand toward getting that Insull stock out of your darky financier's safe, if he has a safe."

"Not me!" Van Derveter announced to the group, "and I'll bet you, Archibald, you're gonna lose your shirt if you try to cash in on that nigger. There's something funny about Mr. Bingo-Bongo and his so-called bank. I wouldn't buy that stock if it were selling for two bits a share."

"Cook says you were out until six in the morning," Elting Archibald said to his son.

"Sir?" Allan replied, thinking that Cook should cook and keep her mouth shut.

Most mornings he and his parents missed each other, sliding one by one down to the breakfast room, where the serving girl had put out the eggs, sausage, and kippered herrings in silver chafing dishes.

"Six o'clock in the morning is when people get up."

"Sir?" Allan repeated. The son could hear a faint noise of combustion coming from the spirit lamps under the chafing dishes.

"Cook says you were acting drunk."

"I was in bed by eleven last night, Father," said Allan, who, during the years of growing up, had become adept at politely needling his father.

"Not last night. I'm talking about last week sometime," Elting said, an exasperated tightness in his voice.

Allan told himself he could not believe what he was hearing, as though his father had been saving this for days, stoking himself up. But he could believe it. His father did that.

"I don't believe in wild oats, Allan. You know that. If a thing is wrong, it is wrong to do at any age. Do I make myself clear?"

Allan tried to judge if this was a passing admonition or whether his father was going to do one of his blowups.

"Yes, sir," Allan said.

"Well, where were you until past dawn? What were you doing? Whom were you with? I want to know."

"I was with a famous gangster, Father. The man who was responsible for the St. Valentine's Day Massacre. I was with Jack 'Machine Gun' McGurn, sir, drinking in a roadhouse in Blue Island, Illinois."

"Don't be insolent, Allan," the older Archibald said, carefully placing his napkin down on the table. Too much on the calendar down at the counting house for a royal rage, Allan thought. "I know what you were doing and don't do it again. No oats!"

Allan was left alone with his mother, who did believe him. What happened? Ottoline wanted to know. Was it interesting? She was always hoping her son would be blessed with what she called "transforming experiences." In art and life, Ottoline was always on the lookout for the higher plane.

"He twisted my ears," said Allan, putting down his own napkin and walking out.

On the drive southward through the city to the university, where he had an appointment with Mr. Park, Allan asked himself again what was happening to him. He did not believe in oats either; he was his father's son in many ways. But his father's head was not reeling with images of nipples and those two pink behinds, and his father's heart was not invaded with an angry memory of humiliation. Made to kneel in front of those people, in front of Irena. Whenever he thought of the night at the roadhouse, Allan remembered the Gunner's mouth, those teeth, and the enlarged pores on the end of his nose, little black pits.

Mr. Park was late. But Irena was there, looking especially beautiful, overcoming the dowdiness of her clothes, and offering him a sheaf of typewritten papers, her notes on the night of the lalapalooza and the Blue Island roadhouse. She had taken to typing up Allan's own notes for him. She liked to do it because she liked him and wanted to do for him, because it brought them closer; she liked to do it because it was a special way of watching him change and take hold of himself. She could see how he was forcing himself to try to see, where he had been blind before, to hear, where he had been deaf. He was changing, Irena felt sure. He was something more than the aloof, snobby person some people in the department had sloughed him off as being.

But when he finished reading Irena's account of the night, Allan was not grateful. He was furious. She had ρ   in everything. This was not like his bitter but mysterious wisecrack to his mother about the ear twisting. Irena had included a blow-by-blow account, Allan on his knees and that bastard doing that to his ears. "You put in everything," he growled.

"You put in nothing," she replied, alluding to his notes, which had omitted a description of the Gunner's behavior toward him. "You can't do that . . . put in what you want and leave out what you want. All of it has to go in, Allan."

"It does, does it?" Allan answered in his calm voice, but underneath his golden tan he glowed red. Taking the sheaf of Irena's notes, he ripped them in half and threw them in Mr. Park's wastepaper basket.

Now Irena was angry. "A social scientist does not act like that, Allan. A young boy acts like that. . . . You know you have to have full notes, everything. Margaret Mead says—"

"Don't talk to me about Margaret Mead. I am sick of that woman, and I want you, if you have a carbon of your notes, to destroy them too. That's an order, Irena. I mean it."

"You'll have to *order* Mr. Park to burn the copy I gave him. What's wrong with you, Allan? What does it matter?" Irena asked.

Allan went to the window, putting one hand on the stone mullion separating the two leaded window frames. Looking down on the quadrangle, he craned his neck upward, then down, then back up in a ritual of self-control he used when he was very upset and wanted to stop himself from shouting at someone. He hated shouting. "You have no right, Irena. You're butting into my life, you're bossy. You had no right."

"I have a professional right. I am not bossy. You are a colleague, Allan. What if something happened to you and I had not told Mr. Park or anybody what I saw, what I knew? That man is dangerous, Allan. He's cruel!"

"What do you know about cruel? You grew up with the nuns. You stay out of my life, Irena. I can take care of myself."

"I know more about cruel men than you do, Allan. You're so sure of yourself."

"Yes, I am!" And this time he did shout as he turned away from the window and, slamming out the door, bumped into Mr. Park. "Pardon me, sir. Let's make it another time," Allan said, his manners staying with him the best they could.

Irena had seated herself on the edge of a straight-backed wooden chair. Her head was tilted back to keep the tears in her eyes from overflowing the rims and coming down her cheeks. Mr. Park put the hanky from his breast pocket in her hand and admired this swanlike young woman. Not an academic disagreement, whatever had happened between those two. McWhorter had told them these kinds of things would happen if a woman was admitted into the department; then Park reflected that these kinds of things happened if women were not admitted. They just wouldn't happen in professors' offices.

Irena knew where to find Allan. He was lying in the grass near Lorado Taft's statue of Time, face down. His right foot hurt because he had kicked a tree and now, when he heard her voice, he teetered between anger and the sulks. She would have to be sorrier than that. Beg a little. "You're right. I was a busybody. I was bossy, but you could get hurt, Allan. You saw what kind of a man he is."

He lay without moving, feeling the grass spears against the skin of his face, and thought that a few months ago he did not even believe there were men like the Gunner. Now he wondered if he had seen real meanness before, whether the worst he had seen until now was only impoliteness.

"You have to find another way to do this study, Allan. A way that gets you away from McGurn."

"No," she heard him say, still face down on the greensward. She did not hear Allan add to himself, "And I'm going to get back at him."

"Don't be stubborn. Listen to others sometimes, Allan."

"Don't be bossy, Irena," he mumbled, turning over to look up at the tower of blondness. He had found the way to intimidate her, so Irena said nothing. Still on his back, but rising up on his elbows, Allan fished awkwardly for match and cigarette. When he had got the latter smoking and had flipped the former away, he looked up at Irena, blew the blue vapor toward her, and told her, "Don't worry about me. I can take care of myself. A man like that can't hurt me."

A red-faced policeman, a real map-of-Ireland face, Mr. Archibald thought, was trying to talk a man in a longish overcoat into moving along. The banker watched out of the rear window of his limousine as it waited for a green light on Michigan Avenue. The man wore a tweed visored cap with a little button on top of it, and his cold, ungloved hands were holding a box on which a printed sign was affixed. It had the circular symbol of the American Legion and the words HELP A VET—BUY AN APPLE—5¢. The traffic light turned.

Thank heavens these downturns didn't last long. He recalled 1907 again and remembered 1920, not so bad, but there had been some bitter days before the rising tide of money had caught them and begun to carry them up. These downturns were like floods on the Mississippi, Mr. Archibald had come to believe, awful but over in a few months. This one would surely be a memory by spring. It had already gone on longer than most, and it was not right that the men who fought in France should be on the street corners like that. He regretted he had not gone. The Spanish war had meant nothing to him, and he was too old at thirty-eight for the Great War. Allan would have no chance to fight for his country, either. Only his own father, of the three, had stood by the flag in the midst of shot and shell.

Unemployment obtruded again as Mr. Archibald passed through the brass and glass double doors of Insull's executive suite. Sam, cigar in hand, was seeing out five or six obsequious newspaper reporters who had just been told by the Captain of Industry himself that he and all Insull employees would each contribute one day's pay every month to help the unemployed. "This, gentlemen, is more than a gesture, this is action."

Insull led Archibald to a comfortable chair, offered him a cigar, and then walked in a hippity-hop gait to his own desk chair, which was placed behind a slightly raised platform. The platform was designed to let the short man sit in a tall chair and yet have his feet on the ground. The effect was spoiled, however, by the way he jumped onto his platform and spread the tips of his swallow-tailed morning coat to either side before alighting on the great wood and leather chair. A business throne. With his habit of cocking his head to one side and tilting it upward, he looked like a somber parrot whose plumage ran to the blacks, grays, and silvers of a man who wore a cravat, stickpin, and spats.

The angle of the head-cock gave him an air of permanent inquiry when he was not talking and of an overconfident didactic fowl when he was. Sam evoked bird metaphors: dodos, ostriches, hawks, vultures, even occasionally puffins. "It is things like my relief program which set me apart from ordinary or even some very very not ordinary, extraordinary tycoons," Sam began the conversation. Mr. Archibald remembered all the things that made this Englishman distasteful to his crowd. "Sometimes I compare myself to Ford. Did you know that on any given day I'm likely to be as rich as Henry Ford? Depending on whose stock is up or down, and his company has been going down for some time, if you ask me."

Insull's stock had not been doing much better, the banker reflected. Saying nothing, he placed his hands softly one on top of the other and looked into Insull's face as the utility magnate groped to place himself properly in history.

"Take Ford. He's a great inventor, and he's a genius at mass production. So's Edison. A genius too, but flameless light would be a magician's trick if it weren't for me. I started an industry, Elting. The electric industry. Ford didn't start an industry. There were motorcar manufacturers before he came along. The difference between him and me is *I* am a national leader. Ford? He's a national eccentric. He blames conditions on the Jews; he's always talking about what the Jewish bankers have done."

Mr. Archibald recalled the references to Jewish bankers at the Chicago Clearing House board meeting. It could be it was Sam Insull who was out of step.

"Ford is not a leader, but you are, Elting. You are a regional leader. You are as big in the Midwest as I am in America."

It seemed a propitious moment to bring up the distress Moncrief Borders's bank was experiencing because the stock in the national leader's holding companies had lost half its value. As the banker went over the details, the industrialist gave off a brooding, birdlike sound. Given his problems with the Morgan gang, Insull did not need people focusing on the drop of the price of Insull stock that this little bank failure might bring with it. Something about the way Elting Archibald spoke told Insull he might be able to avert that embarrassment. He had picked up a second, not-so-altruistic stream in the banker's words, but, good Methodist that he was, he did not call mixing philanthropy and profit hypocrisy as Van Derveter had. No, no. Forget not the tale of the good steward, the parable of the talents. The Bible tells us we serve God when we make money.

"I think about my place in history," the old bird said, a knowing Methodist talking to an itchy Presbyterian. "I'm seventy years old, but I can tell you what I did with my time. I'm not one of those who's surprised by old age. Thomas Alva Edison, Henry Ford: amazing

66

imaginations, but I've had my imagination too, the imagination to make those inventions useful for millions of people. But, Elting, I'm not in a position to buy that stock back just now, so this gives you an opportunity to serve. You buy that stock. It'll be worth three or four times its selling price by the spring. You'll make some money for yourself and do something for the colored people. Service. It's the right thing to do. You help them, and when the tulips send their green shafts toward the warming equinoctial sun your help will be rewarded, your service recognized."

My! Sam did go on, but Mr. Archibald agreed. "It's the better class of colored person who has his money in that bank."

"Oh, you have to see to it the darkies' savings aren't wiped out, and as I say, with my stock selling at two hundred and four you'll make money. Morgan is dumping my stock on the market by the bucket . . . pounding down the price . . . trying to wreck me and take over, but he can't go on much longer. He's drained himself, and when he gives up, the price of that stock will spring back so high! You'll see. And you owe it to those darkies and yourself, Elting. You know that. You're an astute businessman. You also owe it to the Republican Party to save Borders's bank. There is an election next April. We could lose City Hall if the darkies are cleaned out and defect to the Democrats."

"I don't know anything about politics," Mr. Archibald told Sam, who knew a lot about them.

Mr. Archibald had come to get Insull to buy back his own stock and save the bank. Profit and piety, but Sam had a plan to keep from having more of his stock dumped on the market, a plan that would help keep the Republicans in control of the city, a control the silvered bird feared he might need in the upcoming months. His private estimation of the short-term future was not as happy as the one he gave the banker. More troubles, he suspected, would accumulate before the return of better times. "Elting, Mayor Thompson has to have the colored vote. He's going to be hurt if the only colored bank in Chicago goes under. He can have the city deposit some money . . . say a million dollars . . . interest-free in your bank. It'll stay there until April or May, and in the meantime you can use it to buy Insull stock."

"Oh, we wouldn't need that much to save Borders."

Playing to a higher greed, Sam ignored Archibald's last statement to say, "And after the stock goes up, the money will move out." He talked as though the money had a will of its own which had engaged itself to help them, as though, once the money placed itself in Mr. Archibald's bank, it would not move until given permission. "Come spring, Elting, you will be richer, richer than you were before. A lot richer."

No deal was struck. The scheme was left hanging, but when the regional leader got back to his office after lunch, he was told that the City of Chicago had deposited a million dollars in a special account. Mr. Archibald sat with his hands on the armrests of *his* business throne and then called Moncrief Borders to tell him that Great Lakes National would take the stock off his hands. Then, telling himself better a sheep than a lamb, he used the rest of the money as a down payment for more Insull stock, the price of which rallied sharply under the impact of such a large buy order. For that day, at least, Morgan's bear raid was beaten off.

Where Washboard's son-in-law had risked his bank by playing with thousands, Mr. Archibald was risking his by playing with millions. If the stock dropped and he got a margin call from his broker, it would crush his ribs. He did not own the kind of money he was playing with. His wife did, Fenwick did, and . . . but he would not take help, not ask for it. Elting Archibald would not do that; he would have his own money; the stock was on the rise. It was a risk-free deal, one that the darky could have profited on if he had had a little more capital to cover his bet or better luck on his timing. Prosperity would be back in the spring. They were not calling this a panic, or even a recession, but a dip, a declivity . . . merely a depression.

For the son there was pressure to commit an act of altruism also. For a second time, Allan found himself being taken up the Metropole's elevator by the Gunner to see Frank Nitti. This time, Allan deduced from the Gunner's noncommittal attitude about the visit, the idea had come from Nitti, whom he found tilted back in his desk chair. He studied Allan as he made spread webs out of his hands and bounced his fingertips delicately off each other. Then the fingertips came to rest and the closed mouth twisted itself into a porcine shape as an unseen tongue wiped the outside of Nitti's teeth. Each of them had a way of letting you know who was the boss. Gunner did it his way, Allan thought; Nitti makes you watch him as he attends to the details of his hygiene.

The performance concluded, he said to Allan, who stood with McGurn in a subordinate position in front of the desk, "You're learning stuff for your school, huh? Stuff about our operation. I guess you can see we're up to date. We have the latest, whatever it is. You haven't seen our bookkeeping department. There's more you won't see just hanging around with Jack. We could show you some things if you're interested. Are you interested, Archibald?"

"Yes, sir."

Nitti stretched and bent his upper lip down over the tops of his teeth. The polished and softened tips of four fingers felt the bottom edge of his isosceles triangle of a moustache. He stared at Allan as the fingertips moved grazingly back and forth along the evenly clipped black line. "So, you being a social worker and all, you could do us a favor. It's up your alley, Archibald. You will be helping your fellowman. That's what social workers do—help their fellowmen, huh?" In the ensuing seconds, while Allan considered whether the question was real or rhetorical or sarcastic, Nitti's right hand rose to the level of his shoulder; the wrist executed several rotating shakes as if to free the cuff-linked shirt sleeve from some slight bind. "Help us, Archibald, help yourself, help your fellowman, hey, fella?" Hand and wrist reached out for the glass with the milky fluid.

This appeal, if that's what it was, led several mornings later to Allan's being seated on a packing case in a dingy vacant store. He had spread out some papers on which he was drawing while Andy and three other men carried in a large restaurant-size cooking range.

"Rest it there," Allan said. "I want to finish the sketch of where everything will go. I want this place to work efficiently." This was Allan's first experience of being in charge of anything, but he and Nitti assumed that the talent for directing others in worthy causes came with his background.

Andy was not so sure. "What d'ya think you're doing? Opening up the Stevens Hotel?" referring to the world's largest and, to Chicago's mind, spiffiest lodging place, which was not too many blocks away. "Since when did you get to be an efficiency expert, Allan? This is going to be a soup kitchen, in case you forgot. Anyways, you gotta put the stove where the gas pipe is, so what say we move it over by the gas pipe so the guy can make the hookup when he comes?"

"And I suppose you *are* an efficiency expert, Andy? You are a counterman in a coffee shop, and I have studied these things," Allan said.

"You're a real muff diver, ya know that, Allan?"

The two sniped at each other for the next several days until the

69

morning the soup kitchen was to open with a breakfast of coffee and sweet rolls. Allan did not understand how it happened, but with no sign in the window and no other announcement, a long line had formed outside the store even before the coffee was brewed.

Allan had decided that his clientele should earn their keep by providing information about themselves. "Who Really Are the Unemployed?" by Allan Archibald—he had begun to see those words on the cover of the *American Journal of Sociology*. To be published in a scholarly journal at this stage of his career! With all of Irena's success she was still unpublished.

He would have the people on the line fill out a mimeographed form he had devised before they got their eats, but he had not asked the girl in the department's office to run off enough copies and already there were more men in frayed and patched clothes lined up than he had forms for. The world got scruffier every day. Well, when he ran out of forms, Allan decided, he would close the doors.

"You're gonna start a fuckin' riot," Andy shouted.

"Language!" Allan shouted back.

"Sorry," Andy said with an abashed look at Irena, who was standing next to a coffee urn with an oversized apron wrapped around her.

"I was told by Mr. Frank Nitti, not you, Andy, that *I* was to run this soup kitchen the right way, which is having those people fill out the questionnaires before they are given free food." Allan, feeling his power and position threatened, finally agreed that he would go down the street to a pay telephone to arrange for more copies, while Andy stayed behind to see that those on hand were completed.

"Couldn't find no pencils," was Andy's excuse when Allan got back to find four or five soiled but blank forms.

By eleven, they were into the midday feeding, which consisted of soup and bread as well as coffee. The atmosphere was hectic and more rancorous because there was more to cook and more to wash up and because Allan still regarded the questionnaires as the test of his authority. When he would take himself over to admonish the dishwasher or Andy, there was a soft edging of the line of hungry men from the little questionnaire table to the counter where the food was. Not defiance, not refusal, but avoidance, so that only one man in eight fully complied.

As Irena strove to appear to neither look nor listen, Allan struggled with his perplexed respondents. "See here, didn't I tell you . . ."

"Didn't you listen when I told you . . ." "I specifically ordered . . ." "Don't you know how to follow the simplest instructions?" His voice wasn't squeaking, but his piping tone made him sound out of control, a person of rank without authority. Allan felt the ground dropping away, but instead of backing off he pushed harder. He was taken up with the ardor of getting something done for once.

So taken up that he failed to give the Gunner his usual fawning attention when the gangster came into the storefront for a looksee at organized crime's venture into social welfare. The Gunner had jokes to tell and pranks to play, but Allan had forms to fill out. McGurn had an answer for that. He picked up the questionnaires, the completed ones and the blank ones, and threw them all in the garbage.

"You can't do that!" Allan said before he had thought it through. "What can't I do?"

"Nothing, Jack," Allan replied in a room grown quiet. One of the dishwashers made a choked rheumy giggle.

"Hey, Al, don't take it so bad, pal," the Gunner said with unusual solicitude. "Hey, no hard feelings. Put it there." He extended the hand of reconciliation. When Allan shook it, he received such a bad shock he screeched. Now the room rocked with laughter as McGurn took the gizmo off his finger, and Allan had to submit to a demonstration of how it worked, how the wires went to a battery in McGurn's pocket, how you could switch it off and on. "Tonight we go out on the town. No hard feelings, right, Al?"

Allan was able to say, "It was a joke, Gunner."

"I got a great sense of humor," McGurn reminded them as he sauntered out in the general direction of his bookie's wire room over on Clark Street.

"So, come on," Irena said in a voice that was working hard to sound upbeat.

Allan was staring at the garbage can; Andy was looking away and feeling bad for his difficult friend.

"Come on," Irena repeated. "Let's get the train, or are you not coming to my fieldwork seminar? They're waiting for you. You're the star. They want to hear all about the gangsters." She slipped her arm under Allan's in that way of hers and, turning him around, walked him away from his humiliation.

She tried to distract him by telling him she had good news. She had been hired as a "part-time charity inspector." "Rich people adopt an unemployed family through this agency," Irena began, but then stopped. *He* was a rich person. Maybe he had adopted one of these families. No, not Allan. But she did not want to continue.

"Go on."

"The donors make out the budget for the family . . . and other things they want the family to do, and I have to check to see if the family is doing what it is supposed to do." She stopped talking and glanced at Allan. He was walking straight ahead. She could not tell if he was listening. "Oh, well, it's eleven dollars for twenty-five hours. You can't beat that, and I might get a raise," she concluded, though it was difficult as always to refer to that part of her life.

Allan was barely listening. He wanted one more wrangle over his questionnaires, but with someone whom he could beat.

Irena did not oblige him. "What can you learn from that questionnaire? There is only one answer which counts, Allan, and it's always the same—no work."

On the train, they sat next to each other and Irena was conscious of Allan's body, but this semi-boyfriend of hers was acting the distant male. He was reading the paper. At 39th Street, the Oakwood Boulevard Station, his fine, distant, handsome, self-centered self laughed and said, "Listen to this, Irena:

> Police at the Ravenswood Avenue Station announced that Herman Skedsmo, 23, address unknown, confessed in writing to four robberies and a burglary. The holdup man is both deaf and dumb. He told Police Lt. Harry McInerney that the biggest obstacle to his life of crime has been his difficulty in commanding his victims to put up their hands. Skedsmo said that at first he used gestures, then he carried a piece of cardboard with the words THIS IS A HOLDUP printed on it. It was the criminal's deafness that led to his capture. His last victim began shouting and Skedsmo, unaware that help had been summoned, did not try to run away in time.

Irena grabbed the paper from him while he continued laughing, first at the article and then at her visible displeasure at what he had found amusing. They had never talked about money and the lack of it. Money was something Allan took for granted, and on Irena's side, his family's money inhibited her. Before Brundage told her about Allan's Uncle Fenwick being on the university's board of trustees, she had thought Allan came from one of those "comfortable" backgrounds like most of the girls she had gone to college with. Enough money not to have to worry about it all the time as Irena did, but not so much money that you would never have to work in your whole life if you didn't want to. That was hard for Irena to believe, but, once she did, it made her think more highly of Allan for not being a playboy with his family's money. Yet at the same time she sometimes felt that his money gave him certain privileges that were wrong in her eyes. Like the privilege of laughing at Herman Skedsmo, age 23, address unknown. In revenge she started to read his newspaper, though it bothered her to do it. The woman never reads the newspaper in public when the man is sitting next to her empty-handed.

A few minutes later she decided to get even. "Mr. Archibald the Great," she announced, "it says here:

> Westbury, L.I., Nov. 10 (AP)—Miss Ann Ridley Foster was introduced to society at a 'poverty party' costume ball. The grounds of the estate were lighted with Japanese lanterns festooned along the entrance driveway, and the marquee beneath which the dancing floor was laid was lighted in Chinese bamboo. Guests dressed as unemployed workers, hoboes, and drifters. Dinner was served at small tables.

"Do you think that's funny?" Allan asked.

"Is Ann Ridley Foster a friend of yours, Allan?"

Allan grabbed the paper, tearing it; Irena grabbed it back, laughing; Allan grabbed again, laughing. The paper in tatters, their roughhouse ended with them close to each other, lips nearly kissing.

Walking up from the I.C. station to school, Irena tried to instruct Allan, whose talk at her fieldwork seminar would be his first academic performance of this kind. She had asked him to make the presentation, since there could be no field more difficult for a sociologist to gather information about than crime. "Tell them tidbits," she said. "No theory. They'll pull you apart if you do theory. You know how they are about who gets to do the theorizing, Allan. Not the beginners. Do the tidbits. No matter what they say, they like gossip. I live off stories my granny tells me, only I call her an old peasant-woman informant."

Irena wondered what her granny and Allan would make of each other. She was not confident enough with Allan to be confiding about her family. It seemed to her that in the department the students doing work on their own foreign language backgrounds camouflaged themselves in Anglo-Saxon clothing, or so they thought, while their Anglo-Saxon professors looked on them as fascinating exotics. She was sure that, kind as Mr. Park was, appreciative of her abilities as he was (she was the first woman to chair the seminar they were going to), he also looked on her as one of the exotics, a social specimen it would otherwise be almost impossible to capture for the collection. She did not want Allan thinking of her as a foreign language exotic.

As for Allan, he could have done without her coaching. He did not think of her in the way she feared, but he did look on her as the most peculiar girl he had ever met. He had come to realize he resented her and admired her at the same time, that she was in his way, a person he had to step over from time to time, but who was helpful to him; at times he even relied on her.

His dependence on Irena didn't make Allan feel grateful. He had been brought up to take all that he was given for granted, and without thinking much about it, he took her advice on leading the seminar. No theory, no grand statements.

Gangsters had a special cachet; instead of the six or seven graduate students who customarily clustered around Mr. Park at one end of the immense oak oval, every place was taken. Eustis McWhorter, the department chairman, was there, opening and reading his mail. Several strays from the anthropology department had shown up, as well as an undergraduate English lit major who introduced herself timidly.

Allan told the group how he had wiggled himself in with McGurn and Nitti and soon had them in stitches. Irena laughed too and enjoyed his charm and prepossessing good looks, but she was also bothered. The picture he was giving them was amusing and graceful, the way Allan himself could strike people, but it was false. He made what he had done seem easy; he did not let them have a peek at the real McGurn and at Allan's tortured relationship with him. Allan's presentation was a theatrical success, but it left much to be desired as a guide to fieldwork methods.

Toward the end, she lost track of the discussion, her mind distracted by Jack McGurn. McGurn seemed to have no inkling of Allan's social status, and even if he did, she decided, it would mean nothing to him. When it no longer pleased him to have Allan hanging around, pretending to laugh at his jokes—and after the roadhouse incident Irena felt sure McGurn knew Allan was pretending—he would cast Allan aside or really injure him, hurt him badly.

Her body gave a little shudder as her consciousness of the talk around her revived in time to hear several of the senior graduate students and a snippy professor argue over whether sojourns like Allan's in the company of wicked men had a place in sociology. "It's not social conduct, it's antisocial conduct. Deviancy. Leave it to psychology." That got them snarling over distinctions that soon no one in the room could follow. Mr. Park rescued the seminar by congratulating all concerned on their insightfulness and asked Allan what techniques he was using in his study.

"I don't have any," Allan responded. "I improvise as I have to. Only newspaper reporters are conceded the right to ask questions. Anybody else who does is regarded as a snoop, a stool pigeon, down at the Metropole Hotel. Everyone here who has done social survey work has encountered the difficulty. People assume you're either a masher or a salesman if you go knocking on their doors with questionnaires." Allan skipped around events at the storefront to say, "If you cannot count on the social role of a person whose job is to be given information, you have to buy it, pay for it some way or other. If all the world's a stage, you have to buy a ticket to get into the theater."

The currency with which he was presently paying for his ticket was administering Mr. Capone's charitable activities, the soup kitchen. That set off a row. "Well, you're in with them!" said Louis Wirth, one of Mr. Park's favorites, one of the true comers in the field. "You're helping them! You're not studying them as a detached observer. You've joined them, you've made the Faustian deal. That can't be the only way to get these data. If it is, maybe there are data which cannot or should not be studied."

"Oh, Louis!" Brundage exclaimed. "For God's sake, he's not bootlegging whiskey. He's running a soup kitchen, not a brothel but a soup kitchen, a lawful, laudatory activity. Besides Al Capone, the Salvation Army has one too."

"Archibald may be running a soup kitchen, but the people for whom he is running it have different motives than the generals in the Salvation Army, Brundage. The mob is running a soup kitchen to advance their purposes, and that means they're using Allan and, by extension, they are using this department and the University of Chicago. They're buying into *our* respectability, Brundage, and buying in cheap, I might add."

"May I say something here, may I, please?" Allan asked in heat. "The Capone organization employs hundreds, maybe thousands of people—I don't know how many yet; it does millions and millions of dollars' worth of business with every segment of the community. It rents property, it buys bottling machinery, glass, labels, trucks, cars, every kind of product. It may not be as big as Sam Insull, but it is one of Chicago's largest business enterprises, and the proposition that it's too evil to study is one better made across the street at the divinity school."

"Well said, and what does Rabbi Wirth answer?" asked Brundage.

"Brundage, I grew up in a Capone neighborhood. I've seen the mob grow and take over for ten years now, and I'll tell you something. Neither you nor Allan can use these people. No one uses them. They use you. They are bad men, and they are dangerous men. If you play with them you are going to be sorry for it. Allan, there's an old Russian proverb you should keep in mind: If you're going to drink soup with the devil, use a long spoon."

Cook served Allan breakfast alone. Only two chafing dishes with their spirit lamps keeping bacon and kippered herring warm. The day's great gustatory effort was being directed toward the Thanksgiving dinner later on in the afternoon.

The rest of the family slept but Allan had to be up, out, and down to his soup kitchen to supervise the turkeys and receive the boss. Yesterday an underling from Nitti's office had told Allan that the Napoleon of crime would visit his charity operation. The order had come down from Nitti that Mr. Capone's spread was to be more lavish and in all ways superior to the Salvation Army's. Someone had gone so far as to suggest serving wine, but someone else had predicted that if wine were served, Elliot Ness and his federal prohibition agents would stage their first soup-kitchen raid. To Allan it seemed wrong for the unemployed to be given alcohol of any kind.

As he ate, Allan turned the pages of the morning paper until he came across this item:

BANKER TO HEAD MAYOR'S
PROSPERITY DRIVE

Mayor William Hale ("Big Bill") Thompson announced yesterday that Elting Archibald, President of Great Lakes National Bank, the city's third largest financial institution, will head the Mayor's prosperity program, designed to stimulate business. Under terms of the promotion, people may purchase 25¢ coupons to be called "Big Bills," which some Loop merchants have agreed to redeem for a dollar's worth of merchandise. "Big Bills are Chicago's ticket out of the depression," the Mayor said, "and with a businessman of

Elting Archibald's stature heading up this drive, I predict we will get 100 percent cooperation."

Allan first thought the story must be a lie, a Thompson trick. The man had been Mayor for so long Allan could not imagine someone else in City Hall; in that time he amused the rich people on the North Shore and taught them that there was nothing crazy enough that he might not do. Making up a story about Allan's father would not be Big Bill's first lie or his best. The story could not be true. But would Big Bill make such an announcement to have it repudiated the next day? He had gotten himself elected three times. Dumb, crooked, drunken, loud-mouthed, but sly. So it must be true. Yet Allan's father despised Big Bill as much as anybody, even as much as Uncle Fenwick, who put more energy and eloquence into his despising than anyone else Allan knew. "The man's father went to Yale, for God's sake," Fenwick called out to the Presbyterian God, who, judging from the way his uncle acted, lived in the attic above the servants' floor in the mansion home. "He's a Protestant, an Anglo-Saxon, not shanty Irish. The man's a native American, one of us. He chews no garlic, eats no sausage; he's a Republican! Braying, thieving ignoramus. I would as soon see some immigrant paprika sniffer from Eastern Europe in the Mayor's office."

At the soup kitchen Allan put aside his consternation about his father to listen to Andy's consternation about Thanksgiving dinner. "I thought you'd never get here. I was gonna call ya at home. We got trouble. The turkeys was hijacked."

"Aw, come on, Andy. They don't hijack turkeys. They hijack liquor." Nevertheless, the truck with the five hundred turkeys consecrated to the Big Fellow's holiday charity blowout had been stopped in the first light of dawn on Vincennes Avenue, in the heartland of Capone territory, the driver ordered out of the cab, and truck and load made off with.

"We have to buy turkeys," Allan said, lighting a cigarette and looking as though nothing were simpler than buying five hundred turkeys at ten o'clock on Thanksgiving morning. "Where do you buy turkeys, Andy?"

"Where do you buy turkeys?" Andy mimicked him. "Have you ever bought a turkey, Allan? Have you ever been in a grocery store, Allan? Shit, where the hell are you going to buy one turkey today? And we need five hundred . . . five hundred real fast."

77

"We can telephone; somebody must have turkeys in a warehouse. As you pointed out, Andy, business is not exactly booming."

Andy was sent to telephone; it was after eleven before he struck on something. "No turkey!" he shouted at Allan. "Mackerel!"

"Mackerel? You mean as in Holy Mackerel?"

"Yeah, mackerel, Allan, Thanksgiving Day mackerel with candied sweets and all the trimmings. My cousin Gus works for this fisherman. It's the best I can find. Anyways, it's so late you gotta have something you can cook quick. They gotta get it over here too, ya know. That takes time."

"I thought mackerel was a saltwater fish, Andy," Allan said, putting his most.suspicious tones in his voice.

"Don't be a muff diver, Allan. It's special Lake Michigan freshwater mackerel, and you oughta be glad you're gettin' it."

"Pooo-ee!" the Gunner said, banging in the front door of the soup kitchen. It was nearly two in the afternoon. The lines outside were long and space inside given over to the multitude enjoying the Thanksgiving mackerel. The place stunk of fish. With him were a group of men who Allan would learn were newspaper reporters, and seven or eight more gentlemen who unmistakably worked for the corporation. Frank Nitti was there, and Greasy Thumb, and in the center, instantly recognized and cheered by all on the line outside and all working within, the most famous American outlaw since Jesse James.

Allan knew that Capone was short. He had expected that, but what threw him was that Al Brown, as the Bonaparte of gangsterism sometimes called himself, was in color. Heretofore, he had been smudged over, a gray photoengraved picture in the papers, which gave the king of crime a monochromatic similarity to Herbert Hoover.

Snorky was doubly eye-catching against the sooty background of the store and of the men in their dead browns, grays, and blacks, eating their fish and pumpkin pie at the trestle tables. Capone wore a soft yellow suit with faint raspberry stripes, cerise tie, buff shoes, a white hat with brim turned down in front and back. Off his shoulders hung a white cashmere overcoat. Garnished with gold and diamonds, the effect was made more shocking because the face, the pistil and stamens in the center of this arresting daffodil, was so mean and ugly.

"The bankers, they're the crooks in this town," Snorky lectured his entourage. "What I make here I spend here. Nobody can say Al Capone don't give value for money. What did the guys on La Salle

Street do? They took the people's money and they scrammed. I'm still here tryin' to help with conditions like they are. I'll tell ya, receipts are down in our business too. Yet I believe in helping my country and my city. When the President called in 1917, I went. Wasn't I the one that got the army to use the modern machine gun? Not McGurn, here. You're fuckin'-A I did, and I'm feedin' the unemployed in this emergency. This ain't no publicity stunt. I got a guy here, a social expert from the University of Chicago. Frank, where the fuck is that guy?"

"Al, that was twelve years ago you won the World War," the reporter from the *American* said to him. "Why don't you invent a machine that turns bullshit into gold and get us out of this depression?"

"Say, lemme tell you sumpthun'," the diamond daffodil said, making the smallest movement in the direction of the reporter. The white cashmere fell to the floor; the reporter fell backward as Capone reached out and got a hammerlock around the man's head. "Would I shit you, pal?" He dropped his hold, laughed, looked at the man, and said, "Hey! I saw you flinch. Thinkin' about Jake Lingle? I'm only kiddin'." Somebody's arms extended themselves to put the cashmere back on the shoulders, but the floor had smudged it. "Don't put that rubbish on me," Capone ordered. "Gimme another coat."

Nitti was able to tell Allan by a slow snap of the eye it was his turn to step forward. Unhinged by the hijacked turkeys, Allan was not at the top of his form for playing social expert from the University of Chicago, but Capone did not notice him even as Allan came closer to the center of the gathering. The big boss was taken up with itemizing: "Look at that stuff! We got piccalilli. They got that at the Volunteers of America? We got olives and we got beets. They got that at the Catholic Charities? We got mince pie. The Sallies got mince pie?"

"But they got turkey and we don't" came out of Allan's mouth.

"We don't got turkey?" Scarface asked, making a wrinkled expression.

"We've got mince pie, as you said, Mr. Capone, but we got no turkey. Not a drumstick, sir."

Allan was trying to moderate his North Shore accent. What issued forth sounded like an Englishman doing an imitation of an American tough guy. It got everybody laughing, Capone too, who told the room, "Wait'll I get the cocksuckers who heisted my birds. I'll stuff the sonofabitches, roast 'em, and serve 'em here for Christmas dinner. Get some more turkeys. What are you feeding these people?"

"Mackerel, sir."

"Mackerel and cranberry sauce? Makes me sick."

Minutes later, amid billows of wisecracks and braggadocio, they were gone. But Capone had half taken Allan aside to tell him something he could not get the meaning of, except that the sounds were favorable, perhaps laudatory. Whatever it was it had no great significance, but to Andy, Mr. Wise Guy, and the cooks and the dishwashers and the gray line waiting for their Thanksgiving dinner, it must have appeared that Allan was on the inside. He and Cholly were getting someplace. He, Allan Archibald, knew Al Capone, and he knew him on his own, not through family connections. If not on the inside-inside, he and Cholly were on the outside of the inside, getting closer. One or two reporters had asked him some questions, including his name.

Allan left the soup kitchen in midafternoon in a happy state of carbonation. Often, when he would leave the storefront, he would slink a little, not out of any guilt the well-to-do occasionally feel in front of the ill-to-do, but out of apprehension they might notice his well-to-do-ness and hold it against him. This day he bounced unmindfully past the line without end. Heading along the street to where he had parked his car, he looked up and saw a dark red, liver-colored sky, full of ores and oxides and particulates. The droughts of last summer had been followed by the winds of November.

Although Allan did not know it, he was seeing the State of Oklahoma blowing past Chicago, traveling east. The Dust Bowl had begun.

Chapter 5

Chicago fled toward the holidays as if the city could hide among the Christmas trees and the mistletoe. To make it like Christmases remembered, the State Street department stores, Marshall Field and Carson Pirie Scott, had taken over and decorated the windows of other stores on State Street that had gone bankrupt. As long as you did not try to walk through the padlocked doors, you could think you were back in 1927. At State and Randolph, the Chicago Association of Commerce and Industry had rented a billboard on which Santa and his reindeer could be seen in full flight under the legend BUY SOMETHING FROM SOMEBODY—WE ALL PROSPER TOGETHER. The papers were full of articles comparing prices with a year or two ago. Coats, jewels, toys were 40 percent off what they used to be, but who had money?

Irena didn't. Setting aside any money for Christmas presents was the besetting problem. Her little brother, Robert, must have something, and her sister, Steffy. Granny would understand why there was no present, and her mother would say nothing. Allan was the big puzzle. She had never given a man a present, and, anyway, what was Allan to her? Colleague? Boyfriend? Companion? He had invited her to spend Christmas with him and his family and that meant something—but did it mean a present? Was he going to give her a present? If she did give him one, what should it be? Shaving lotion from the five-and-dime was out of the question. Perhaps a secondhand book, something out of print, something he wanted and she could afford, but who had the time for such careful shopping?

Her question about Allan was solved when the charity agency cut her salary. The director of the Goodfellows of Chicago had been told that another member of her family had a job. She suspected it was

Mrs. Boll who had snitched on her; in the early days of their relationship she had told Mrs. Boll too much about herself.

The policy at the Goodfellows was one job to a family, and Irena had too much pride to beg the director and tell him that Morton—she could not make herself call that man uncle—seldom brought home his paycheck. Mr. Park intervened to save the job but at a two-dollar-a-week pay cut, since, after all, the director said, Irena was only a student and a female one at that.

The Goodfellows of Chicago "adopted" deserving poor families by giving money through the agency; Irena's job was to visit seven needy families and report to their patrons by phone. Six of the families were no trouble. The calls were perfunctory and relationships were routine as long as Irena made sure the families and their children wrote thank-you notes to their benefactors.

It was the horrible Worthingtons who were difficult. Mr. and Mrs. Worthington were fearful they were being taken to the cleaners; Mrs. Worthington in particular was still convinced that any ablebodied man could find a job "if he tries and if he is not too persnickety." The Worthingtons insisted on detailed reports from Irena and passed on endless instructions to their foster family, the Bolls.

The Bolls were as horrid and difficult in their way as the Worthingtons. A German family, they reminded Irena of what they said in her neighborhood: "As long as the world is going to be a world, a German will never be a brother to a Pole." Irena could sympathize with Raeder Boll, the father. He had come from the old country after the World War and worked as a room service waiter at the Blackstone Hotel for years. When the hard times hit, the management wanted him to stay on after his shift and work in one of the dining rooms. For the same money his nine-hour day became a thirteen-hour day, the last part spent under the supervision of a French headwaiter Mr. Boll disliked. "These guys, they come here with their French accents," Mr. Boll said in his German one, "they fool everybody they know about service. You couldn't tell that man nothing, he was that ignorant." The morning after their last fight, Mr. Boll found his time card had been plucked from the rack. He had been canned, and when he went over to the waiters' union hall, they told him that in a depression stiff necks bend.

Irena made an effort, and so did the Bolls. But the humiliation Mr. and Mrs. Boll felt at having to account for their lives—and in front of their children—to a woman much younger than themselves broke into open resentment. Irena talked to the Bolls in German, which at first they seemed to appreciate. Later they accused her of thinking that she was better than them, that they could not speak good English. At the beginning she had told them something of her background in the hopes that they would be less bothered by her prying into their lives. But, as relations soured, Frau Boll used the information against her; she would call her Fräulein Polack, as she threw open the cabinets in her kitchenette to prove they were as inhumanly clean as the Worthingtons expected and a German hausfrau could make them. The director of the Goodfellows of Chicago had been known to drop by his foster families to make sure his charity workers' reports were accurate, so Irena didn't dare to omit the inspections. After she had come to hate the adult Bolls, she used the inspections as her way of getting back for the insulting names they called her. Irena would come away from her visits with a sense of degradation, her own and theirs.

Shortly before Christmas, the director gave Irena a Kodak camera with instructions to take a picture of the members of the Boll family, so that the Worthingtons could see that their largesse had not been misplaced and could determine if they had anything "suitable" in the way of castoffs to give their wards. "Mr. Boll needs shoes," Irena told the director as she took the camera to go for another encounter with the family. She did not tell the director that she had never taken a photograph and that when she asked the Bolls to submit to this new indignity they would call her a Polack bitch and she, in her anger, would lower herself to their level.

Mr. Boll's shoe situation was acute. Mr. Boll, whatever his faults, was not given to sloth. He got up every weekday and was out of the house, going everywhere he could think of to ask for work. To save the nickel carfare, he walked. He walked the shoes beyond any clever cobbler's ability to repair them; the slush and bad weather made the wet come through the cardboard he put inside them. But Mr. Boll was tough and sustained by a Teutonic belief that icewater applied to the extremities was invigorating. It was the nail coming up in the heel that made the shoes unusable. The cobbler would fix them, and the nail would work its way loose and start pressing its point against Mr. Boll's foot. He tried putting a paper wadding between the sole of his foot and the place where the point of the nail penetrated. Nothing worked.

When Irena arrived at the Bolls' apartment with the fifteen dol-

83

lars the Worthingtons had allotted the family for the week, the fact that Mr. Boll had given up on the shoes, that he acknowledged the shoes were beyond saving, was vouchsafed by their place on the table. It was as though they were dead and being mourned. Then Irena saw what the man had fashioned for his feet and realized it was possible to hate somebody and feel sorry for him at the same time. He had gotten a pair of undersized tennis shoes from somewhere, slit them so he could insert his feet, then put his rubbers on and roped this grotesque footwear together.

Irena tried to hide the Kodak. Mr. Boll looked at her, calm as he could be, and said, "You Polish slut, get me shoes."

Irena drew herself to her full height to answer, "You are a German pig. I do not have to take that from you."

She too had not raised her voice but had turned and walked down the two flights of stairs and outside onto Armitage Street. She heard Mr. Boll coming after her, heard his strangled voice say, "Fräulein Giron, I was not the same man when I had work."

Irena turned to face him. As she did, she began to weep, as did he, still coming down the steps toward her with those contrivances on his feet. He stopped a step above her; Irena was so tall their eyes were level. Neither of them would say an apology; at the same time they stuck out their hands.

"Merry Christmas, Fräulein."

"Merry Christmas, Herr Boll," Irena answered. When she had gotten down on the street she remembered she had not taken the pictures. She would tell the director the Kodak had jammed. She had to chance it.

Elting Archibald wanted the holidays to come quickly. He was counting on an end-of-the-year market rally, which the brokers believed was as certain to occur as New Year's and which, sometimes, did occur. This year it was a necessity, for Mr. Archibald had gotten two margin calls from his broker on the Insull stock.

Since October, the jangle of the telephone bringing news of a margin call made investors dread the sound. If you had no money to put up, your broker sold your stock and you lost everything to satisfy the debt. "Just to keep the account current" is what the broker had said to Mr. Archibald when he called the first time to ask for $250,000. Either the banker found the money or he would lose a million or millions—it was so complicated he could not be sure. He had to go deep into his portfolio of other stocks and sell them off to meet the margin call. But the price of Insull stock continued to go down. A few days later Nadja Pringle told Mr. Archibald his broker was on the phone again. Again, "just to keep the account current," another margin call for several hundred thousand.

"I'll get it over to you," the banker had said, but his voice was tight. This newest margin call would be painful; it would require using some of his wife's money. The price of the Insull stock was bound to go up in the spring; prosperity was around the corner, prosperity was named April or May or June at the latest, when he could sell Insull and put the money back, but how to get through the winter? As of now, he had no money of his own left, the City of Chicago account was empty, and he would have to borrow from Ottoline without her knowing it. He had forgotten the scenario he had sketched out in his mind with the curtain coming down on an astonished Fenwick being told that his brother-in-law, with consummate financial skill, had scored a five-million-dollar stock market steal. Men up and down La Salle Street were shaking heads in admiration, saying, "I'll admit it. I underestimated Elting Archibald. In his quiet way, he's a shrewd businessman, every bit as good as his brother-in-law, but not so abrasive, a credit to the community."

The actual Mr. Archibald put in a call to Sam Insull. He dialed the number himself, not wanting Nadja Pringle to know about too many calls to the utility tycoon. But the tycoon was not to be talked to. A perky secretarial voice explained the entire day and night was given over to celebrating Mr. Insull's fifty years in business in America. Mr. Archibald read about it in the paper the next day.

The broker, obsequious but persistent, had called to say the check had not "gotten over here yet." Mr. Archibald was just finishing the account of the elaborate public honor done Mr. Insull: the luncheon of dignitaries at the Congress Hotel with an oversized replica of the original Edison incandescent lamp decorating every table, and at night a gala at the Civic Opera House, the massive art deco auditorium skyscraper Insull had built. That must have been a sight, with every one of the hundreds of companies the magnate controlled represented by a papier-mâché figure.

When the banker did get through to Insull, the Englishman was not curt, but he was not as reassuring as usual. He listened to Mr. Archibald's politely pointed complaint that the margin calls on Insull stock were pushing him to the wall, and then said in his cockney voice, "Elting, you did know about the stock market when you got into this."

"How's that, Sam?"

"You remember J. P. Morgan's remark. That's Morgan senior, not the unmentionable junior who is trying to ruin me. You remember what he said when he was asked what was the future of stock prices in the market. The old boy said, 'They will fluctuate.' Elting, they are fluctuating. . . . Never mind. I will see to it that another million is made available to you on the same terms as before. No more after that, though, Elting."

But it was not as before. There was no quiet notification that a million interest-free dollars had been deposited without ceremony or understanding about specific undertakings. Rather, Mr. Archibald had to meet Mr. Insull's man at City Hall in a grimy coffee shop, where he was told the sum would only be $750,000, with the proviso that $100,000 would be used to meet the margin call and the rest would be used as 10 percent down payment on more Insull stock. The banker was troubled about getting in deeper, but deeper seemed to be the only way back up to the surface. No talk of helping the coloreds or the little investors now. It was a big investor who was getting helped. The representative pressed the point that the price of Insull stock had to be supported and that could only happen if people bought it. Who was buying it besides Allan's father? It seemed to him that he was a lone bull in a market of bears.

Sam's man also told Mr. Archibald that the Insull-owned gas and electric companies owed the City of Chicago millions in back taxes and franchise fees. "No problem with Big Bill in the Mayor's office, but he better get re-elected next April, Mr. Archibald," the man said. The banker left to get back to the security of his marbled and arched building, where, with tense eyes, he looked on as his customers and employees went about their business.

Insull had lied to him. There was more to what was wrong than Morgan's bear raid. If those two apparently strong and profitable Insull utilities could not pay their taxes, then, Morgan or no Morgan, the great horizontal expanse of interlocking companies and holding companies might be hit below the waterline. It would be tantamount to the United States Steel Corporation sinking: the billions of dollars, the tens of thousands of people. The losses would be so large Mr. Archibald could not guess at them. But it was impossible; companies the size of Insull's do not flop over in the water, not in 1930, not in modern times. Yet when Mr. Archibald's big buy order hit the market, the stock tape coming out of the glass bell in a corner of his office did not show any corresponding jump upward in the price of Insull securities.

An order that size unable to push the price up a penny? Mr. Archibald sat stiff at his desk, looking straight ahead. But then, several hours later, the stock did rally. The bears had been pushed backward for the nonce. Nevertheless, Mr. Archibald had been so scared by what he had learned that he decided to begin bailing out, to start selling Insull stock as soon as the price ran up somewhere near where it had been when he bought the first batch. He would have to feed it onto the market a little at a time or risk depressing the price to yet lower levels and aiding in his own ruin. He needed the year-end rally. He needed Christmas. But he got something else first. Several days after he had bought his second batch of Insull stock, the back page of the paper carried a smallish article under the headline "Colored Banker Indicted." The bank examiners had moved in, closed Moncrief Borders's bank, and indicted the black man for embezzlement. The colored people's savings were gone. That damned darky had lied. He had to have known that taking the Insull stock off his hands would not save him—but, as Mr. Archibald ruefully told himself, a man will try anything when he's being closed in on.

Once it had been juiced for publicity, the soup kitchen was closed, but Allan, though he was slow to realize it, had been awarded his own place in the world of the Metropole. He was told he could use the exercise rooms on the ninth floor, installed some years earlier after Nitti had read that big companies of the modern, up-to-date sort supplied such rooms to their executives to keep them in fighting trim. Nobody used them, but having access to them conferred a degree of status, certainly in Andy's eyes. It meant that Allan had a right to be present whenever something on the up-and-up was going on, and to socialize, most of the time in painful humiliation with Gunner. What do you get when you cross a cow with a duck? Milk and quackers. Allan kept on laughing. He also kept on hoping he could make a solid connection with someone else in the organization to escape McGurn, but, although he would go out from time to time with a few of the others, none of them had an interest in palling around with him. He had nothing to offer them, he came reluctantly to realize. This came with a twinge to a young man who had been welcomed wherever he had gone until he came to the coffee shop of the Metropole Hotel.

He was spending a large part of his life with people he was not sure how to act with in situations of precarious ambiguity. They spoke English but the words sometimes meant something else to them; they laughed when he would not; they were solemn when he would have laughed. The strain did not lessen as their view of him shifted from a stranger, a student from the university, to a familiar person, a given in their lives.

"Being in the field is helping you, if you'll permit a friend to say," Mr. Park said with a pleased, almost parental manner. "And you're beginning to get some information, not bad stuff. Keep at it, Allan."

Allan told Mr. Park how he had gone out the other evening with the Gunner and Mona Jupiter to the Near West Side, the Genna brothers' territory. The Gennas themselves took them around to some of the tenement apartments where the Italian families had little stills in their kitchens. Gunner laughed at Allan's amazement while the two alky cookers bragged that Elliot Ness and all the G-men in Washington could not close down alcohol production, because it was being carried on by families from Halsted Street to Ashland Avenue. It was an astounding system, combining cottage labor with modern high-volume distribution, a system depending on runners bringing the new material and taking away the alcohol for the synthetic scotch, rye, and bourbon that was sold to the masses who could not afford the more expensive stuff that came over the border from Canada. They did not fear to tell Allan how it was done—many people knew—because the authorities could not stop it even if they wanted to, which a substantial number of the authorities were not fired up to do. "They gotta put forty thousand of these people—the kids too—in jail to close down our operation," one of the Gennas said in the speakeasy where they spent the latter part of the evening.

That's where Allan stopped the story which Mr. Park called rich, anecdotal material, "the sort of illustrative material we have never had on organized crime." He seemed to be telling Allan that Cholly was getting there, but Allan had stopped short of relating all that had happened. He did not tell Mr. Park, for instance, that they had gotten snockered. He had also been goosed, something that had not happened to him before. McGurn did it at the end of the night, in front of

Mona Jupiter and several others, men and women, as Allan was carrying drinks over to the table, the waiter having gotten so drunk on the whiskey the party had bought him he could no longer stand. The drinks Allan was carrying had splashed every which way, but that was nothing to the humiliation of bending over protecting his privates in public. Everyone else thought it was funny.

That was a story Allan was incapable of telling anyone. Instead, he said to Mr. Park, "I'm getting into situations I don't know about. It makes me tense. I'm edgy a lot of the time."

Mr. Park reassured him that the new person in any group, the person who is being judged acceptable or unacceptable, is bound to be nervous. "Your nerves are your friends in such a situation, Allan. It's the nervousness that keeps you on your toes, keeps you from making a mistake."

Allan got more useful advice from Andy, who, now that the soup kitchen was closed, was back at the hotel coffee shop. The two had taken to passing evenings together in a beer flat in the neighborhood, a block from the rooming house where Andy lived. A beer flat was an apartment converted to sell brews to working people at prices well under those of the more expensive speakeasies.

"You're gonna get in trouble," he announced to Allan one evening out of nowhere. "You think those guys just kill for money. They kill for their women too."

"What are you talking about, Andy?"

"You know fuckin' well what I'm talking about. What d'ya think, I ain't got no eyes? You wanna play innocent with me, go ahead. But you're the one that's gonna get pushed, buddy. I'm not gonna say no more to you about it. And I don't want to know nothing about it, but, pal-o'-mine, you goin' straight for trouble."

Allan knew Andy was talking about Mona. Mona the mysterious. There were two items that were often in the newspaper stories about the Gunner. One concerned his connection with the St. Valentine's Day Massacre and the other said the only time he had been arrested was for taking his wife, the then fourteen-year-old Mona Jupiter, across a state line for the purpose of marrying her. That was supposed to have happened in 1926 or '27, but Mona did not look that young. But then Mona did not add up in any way. She could act childish, she could act smart and old, she could act loud or soft, coquettish or brusque; she seemed to have no past beyond the Gunner, no place of origin geographic or social. Mona was Mona, a peroxide phenomenon whom men saw and wanted to fuck.

Allan would have liked to ask Andy for some advice. His father was right about how it should be—no oats—but he did not seem to understand how it actually was with his son, the urges which were washing away his consecration to living the clean life. He had been tortured since the night of the lalapalooza. He had not been able to get women out of his mind. Those two dancing trollops had cut a restraining cord in his soul; he thought about the act of mating every idle hour; he listened to yowling cats and watched dogs in pursuit of hot bitches with new empathy.

Allan's libido was rising as everyone else's sank. The joyousness of the swelling bull market had shriveled, giving way to tightness and caution. The papers carried stories that marriage licenses were off 15 or 20 percent. Announcements of pregnancy were an occasion for condolences. Allan, who had not engaged in heavy petting in the rumble seat of a Stutz Bearcat under Coolidge, found the flappers had flitted away under Hoover. In the year after the crash, chaperones had been rendered unnecessary; men were too confused, too timid, too worried to slip their hands under women's garments.

"Sounds like a very, very hot and very, very naughty lady to me," Brundage had said, combining sneer and leer, to Allan, who had been sitting in the student lounge talking about the Gunner, Mona Jupiter, and social life in gangland. Naughtier than Brundage knew. Mona had taken to appearing near Allan at strange moments and places. When he had been in the ninth floor exercise room working out, he saw her face through the oval glass window in the door. Allan had on trunks and a tank top, he had been doing a drill with the dumbbells, but her stare had bothered him enough to send him hiding among the lockers of the adjacent shower room.

When the Gunner was upstairs in the headquarters suite, Mona would sometimes come sashaying into the coffee shop in her spectacular fashion, pretending she was waiting for her husband to come down. By the customs of the organization she should not have been there. The wives did not come to the Metropole, save Mona, who gave the impression of being permanently and irresponsibly out of control, a savvy and experienced woman one minute and a nutty young chorus girl the next. When she saw Allan she would sit down at the table and talk to him in the friendly, familiar way she would never use with the other men in Gunner's world. To them Allan was no threat; he did not give off the scent which made them competitive and wary. His upper-class ways, his clothes so dull compared to their fine feathers, his hoity-toity fruitcake accent, his student's eagerness, his manifest softness put him in the eunuch category. No balls, no status; hence he was allowed around the women. More than allowed. They liked it because they presumed that if he was around, other men would know to stay away; Allan was the castrated sheep dog. He had even been allowed to meet the real Mrs. Capone, whom few knew. A thirteen-year-old boy from Cleveland had run away from home and succeeded in arriving at the boss gangster's residence; Allan had been dispatched from the hotel to the South Shore to fetch the runaway and turn him over to the Chicago Police Department, an incident that also got into the newspapers.

Andy saw what was happening. He would serve them coffee and watch Mona make her play. She would ask Allan about Irena and their dates. "What did you do *after* the show, Allan? Did you take her right home or did you go somewheres?" She'd wink at him, and Allan would wriggle away from answering her directly. Then one afternoon when the coffee shop was deserted and Allan was thumbing through a movie magazine left by a previous customer, Mona got him.

She appeared from out of the cold, the smell of snow clinging to her furs. He would turn a page and she would lean over the movie star's photograph to ask, "Is she your type, Allan? Do you go for her? Would you like her, would you like to get off alone with Norma Talmadge? I'll bet you would." The cardboard Santas hung from the ceiling twisted in the quiet, heavy air, and Mona spoke in a tone that claimed Allan. He could not look at her; he was scared to stop turning the pages as Mona talked to him, her lips seemingly close to his ear.

The more she talked, the more embarrassed he became. He had a fierce erection. Her words were purring over his skin. As Allan put his hands together on his lap, Mona stopped her banter. For a full count of two she said nothing. When she spoke again it was in a mocking trill: "Al-lan, look at me." He did, but barely. "Allan, have you ever been with a woman?" Allan turned away from Mona to study the movie magazine, blushing; Mona Jupiter leaned away from him, but only to study this young male, her teeth pressing her lower lip, pretending to bite, her face becoming satanic dimples.

Midafternoon of Christmas Eve, Irena was walking up Marshfield toward home with Christmas presents: a toy for Robert, a blouse for

Steffy, gloves for her mother, a scarf for Granny, and a tie—it was ugly but he would like it—for Morton. There was something for Morton's wife, Irena's Aunt Helen, who had two customers in her beauty salon, which had once been the Giron living room.

People had started using their parlors as their places of business. Barbershops, groceries, dairies, candy stores, all manner of minor enterprise were located there. The country, thrown out of work by the big guys, was going into business for itself. Every other knock on the door was a salesman offering dishes, brushes, cosmetics, subscriptions, home repair kits for anything that gets broken that people could not afford to replace. America had become a nation of sellers; buyers were nowhere to be found.

Helen, Morton, and the obnoxious Jerzy had come to stay some ten years ago, after Irena's father "left," as the family still referred to his absence. Irena's mother couldn't keep her sister Helen out. She needed Helen financially and she needed Helen to tell her what to do with her husband gone and no man to depend on. She could not stand alone; she never could.

Morton became the head of the family, although the house belonged to Granny. She had intended to give it to her son, Irena's father, but once they had moved in, Morton and Helen tried to get her to sign it over to them because "it would make things easier." Granny understood it would not make things easier for her. "When you are an old woman," she told Irena, her favorite, "your power is property. They don't respect age." Sometimes when they came after her, she would tell Irena, "A Pole never gives away a house or land." To their faces, Granny did not tell them no; she said not now, she would think about it. She would rattle the pots and pans and have small conversations with Panna Maria, Holy Mary on the kitchen wall over the sink, the figure of Our Lady of Czestochowa, the much-venerated Black Madonna of Poland. The content of these conversations with Panna Maria was more complicated than simple peasant idolatry. Sometimes Panna Maria would be turned to the wall for having failed to answer what Granny considered a reasonable request. "I don't pray for miracles," she would tell Irena in Polish. She always spoke to Irena in Polish. Yet, though Granny owned the house, had the most influence with Panna Maria, and was the only one Irena would listen to, this grandchild for whom she held the hope of a special future, the brutal Morton headed the household.

The dislikable Jerzy shared half a bedroom with Irena's dear but sadly dull brother, Robert, while Irena and Steffy lived on the other side of a blanket hung up on a rope dividing the room. Irena's mother slept with Granny so Helen and Morton could have her room. Helen's beauty parlor took away the use of the living room. There was no privacy, no place for Irena to study, and no sympathy. When she would demand some quiet they would tell her she was stuck-up.

As Jerzy got to be a teenager, he began peeking at his two cousins around, under, and over the blanket. Of late he had begun to brush up against Irena with his hands. "You know what I mean," she and Steffy, who was having the same experience, said to each other. They did not know he was selling squints through the crack in the drawn kitchen shades. For a penny a peek his pals got to see the girls washing themselves in the corrugated tub on the floor.

"Irena completely! Oh, Jesus, not a stitch! Look at that broad!" Granny had heard these gargled whispers of lust as she stood by the window one night. She may not have understood much English, but she didn't need to, and from then on she stood in front of the window whenever the girls bathed. A bathroom with its own frosted glass window was what the family needed; it had been part of the plan when the flush toilet was installed shortly before the lumberyard accident. After Irena's father had gone away, they had gotten a new radio with part of the settlement. They were arguing whether they should get a bathroom or a refrigerator when the market crashed. They were still arguing but they had no money now.

The girls were afraid to say anything about Jerzy. Granny was afraid to talk to his parents. The idea had taken hold of her that Morton was somehow going to get the house from her; he was going to trick her, she felt sure, and then Morton would send her to Holy Guardian Angel Home for the Aged. The old lady made Irena promise not to cross Morton.

"She's too good for us. She's going away for Christmas, going away from her family," Aunt Helen said as she applied elastic, metal, and wave set to a neighborhood lady's hair. This needling was to be accepted as good-natured teasing, so Irena tossed an insincere smile at her aunt and took herself, the Christmas presents, and the overnight case she had borrowed from a friend on campus to the semi-privacy of her room. She had wrapped the presents and was getting dressed, struggling to hook her brassiere, when she saw Jerzy's eye at one end of the blanket. She screamed as she swiveled her back to him and covered herself in a terry-cloth robe. Jerzy fled downstairs.

It was Christmas Eve, Irena told herself. She should finish getting dressed and get out of here. But she couldn't make her hands work. Twice she started to put on the rest of her clothes, only to discover that she was sitting stock still on the bed. She ordered herself to forget it, to remember she had promised Granny not to say anything.

Cinching the belt on her robe tight, Irena threw the blanket aside and stamped downstairs into the beauty parlor, caught up with Jerzy, and slapped him as hard as she could. She shouted, "Creeping peep! Peeping creep! Don't ever do that again!" Jerzy took the blow and cowered, making a pleading gesture for silence from Irena as he did. Jerzy was aware of Morton's having come into the room and was frightened of what his old man might do if he found out.

"Don't you hit my kid. Not now, not ever. Don't hit my kid," Morton yelled.

"He saw me! He was peeping at me. He saw me without my clothes on. He's a peeping tom," Irena yelled back.

"He's a kid, for chrissake."

"He's *not* a kid! He shaves, for chrissake yourself. I'll hit him every time I catch him. I'll report him to the cops."

"Your goddamn tits. Your *tits!* Have ya got any?" Morton came back at her and went for her. Irena fought him off as he attempted to open her bathrobe.

"That's enough out of both of you!" Aunt Helen shouted louder than the rest, a hot curling iron in one hand. "You're not as precious as you think you are, Irena. You're not such a hot number. And you," she said, turning to her husband, "you stink."

"She ever lays a hand on Jerzy again—" Morton replied to his wife. "You ever lay a hand on Jerzy again," he said to Irena, "I'll turn you over my knee. I'll take your panties down and beat you black and blue."

Her brother, Robert, the slow one, came to her upstairs after Irena had returned. He stood by his sister as she sat on her bed, gulping air. She had made a mistake by slapping Jerzy; she had broken the arrangements that held the family together. She had made it easier for Morton. She had controlled him by conning him into sticking to polite forms, by acting as though force was unthinkable. Now she had let her temper take away her advantage.

Irena gave Robert his present and told him, "Don't open it now, not until tomorrow." The little boy nuzzled his face into her bosom. Irena found she was still furious. She picked up the paper bag with her other gifts for the family, came downstairs, banged the bag on a little table in the beauty parlor with such force it split, spilling its contents of small, earnest Christmas packages on the floor. The table tipped over. "There!" said Irena, who kept on going past the permanent wave, out the door of the house, and up Marshfield Avenue.

Irena kept walking until she came to the convent of St. Thomas of Canterbury parish, where Sister Mary William was now teaching. As soon as the nun sat down in the small visitors' room with the Sacred Heart lithograph on the stippled beige wall, Irena knelt beside her, put her head in Sister Mary William's lap, and cried. Irena cried herself into a condition in which she felt nothing but her tears, nothing but the act of crying. She gave herself over to her unhappiness until she felt Sister's hand on her head, noted her sobs were tapering off, and saw with a third-party interest that one of her fingers was idly playing with the cross on the nun's rosary.

It seemed to Sister Mary William that Irena was going through something similar to what she herself had experienced with her family when she went to the novitiate. She told Irena that her parents had been proud of her, but also resented her; they were glad to see her answer this call, yet they knew they were losing a daughter who was going on to a different life. Sister Mary William was inclined to think of Irena as having joined a scholarly order, a secular body run along the lines of her own religious one.

Irena reverted to the respectful attention of her high school and college days. Sister Mary William's strength was not in counseling but in practical advice and help. She said she would find a parish convent near the university where Irena might live in return for secretarial duties; as for the pain of her spirit, Sister urged Irena to "offer it up." It occurred to Irena that she had been hearing that suggestion her entire life and that it meant no more to her now than it did when she was in first grade. She was outgrowing Sister Mary William or growing apart, she thought, as her self-confidence and emotional balance began to return.

On the drive up to Uncle Fenwick's estate, Allan said he had been doing his part to end the depression. Following the advice of the newspapers, he had been spending money. Irena decided against telling Allan about her new problems. But after the next two days, living with Allan's family, she did venture to say, "Our families are the same in one way, anyhow. Neither of them have company manners."

Allan's relatives were rich, obtuse, and bereft of any understanding of people unlike themselves. The several distant cousins who had come for the holidays were braying alcoholics or pale, fumbling wraiths. Uncle Fenwick was so thoroughly insensitive that Irena got a kick out of him and ended by liking the old bigot, who met her in the drawing room bellowing, "Allan! She's gorgeous! But you told me she was Polish!" Irena, easy with him on first sight, stepped in to say, "Wait! I *will* look Polish. In thirty years I will have piano legs and a babushka." That tickled Uncle Fenwick no end and he took a great liking to her, showed her all over, and lectured her about the dangers of Coast Guardsmen getting drunk on confiscated bootleg whiskey while on duty patrolling the nation's sea boundaries. Irena realized it was no accident when he brushed up against her fanny and her breasts, but she didn't mind. They liked each other, these two.

She did not like Elting Archibald. She caught his high opinion of himself and thought Allan was in danger of copying it. "You may find Presbyterian services drab compared to what you are used to," Mr. Archibald told her in the back of his limousine on the way to church. "No incense, no statues, and we don't kneel, you know."

"Oh, I know you do not kneel," Irena replied, but it was lost on him. She turned to look at Allan and move nearer to him. Handsome profile. He came by it and some of the other not-so-handsome Archibald traits naturally, she was reminded. Deciding he could be trained out of them, she gave herself up to her first Presbyterian Christmas, which she found to be more good taste than faith.

They spent much of the holidays together and exchanged their first, sweet, chaste kisses. When Allan held her and Irena did love's puzzling inquiry into the face of the beloved, she thought of Leslie Howard, the new, sensitively featured English movie star who spoke quiet, elegiac words to his leading ladies. Irena's dreamy moments were not of men who grabbed their girls. No Clark Gables for her, no swashbucklers who ordered their women to "Come over here, baby." She wanted Leslie Howard and the soft touch, and Allan touched her as she imagined Leslie Howard would.

They enjoyed each other and began to learn how to enjoy being a couple. Irena had been pleased with how they looked together since the first day on the Midway. Allan was getting to know the feeling of having other men envy him his girl. "You're a lucky boy to have *that*," Uncle Fenwick informed Allan, making his eyebrows go up and down once or twice. It made Allan plucky. It did not, however, open the way for him to talk to Irena about his private tortures and temptations. He was not going to mention Mona Jupiter to her, or to anyone. Was he going to ask Irena about sowing one wild oat? to see what it was like one time, to try it, to know it, to feel one nipple, to get it out of his system once and for all? At last a girl had come into his life whom he felt close to and worked closely with; but he could not talk honestly to her, could not discuss his morning guilts and his midnight erections.

Allan had been driven to trying prayer, not the perfunctory prayer he said nightly but ardent, sincerely meant petition. "Thy will be done," he had prayed one night and stopped. A bulging erection was pushing out of his pajama pants. The restraining effect of the prayer was gone, worn away. He rose from his bed, turned on the lights, took his pajamas off, and looked at himself in the mirror as he undressed Irena in his mind. God, she must be fabulous stripped, he said. His mind returned to the Father who art in Heaven, and he reproached himself for having such thoughts about Mona and about the girl he had begun to think he loved. He would never be able to tell Irena, though. He was sure he could never get the words out of his mouth.

Neither could tell the other what was uppermost in their minds. Sister Mary William had found a place for Irena at St. John of God, not too far from the university, but Irena was uncertain, in and out and back and forth about leaving her family. Morton harassed her. A barrier had been broken there. She was afraid of what he might do if he got her somewhere where he could do it, but she hated leaving Granny and dear Robert and poor, ugly Steffy. Sometimes she thought she had pigged up the family allotment of brains and looks. Then she would reproach herself for being conceited until she looked at Steffy, acne down to her shoulders, though she did have a nice body.

Living in the convent would restrict her freedom. She would have to be in by a certain hour; there would be social pressure to go to Mass every morning, pretend to be a better Catholic than she was. If she moved to the convent, she would have to explain to Allan why; she would have to tell him what went on inside the clapboard house on Marshfield Avenue, which would confirm what people like the Archibalds thought about people like the Girons.

In *Zgoda*, the paper published by the Polish National Alliance, they said to be proud of your people, but what did they know of

Winnetka, the North Shore, Mr. Rockefeller's school, La Salle Street banks, or going to the Onwentsia Club for lunch with the Archibalds? Three spoons, three forks, two knives, and no prices on the menu. What did they know about that in Polonia, going up and down the steps of St. Stanislaus Kostka to pray in the flickering candlelight of the Baroque and Romanesque basilicas the Polish people and their pennies, so painfully earned, erected to the honor of God and their own dignity? What did they know of an Uncle Fenwick around St. Stan's, around the Stanistawowo? And how is a girl going to explain her Aunt Helen to Lake Forest when she doesn't exactly understand her herself? How is she going to explain Morton to Allan or ask him to skip lunch at the Saddle and Cycle for a bowl of Granny's *kapusti i groch*. They do not serve sauerkraut with peas at the Tavern Club.

Allan and Irena preferred to meet on neutral ground. Not your house, not mine. It was a love affair conducted in public places, one of which was a dance marathon at the Tivoli Ballroom on Cottage Grove Avenue.

"I've never seen one," he said, when Irena said she could think of better ways to spend New Year's Eve than watching broke, out-of-work people pushing hurting feet and defeated bodies about a dance floor for a few bags of groceries and sacks of coal. "They say it's fun. Lots of people go," he added, and they went. The man gets to choose, and there were a lot of people who thought watching a dance marathon was a jimcracky way to spend New Year's Eve.

Amid the shouting and yahooing by the audience—the employed watching the unemployed enduring the unendurable—and between titters of enjoyment from Allan, Irena thought she saw a girl from Our Lady of Victory Academy on the floor. It was, definitely, a girl who had graduated a year earlier. Irena did not know her name but she had seen her often at assemblies sitting with older girls in her class; it was the same face Irena now saw on a somnambulent young woman shuffling through her seventeenth consecutive hour for a dozen eggs and half a dozen cans of baked beans. Their eyes met, but the girl did not recognize Irena; though the girl's eyes were open, fatigue had stolen their sight.

After Irena pulled him out of the Tivoli's Venetian decor over to the New Year's Eve party at a young assistant professor's apartment, Allan was charming. He made for the piano and did his performance with the highball and cigarette, attracting two or three pretty young women, whereupon he stopped playing, thereby incurring groans and protests, but he would not begin again until Irena sat on the bench by his side, and then, dropping his cigarette into the ashtray, Allan looked at her and sang:

> And that's why the Chinks do it, Japs do it,
> Up in Lapland, little Lapps do it,
> Let's do it, let's fall in love.

The gin, supplied by a physician from the university hospital, got to Allan. His let's-do-it began to slur before he spilled his drink down his front, and Irena guided him toward the bathroom to spruce him up. When he was inside the room with her, Allan leaned toward Irena as he said, "The Shinks do it, the Shaps do it, do Polack girls do it?" With which he made a grab for her. He hadn't called her that, had he? He was grabbing at her again. But she was strong and Allan had had too much to drink, so Irena held her own. He *had* called her that. Her blouse was going to rip, her best blouse, and then she remembered Alma, Alma Jakucki.

"Wait," Irena said quietly to Allan, "wait, Allan, I'll show you what we—we girls, how we do it," but Alma had never explained precisely how. Allan came at her again, and again Irena asked him to wait, pushing him against the bathroom door, her hands trying to find the space between his shirt and his pants. He had called her a Polack. She could not stand seeing him or it and, oh, God, she recoiled; her fingers were touching it, she could feel his pubic hair and, unmistakably, his penis. Alma had not said how hard it would be.

Irena was leaning against Allan, her head averted from his, her eyes teared over, her cheek on his shoulder, the fingertips of her free hand resting on his lips as though she had to have some other kind of contact with him at the same time, as though she were hushing what they were doing out of existence. Someone in the hall knocked on the door.

"Occupied!" Allan shouted, not so drunkenly, it seemed to Irena. She felt Allan's breath slide out between his lips as she manipulated him, wondering if she was touching him correctly. Whatever the task, Irena had been trained to do it right. Alma had said behind the packing cases it was like milking a cow, but Irena was a city girl with only theoretical knowledge of how that might be done. As Allan's breathing got harder, Irena decided her hand job must be satisfactory except now she was startled at how his muscles were tightening. How could he have called her *that?* It was as though he were going into a spasm, epilepsy. My God! Will he hurt himself? Will he hurt me? She understood now why the sisters had warned them against the arousal of the male. She remembered reading years ago, when she was a little girl, that bull elephants go mad at certain times of the year and girl elephants never do. Even Allan's lips were drawing back, like the male elephant, but, but, why had he called her that? Allan was making a noise almost like he was having trouble breathing; as he bowed himself away from the wall, gurgled, and ejaculated, Irena moved her fingertips across his lips, as much like a nurse as like a lover. It must be painful for the man. More banging from without.

"In a minute, please," Irena called through the door. Her voice was scratchy. Allan was speechless and then Irena exhaled a small yip. That stuff was on her hand. The rash. She took her hand out, looked at it as though she had suffered a cut, muttered, "Oh, goodness, it's venal," and went over to the sink. She stared at Allan's semen as though it were pearly poison ivy lotion.

As Irena washed and wondered what she had done to arouse him—she had probably sat too close to him on the piano bench—he balanced on the edge of the bathtub, his head lowered, repeating, "Irena, I'm sorry. I'm sorry, Irena." Outside there was a modicum of whoopee and bells, Happy New Year, thank God the last one is over, let's hear it for 1931.

As she dried her hands, Irena wanted to cry in her anger at this boy she was falling in love with and in the confusion of emotions working on her. Allan too was close to tears, still begging to be forgiven, when Irena looked at him and asked, "Sorry? Sorry for what, Allan? For what you did? You are a man. I guess it is hard for you to control your nature, but not for what you said. You can control your tongue, Allan. You hurt me." Irena, who cried without changing expressions, could feel her face breaking up into a look of injury.

"Oh, God, what did I say? I've had too much to drink. Please. . . . What, Irena, what?"

"What you called me, what you called me. You called me a . . ." She could not form the word. She hated it and never used it, and when she heard Polish people calling themselves dumb Polacks, she told them what she thought of them. "I cannot say it. I cannot say that name," Irena sobbed.

Now Allan did remember. "I did not mean it," he told her, as slowly, as seriously, as soberly as he could. "I am sorry, Irena. I will never say it again. I didn't mean it."

"You didn't mean it?"

"No."

She paused. "Well, get up," Irena ordered Allan, and he did, "and let me fix you," and she did. After being reassembled, Allan hugged her, kissed her, not in the blouse-ripping way but in the Leslie Howard way, and she heard him say it very, very quietly, almost inaudibly, like a stolen military secret passed in the dark. "How could I mean it when . . . when I love you, Irena." They hugged tighter, and Irena was astonished to feel she wanted to push her pelvis against him. Her breath was starting to come harder. Just like the man.

Chapter 6

The naked man was enjoying his morning *Chicago Tribune,* knees spread apart, mounted on his throne. This throne was more than metaphorically regal, for it was made of a glistening black stone with what looked like stylized swan's wings on the curvature of the bowl. The handle was gold plate and the flush, when it came, was almost inaudible, the whoosh and gurgle of water muffled.

Barefooted, the naked man, a lanky figure in his early sixties, plotched across the floor to the sink, where he tweezered a hair out of his nose and then wapped his face and neck a couple of good ones with a scented powder puff. The man came into his sleeping chamber. The posts on his unmade bed were carved columns of darkly formal wood supporting a baldachin of somberly draped, heavily gold-fringed velvet, the commanding piece in a suite of bombé and inlay, of marquetry and tapestry, of brocade and swag.

The naked man proceeded through this splendor to his dressing room. At the mahogany chiffonier he halted and put on a ring of platinum and gold that climaxed in a ruby the size of a jumbo marble, set in a circle of emeralds. Next he donned the monogrammed silk underwear set out for him, and his shirt, the collarless kind, and his black trousers. Instead of shoes his feet went into slippers, red ones with silver bows. Next he stepped into his silk moiré cassock and began the labor of buttoning up. The matching zucchetto went on his head like the top of a coffeepot; and lastly the now completely dressed George Mundelein, Cardinal Archbishop of Chicago, took up a weighty gold chain and, putting it over his head, adjusted the diamond cross so that it lay flat in the middle of his chest.

Then, with an energetic rustle of skirt, this princely figure went quickly through the bedroom and down a gallery to the small robing room, where an assistant waited to help him into the vestments of black and gold cut from material originally woven for Duchess Anne of the Palatinate. The assistant opened the far door in the robing room and the Cardinal walked through it into a chapel where fifteen or sixteen nuns, the women who ran his household, waited, kneeling in meditative rows.

His Latin pronunciation was unhurriedly Italianate, his gestures careful. The Cardinal, who considered the abracadabra mumble of a priest rushing through Mass sacrilegious, set an example of how it should be done for his clergy. *"Introibo ad altare Dei"* (I will go to the altar of God), he chanted, and the priest assisting him answered, *"Ad Deum qui laetificat juventutem meam"* (To God who did give joy to my youth). He was a butcher's son, born in the diocese of Brooklyn, and his had been more a diligent than a joyous youth, a short one that ended with his attending a minor seminary when he was sixteen. No girls and few pranks. By eighteen he had stopped having wet dreams, a sign spiritual advisers believed showed a priestly vocation. *"Judica me, Deus . . ."* he called out loudly, hammering the first syllable (Judge me, God . . .), *"ab homine iniquo et doloso erue me"* (take me away from cruel and treacherous men). That prayer had not been vouchsafed to George Mundelein, for he was taken away to the Holy City to finish his studies, one of a picked group of promising young men to be ordained by the Pope.

"Nowhere in the world am I so much Pope as I am in America," said Pius XI of his North American flock in the year of our Lord 1926, and nowhere in the year of our Lord 1931 was a cardinal more a Prince of the Church than George Mundelein in Chicago. As Pope Gregory the Great imposed Roman law, Roman order, Roman discipline over the Catholicism of Medieval Europe, Archbishop Mundelein imposed Roman rule over the Catholicism of modern Chicago, the anarchic and fractious church of the immigrant millions, distracted and disordered by a score of different nationalities and languages, rites and rituals. Mundelein was mastering pastor to more sheep than even his rival in New York.

"Emitte lucem tuam, et veritatem tuam" (Let thy light and thy truth to shine). In Chicago it had been darkness, lies and envy and schism before the Cardinal. The Poles were threatening to start their own religion if one more Irish bishop was set over them; the Serbians and the Italians and the Croatians and the Ukrainians and the Lithuanians were quarreling with and between and among one another over

104

the boundaries of their parishes, what language was to be spoken in their schools, how the money was to be divided, what priests were to be made monsignors; and the Irish were fighting among themselves, the American-born clergy versus the FBI, as they called the foreign-born Irish. Some of the things that went on—tacking bulls of excommunication on church doors—were more akin to the struggles of the Reformation in old Europe than up-to-date industrial Chicago where the One, Holy, Roman and Apostolic Church was undergoing a new experience. Its oneness was being tested. Never had so many of Holy Mother Church's children of such diversity dwelt cheek by jowl in one city.

"Credo in unum Deum, Patrem omnipotentem, factorem caeli et terrae, visibilium omnium et invisibilium" (I believe in one God, the almighty Father, maker of heaven and earth, and of all things visible and invisible). A petrified tone gave his pronunciation of these words a hard definition. This part of the Mass was the profession of the faith and doctrine which had formed the Cardinal, the Counter-Reformation faith, the doctrine of Pius IX, of the Immaculate Conception, of the Infallibility of the Vicar of Christ.

Bells with pointy sounds, small hand bells, jingled in the chapel. *"Hic est enim Calix Sanguinis mei"* (For this is the chalice of my blood), he chanted, holding the jeweled cup up above his head as the nuns cowered before God and his archpriest. He who had ordered his clergy never to appear on the streets of Chicago again without wearing a hat and regulation clothes—no incognito at the racetrack with the officers of the Holy Name Society—he who had taken all into his hands, he who had made order and, beyond order, grandeur in the Midwest, he whose opulence was a scandal to the Protestant Gentiles and therefore a source of pride to the immigrant faithful, he was a prince. For Polish slaughterhouse workers, Croatian open-hearth men, Irish gandy dancers and their wives who cleaned house for the Gentiles, for Italian hod carriers, garbage collectors from Calabria, for Swabian butchers in the stockyards, for the Ukrainian ladies who cleaned the Loop's office buildings, the Cardinal's *grandesse* was their vicarious greatness. If his limousine was longer than Sam Insull's, they rode in it; if the banquets at his turreted house on North State Parkway were more splendid than those at the McCormicks', they supped at his table. If the pennies of the poor went to support a princely way of life, the poor thought their pennies well spent. When the silver-trumpeted fanfares announced the Cardinal was entering one of his hundreds of parishes, the notes sounded a triumph that was theirs as much as his. "I've built more churches than Innocent III," he had said to Father Hildebrand, his secretary.

"Benedicat vos omnipotens Deus, Pater, et Filius, et Spiritus Sanctus." (May almighty God, the Father, the Son, and the Holy Ghost bless you.) He prayed as Marshal Ney might have addressed Napoleon, as one power to a greater one.

Minutes later, wearing a full-length coat and a red biretta, the Archbishop—or "Cardinal of the West" to Chicago's newspaper readers—walked out under his porte cochere, where his chauffeur, in leather puttees, jodhpurs, and high-collared tunic, held the limousine door. At the chauffeur's signal two motorcycle policemen kicked the starters of their machines and His Eminence was off, down North State Parkway on his way to work.

The Chancellor, Monsignor Cavanaugh, who corresponded to the executive vice-president of a modern corporation, was wearing what they used to call in the seminary a scatophagous or shit-eating grin.

"Father Bonura called to ask for a special dispensation, Your Eminence."

With hundreds of churches and four thousand priests from the Wisconsin border to the Indiana line, Mundelein no more knew the names of all the people who worked for him than Sam Insull knew the names of those who worked for his utilities. The Cardinal knew the names of the archdiocesan consultors, the official circle of advisers, and he also knew the names of the men who gave him problems—the drunks, the priests who were having affairs with their housekeepers, and Father Carlo Bonura, the pastor of St. Nicholas of Tolentino Church on the Near North Side.

"Father Bonura wants permission to say a Funeral Mass for one of his assistants, Father LoPresti. The man's been sick for a long time," Monsignor Cavanaugh continued, a smile turning his face into a happy moon.

"Well, Monsignor?" the Cardinal asked, going along with the joke.

"Father LoPresti isn't dead, Your Eminence, at least not yet."

"Isn't dead? Why would Father Bonura want to say a Funeral Mass for a living person. Isn't that a sin against hope, Monsignor?" The Cardinal Archbishop's famously hard face began to crinkle at the eyes.

"Bonura tells me that LoPresti's doctor assured him on Monday that Father LoPresti wouldn't live out the night. So Bonura gets himself a special deal on the printing and sends out funeral announcements to every priest in the archdiocese . . . for tomorrow morning. Every priest! Does he think the Poles are going to go to a Dago funeral? I got a spy over at Tolentino. He says Bonura runs up the rectory stairs to LoPresti's bedroom every five minutes to find out if the guy's dead yet.

"And, Your Eminence, the sonofabitch got a deal on a coffin too! Only there's no place to hide a coffin in the rectory, so he's got it in one of the other assistants' bedrooms."

Mundelein was laughing.

"He says if you don't give him a dispensation, it'll cost him a fortune. He'll have to send out a card saying that, due to circumstances beyond his control, Father LoPresti's funeral has been temporarily postponed and then, when he dies, Bonura will have to send the announcements out all over again. . . . He says he'll never trust a doctor again, and this doctor is a Guinea."

"Monsignor, you tell Father Bonura he can have his funeral tomorrow as long as he's got Father LoPresti, dead or alive, with attending physician or without, in the coffin." The two of them laughed, picturing the Italian celebrating the Funeral Mass with bumps and groans coming out of the coffin banked in flowers on the other side of the communion rail.

Around the archdiocese they used to say that if Mundelein wanted to know what you were up to, he could see you in his ruby. But besides reading the secrets of the human heart in his smoky red stone, the Cardinal had spies. "Fast Father Frank is in the small waiting room, Your Eminence," the Chancellor said.

"Don't call him that. They're calling him that all over town. He's getting notorious."

In came Fast Father Frank, who did walk and talk as fast as his nickname. Moving across the room on paddlewheel legs to the carved wooden chair where the Cardinal sat, he dropped on both knees and with both hands grabbed the ring hand and kissed it with ardor.

"Up!" said Mundelein. "I should have exiled you to an Indian mission in Peru, Father," he continued, shaking his head slightly and looking the runt-stump man full in his ugly face. Low hairline, straight black hair greased tightly to the rear, acne-scarred red skin, here and there a fresh pustule, the nose a lacework tracery of purple capillaries. "Now, what did you find out about Insull?"

"Broke, Yer Eminence."

"He can't be. How?"

"There's nuthin' left. It's a shell, Yer Eminence. Everything's gone fighting Morgan and the eastern bankers."

"How can that happen, Father? That is a two-billion-dollar holding company. How can Morgan do that?"

"Morgan dumps the stock on the market. That pushes the price down. Insull borrows to buy the stock to push the price up and then Morgan dumps more on the market, or he spreads rumors that Insull's sick, or there's doctoring of the books been going on, or something else which drives down the price so Insull's got to come up with more money, and he don't have no more."

"Doesn't."

"Doesn't what, Yer Eminence?"

"Never mind. . . . What you're saying, Father Rooney, is that the Insull utility empire is going down? It's hopeless?"

"Yes, Yer Eminence, as far as I can make out, which, Insull bein' Insull, isn't easy with his holding companies and the convertible stocks, the debentures and the swapping of so many shares of this for two thirds of the shares of that. He's a genius at shuffling money around, Yer Eminence, but since you asked me, I think he's broke an' I think the utilities are going under."

"When, Father? When are the utilities going under?"

"Well, he's always been a lucky son of a gun, Yer Eminence. He could make it if he gets a little help from City Hall. If the utilities can defer their taxes and franchise fees—there's a lot of money owing there, millions—if City Hall gives 'im that, he might make it. He just might do it. He's got a chance as long as Big Bill is in there. Even if he couldn't pay the cops, Thompson wouldn't try to collect that money. He owes too much to Insull."

The Cardinal looked into his ruby. "The families that have their money in those holding companies, Father. How many thousands?"

"Those families are gonna vote Big Bill outa there, Yer Eminence, 'cause he's crazy, he drinks too much, an' he can't win no more."

The Cardinal studied the ring on his flattened hand while Fast Father Frank and the Chancellor studied him. Then Mundelein returned from wherever he'd gone, leaned against the upholstered oval back of his chair, rubbed the lion heads on the ends of its arms, and, staring up into the veins, the pimples, and the blue eyes, "If you can't stay out of trouble, stay out of sight," he told Fast Father Frank.

When the little priest was gone, the Cardinal walked over to the French windows, looked up and out at a nondescript winter sky.

"The bonds," he said.

The archdiocesan bonds, there were millions of dollars' worth of them. When Mundelein had been doing the work of imposing order on the chaos of Catholic Chicago, he had made every parish invest its savings in bonds issued by the archdiocese. The money, invested in the safest of stocks, gave the Church a greater return and the Cardinal greater power. The money from the parishes had been put where the analysts said it would grow and be protected; the money had been put in Insull Utilities stocks. If Sam went down, so would the schools and the hospitals and the orphanages.

"Big Bill better get himself re-elected," the Chancellor remarked.

"*Virtus post nummos,* eh, Monsignor?" The Cardinal was proud of his stock of quotations from Horace and the other Golden Age poets. This one roughly translated into: First money, then ethics. Having so said, he allowed an archepiscopal sigh to pass his lips and, clasping his hands behind his back with such force that the diamond pectoral cross clicked against the buttons of his cassock, he said, "Now bring in our friend for his blessing."

The next man to traverse the orientals was bowlegged and barrel-chested. He had an arthritic hip that made him limp and lean, but he knelt and kissed the ruby.

"I can guess why you're here, Anton Joseph."

"For your blessing, Your Eminence." The two had known each other for years. Anton Joseph was on the receiving line when Mundelein first came to Chicago and also when he came back from Rome with the red hat. Every politician in Cook County was down at the La Salle Street Station to see the prelate descend from his private Pullman car. Amid the hissing of steam escaping from hose couplings and the clang of passenger trains being backed under the high-trussed iron shed, the Governor had presented the Cardinal with a special red license plate that had "1—ILLINOIS—1924" printed on it. Big Bill had congratulated him and so had Anton Joseph, the President of the Cook County Board of Commissioners.

"*Hoc opus, hic labor est,* Anton Joseph. That is from Virgil and it means the job you are hoping to undertake is a difficult one." Instead of saying thank you, Anton Joseph made a humble grunt. He could not pronounce the *th* sound that abounded to torture him. In Kladno, in the Austrian emperor's province of Bohemia where he was born, the *th* sound was as unknown as it was in the Czech settlement of Braidwood, Illinois, where his father had worked in the mines with the other Bohunks, or in Chicago's Pilsen neighborhood, where Anton Joseph had come to escape the life of a mule skinner in the same mines and where he had begun by selling firewood door to door from the back of a horse-drawn cart. It galled Anton Joseph to have to allow the Cardinal to do a job on him. He had pains in his gut without Mundelein.

"I can appreciate what you want to take on," the Cardinal said. "I have secular responsibilities as well as the cure of souls. Did you know, Anton Joseph, there are more teachers in the archdiocesan school system than in the public school system? More priests than policemen? More sisters than firemen? Hospitals, colleges, universities, seminaries. The Mayor can tax to support the city government; the Cardinal must beg."

Anton Joseph remembered the Cardinal, in gold and silver vestments, with a choir of a thousand, giving the final blessing at the Mass of Millions, the ceremonial climax of Mundelein's Eucharistic Congress. He remembered a private train, painted cardinal red, with Mundelein's coat of arms on the linen, on the silverware; this Red Express, outfitted to take the cardinals of Rome from the high ocean liners to Chicago to sing *cum spiritu tuo*'s to his *dominus vobiscum*'s. The semicircle of men in red robes on gold thrones in Soldier Field football stadium presiding over two hundred thousand kneeling people, wielding the cross keys of the papacy, the power to give or withhold forgiveness, the power to take away sin, the power to open the doors of heaven. Anton Joseph, ward and precinct politician, chairman of three decades of committee meetings and as many years of trading favors and saving up chits and markers, he knew who begged and who gave orders.

"Everybody knows what Chicago would be without you, Your Eminence."

"Do they? It's not me. It's the archdiocese. Do you know what a load would be thrown on the city government if the archdiocese could not carry on? Have you thought of that? I hope you understand that when you help us, you're helping yourself, the city, everyone."

"Yes, Your Eminence."

110

"Well, *Deo gratias,* you've worked for this chance. You have my blessing. Privately, of course." So said the Cardinal's mouth. The Cardinal's mind was calculating on the rescue of the bonds, the disadvantages of a Bohemian, their tendency toward anticlericalism and Protestantism. An Anglo-Saxon, what the Cardinal thought of as a true Protestant, could be bluffed, humbugged, and bullied. Like Big Bill.

"It means a lot to me, Your Eminence, your blessing," Anton Joseph said as he rose to leave. The Cardinal couldn't recollect, after years of distant association, if the man was a Catholic or not.

"You have it, rest assured," Mundelein said, noting the layman had given up his old-fashioned celluloid collars for the campaign. But his suit looked too small for him. Was this Bohemian going to be the first Roman Catholic mayor of Chicago? Was he a Catholic?

"The sonofabitch is being cute again," Anton Joseph said to his coat holder as he climbed into the back of his limo. He took up a pile of papers, started to look at them, but, instead, glanced out the window at the Water Tower as his car rolled down Michigan Avenue and across the Chicago River Bridge which Big Bill, the Builder, had built. "He can wipe my ass," Anton Joseph Cermak said.

The men stamped their feet in the driveway, six or seven of them, inside men, plasterers, floor finishers, men not accustomed to standing around in the foggy cold. They flapped their arms and occasionally glanced up at the handsome fieldstone house they had built in this, the nicest section of Princeton, New Jersey. A home for a stockbroker or some other rich guy who commutes to New York City to work inside a heated office. The men were waiting for the contractor. He was there every morning at six thirty to open the temporary lock on the house's front door; he was there every Friday to give them their wages, in cash, in small envelopes with their names written on the outside. This morning he was not there.

He was late, they said; damn him, for this was the Friday before Christmas and they wanted to start early and finish early to begin the holiday. Eight thirty passed and the man had not come. By ten they knew he was not coming and they began to leave, climbing into an old car and a truck to look for the union business agent or to find the contractor if they could remember his name rightly.

Joe Zangara was the marble man. Joe was from the old country, a journeyman of a vanishing craft Americans had not taken the trouble to learn. Not enough money, not enough steady work. The men hoisted Joe into the back of the truck and took him along, although he did not seem to care that he was being cheated out of his wages, and on the weekend before Christmas. The men hoped they were being cheated, for that would mean the foreman might have their money; they feared he had gone bankrupt with everybody else and had no money for them.

Of this Joe said nothing. For Joe the membrane between past and present, between time was and time is, was spongy soft, not a barrier; new things seemed old, old things seemed new. This morning, when the paymaster did not show up, the little stonecutter's attention had wandered back to Italy. The New Jersey fog melted into the fog at the crossing of the Isonzo River—wartime: He expected to see the Austrian soldiers in front of him on the plain; he anticipated they would be of the Edelweiss Division and they were.

They made the Italian soldiers in the truck get out and line up, and they told them they were being taken prisoners. But not Joe. They saw him in his oversized uniform, a mite too large to be a dwarf, a foot too small to be a soldier, his head out of proportion to his body. They pulled him out of line, shouting that the Italians were not fighting fair. "You guys are using monkeys. It is strictly forbidden for a monkey to carry arms. Geneva Convention rules," an Austrian said in broken Italian. Joe's own people laughed. The men of the Edelweiss shouted at Joe and, when he did not move, they drove him off by throwing sticks and mud balls at him. "It is against the regulations for prisoners of war to have monkey mascots." Joe heard them saying these things as he stood in the field between the road and the Isonzo. On the riverbank, there was a dead cow.

Now the river was gone and Joe was being lifted out of the truck in Princeton. The scene at the Isonzo had failed him, leaving him with the feeling that his past had been another life, another birth, a different suffering. Joe was like one who believed in reincarnation, invaded by the conviction that he had lived once before. But he could summon up no names, no faces. Only certain emotions prevailed from one life to the next, emotions such as rage.

The ice hawks of winter flew through Chicago's streets bringing silvered black clouds off Lake Michigan: arthritis and influenza weather. The unemployed, camping unseen in cardboard and corrugated-iron lean-tos on the lower level of Wacker Drive, felt the ice crystals in their joints as they stood around steel barrels in which trash fires burned when there was trash to burn. In the last few weeks, women's hands also stretched toward the sulky flames and people discussed the rumors that, out in the country, farmers were pouring milk on the ground and splashing cream in hog troughs because the cost of getting it to market exceeded what it would fetch.

The ice hawks flew down Randolph Street with such force Allan went limp against the wind and let it march him forward toward City Hall. Glancing up at the high stone front of Marshall Field & Company, he saw white snowflakes against the dark facade and felt a fine, grainy, frozen moisture against his cheek. As he brought his eyes to street level again, he saw a double-humped camel being led by a man in what was apparently meant to be puffy Turkish pantaloons. The man wore a leather jacket and a fez that was more Shriner than Seljuk. As the camel clip-clopped off Wabash onto Randolph Street, a sign strapped to its belly told any passerby not too frozen to read it, I CAN GO 8 DAYS WITHOUT A DRINK BUT WHO THE HELL WANTS TO BE A CAMEL? That point was developed by the sign carried on the sides of the elephant which followed the first beast: STAMP OUT PROHIBITION—TRAMP OUT THE DEPRESSION—VOTE FOR WILLIAM HALE ("BIG BILL") THOMPSON—VOTE REPUBLICAN.

The campaign was on for the April election. Big Bill, the biggest of all of America's Big Bills, Honest Johns, Giant Jims, and Joltin' Jacks, was trying to get himself re-elected one more time. Allan was on the way to the office of one Daniel Serritella to help Big Bill do it. As with the soup kitchen, he was going because Frank Nitti had sent him.

McGurn had taken him up in the elevator. "Didja hear the one about the guy on Wall Street, Al?" The Gunner was the first person in Allan's life to call him Al. "He made a killing in the Market. He shot his broker." As Allan inhaled to pump himself up for his belly laugh, the elevator door slid open onto the corridor where the bodyguards waited and smoked, vests open, guns visible in shoulder holsters. They seemed less disciplined and more tense than before, giving Allan the impression that things might be getting out of control.

In dress and manicured attention to himself, Nitti was as immaculate as ever. Opening a box, he took out a gilt-framed, lacy, red-satin Sacred Heart of Jesus. "For my mama," he said with no self-consciousness. "For Valentine's Day, and it's a beaut. A beaut."

"A beaut," the men in the room agreed.

"No guy's too tough not to be good to his mama. . . . Know what, Archibald?" the Enforcer went on. "When a guy dies, the last word outa his mouth, it's always Mama, Ma, Mom, Mother, Mommy. See, your word for mother, it's the same in every language. Italian and English. There's no other word like that which is the same in all languages. That's a fact, Archibald, and there's a reason for it. When ya die, ya say 'Mama,' the one person you can trust. You never heard of a guy's mama doublecrossing him. I know times when a guy's old man has turned him in, but a guy's mama—it could never happen."

Allan wondered, if he were to die in the next few minutes, what his last word might be. "Mother?" Sounds stilted. "Mama?" Sounds coarse. Maybe "Irena."

"Guys die cursing. Sometimes. I saw a guy—he had three slugs in him. I saw him croak an' he bit a police lieutenant on the ankle just as he was croaking. The last thing he did on earth. I saw another guy die, an' the last thing he ever said was 'cocksucker.' Ain't that a helluva way to go out, with a dirty word like that in your mouth? But, Archibald, I seen a lotta hoods go, and most of the time they say 'Mama' or some other word for their mothers. Ya know what I never heard was a hood whose last word was the name of a broad. Not even his wife, the mother of his kids. I never heard a dying guy say that. It's Mama what they say."

Then, with the same care he used in adjusting his clothes and coiffure, Nitti put the Sacred Heart back in its box, took up the glass with the white fluid, and, fastidiously using a thumb and index finger to hold it, took a measured sip and told the men gathered in front of his desk, "My stomach's killing me today. Mama, Mama! I could get shot any time. That's the kinda business we're in, you know. The beer business is lousy; who's got money for whiskey, booze? I heard there's whores on South Clark Street askin' a quarter, good-looking dames, an' they can't get it. You ain't horny when you're hungry.

"Business this bad an' I could still get shot walkin' out to the car, in the restaurant. For what? I could get shot here. You, even you, you could have heat on you. Everybody trusts you. The banker's son. You could be packin' a howitzer, for chrissake. You could push me five minutes from now. *That's* why I got a bad stomach. If I was in another line of business, like banking, like your old man, Archibald, all I'd have to worry about is getting hit by a taxicab or a trolley or listening to the latest banker jokes. Gunner, tell him the one you told me. First good joke this guy's told in five years."

Machine Gun's minute: "The one about the banker who says, 'Don't tell my mother how I make a living. She thinks I play the piano in a cat house.'"

Allan watched them laugh. The papers were saying that Snorky was on the lam. The world's most famous gangster was placed in Florida one day, Texas the next. In Chicago the police were waiting for him with one of Judge Lyle's vagrancy warrants. There were other stories about the government seizing and impounding beer trucks, vats, and bottling equipment, and a rumor that a federal grand jury would soon employ a novel tactic and indict Mr. Capone and some of his business associates—possibly Frank Nitti, even—for income tax evasion. Nobody was rich enough or tough enough or lucky enough to sail on without worries these days.

"I got a race on between a bullet and my perforated ulcer. I'm a Guinea who can't drink vino. Ever heard of that before? Vino rips my stomach. Like vinegar. A bullet couldn't be worse sometimes."

During these audiences, Allan said as little as possible, concentrating instead on committing what others were saying to memory until the words could be transferred to his notebook. Silence in subordinates was taken as a sign of intelligence, and in a minor way, Allan had found a place in the organization.

"I got something for you to do, Archibald," Nitti told him, leaning forward.

"Yes, sir, Mr. Nitti," Allan answered. This was not a crisply self-contained Nitti. This Nitti had problems.

"This'll help us. Help your old man too. You go to Serritella's office and you do what he tells ya. You'll be workin' on the campaign with him. Nice for your dad, him being chairman of the Thompson Committee and all. An' get your mom something for Valentine's Day, Archibald. She's your best girl. Believe me."

"Serritella's office, Mr. Nitti?"

"Yeah, Serritella. The City Sealer. Fourth floor, City Hall."

The meeting with the dyspeptic gangster had sent Allan running before the winter's wind down Randolph Street to Danny Serritella's office. The work of the City Sealer was to make sure that Chicago's butchers and grocers kept their thumbs off the scales. Next door to the City Sealer's office was that of the Chief Inspector of Stationary Boilers, and next to him was the Elevator Safety Inspector, and hard by him was the Recorder of Utility Hook-Ups, and the Hack and Cab Commission and Traction Franchises Division and the Recorder of

Liens Office, the names painted in ornate gold and black on beveled opaque-glass doors. In and out the doors, Allan came to recognize a distinct type of ward heeler, pot-bellied men who wore waistcoats and carried a pocket watch on a chain in preference to the wristwatch that younger men thought was spiffier. They occasionally still wore bowlers; their overcoat pockets were deformed from jamming folded newspapers in them; they had cracked fingernails and eyebrows that beetled and a wild gray hair coming out of a nostril; their shoes were black, polished and high-topped, laced up to the ankles. Some were famous. Allan had Umbrella Mike Boyle pointed out to him, and wouldn't you know it, Mike was carrying the bumbershoot into which, it was said, you were supposed to drop the money. Danny Serritella came out of his office in a bustle. He'd heard what a great guy Allan was, "and say, pally, that's a suit you got on, I could tell you know how to dress the minute I saw you; pally, we're gonna make a great combo so I'll be right back to you, don't go away, we'll get you started in a jiff, don't even sit down, pally, I'll be back that fast."

It was two days before Allan saw him again, the passage of which Allan spent reading newspapers.

> The Williams Mfg. Co., Portsmith, O., hopes to banish any lingering doubt as to the manliness of wearing spats by a series of radio programs in which football and spats will be associated. Each program will feature a famous football coach, beginning with Fielding H. Yost of the University of Michigan.

Was this the end of spats too? Almost all the gangsters Allan knew, and by now he knew a wagonload, wore spats, and gangsters were the epitome of barbaric masculinity. So why were spats increasingly regarded as effeminate? He recalled a squib in the paper about how they were wearing fur spats in Germany. When he was a little boy his father put his plug hat square on his head before going to work in the morning. Where had the top hats of childhood gone and how come? Where had the father of his childhood gone, the friendly father, the talkative one, and whence came this man who alternated between hypertensive trances in the living room and whispering, maniacal activity at the office?

While he waited for Danny Serritella to come right back, Allan would take himself downstairs to the City Council room with its wooden Corinthian pilasters and coffered neoclassical ceiling. On this day Bathhouse John was offering his colleagues a remedy for the depression:

"I rise, Mr. President, to introduce an ordinance which I believe will go far to lift the unwarranted gloom infecting our fair city. I do believe conditions are what they are on account of a poor mental attitude. Laughter and a light heart makes prosperity. 'Tis a motto I've adhered to at the racetrack, but I have reason to think it has wider application.

"I rise, therefore—"

"You already rose once, Bathhouse. You wanta do it again, you gotta sit down first," the alderman from the 35th Ward shouted.

"Be that as it may," the Bath continued, "I'm introducing an ordinance for twelve-foot-high stone walls to be put around all cemeteries. This is no bosh. A graveyard has a deadening effect on a neighborhood and I want 'em covered up. Men who have to forgo breakfast don't need to be lookin' at a forest of tombstones on their way to go seeking unemployment. Alas, poor Yorick comes soon enough without our being reminded every time we buy a quart of milk. What the people need is cheering up, so my ordinance calls for the cemetery walls to be ornamented on the outside of 'em. Sell the space for advertising. It'll stimulate conditions, you know, and, heavens! the city can use the money. The school board's down to thirteen tons o' coal and, the winter being the worst of the century, they say, I want an amendment to me ordinance saying all revenues, royalties, incomes, emoluments, fees, payments, and moneys whatsoever and howsoever derived from the selling of these advertisements is for the one and specific purpose of buyin' coal.

"I close by askin' what's the use of a whole neighborhood having a job lot of tombstones in sight when you can just as well fence them? I close a second time—"

"You never closed that hippo of yours in your life, Bathhouse," his colleague from the 35th Ward shouted.

In the fullness of time a task was found for Allan. He was to proofread and lay out the program for the final pep rally the Saturday night before the election. Allan's father, chairman of the Citizens Committee to Re-elect Thompson, was to be there, which Allan learned from one of the men in high-topped shoes in Danny Serritella's outer office. The family was embarrassed by Elting's conspicuous place, but Allan was more resentful than discomfited by his father's arrival in the world that Allan thought he had discovered, a world exotically remote from Winnetka. The small cachet of being the only one in his circle whom the newspapers said was an associate of the deplorable Mr. Alphonse Capone was at risk.

The work Danny Serritella had set for Allan was tediously easy. Most of the ads for the program simply said "Compliments of a Friend" or its variants. Every once in a while there would be something like "Best Wishes from the Gang at 47th and Homan," but most of the people who gave Big Bill their money preferred not to lend the gentleman their name. Not so with the Great Lakes National Bank, which had placed a big ad with his father's name printed conspicuously on it. There was another from Sam Insull and one each from every one of Sam's myriad corporate shells, dummies, subsidiaries, and holding companies. His father and Insull were both listed as patrons and honorary co-chairmen of the pep rally that would be held in the Civic Opera House, which Insull had built and Chicago society hated. The mischievous Englishman had directed the architects to build the dress circle so that the ermines and diamond tiaras in the grandest boxes were invisible to the audience.

And what of his father? When his eyes were not rigidly focused on invisible objects, he had taken to calculating with pencil and paper, spending entire weekends filling up large ledger sheets with numbers. No one could break through, not even Uncle Fenwick. Fenwick had violated his political principles by sending a check to the Cermak campaign. Colonel McCormick's *Tribune* and everybody else on the North Shore had abandoned the candidate of the party of Lincoln. His paper was printing stories that Capone's thugs were out to get him. The Colonel had bought a bulletproof limousine and went about town with two thugs of his own from the *Trib*'s circulation department. As Uncle Fenwick explained, "Thompson has no one left but the darkies and the dagos."

Whichever way the campaign was tending, Allan found himself seeing it from afar. He had told the seminar that he would be standing at the point where organized crime and organized politics met. Instead, he was sitting at a spare desk in Danny Serritella's waiting room playing with a printer's dummy for a pep rally program. He had yet even to see Mayor Thompson.

Six or seven times a day Serritella would pass Allan at the spare desk, his porkpie hat popped on the back of his head, his fists, with thumbs pointed upward, pumping with each step. He never passed without saying something to Allan. "Hey, Al, rhymes with pal," or "Doin' a great job. You're really givin' it to 'em, Al." So Allan followed the campaign like everyone else, by reading about it in the newspapers.

118

Allan was surprised one Wednesday morning when the papers made it look as though he truly was on the inside. One of the themes in Big Bill's career was a hatred of things English, including the king, whom he had promised to punch in the nose four years previously. There was also Big Bill's program to eradicate the British national animal. Lions were chiseled, hammered, sandblasted, or otherwise removed from every public building discovered by the Mayor's beaters.

It was consistent with Big Bill's campaign that in a speech to his cheering partisans in the Eighteenth Ward, he hit the bell three times in one night by saying (*a*) that if a certain Jewish candidate was elected, "the price of pork will drop fifty percent in this town," (*b*) that contrary to his claim, Colonel McCormick had not introduced the machine gun to the American army during the Great War, and (*c*) that, if re-elected, he would "purge the public library of British propaganda."

It fell to Danny Serritella to explain what the Mayor had really meant. "Your Jew," he told the reporters from the city's seven dailies, "has no better friend than Bill. The thing about pork was to get some more jobs in the stockyards. Ya got it all wrong, fellas." But on the British menace, there was no backing down. "America First, fellas, you know how the Mayor is on that. With people outa work we're not gonna stand for importing English books when Americans could be makin' a living makin' American books. That's a fact. We got a guy from the University of Chicago in my office working on it right now. . . . No, I'm not kidding you guys. He's a doctor of, ah, divinity. The guy's got all the diplomas you'd ever need."

"Whazzis name?"

"Allan Archibald is his name, wise-ass. You thought I was bullin' ya. The Mayor's appointed him to head the commission on it."

Soon an efflorescence of newspaper clippings bloomed on the Sociology Department's bulletin board. Next came some student-made cartoons, the best of which, to Irena's way of thinking, depicted her handsome Allan in a pith helmet tracking a lion with a hunting party of Chicago mobsters and cigar-chomping precinct captains. The episode threw Allan into one of his impenetrable funks. What particularly rankled was that the stories in the papers showed him to be a nobody in the campaign. The *Morning Post* called him an unemployed social worker. The *Daily Illustrated Times* referred to him as a student writing a homework paper. The *American* connected him with his father, which got to Allan almost as deeply as the *Journal*'s description

119

of him as "a fan of politicians and well-known stage-door Johnny to gangsters." All the articles had the same quote from the Mayor: "I never met the guy, never heard of the character."

For two days Allan took to his bed. Cook had the girl bring up trays he did not touch. The bread of humiliation was his portion, and the digesting thereof paralyzed his other appetites. His demanding libido left off tugging at him. When Irena called they had a fight, the silent variety with them both sitting wordless on either end of the telephone wire. Irena gave in first. "Allan, are you all right?" she repeated to her mute boyfriend. Finally she lost her temper and told him, "It's your own fault. Thompson's against the ordinary people, and you hang out with him." She hung up on him after telling Allan he was spoiled and then felt sorry she had. Going out with a girl who lives in a convent is a pretty poor joke too, she thought, remembering the number of exasperated times he had had to get to the doors of St. John of God by ten o'clock, when Mother Superior locked them. He sent Irena flowers. It was the first time in her life. She kept the card on which he had drawn a comical stick figure down on his knees begging the forgiveness of a stick figure princess.

Newspaper storms, however, subside faster than meteorological ones. They had to clear off the front pages to make room for the next turbulence, which Big Bill was not slow to supply. While Cermak moved this place and that, dropping his *th*'s and putting people to sleep telling them that what the city needed was a "master executive," the Mayor chose the Rogers Park neighborhood on the North Side to tell the world it would demean Chicago to elect a man who could not pronounce those consonants. Also, he objected to Anton as a first name. Anton was not an American name. No one named Anton had ever been elected to high office, and no one ever should.

The reaction to this last locution was so bad that Elting Archibald, whose knowledge of politics was limited to what he was told at his club, called Sam Insull.

"You've forgotten," the tycoon chirped in his cockney, "every time he runs, they say Thompson's going to lose. Now you stick there, Elting. Be ye not of little faith, I say. We'll hold on, us two, we'll hold on, and the day after the election our friends can buy us drinks. Buy you drinks. Sarsaparilla for me, of course."

"I don't have your confidence, Sam."

"You're a banker, Elting. It's the business of bankers to be nervous. The more they make, the more they worry."

120

"Nevertheless—"

"Nevertheless, Elting, we have no choice." The line went dead.

At the Chancellory, Fast Father Frank waited in Monsignor Cavanaugh's office and discussed the pungencies arising from the case of a forty-eight-year-old priest who had been arrested by the vice squad in a room at the Princess Hotel on South Clark Street with a fifteen-year-old boy. The arrest had been expunged from the books, Father Rooney reported, and he had also arranged, as per instructions, to have two detectives put the priest on the Union Pacific's *Sundowner Limited*. Two Carmelite monks would take charge of him during the train ride to Provo, Utah, whence the disgraced man would be taken to a monastery in the desert.

"I should send you to Provo, Utah, Father," the Cardinal said as the clerical fixer, his coat, his hat, his muffler in hand, churned across the orientals to flop in front of the episcopal seat, take the ring, and kiss the hand. "In three weeks, we're having an election, Father Rooney. Who is going to win it?"

"Cermak, Yer Eminence. Thompson's crazy. He's on the sauce. He's goin' around like a wild man."

"He always goes around like a wild man and he wins."

"Not this time, Yer Eminence. He's only got the niggers and the Guineas this time, and maybe not even the Guineas so much as they say. Cermak's got the Bohunks, o' course, and all the other foreigners, natchurly, the Polacks, the Lits and the Lugans, the Krauts and the Hunkies."

"The Irish?"

"Well, Cardinal," said Fast Father Frank, slipping into an informal Americanism that Mundelein detested, "the Irish ward committeemen would hate to see any Bohunk get to make mayor, Tony Cermak worst of all. The guy is a real—well, nobody likes 'im, Yer Eminence. But Cermak's got the Irish by the short hair."

"He does?"

"See, he's got a secret grand jury indictment on Ed Kelly, Pat Nash, Mike Igoe—all the guys—for stealin' from the Park Board, as though all of a sudden that got to be a sin. He's holdin' it over their heads, Yer Eminence." Fast Father Frank's voice rose with indignation. "If they carry their wards by the quota assigned to them, the indictments are supposed to be quashed. If they don't, Cermak might lose, but they go to trial. The way I see it, Thompson'll be lucky if he carries the River Wards. The smart people are makin' their deals with Cermak now, before the election. With Tony, particular, you gotta be able to say, 'I was with ya when.' So if you ask me—"

"*Sufficit,*" said the Cardinal, and Fast Father Frank knew enough Latin to know that meant shut up. Mundelein put his palms together, the tips of his middle fingers just touching his chin, eyes focused on a point of perspective beyond the French windows. Then he looked into the ruby before he asked, "So have you gotten out of promoting prize fighting as I told you, Father?"

"How could you ask, Yer Eminence?"

"Hmmm. And the one-arm bandits in front of your church?"

"In the basement, Yer Eminence, and half the handle has been given to the missions."

"Father, you're a barbarian."

"Yes, Yer Eminence, but a barbarian for Holy Mother Church, Yer Eminence."

Joe's mother would have nothing to do with her son. The first time she saw Joe, she turned her head away; she told the midwife to give the child to anybody who would take him. Her husband put a stop to that, but he could not make her nurse the baby. Whatever was done for Joe, the father did. He was the one who taught Joe his trade. The mother did not hate the child, beat it, or pinch it; she did not see it. It was as though Joe had not lived nine months in her womb and come out between her legs to life.

When the news reached Paterson, New Jersey, where Pasqualina D'Amico had immigrated, that her uncle was dead, she thought of her cousin Joe. She knew he would have nobody, and she formed the idea of bringing Joe to America. "Blood," she told her husband, who had heard the aphorism before, "is thicker than water."

"Not with them. Not with that family. If it isn't thick for his mother, why should it be thick for you?"

"For the memory of my uncle," she said, but when they saw Joe, Pasqualina's husband understood why the mother had been unnatural. So ugly, so strange. "He sleeps alone in the room behind the kitchen," the husband said. "My final word."

Joe tried to fit in. He did so in the most important way; he worked. Mr. D'Amico conceded him that. Joe was a worker, and he gave most of his pay to the D'Amicos for his room and board. Joe could have rented better for less. They knew that. But after Christmas when neither he nor the other men who built the stockbroker's house got paid, there was no more work. Joe looked, but who was building houses?

In a crowd of casuals in front of an employment office, Joe would not be chosen. When Joe did work for a day, hauling trash, sweeping out a warehouse, he gave the pay to the D'Amicos, but the days were few. The family was at him to go over to the relief station and line up for the food they gave away to the unemployed two or three times a week. The extra food would help the family.

Joe resisted. He would say he was going over to the relief; sometimes he would leave the house, but he never went. When he came back to the house he would tell the family he had been at the end of the line and there was no food left. "It was the bosses, the goddamn bosses," he said.

Mona had called Irena at the university, insisting that they have lunch on this particular Saturday. It was the Saturday before the election, the night of the Civic Opera House rally, which Allan had insisted she attend. He had been put in charge of the ushers, a corps of wheezing, addled school secretaries and clerks at the Board of Education Commissioners, who had been ushering Republican Party rallies since William McKinley carried the city in 1896.

It annoyed Irena to have to go. Allan knew what she had come to think of Thompson. He irked her so much that on Saturdays, after visiting her family, she had taken to dropping in on the Fourteenth Ward regular Democratic organization to help Mildred Wajciechowski with the paperwork. Often there wasn't much to help Mildred with, but it was low-keyed and sociable. Mildred made her coffee and the men made over her, telling her she was "a smart Polish girl making something of herself. The University of Chicago! Won'erful place. After the election we're gonna find something for you. At the School Board, maybe."

The second time Mona called she told Irena Saturday was her birthday, and that Gunner wasn't going to be around and she didn't want to be alone. "It'll be my treat," she added, striking a chord of pathos and imperiousness that prevailed on Irena.

They reached for the handle of the door to Henrici's restaurant at the same time. It was Mona that the men stared at. Silver-tipped foxicles danced around her shoulders and over her bosom. Ample and platinumed, Mona already had the shape and style that were to become the ideal feminine type of the decade.

Conscious and oblivious, cunning and guileless, Mona was impossible for Irena to read. She gathered that Mona was the daughter of a southern Illinois farm family that got foreclosed in the early twenties and moved to a shaky cabin alongside the railroad yards in East St. Louis, that hub of transportation and vicious degradation across the Mississippi from the better known St. Louis. "My home town is where you get the real St. Louis blues," Mona said.

Irena could pronounce the German words on the menu correctly, but Mona was familiar with the dishes. You could never tell what she might know and what she might not. She'd know surprising, sophisticated things, Irena came to realize, and then be ignorant of something a high school junior should know. Mona wasn't outside of her context, a feeling Irena often had about herself; Mona didn't have a context.

"It's like being married to a ballplayer," Mona said suddenly.

"What is?"

"My life. You think about your life on your birthday. I got to know this girl. She's about my age. Her husband is *the* Mat Selwyn, on the Cubs. The baseball player."

"Mona, how old are you really?" Irena asked. Mona said she was nineteen.

"The other wives are all older, so Loretta doesn't have anything in common with them. It's like with me and Gunner. A man's world, if you know what I mean. The wives friend with each other 'cause their husbands are famous. That's how come Loretta and me started friending together. Ya know the Gunner's famous too. More than Mat Selwyn. But the manager said it would look bad for baseball if it got out Mat's wife was friends with me. He called me a moll. Like I wasn't married. I guess they think that because I don't use his name, I don't want to be Mrs. Machine Gun. Anyways, I might want a career, like in singing or something, and then a girl has got to have her own name."

Irena was trying to memorize what Mona was saying for Allan when the platinum girl stopped herself, put her hands under her chin and her elbows on the table. "So tell me about Allan. I want to hear everything."

"There's not much to tell," replied Irena, who hadn't had a chance to learn how to talk boyfriend talk.

"He's so handsome," Mona said, not with a gush but with a tone of decisive judgment.

In one of her articles on the art of doing social research "in the field," Margaret Mead had said you have to give to get, trust to be trusted, confide to be confided in. People are not going to keep up a one-sided relationship indefinitely.

"What's he like?" Mona was saying. "I mean, what does he like and what does he hate?"

"He loves French toast, but they don't make it the way he likes it at home," Irena began and, to her surprise, felt the blood beginning to rise to her cheeks. "If we get . . . well, you know, *if,* he says he's going to show me how to make it." By trying to talk to Mona this way, Irena discovered thoughts she had not spoken to herself. By telling Mona that she loved Allan, that, no, he had not asked *the* question, she was for the first time admitting to herself that she hoped he would, expected he would.

Mona, for her part, told Irena about "the mamma mias," the wives of the executives in Mr. Capone's corporations, who were older, who thought she was a chippie, who had babies, lots of babies, and were always telling McGurn, "If you wasn't gonna marry an Italian girl, leastways you coulda married a Catholic."

"But why did you marry him?"

"You never been to East St. Louis," Mona answered. "I woulda married the Loch Ness Monster to get outa that burg; so would every girl I friended with back home. But the Gunner's OK, an' he loves me, which I can tell on accounta he gives me lots of money. So let's go spend some of it."

Against Irena's better judgment she let Mona drag her over to Saks, a store that Irena knew about but had never been in. Practical young woman that she was, working at getting on, she did not cultivate tastes she could not afford or appetites that would make her feel frustrated. Irena had seen her mother, Aunt Helen, and Morton make themselves sick wanting what they weren't going to get, so she practiced an economy of desire, even to some extent with her feeling for Allan. As she watched Mona order the salesladies around and buy one of this, "or maybe I'll take two of them," she did not envy Mona her clothes but she did begin to see how shabby her own were.

"I can't get over you living in a convent," Mona said, sashaying over to Irena and holding up a dress against her. "Jeez, you'd look great in that. I'm gonna get it for you."

"No. I couldn't."

"Will you shut up, Irena? It's a birthday present to you. Ha! That's a good one, a reverse birthday present. Take it in the dressing room and put it on." She pushed Irena toward the curtained cubicles, and when Irena didn't move she whispered, "Shhh. The floorwalker's looking at us. He'll think we're up to something." When Irena came out in the dress, Mona sucked in her breath and said, "Allan's going to love you in it. Next, accessories. Didja know that's what the fashion magazines are calling gloves and belts and stuff? Well, you probably read books, Irena. After that we're going to my place, and I'm gonna do your hair. You might live in a convent, but you don't have to look like a nun."

It was a dress such as Irena had never worn. A confection, sleeveless, with a wide scalloped collar that came down over her shoulders and triangled to a point far enough below so that—Irena was a little dubious—there was some cleavage. The bodice was light blue, and the silk of the skirt clung to her hips and dropped straight down to give a transition look between Wonderful Whoopee and the Depression, which a few people had begun to spell with a capital D. Gorgeous, but Mona was right. There would have to be accessories.

"I don't know how I could pay you back. It would be a long time."

"It's bootlegger's money, gangster's gold, so shut up, Irena, will you, please? Gotta spend it before it gets away from you."

The McGurn family, as the desk clerk referred to them with a roll of the eyeball, lived at the Edgewater Beach Hotel on Sheridan Drive. After the bellhop had left them in the living room with their packages, Mona kicked off her shoes, poured herself a drink, and exclaimed, "Jeez, I wanta see Allan's face when he sees you. I can come, can't I? Just to the rally, I mean?"

The bathroom was such as Irena had not yet seen even in the talkies. There was special upholstered bathroom furniture suggestive of lotions and potions, luxurious sybaritic hours. After Irena had bathed, Mona did her hair and helped her with her makeup. Then she stepped back to study Irena as she stood near the lights and mirrors, a fluffy bath towel wrapped around her.

"Terrific! But you're hairy."

"What?"

"You're hairy. You can't wear that dress looking like that," Mona said to Irena, who put her arms straight out and beheld innocuous peach fuzz. "No. Under your arms. You can't wear a sleeveless dress that way. Gosh, you can even see the hair coming out when you have your arms down." When Irena protested, Mona went out of the room and came back with a copy of *Silver Screen*—"The New Talking Movie Stars," it said on the cover—and a copy of *Vogue*. Both of them contained pictures of great and glamorous ladies who, one could plainly see, shaved their armpits.

"You're too tall," Mona said, gesturing for Irena to sit on the stool. "The first time I did it I used the Gunner's straight-edge razor." Irena wiggled. Would Margaret Mead call this going native or would she say it was ritual mutilation? Irena did a slight groan, causing Mona, who was about to begin the surgical procedure, to say, "Will you please hold still, Irena? . . . So anyways, I learned the hard way; you gotta use cream and a safety razor like a guy does. A Gillette."

Irena cooperated, closed her eyes as Mona finished up by rubbing a sweet-smelling cream into her armpits. "That way you won't sweat. No body odor. No B.O." She left Irena alone in the room, where the young woman leaned forward with her face in her hands. She began to tremble, as the imp of guilt and insecurity tossed her soul around inside her body.

She had spent the afternoon with the wife of a gangster instead of visiting Robert and Steffy and her grandmother. She had moved away from home. She did think she was too good for her people. She let somebody buy her clothes which cost as much as the family lived on for two months. She had spent hours, almost naked, prettifying herself and had let Mona shave the hair off personal parts of her body. Wouldn't all that be a sin? All the women in Winnetka probably shave under their arms, Irena thought, in a haphazard association. She sat up, her hands tightening on her elbows, trying to master her shakes.

Mona gave Irena a thimbleful of gin and showed her a set of panties and brassiere in apricot, trimmed in lace, that she'd gotten Irena, but Irena said no. Around South Marshfield Avenue girls and women wore corsets, unless they were that kind of woman who didn't and who did those other things.

"Girdles are for middle-aged women who bounce," Mona said.

"I can't. No."

"Will you please shut up and put these on?"

In the last few years some of the women in Our Lady of Victory parish *had* stopped wearing corsets. "I'd feel too . . . too naked."

To catch the Saturday movie-night crowds in the Loop, the *Trib*'s green trucks dumped early bulldog editions beside the newspaper kiosks. The big headline across the front page of the paper was:

CARDINAL HITS THOMPSON TACTICS

The text of a pastoral letter to be read from all pulpits Sunday morning was printed in full. No names were mentioned in it, for none had to be, in the message warning against "those who would fan the animosities of ancient and outmoded European nationalism and anti-Catholicism in our city."

Andy, in a rented fish-and-soup, as he called his dinner jacket, had seen the papers as he stood in the lobby of Insull's opera palace. Posted in this art deco opulence, Andy was waiting for Irena, stationed there by Allan, who was off directing his ushers. Andy read the Thompson story and considered how everybody else seemed to be going down while he was going up. Andy had promoted himself into being the runner and all-around assistant to the bookie who did business in the cigar store at the corner of Dearborn and Madison. Words had been spoken about a job in the County Clerk's office: "The lawyers gotta tip you to look up some paper or somethin' for them. Otherwise you make 'em wait for service. It's a good job. 'Course a guy with his own book makes a helluva lot more."

Allan had just returned when the two young women appeared at the other end of the lobby, the platinum blonde and the taller golden blonde, laughing, arms hooked around each other. "Too much of a good thing, pal," Andy said. Allan gave no sign he heard him. "You better watch it."

Andy's words slowly registered on Allan. "Can't you ever keep quiet, Andy? You always have something to say."

"For your own good, pal." Andy raised the palms of both hands. But the two women, in smiles and high spirits, were in front of them, with Irena speaking words you would have expected from Mona. "Well, Allan, which is the prettiest? Who do you like best? Tell us."

"Yes, Al-lan," Mona chimed in. From Andy a half-heard "Oh, boy."

"Too beautiful to choose from," Allan said, causing a hurt disappointment in Irena, and then irritation that she had said what she had. These new clothes made her untrue to herself; they were other people's costumes and she was playing other people's parts. The convent was better; it reminded her of who she was.

In the hall itself four thousand people had been crowded in to sit gazing at the gold-curtained stage, in front of which hung a huge cutout of the Statue of Liberty, torch illuminated. Next to it was an equally large representation of Chicago's tallest structure, the Palmolive Building, on top of which, just as with the real one on North Michigan Avenue, the Lindbergh Beacon revolved. Between and slightly above these two figures was hung a full-scale but heroically slimmed painting of Mayor William Hale Thompson, bearing the caption: BIG BILL—CANNOT BE BOSSED—BULLIED—OR—BOUGHT.

Behind the curtain and to one side, where on other nights the Valkyries, picadors, and courtiers waited, a civic chorus had been assembled. The honorific notables who headed the commissions, committees, and blue panel investigations had come to the night when they had to return the favor. In a pink and white organza gown, Hortense O'Neil Conkey, the 240-pound Republican National Committeewoman, clasped her hands just below the Grand Tetons and said in a contralto to Elting Archibald, "I think it's wonderful that these old families that go back hundreds and hundreds of years are getting involved in the politics of our fair city. The old aristocrats, Mr. Archibald, that means the rule of the finest. How far back does yours go, Mr. Archibald? To the Norman Conquest, I'll bet. And now you're putting your shoulder to the wheel for our great mayor. It's won'erful."

"My father is a farmer outside of Galena, Mrs. Conkey," said the banker, who could not know if he had been hit with an oblique insult or lower-class Dickensian ignorance.

"And I'm sure he's a good one," said the National Committeewoman, as she walked away in a slow waddle.

As the farmer's grandson and the three other young people made their way inside, Danny Serritella, recently indicted for taking money to let merchants shortweight their customers, went by like the *Broadway Limited,* calling out, "Great, Al, great. 'Member we're goin' to the private party on the Mayor's yacht. Catch ya later."

Then the houselights dimmed and the Police Department Octette, turned out in dress blues, buttons shined, walked onto Mary Garden's stage, where spotlights picked them up as they began to sing:

> Scanning history's pages
> > we find names we know so well;
> Heroes of the ages,
> > of their deeds we love to tell. *(vibrato)*
> But right beside them soon there'll be a name
> As someone we all acclaim.
>
> Who is the one,

Chicago's greatest son? *(fortissimo)*
It's Big Bill the Builder.
(the whole company, all four thousand)
Who fought night and day to build the waterway?
To stem the flood he stood in mud
    and fought for all he's worth.
He'll fight so we can always be
    the grandest land on earth.
BIG BILL THE BUILDER, WE'RE BUILDING WITH YOU!

With the stage in darkness, the band hit the first chords of "Chicago," whereupon three or four spotlights zigzagged through the audience until they converged on the big man himself, standing at the back of the main aisle, and followed him as he marched in his cowboy boots and Stetson to the stage. It was the first time either Allan or Irena had seen him in person, truly the biggest of the Bills, well over six feet tall, a once-athletic man gone to bags of fat and flushed by alcohol, yet still alive, still giving off something of what had made him the pre-eminent Jazz Age politician, as Babe Ruth was the Jazz Age athlete and Fitzgerald the Jazz Age novelist. None were known for self-control.

On the stage next to the podium was a table with two boxes on it, both draped in purple plush. As the Mayor arrived at his rostrum, the band switched to "There'll Be a Hot Time in the Old Town Tonight," which set off another uproar. Big Bill responded by standing, legs apart, grinning and waving the Stetson. The song did not end, it gave way to a simple one-one time beat on the kettledrum—*boom-boom-boom-boom*—as a chant arose throughout the house: "jobs, jobs, *jobs, jobs,* JOBS, JOBS, JOBS." Big Bill picked up the gavel and pounded it in time with the drum, leading the thousands of politicians in their incantation for boodle.

"Meet my committee," Big Bill said when the hall had quieted, and to Allan's embarrassment there came out on the stage a single file of men in dinner jackets and two or three women in formal gowns. The first in this lineup was Elting Archibald. The expression on his face was of a man trying to be brave in the dentist's chair. Immediately behind him, and suffering no similar strain, was Hortense O'Neil Conkey. "There's as great a bunch of boys—and girls, too—as you could want. Civic leaders, all of them. Give 'em a big hand, and I do mean a big one."

130

The honorary chairman, he of the Galena childhood, U. S. Grant country, was made to step forward "to say a coupla words." The piece of paper he held was so badly crunched it had to be smoothed first. Allan was burning. The superlative acoustics made it possible to hear his sire's words with clarity. It was good, the elder Archibald observed, that what he called the better element was shouldering responsibility at this critical time in the city's life. Irena turned to glance at Allan in the dimness, started to say something, and, touching his cheek with the back of her fingers, felt his jaw tightly clamped. She took her hand away. The older families, Mr. Archibald was saying, having gotten more, were required to give more to the community. Mona noticed Irena take her fingertips away. He ended his peroration in a mumbled reminder to the throng that "merble, merble code of civic honor, public service merble code of merble and the merble of the community, merble why, merble, merble Chicago takes as its motto the phrase *Urbs in hortu* or merble in the garden."

The line then turned on its heels. First in, last out was Allan's father, and then Big Bill was starting his performance. Taking the purple wraps off the boxes, he revealed them to be cages, in each of which was a rat, one labeled McCormick and the other Cermak.

Irena set herself in the seat, told herself that Thompson was crazy, a drunk, that it did not matter what he said. But it did matter. She was sure he would be calling Cermak a Bohunk in another few minutes, and she would not sit still and listen to it. She blamed Allan. He knew her feelings and yet he had insisted on her coming. She looked at him and decided he did not know her feelings. He did not understand what she had told him. There were pejorative names for every group in America except the one Allan came from. If you wanted to insult *his* people to get back at him, what would you call them? Yankees?

Passing on from the rodents, Big Bill's discourse, meandering from shouts to grumbles, made its way out of his big, bad mouth:

"I built the schools and the playgrounds too, made the drinking water pure. . . . That skyline, Chicago's skyline, that's my skyline, and the *Trib* says to vote for Tony. Antony. Tony, Tony, Tony, where's your pushcart at? I won't take a back seat for that Chairmock, Chermack, Chormocksi, Mocki, or whatever the hell the guy is. You want that to represent our city?"

Irena turned to Allan in her seat but his was a stoneface in profile. "Take me out of here," she whispered, but Allan was too withdrawn to respond.

Big Bill's big voice amplified by the hall filled the air, and the muck it rained down covered Allan like drops of fouled rain. She drew an elbow back to ready a poke when her anger lifted her up.

"Pardon me!" Allan heard that. He felt Irena push by him and saw her outline walking up the aisle as Big Bill lost himself in the elaboration of his theme: "Tony, the Jew hater, gets money from that faker philanthropist Julius Rosenwald." Now Allan, bumping up against knees and stepping on toes, got to the aisle against the background of Thompson's voice saying, ". . . calls himself a master executive, Tony does. Well, I needn't tell you Negroes what a *master* is. . . . Wasn't it he who kicked all the Negro caddies off the golf courses? Sure, it was, and he can't say *th*. Hey, Tony," he called out, looking into one of the cages, talking to the rat, "put the tip of your tongue here on your teeth and go *thhhhh*." Except in the very front rows, where the distinguished personages such as Allan's father were now seated, the audience could not see the spit come out of the big mouth with the curled-down ends that gave the Mayor the sour look of a just-hooked striped bass.

Allan caught up to Irena and touched her arm as she was about to walk through the doors into the lobby. She turned around, saw Allan, and saw Big Bill behind him, his sour fish mouth, holding up one of the rats. "God, why!" She shouted the interrogative word as though it were an interjection. Allan followed Irena, calling at her in the strident whispers of someone brought up not to make a scene, "Will you please listen to me, will you, please?"

"Invite me here to listen to that! Allan—" She turned on him and then stopped, too overwhelmed to speak.

"I didn't know he was going to talk that way."

"He's been talking that way for weeks."

"You know the only reason I'm here."

"What's the only reason your father's here? 'Civic duty! The best elements!' Oh, Allan, you people, you make me sick. I don't know what's wrong with me, I don't know how I could care for you." She made a gulping cry and, holding her hands against her mouth, turned and ran away from him as Mona came up, stopped, looked at Allan, looked at Irena vanishing, lit a cigarette from a gold lighter, and said, before she followed the other young woman out into the night, "Bad taste, Allan, real bad taste."

Behind him Allan could hear doors opening. Irena's face stayed with him, and Mona's words, strange words, like stage lines. The rally was breaking up. Band music in the hall coming into the corridors and Danny Serritella chugging up, taking him by the upper arm, moving Allan forward. Thompson was much worse than had been reported in the papers. How was Allan to know? "Al, we're number eleven in the motorcade, boy. We gotta get to the car. Don't want to miss the yacht party. You never seen whiskey get poured like this—and the eats! Big Bill knows how to do it."

Allan almost shook the City Sealer off to lunge after Irena, but he allowed himself to think he had no idea where she'd gone and this might be an important evening. So he stood next to Serritella while he screamed at a motorcycle cop who had demoted him from eleventh to fifteenth in the motorcade. Even from number 15 Allan could get a look at Big Bill's Lincoln touring car, equipped with the rear seat that elevated and had mini spotlights to shine up upon him and his splendorous waterfall of chins.

With a toot and a yahoo they motorcaded northward to the Belmont Park Boat Club, where Big Bill's yawl, named—need it be said?—the U.S.S. *Big Bill,* was moored, its carved wood likeness of Big Bill on the bow rising up and over the dock. On the stern a band was playing fox trots, and it looked from a distance as though about one thousand of Big Bill's guests had skipped the rally and come straight to the party. There wasn't room for another sailor on the vessel. Even the Admiral of the Great Lakes, the yawl's great-bellied captain, had difficulty forcing his way up his own gangplank. Allan, who had thought this was going to be a very different, smaller gathering, had no spirit to try to push his way on board. The packed people made him think of boyhood afternoons lining up between doubleheaders at Wrigley Field for the men's room. Beer, urine, and jostle. He should have gone after Irena. He knew it as he studied the distasteful mob pushing against each other for drinks. Serritella was gone into the pack and Allan began to think about going home when he heard a shrieking noise, one he took to be the throng recognizing and greeting its host, but, instants later, no doubt about it, he could tell that those were cries of panic and fright.

The deck of the *Big Bill* had yawed to one side and was sending orchestra, fancy gents, and spiffy ladies sliding into Lake Michigan. Within minutes the yacht had rolled almost all the way over on one side, settling into a shallow, muddy bottom, and what had been shouts of fright turned into lamentations over spoiled frocks and cries over lost earrings as the company splashed and coughed, grabbed tussocks of grass to pull itself out of the shivering wetness onto the dry ground of an early spring night.

The last time Allan saw Big Bill, that night or ever, the cowpuncher Mayor was dripping in mud up to his hips, wading ashore assisted by an inebriated state senator and a lieutenant of police. William Hale Thompson, thrice Mayor of Chicago, was waving his Stetson in one hand, a whiskey bottle in the other, shouting as loudly as his fish mouth could, "We ate 'em alive! I told you we would."

Chapter 7

Shoot the faces, blow up the places. The words in Joe's brain were a message from a previous incarnation, a confirmation of the conviction which abided within him.

Pasqualina D'Amico's husband had gotten Joe a job at the diner. "He's a good worker, don't mind how he looks. He's OK. He does his job. Where are you going to get a man like that: washes, cleans up, and in between he will tile the toilets . . . the kitchen too, if you want. Make it look like a downtown hotel."

Joe went to work, but one of the D'Amico boys did not like it. He wanted the job. He wanted the room that Joe had all to himself. Mrs. D'Amico told the boy, "You shut up. Joe is a cousin." He shut up, but he did not give up trying.

Joe went to the diner every day; he was on time; he began the preparations for tiling the toilets; he did his work. The man asked his daughter, Bettina, "Do you know what it costs to have a regular tile man do the job? It's going to look like a downtown hotel, this place. People are going to come."

When Joe was not working he lay on the bed, waiting for more words. Shoot the faces, blow up the places . . . and something of money. The faces of the bosses, blow up their places? Pasqualina sent the boy to tell Joe the food was on the table.

The boy knocked on the door. Joe had his eyes open; he was naked on the bed, the room a gloomy bottle blue, waiting for more words to come to him from the other time, the other life, the other side of the connection. The boy knocked again. Joe focused on the electric light bulb. The boy opened the door. It was dim but he could see.

*

"I said to him, 'Gunner, sometimes I don't feel like it; sometimes it don't feel good,' an' he says to me, 'I never had a bad lay.'"

"Such language. So what did you say back to him?"

"I looked him in the face an' told him, 'You wouldn't say that if you was a woman.' That got him mad, but I waltzed off into the can. I mean the toilet."

The Chicago Cubs were playing in St. Louis, allowing Loretta Selwyn to share an evening of inebriated women's talk with Mona. Loretta was the only woman Mona could discuss intimacies with. Irena was too virginal, too unmarried, and, Mona decided, too dense about men.

"Sometimes Mat gets like that and wants his way with me," Loretta said, lighting a Lucky Strike cigarette. "I don't say anything. I let him."

"Ya do? When I'm not in the mood, I tell 'im I got the rag on."

"I never use that kind of language. It lowers you down to their level. Then they truly do think they own you. I think it's like what happens to a woman if she swears. Usually I call it "my monthlies," but sometimes I call it 'ninky-no-no-time.'"

"Ninky-no-no-time?" Mona asked.

"That cools Mat off, and so he's not too disappointed—you mustn't ever tell—I say, 'For tonight, we'll pretend I'm your mommy, and you're my baby'—which he is in a way—'and you can suck.' Do you think that's horrible, Mona? I mean, it does calm him down, you know?"

"He'd crack my face open," Mona said out loud after thinking about trying out ninky-no-no-time on the Gunner. Loretta let it pass, though she didn't understand. Mona tried some more of her Tom Collins and remembered that she'd spent the first money she'd earned to buy a box of Kotex. Her mother had told her only a harlot would go into a drugstore and ask a male clerk for something like that. She continued to use and wash out the rags which hung on the backyard laundry line for anybody to see, until shortly before Mona left home. "Since you're going to the store, pick up a Kotex, will ya?" she had asked Mona one day. One of Mona's younger sisters was running that errand now.

"Do you ever like it when Mat does it?" Mona asked. She considered it possible that it might be enjoyable with Mat, who did not have one eyebrow that went straight across above both eyes and who did not come home with the smells of the speakeasy to say to her, as he stood by the side of the bed with nothing on save his socks and garters, "Over! Over on the backside." She would then pull her nightgown up around her neck, throw her legs, bent at the knees, apart, close her eyes, and wait to be done to. Mona was sure the other men in Mr. Capone's corporation treated their wives with more respect.

"You mean do I ever enjoy . . . like it? . . . like introcourse?"

"*Inter*course," Mona corrected Loretta. To make love to, to sleep with, were expressions used by the Bohemians who lived on the Near North Side, Chicago's Greenwich Village. Elsewhere in the city women who might know the right words hesitated to use them. "The Gunner is a beast," Mona remarked.

"Ya could do worse, ya know," said Loretta, her eyes indicating the swank of the McGurns' Edgewater Beach Hotel living room. "Mat's in the big leagues an' all, but we couldn't afford a place like this, Mona."

"Sometimes he leaves the light on and hurts the hell outa me," Mona replied.

Loretta didn't follow the meaning. "Golly, you live like a millionaire."

"I want a hero," was Mona's cryptic answer to that.

"A lotta girls would give everything for what you got. You live like a millionaire, Mona," Loretta said again, sounding like Mona's mother.

"I earn it," was Mona's answer, as she recalled her mother's letter telling her to put what the Gunner gave her in the bank.

They had drunk more Tom Collinses than either of them needed before Mona put her friend on the elevator down to the lobby to woozy her way home. Mona herself bumped against the corridor wall returning to her apartment; after undressing and wrapping a lace-trimmed, plum-colored chiffon negligee about her body, she found new energy, stood in front of her mirror, tousled her hair, stuck one leg out from the peignoir, and exclaimed to the glass, "You're gorgeous, you're glamorous, you oughta have the best!"

With that she put one hand on a hip, one behind her head, and gave her rear a little shimmy and her bosom an outward twist as she sang:

> Well, in the town of Louisville
> They got a man they call Big Bad Bill.
> I wants to tell you, he sure was tough

137

And he certainly did strut his stuff.
He had folks all scared to death,
When they walked by they held their breath.
He was a frightening man, sure e-nough.
Now Bill's took himself a wife
And he leads a different life
'Cause Big Bad Bill is Sweet William naaaaow.

Mona lurched. "Married life has changed him somehow," she continued. "Well, he's a man they all used to fear." She stumbled against a little table with a lamp on it. "But now the people call him Sweet Papa Willie Dear." She failed to catch the light before it went over onto the floor, its shade cockeyed, filling the room with elongated shadows and unusual stripes of light. Squinting at the ceiling, on which were projected strange patterns of light and darkness, Mona mumbled "I want a hero" and passed into intoxicated sleep.

She woke several hours later, sick, headachy, thirsty. Rearing up to make a bathroom run, she was stopped mid-motion as her face brushed into Gunner's genitals. Her eyes still closed, Mona fell scrambling back on the bed, parting her negligee, spreading her legs, the palm of a hand against her lips. No kissing, God, no kissing. The pain of the Machine Gun's insertion was masked by the scratches his beard made across her chin. He made the piston grunts of his sex; she held her mouth closed, scratched the bedcovers with her free hand, held her breath, tried to relax the lower muscles of her body to let her accept his ramrodding with less pain. Mona's eyes were open, nearly bulging; she saw but could not register the triangle of shadow on the ceiling; from her own throat she heard a rupturing, spasmodic sound. She was getting sick.

When he was done the Gunner rolled over somewhat, allowing Mona to sidle out from under him and make a swift crawl to the bed's edge. More drunk than she but able to execute, Mona's husband, mistaking her distressed, heaving sounds for ecstasy, reached out a palm of lumber, whacked her on the ass, and said, "Ya like that, don't ya?" The hit was so forceful Mona was thrown off the bed headfirst onto the floor, from where she ran crawling into the protected isolation of the locked bathroom.

She saw a smidgen of blood on her thigh and, leaping up, making pizzicato O-shaped sounds, she ran across the bathroom and hopped on her dressing table to get as close to the mirror as she could. She examined her vagina with slow care and saw that it was a superficial abrasion, not a tear. Still on the dressing table, she studied the scrape on her cheek and then drew back her robe and considered the bluish-red welt rising on her rear end. "Aw-w-w," Mona said in the tone of commiserating sympathy people use when beholding an act of incomprehensible vandalism. It was incomprehensible to Mona how anyone could injure her beauty.

"But," Irena said, putting both a question mark and an exclamation point behind her enunciation. They were standing on the steps of the Art Institute. Part of Irena's body was in shadow but her face was in the soft beam of an autumn sun. The light was so clear he could see the pores of her skin, and her face and her hair were precise and full, Pre-Raphaelite. One minute, Allan thought, he wanted to worship her and the next he wanted to hurt the yellow and peach and rose symmetries that the sun seemed to note and then illuminate.

"But I was going to say," Allan said, "someday you are going to have to settle down."

"I am settled down. I have my plans. I know what I am going to do, Allan."

They had been pecking at each other as they attempted to look at an exhibit of medieval altar triptyches. Having drifted out of the gallery without agreeing to do so, they were carrying on this irritable conversation on the steps when they heard coming down from side streets to the boulevard the *boom-boom-boom* of drums and the martial brass under which were hidden sad, candied notes of regret and loss.

"When are you going to have Polish babies? Blond ones with their mother's eyes?" Allan asked. He had been baiting her about settling down since Mr. Park had told her she had been awarded a $2,000 research fellowship to go to Poland. He brings it up, he brings it up, but he never asks the question, she thought, squinting at him, thinking that only Mona Jupiter had more perfect eyebrows and she knew that Mona plucked hers. She leaned forward so that her cheek gently touched his. Irena thought for a second of proposing to him.

Allan stood in the sun and let himself enjoy the softness. He was thinking about making a leap from young manhood to husbandhood, for that was what it seemed to him he would be doing if he were to propose. He would skip bachelorhood, that post-school, early-career phase he had sketched for himself. His plan had been not to marry until he was thirty. That's what he had always told his mother. But if Irena was going to Europe . . . she would meet other men. Well, then he should go out with other women. It had begun to seem to Allan that marrying Irena was akin to marrying his high school sweetheart, but on the autumnal steps that had a strong appeal for him. One life, one love.

They held hands and drifted across a Michigan Boulevard empty of traffic on this Labor Day, 1931, toward State Street and the music from the parade. Mayor Cermak, in the lead, had already passed on the way to the rally at Soldier Field, built in honor of the doughboys who had served in that war which had ended only thirteen years but a long time ago.

Whirling off to Europe to make a place for Uncle Sam in the world, and spinning through the golden nonsense of the aftermath, a distant and industrious Republic on the western rim of Christian civilization had cantered off on a decade-long spree. But that was past too as Allan and Irena stood on the corner of State and Monroe, watching the members of the International Brotherhood of Telegraphers walk by, carrying their banner that said WORK NOT CHARITY. The onlookers concentrated on the three words in near silence. No applause, no talking; the onlookers looked, the marchers marched, and the sound which dominated was that of feet, the arrhythmic shuffle of shoes on asphalt.

"I want you to change your thesis topic, Allan." Irena had been brooding about it. "You can't get closer through McGurn, I do not think, and it's too dangerous with him."

"You're the one who told me how good this was going to be for my character. Didn't you, Irena?" Allan said, teasing.

"That was before," Irena replied. She was in earnest.

The Brotherhood of Egg Inspectors—there were less than a hundred of them—came along, preceded by a man in spangles doing cartwheels. They were immediately followed by the members of the Butchers and Meat Cutters Union, looking almost medical in their white working smocks and trying to look military by staying in step and wearing their campaign caps from the Great War. PLENTY OF WORK STOPS DEPRESSION they wanted the world to know.

"Before what?"

"You know before what, Allan. Before we found out what he was like. Before we found out how dangerous he is. Andy says so; everybody says so."

140

"I can handle him."

"He can't be handled, Allan. Nobody can. Can't you see how he uses everything to hurt and injure?"

"If Mona Jupiter can handle him, I can."

"You just think she can, Allan. I wouldn't be surprised if he killed her some day. I wouldn't. Truly, I wouldn't."

A cheer went up. An enormous banner the width of State Street, held aloft by twenty men laboring under ten poles, proclaimed the INTERNATIONAL BROTHERHOOD OF EX-BREWERY WORKERS—GIVE US BEER AND EMPLOY A MILLION WORKERS. Trailing them was a float on which was a tableau vivant depicting a beer garden with shrubs and an oompah band. At the tables men were seated in poses of dejection, contemplating their empty schooners. "Looks like before the war," someone near Allan and Irena said, while the sign on the side of the float declared that WHAT THIS COUNTRY NEEDS IS A STEIN OF REAL BEER.

"Allan, you are handsome, intelligent, and have a nice personality—and I don't want anything to happen to you."

"You're extra pretty when you have that sincere worried look," Allan told Irena, touching her cheek in the experimental way of someone feeling the contours of a statue.

"Oh, Allan," Irena said, wanting to tell him, I love you.

The laundry workers union was abreast, skipping, limping, wizened, pallid little people, heretofore invisible, driven out into the light from their nether places of work and habitation by hard times. They bore the sign on which they had painted their respectful message: TO RETURN TO NORMAL CONDITIONS, REPEAL THE EIGHTEENTH AMENDMENT.

"This bunch looks like they live under a rock," Allan said.

"You should feel sorry for them, Allan."

After the laundry workers came the carpenters and joiners, preceded by the American flag and the emblem of their craft; and so with each group that followed, first flag, then emblem, then the banner with its stilted slogan: WE ARE PROUD TO WORK—GIVE US EMPLOYMENT. Those who had uniforms, like the elevator operators or the conductors and brakemen and porters from the railroad brotherhoods, wore them. The printers were in their best clothes but wore the folded newspaper hats which were the badge of their trade. Post office clerks, boilermakers, the teamsters and warehousemen's union, the boot and shoemakers, the glove makers and the millinery workers, the steam fitters and the plumbers—first the masters, then the journeymen and the apprentices—the stereotypers, the window washers, the pipefitters, the gas workers, the iron workers, and the trolley car men. The members of the Chicago Civil Rights League, portly men whose biceps strained the fabric of their suit jackets, carried a platform on which sat a giant replica of a foaming mug of beer. SAVE THE CONSTITUTION—REPEAL THE 18TH AMENDMENT.

"I'll try to feel sorry for them, but they *are* a scurvy-looking bunch, Irena."

"That's why you should feel sorry for them, and you most of all, Mr. Archibald, considering all the blessings you have. Blessings, Allan, not things earned."

"Ye olde silver spoon, huh?"

"Exactly."

"I didn't earn the silver spoon, but I deserve it."

"Allan, I was being serious," Irena told him, looking into his smiling face. Sometimes he could be as bad as Uncle Fenwick. Yet when either of them behaved like that, it was endearing. She couldn't say why.

Coming into view was a team of six Percherons. "Even with the Gunner," Allan said, "I'm against a blank wall. Since the election, I'm more out than ever." Their hoofs, sequoia sized, had been shined. "I'm on the outside again. I'm not getting anywhere." Their manes and their tails were braided and tied with blue ribbons. "I haven't gotten any useful new material in a long time." The black leather of their harness had been made to look smooth and supple; the nickel trim was polished. "With Andy gone from the coffee shop . . . I don't know . . . and I can tell, a lot's going on upstairs, I'm sure. I sense it." Behind the Percherons was a flatbed wagon on which a forge had been set up, where two blacksmiths from the Horseshoers Union used their tongs to hold up pieces of white iron. "You have boxes of material, Miss Giron. You're the one who's rich." One of the blacksmiths lowered the iron onto the anvil. "I'm poor." The hammer came down. "I mine nuggets of information as though I were panning for gold. But I'm going to keep on, and I'm certainly not going to let a dumb brute like McGunner stop me." A few taps, bends, and twists accompanied by clangs, sparks, and steam, and the craftsmen displayed a finished horseshoe to the crowd.

"It's the latest. It's the best. It's an Emerson with one of those new super hoojies," said Uncle Fenwick, adjusting the dial of a radio almost the size of the Sheraton sideboard near which it stood. "Ah!" He exhaled, either because he had gotten the twits and tweets out of the reception or because he was enjoying his first sip from the martini the butler had given him. "Rudy Vallee and the Vicks VapoRub Quartette."

"Yes," said Ottoline, who took Irena's hand and led her to another grouping of sofas and chairs away from the Emerson. "Your fellowship," she said to the younger woman, "must make you proud. When I was your age I wanted to go to college. They mostly had women's colleges then. I'm not that old, but Papa and Mama said school ruined a girl for being a wife. I came out instead. Irena, you're so lucky to be young now. Women can do so much more."

"A girl with your looks doesn't need a Ph.D.," Uncle Fenwick shouted over Rudy Vallee, the VapoRub Quartette, and a choir of plinking ukeleles. "A figure like that! Built for babies."

"Will you keep quiet? Or turn that thing off or stop shouting or something," Ottoline said to her brother. "He doesn't mean it," she added to Irena.

"Yes, he does," Uncle Fenwick let go. "If Allan doesn't marry her, I will. Leave her all my money too."

"The radio is blatting, Fenwick, and so are you." At the appointed time Rudy Vallee vanished from the air and the radio's owner turned it off. He and Allan, whose interest also was taken by the Emerson, walked across the drawing room to the two women. "So you saw the parade?" asked Uncle Fenwick. "Were the Bolsheviks out in force? I suppose so. They're making trouble all over, and in Europe too, young lady, precisely where you are going. We're getting ready for them here. I have another man with a shotgun on duty, and you saw the new gates. Let's see Mr. Lenin try to bust in here."

"Mr. Lenin is dead," said Ottoline.

"Sister dear, why don't you use your real first name, the good homespun name our parents gave you: Elizabeth?"

"Don't, please," she said, her finishing school diction and her grande damely poise leaving her as she reverted to the tormented and defenseless older sister of their childhood.

"Ottoline! It sounds like some kind of beaver. Or the name of an automobile."

"Elting called. He can't come. He has to stay at the bank." Using ancient sisterly knowledge, she diverted Fenwick, who had had one

143

more martini than he needed, to another topic he enjoyed ranting about.

"Elting!" he declared. "Elting looks like hell these days. He's losing his hair, I swear to God he is, and you married him for his looks, Elizabeth. I mean Ottoline. And listen to this," he said to them as he led them out of the drawing room and down a coffered gallery in the direction of the dining room. "He goes down to that bank of his every day, works twelve hours, and loses money. I stay here, I don't go into the office, I don't invest my money, I simply keep it, and I'm worth more every day. Tell you how I do that sometime. I stay out of the office. I tell them to say I'm not in and not expected. I have three girls down there to answer the phones, Irena; they all have their college degrees, which shows you what you need is a good husband, and if this one can't pull himself together to propose—you come and walk by me, dear—if he can't pop the question, I damn well can. Ha!"

After Fenwick had banged his way to his room and Mother Ottoline had said good night, Irena and Allan went to the solarium to smoke. A milky harvest moon fell through the glass panes so brightly they could see each other's features. Allan wondered how such intensity of light could be so without color; it was like the movies. Irena studied the outline of the broad-shaped leaves of Uncle Fenwick's plants, noted their exotic dentations, so unlike anything to be seen in Grant Park, and smelled the humus in the damp room.

"Like a frog in a terrarium," Allan said, as if he were thinking with her. Sometimes he could do that. Irena opened the cigarette case he had given her and, taking one out, tapped the end on her case as she had seen Ottoline do and lit up. She caught a look at herself in the mirror of her mind, the way she was standing, the heel of one foot slightly angled out from the arch of the other. Women did not stand that way when talking to each other on Marshfield Avenue. They did not tap cigarettes against their cigarette cases. Irena extended her tongue the smallest tip over her teeth to pick up a fleck of tobacco with her thumb and fourth finger. Another Ottoline gesture. They did not do that with cigarettes on Marshfield Avenue either. They did not smoke cigarettes, not women. "I'm surprised you still come home to visit, Irena," her Aunt Helen had said last Saturday through the stink of the wave set she used to torture her customers' hair.

"Maybe the next time Uncle Fenwick proposes, I'll accept, Allan," Irena said, attempting a flirt which wasn't successful because her voice had no lilt or mockery to it. No matter what she said, Irena always sounded sincere.

Allan took it as a cue to talk about themselves, to complain that she would have her Ph.D., "be a sociologist," and he would be carrying on his prolonged minority, living on his allowance, not yet a man, not able to marry. He looked at Irena when he said that. She had seated herself on one of Uncle Fenwick's white wicker chairs, her long torso bent forward, her elbows on her knees, her hands in her hair, the fingers of one hand ever so slowly moving, the other hand rigid, holding the cigarette. "A man has got to be somebody before he gets married, Irena."

She ground out her cigarette, came over to him on the couch, and kissed him with unplanned vehemence. Both her hands caressed his cheeks as Allan responded with such force they could hear their teeth click. When they stopped, Irena was short of breath and she recognized in herself what she had felt and been frightened of so often in Allan when he "got that way." Now it frightened and beckoned her. "I love you, Allan," she said. Allan told her that he loved her. "I love you, Allan," she repeated, remembering the article quoting Margaret Mead and John Dewey in favor of "trial marriage." Did they mean just doing it or did they mean renting an apartment together? They kissed again with the same vehemence, and she felt Allan's hand on her breast. Irena broke off her kiss to take his hand in both of hers and bring it to her mouth. Irena kissed Allan's hand and rubbed the knuckles softly against her teeth.

"Why *not?*" her lover said to her, short of breath, in whining, angry suffocations.

"Darling," Irena whispered, putting her hand on his fly. "You know why." She put her lips to his ear. In a moment he was ejaculating without satisfaction, without pleasure, without relief. He pushed Irena's hand away, and she turned from him, saying, "What do you want?" She was sobbing. "What am I supposed to do?" Getting up, she walked out of the solarium, her hands to her face.

Allan was reading the *Chicago Daily News*.

> Mayor Anton J. Cermak ordered the controversial chalked signs over the old Municipal Jail at Dearborn and Austin erased. The building, being temporarily used as a shelter for the jobless destitute, had been re-christened Hoover Hotel over much of the facade. "I regard this as an insult to our president and an act of disloyalty to our country," said the riled-up mayor, who added, "Such conduct in my opinion tends to promote sedition and communism." Asked if he planned to evict any of those now lodged in the building for

chalking up the sign, Cermak said, "Yes, if it happens again. The city and organized charities are ready and willing to feed the hungry and lodge the homeless who are orderly and gentlemanly." He warned that "For the disrespectful and the riotous, we have built jails and the penitentiary."

Allan was back in the Metropole lobby on a late September afternoon, getting nowhere with his thesis but telling himself as long as he was at the Metropole he was working, trying at least. He missed Andy. Andy had gossip and exciting surmises; he gave Allan the thrill of being close to the gangsters.

To replace Andy, Allan was cultivating the house detective at the Metropole, who was called Sailor in recognition of the anchor with a snake coiled around it on the top of his left hand. To Sailor nothing was as good as it used to be and everything had been at its best when he and the rest of the American Expeditionary Force was at Belleau Wood under the command of Gen. Black Jack Pershing—"There was a man who could clean up Chicago." Therefore Sailor's other boast, that he had been "captain of the first precinct of the First Ward," confused Allan.

He owed his position at the Metropole to the notoriety of the hotel's most important tenants, who wanted him there to shoo away sightseers, crackpots, and other nuisances, so if Black Jack Pershing did clean up Chicago, it would clean Sailor out of a job. Nevertheless, Sailor would inveigh against "those goddamn gangsters upstairs" and tell Allan that "things around this town would be different if they'd let me on the police force. The goddamn Heinies squirted me with their mustard gas. Wrecked my goddamn lungs," he would add, lighting up another Wings cigarette. "They're air-cooled."

Sailor had a whispery gravel voice which added a certain nautical something to the man. He carried a ten-pound revolver, a foot long, with a wooden handle, which, he said, he never had to use because of its visibility. As far as Allan could see, Sailor didn't use his gun or do anything else except sit in the lobby and tell stories. Spinning yarns was a maritime activity.

It was Sailor who told Allan about Bathhouse John and Alice, the elephant. In the days of Alice's pre-pubescence, when she was a sprite of a thing weighing in at seven or eight hundred pounds, she had a disfiguring run-in with the cowcatcher on locomotive number 1127 of the Chicago, Burlington and Quincy Railroad. Baby Alice, tethered by the trackside, stuck her trunk under the cowcatcher, thereby dooming herself to look different from the other elephants in the circus, and she was banished to the Lincoln Park Zoo by a management that saw no profit in physiological anomalies.

Bathhouse, who never left the First Ward except to go to the racetrack, would go to visit Alice. For this elephant with the foreshortened trunk he had love and pity and indignation at the taunts aimed at her because she couldn't pick up the peanuts. He decided he would take her away from insult and humiliation and, gathering up his precinct captains, carpenters, wagons, dray horses, and teamsters, one night he put the snatch on Alice. By noon the next day she was in a place he had in the Wisconsin Dells, to the admiration and delight of the farm boys.

Alice did well in Wisconsin until she came down with pneumonia. "Me pachyderm's dyin'!" cried the Bathhouse when he saw her. "Fetch the whiskey." A quart of the best Irish was poured into Alice, who recovered on the spot but, as a result of the good effects of her medicine, fell into dipsomaniacal ways. The elephant who could not pick up a peanut was able to use the mutilated stump of her trunk to sniff out and extract hip flasks from her visitors. "The Bathhouse went to court on Alice. Sued for her right to whiskey, as medicine," Sailor said. "It was a well-known case: John Coughlin DBA Bathhouse John in loco parentis for Alice, an elephant, versus the United States of America, a country."

Sailor's stories were about the way things used to be, tales of long-ago mayhem and lunacy. Andy was up to date, and what he didn't know he could guess. Andy told Allan that Snorky was going to be indicted for income tax evasion. "Everybody in the Loop knows about it," Andy said to Allan, who, though hanging out at the Metropole, even passing the time with some of the main players, had no hint. "Not an inkling, huh?" Andy crowed.

He told Irena he was spending his best years pressing his face against a plate glass window, on the other side of which persons whose voices he could not hear were living out the important dramas. In response she made him get out his notes and files. "Allan, you have a lot more here than you think, but it isn't organized. Go over it and draw up a list of questions suggested by the material. The time for hanging around and soaking things up is over. Now you have to formulate specific questions so you can go out and try to get the answers."

She talked to him as though he were one of the students in her seminar. When Allan went off and thought about it, he could see Irena was right, which made him resentful and anxious. She would be going to Europe in a few weeks for months and months, and Allan acknowledged to himself he had come to depend on Irena for advice, for approval, and for loving friendship. "She's got you, Archibald." Brundage sniffed. "I don't suppose you can do anything without her permission. You're too far gone."

Allan would not reply to these taunts because, though he did not say it, he did think it was a little unmanly to talk everything over with his girlfriend. "She'll have you henpecked into a condition of servile docility," Brundage predicted in a voice heavy with condolence for a fallen friend. "While you slip a ring on her finger, she'll be putting one through your nose." Once Allan tried to rejoin, "But Irena is different." He could not explain how she was different. Brundage was making too much noise laughing. Brundage's prophecy bothered Allan, as it bothered Allan when Irena disagreed with him in front of the men in the department. It was worse when she was right, when they sided with her. Irena wasn't like other girls; she didn't build him up the way they did. It wasn't that she was disloyal; Allan knew she was loyal as could be; she stuck up for him when she thought he was right, but she did not seem to care or know how something she might say or do would make him look. She stuck up for him, but she did not respect his position as the male, the one who must make the decisions and bear the ultimate responsibilities and burdens.

"Never marry a smart woman, don't even go out with one," one of his fraternity brothers used to say. Allan repeated the words to himself and then went to Von Lernicke and Antoine's to buy Irena a set of luggage. At least Irena always knew what he was talking about and, if she still couldn't play cards or tennis, she had turned into a fair dancer.

Irena asked him for a picture to take with her to Poland, and he gave her a silver locket with his photograph in it. Irena kissed him strongly, as she had done in the solarium, but Allan kept himself under control and then spent the next day or so wishing she would let him touch her. That weekend he went to a college friend's wedding, where one of his chums whispered the bride was "easy" and how there ought to be a law preventing girls like that from wearing white. Irena was pure, keeping herself for him. He ought to be so thankful. God, she would look beautiful in her wedding dress. Pure.

In the autumn weeks of 1931 when so many other lives were fall-

ing apart, Allan and Irena's were coming together. He had not proposed—he had decided he would do it the night before she took the
train to New York to go to Europe—but they began to behave like
engaged people. They spoke of themselves as we and granted each
other liberties to know the other's mind and soul. They told each
other of their love and tried to explain it.

Allan's family, other than Elting, assumed they would be married. "She's a Catholic!" he said, calling to Ottoline from the bathroom where he was looking at himself in the mirror.

"No, she isn't. She told me she doesn't go to the Catholic church
often. She doesn't go to any church, E."

Gargles and mouth swooshings. "I think I *am* losing my hair. Oh,
Jehoshaphat!" An inexplicable *ouch* sound next reached Ottoline's
ear, followed, after a pause, by, "She's Polish, and you can't stop
being Polish. Polack, Ottoline. Do you want Polack grandchildren?"

"Fenwick will take them."

"What?"

"I didn't say anything, E."

"He's trying to steal our son from us."

"No, he wants our daughter-in-law. I know my brother."

"Why didn't he get married and have children of his own? This
thing is not suitable, Ottoline, not suitable."

"I know that, E. But it is going to happen, besides which I've
gotten to know her. She's a nice girl. Brilliant, too."

"Poor Allan."

"I'm going to my room. Good night, E," Ottoline said, rising
from a chair and gathering her peignoir closer to her.

Allan's father's disapproval, never voiced but audible nonethe-
less, encouraged the two to shun his house for Uncle Fenwick's,
where one of the bedrooms was informally assigned to Irena. There
would be flowers in it when she went upstairs after greeting her uncle-
in-law-to-be, who would tell her how beautiful she was and then fall to
talking about making babies. It was disconcerting the way he did that,
and, though kind, it was also disconcerting when he would send a car
all the way down to the university to pick her up. She'd arrange to
meet it at 55th Street and Lake Park Avenue, well off campus, in
hopes no one she knew would see her entering the rear of the Rolls-
Royce, which had two small crystal bud vases in the back with a little
tea rose placed in each.

Then an envelope arrived in the mail at the convent. It was from

Uncle Fenwick, saying, *First class all the way for a first-class babe.* Fenwickian eccentricities included occasional slang. With the note were tickets for a Pullman compartment on the *Twentieth Century Limited* and the same for a stateroom on the *Leviathan.* Irena would be able to give the money from her fellowship she had budgeted for transportation to her family, but the joy of that thought was moderated by the picture of her farewell in the train shed of the La Salle Street Station.

The two families meeting at last. Morton in his short jacket and cap; Mr. Archibald in his Chesterfield, gray gloves, and bowler; Steffy staring at Allan and giggling to Helen how handsome he was; her mother might curtsy or do something of the kind to Ottoline; Allan would be staring at Steffy's acne; Robert hanging onto her mother's hand looking slower than he truly was, and Granny asking in Polish who was who and what everybody was saying. Irena was embarrassed by her natural family because they were poor and Polish, and she was embarrassed by the family she was going to marry into because they were rich and non-Polish and non-everything she was or her friends at the university were.

It would have been better, Irena thought, if she could have married into one of those societies described by the anthropologists in which the bride loses her own family upon marriage and becomes a member of the husband's. Later that day she put her head in Mr. Park's door and asked for a few minutes. To a not wholly confused Mr. Park, who had heard talk around the department, she gave emphasized expression to sentences containing words like exogamous and endogamous marriage, the role of marginality, and the strain on the personality of the migrant, the foreigner or stranger. Moses among the Egyptians, for example. Irena's words were as incoherent as they were urgent, but the last thing she said was plain enough. "Why do we study sociology, Mr. Park? Why the social sciences? Isn't it to live better lives?"

"Irena, you're going to Europe in a few days. You're going to do very good work. You always do, but I don't want you to do good work all the time you're there. Spend some time in Berlin. Go to the theater. I'm going to give you introductions to friends there. You'll be back in February or March," the professor said, walking around his desk to put his hands softly on her shoulders as she sat in the chair looking up at him, "and then you will finish your thesis—and it's going to be very good—and then those other things, you know, which you have on your mind: believe me, Irena, they will work themselves out."

Irena was susceptible to cheering up. She left Mr. Park's office using her longest stride, the most enthusiastic one, which tended to draw her torso slightly forward as she walked. She shortened up when she caught a reflection of herself in a windowpane and was almost Ottoline-like entering the coffee shop where she bought two friends coffee. A nickel a cup but all the refills you want. For the first time in her life, Irena was working off a small surplus. Thank you, Uncle Fenwick.

With headshakes and snickers, she and her friends passed around a paper with an article that told them:

YOUTH CODIFIES RULES OF CONDUCT

> Petting is permissible, if young people have their way. The younger generation has codified its own rules of social conduct, based on a symposium of college men and women, Park Avenue and Palm Beach debutantes, and members of fashionable Junior Leagues throughout the land, and these will be published shortly by the Century Company in a book entitled "Mrs. Grundy Is Dead."

One of the students was insisting that the way out of the Depression was through the new science of government and economics called Technocracy. Instead of old-fashioned money, all values would be expressed in terms of the energy it cost to produce them. The present dollars-and-cents currency would be replaced by money denominated in joules and ergs. "A cup of coffee might cost two joules, don't ya see?"

"Mom, he's wasting electricity," Joe heard the boy say to Pasqualina D'Amico. "He's got the shade down and the light on and the sun's shining."

Joe turned the light off and went out. He walked through the Sunday streets of Paterson, making a malediction on the boy, on the bosses. He thought on the words shoot the faces; he thought on where they had come from. He walked to the Paterson waterfalls, where there were many people and a man's voice amplified over them. Someone said it was Governor Moore, one of the bosses. Joe eased a way between hips and thighs, as an animal moves in heavy undergrowth.

151

The Governor spoke his words from a simple platform that held him and one other man. In front of the platform New Jersey state highway patrolmen stood by, their motorcycles drawn up in a half-moon. Their motors were turned off, but not their lights, blue flashers on the handlebars.

Joe wiggled through the crowd inside the Milan cathedral. The ceremony commemorating the martyr's death of King Umberto Uno, shot by anarchists July 29, 1900, at Monza was taking place at the high front doors so that the larger crowd out in front of the Piazza del Duomo could hear Archbishop Visconti saying the prayers. The golden statue of the martyred king's son, Vittorio Emanuele Due, seated on a warhorse, competed for attention.

"Watch out! Dwarf!"

"Ugh! A midget!"

"Dirty monkey! What's he doing? Smells."

Joe attained the front row where the carabinieri, in blue uniform with red sash, held the line. On the other side, empty marble reflected the sun coming in over the archbishop's mitre as he stood in the largest of the doorways. The crozier cast a crooked shadow on the gleaming.

"God, who did vouchsafe to raise up Umberto so that he might make Italy whole; God, who took Umberto from us before the work of national unity was done, as he took Moses from the Israelites before coming to the promised land, God who—"

Joe, crouched between the feet of two carabinieri, could feel the vibrations before the crowd could hear their noise. In the crypt below, where Cardinal Saint Carlo Borromeo, in the jewels and robes of his office, had slept since the Counter-Reformation in a silver coffin with a rock crystal top, there was a smashing. The rock crystal was shattered and vibrations came up from below to the ears of the crowds honoring the memory of Umberto, the king; the noise of the desecration sounded like a pipe organ in the center of the earth being torn apart as it was being played.

The soldiers, Italians from the Isonzo, a band of them, broke through the line of the carabinieri. They carried hammers and axes. Running across the marble, one of them, a sergeant, cried, "Shoot the faces, blow up the places." They smashed at the face on the statue of Archbishop Otto, ran past the living archbishop; they attacked the gilded legs of Vittorio Emanuele's warhorse.

"Anarchists!"

"Iconoclasts!"

"Protestants!"

Joe turned around, seized the hand of a woman, and bit down; he clenched his jaws until the tendons on their hinged joints stood out against the skin.

An October day of gold and blue, the best time of the year in Chicago, clear and humidity-free so that Mona could sit at the table in her breakfast nook, drink coffee, smoke a Lucky Strike—"It's Toasted"—and see down the lakeshore past the Loop to where she supposed the University of Chicago and Allan might be. Her hero ought to discover her and make arrangements to take her away, to rescue her, to bring her off to a gentle place of caresses.

Instead Mona would trap her hero. It gave her a tingle to think of cheating on the Gunner. It gave her a shudder, too. Dangerous. She could do it though. She was smart enough, smarter than her hood husband. Getting to Allan, however, was like shoplifting. She had called him once on the phone with her approach memorized, but he wasn't there, and when he called back she had lost her confidence, blew her lines, and told him she'd called to see how he was doing, that "they" hadn't heard from him.

She invited Irena for another lunch, giving her her first taste of Swedish food in a Rush Street restaurant where everything seemed to be light blue with red hearts and lace. Mona would get to Allan through Irena, by inviting the couple out as she and the Gunner had before. If she could get him alone on the dance floor, she had him. Irena said she'd like to when she "got back." Her conversation was salted with time, distance, and travel, which Mona didn't follow and wasn't interested enough to ask about, once she realized that soon Irena would be out of the way.

For her part Irena was as self-absorbed as Mona was. "Now!" she said. "Petting." She spoke as though it was the next thing on the agenda, though it had no connection with anything said before. "Did you and the Gunner pet before you were married?"

"You went to college," Mona answered. "I thought all college girls pet."

"I went to a girls' college. Nobody petted. The priests said it was a sin. So you don't think petting lessened his respect for you?"

"Shut up a minute, will ya, please? Irena, you know, you got so much to learn, and there's a lot you can't learn about by asking questions. It just depends. You can't keep a guy if you don't give him nothing. Men are human too, you know."

"So you think I should?"

"You never petted. You never let Allan touch you, huh?"

"No."

Irena looked across the Swedish pickled things and was not able to tell Mona about what her hand and Allan did together. Her hand had done it four times now, the last at night, parked in his car down the street from St. John of God convent, the two of them sitting side by side as if in a classroom.

She had not kissed him when she got out of the car. They could not talk about their courtship to each other, and Irena realized that she could not tell the painful, divisive details to Mona. But Mona, she sensed, knew about men and women, so she went on. "Allan wants . . . well, you know men, and of course I can't and we get upset. Very nervous. It must be better when you're married."

Mona gave out that it was, told Irena she was a "poor kid," and explained that "Everybody goes through it."

Irena said that "Allan, well, I love him, but he can be, I don't know, very passionate, if you know what I mean." Mona said she guessed she thought she did, and Irena wanted to be more specific but she was too ashamed; she told Mona she was a good friend.

Mona told Irena to "please shut up, will ya?" and they parted, touching cheek to cheek and promising to see each other the first thing after Irena got "back" from wherever it was she was going. Mona watched her stride off in the direction of the El. Her steps were too long, Mona thought, puckering her mouth in an expression of distant disapproval, and she shot her hand up for a cab to take her to Marshall Field's.

The glove department held nothing for her. She bought some notepaper and dawdled through twenty minutes with the salesgirl choosing a monogram to be printed on it. She looked at a display of imported crystal and lost herself musing over the differences in the look of common things like glasses or ashtrays if they came from abroad. Almost nothing did. An English car was so rare that a girl like Mona, who was indifferent to all automobiles except those she thought were snazzy, would take a quick gawk when once or twice a year she might see such an exotic roll by. Buy American.

She took the elevator up to the department store's tearoom, and looked at beachwear for Bermuda. The more she did these aimless things the more she put herself in a tingle. She left, saying to herself she didn't care; for once, just once, before she lost her looks, she was going to have a hero, her own three hours with her own hero. Frightened and excited, she began to carry her plan out, leaving the store to hail another cab to go the few short blocks across a segment of the Loop to Dearborn and Madison. "People who walk, sweat," she informed the skeptical part of herself, entering the cigar store. A customer threw a wrapper on the white octagonal tile floor and stuck the tip of his cigar in a little gas jet, housed in a nickel-plated protective container, and lit up. There was another man at the counter, a clerk, a fat man whose diamond rings made his fingers bulge.

"You're late, Artie, you're canned, Artie," said the fat man, who had wide and widely spaced eyes, which saw but appeared not to see.

"Zep, it's Shove Day on the South Side. The El was late."

"Huh?" Zep said, and Mona, looking at the gut, the hips, and the rear, tried to guess how he could get behind the counter, back there in between the glass cabinet doors and their modern-looking nickel frames. "Artie, I gotta have somebody on the fuckin' phones workin' the hour before the first race at Belmont. I told ya that a million times." Zep pushed a flier toward the cash register, on which he hit the no sale key. "Here's what ya got comin', Artie."

"I keep tellin' ya I was late 'cause it's Shove Day. The shines had the system gummed up like they do." Among the sons and daughters of the immigrant whites on the South Side, the belief was nursed and nurtured that, from time to time, the Negroes would pluck a number off the calendar and pass the word that it would be Shove Day, when blacks were supposed to elbow, shoulder, pinch, nudge, and step on the shoes of every white traveling on the elevated trains or trolleys on South Park Boulevard, Wabash Avenue, or the other arterial streets of the black section of the South Side.

"Go fuck yourself, Artie," said Zep, who wasn't from the South Side. "What'll it be, miss?" he asked Mona as he looked around Artie, who had not moved. Mona drew herself up into the bristling position indicating she had heard *the* word. Either a girl did not know what it meant or she had to show she wasn't the kind to allow such language around her.

"Is Andy around?"

"He's working. . . . What's your name?"

"Just a friend," Mona answered, noting little islands of stubble which had escaped his razor, on his second and third chins.

"Just a friend, just a friend," Zep imitated in the manner of one who derides everybody.

"Ya gotta give your name to strangers when ya want to lay down a bet on a horse?" Mona gave back.

But Zep, as though he hadn't heard her, said it again, "Just a friend." As he spoke the words, he tilted around Artie to give Mona a good look, and then he pushed his obese way between counter and glass merchandise cabinets until he came to a mirror underneath the La Primadora cigar sign. A Spanish lady with combs in her black hair and rouged cheeks was painted on it. At a touch which Mona could not see, the mirror swung away and the fat man squeezed into the space where it had been. The doorframe's pressure against his body forced a trumpet fart out of the vanished fat man. The mirror had clicked back into place and where Zep had been there was nothing but a bad smell.

"Shit, what a pig!" said Artie, giving up his post. "Zep is short for zeppelin," he told Mona as he moved off, counting his money. "If he didn't have so much crap in him, that fart-filled blimp would be floatin' over the Lindbergh Beacon." He was out onto Dearborn Street before Mona had organized herself into looking shocked at his language.

Andy, not Zep, came through the La Primadora mirror. Mona was ready for him. She had fanned out an arc of paper money under her gloved hand on the counter. In the loudest of conversational voices this side of shouting, she said, "Andy, put this one"—shoving one of the bills across the counter—"on Water Tower at Arlington tomorrow, third race." As Andy began to write the slip, she whispered, "I don't wanta bet. Andy, buy a suitcase with this." He accepted the bill. "When money is offered," Andy always told Allan, "take it."

"Fourth at Rockingham," Mona shouted again and added in hushed exhilaration, "Buy stuff, anything you want, clothes—it don't matter—to make the suitcase feel like it's got stuff in it."

"What's all this about, Mona?"

"Will you shut up, will ya, please?" The quieter she spoke the faster the words came out. "Now with this one, you go to the Stevens Hotel and you rent a room, a nice room, under a phony name. Like Al Brown."

"Capone uses that name."

"He's got it copyrighted? . . . Whatchamacallit, first race,

Pimlico. . . . You get *two* keys. One of 'em, you give me tomorrow morning. I'll drop by to make another bet. The other, you keep, an' you phone Allan and—"

"First race at Pimlico? Yes, ma'am. . . . Not on your tintype, Mona." Andy was whispering the important sentences now also. "Jack McGurn'll kill ya. You know it, Mona."

"I got a good feeling about a California horse, but lost track of 'im. . . . Andy, goddamn you, you call Allan, tell him to meet me between two and four. Give 'im the key."

"You can't pull that on a white man, Mona. That wop'll cut your throat."

"He's got no way of finding out 'less you tell him, Andy." More of a hiss than a whisper, but she looked at Andy in a full, flat way that was calm and bold and exciting. Allan, that lucky sonofabitch! "An' this bill use to bet me some horses to make it look right, and this last one is for you, Andy." It was twice what Zep paid every week.

"Hey, Mona, no."

"Will you please shut up? I'll see ya tomorrow."

He watched her, listening to the click of her heels on the white octagonals, wondering if he could ever get rich enough to get a piece of something like that. Goddammit.

After the last race at Arlington, Zep let Andy get away early. It was a bad night for him in his furnished room. The sight and sound of Mona's walking across the octagonals infused his sleep with a waking excitement. Tomorrow morning, he reasoned, he could do what she had told him, but come himself instead of Allan. Wouldn't she have to comply? She couldn't shout or anything. He could make Mona walk around with nothing on but the shoes, make her dance for him like that.

You've got to be a gangster or a millionaire for quality snatch. If he tried that on her, she'd get him. She'd figure some way to have Jack McGurn put him down. That's a smart broad; she's got a fool-proof scheme. She don't rent the room; her and Allan don't go in together and don't go out together. The one guy in the world who knows is me, and Andy, friend, you can't blackmail her 'cause you'd have to go to Jack McGurn and tell him it was you who was fixing it so his wife could put the horns on him.

In the last days before Irena's departure, the news of the Big Fellow's indictment for income tax evasion broke across Chicago.

How did they dare? Al Capone was bigger than President Hoover and a lot more popular, or so it was thought until he and the Gunner were booed as they watched the Northwestern–Nebraska game from their box seats on the fifty-yard line at Dyche Stadium. It got to Snorky, who walked out before the end of the third quarter. The crowd saw him get up to leave and began to boo again as the Northwestern cheering section chanted, "Bail, bail, the gang's in jail. What the hell do we care, what the hell do we care now? Hip, hip for Scarface!" The Sunday papers said that on the way down a passageway toward the street, Chicago's most famous citizen told a reporter, "I'm sick and tired of being made the goat of every politician and reformer. I guess I'm going to retire."

Allan was at the Federal Building, a spidery cast-iron structure with a colored glass dome and elaborate wall sconces and doorknob plates, out of which fierce war eagles glared. Outside the courtroom, beneath the dome, stood Alphonse Capone in a lime cashmere coat, the wraparound sort, with a belt, canary yellow accessories, and shoes of a muted grayish puce.

He seemed the same man he was the previous Thanksgiving, the last time Allan had seen him long enough to make a judgment. The violent splendor, the theatrical self-confidence were intact. "It's not me that's the trouble. It's prohibition," Mr. Capone said. "Prohibition has done nothing but make trouble for us. It is the worst thing that ever hit this country. If I say I don't give it more than five years, you can bet I'm right."

"Hey, Al, how come ya don't pay your taxes?"

"Who's gonna pay for the army if you rich guys don't pay your taxes?"

Mr. Capone struck a pose more suitable for grand opera than the federal courthouse to answer, "Rich guys? Big business? Big business is after me. I don't interfere with them. None of those big business guys can say I ever took a dollar off 'em. I only want to do business with my own class. I don't interfere with their racket. Why can't they leave my racket alone? They're the guys that got President Hoover on me, getting the government to seize my trucks, smash the breweries. Income tax? Ya know how much money I lost to the government the last couple of years?"

"Al, we'll take what you got left."

"I'm serious. These big business guys are always after me. Why can't they leave my racket alone? Now they got me framed on this income tax charge. And if that don't stick, they're gonna have me arrested for vagrancy."

"I thought you said you were broke, Al. Doesn't that make you a vagrant?"

"Anyways, it ain't fair," concluded the only American criminal to rival Jesse James and Billy the Kid in story and legend.

How well or how poorly Mr. Capone's conglomerate was doing occupied Allan less during this audience than whether or not the chief executive officer would recognize Allan, by so little as a wink or pointing of an index finger toward him. Nothing. Allan stayed on the edge of the circle of reporters; after Snorky and retinue had left, they scattered to phones or meandered away to get a sandwich and a cup of coffee at Thompson's. Allan looked up at the dome, experiencing the particular smallness a person can feel alone in a large man-made structure.

Irena was right. Hanging around made no sense. He should draw up his list of questions and start seeing people for answers. Snorky might not know him, but Allan was remembered by more than a few in the organization. Nitti for one. He might be able to get Nitti to let himself be interviewed. One or two sessions with Frank Nitti, and Allan would dazzle them in the Sociology Department. And there was Gunner. He had not gotten enough for his pain from that s.o.b. Irena was right, Allan reflected again, admitting to himself he needed her; he was able to recognize the part she played in his work without immediately resenting it. That was a change for him. Walking away from the echoing marble of the rotunda, Allan aimed a course across the Loop toward Peacock's, the shop where the young men of Allan's background had, since the time of the Great Chicago Fire in 1871, bought their engagement rings.

There would be a family dinner at Uncle Fenwick's on Irena's last night, and the next morning, when they took her to the station, Irena would be wearing his ring. Allan also thought of their two families meeting, of his father's indubitable chilly rudeness and his uncle's tasteless bonhomie. The meeting would be excruciating and so would the wedding. "If they go through with it," his father had said when Ottoline had mentioned Irena, "the papers are going to have a field day." Brundage, with an irritating vividness of imagination, had already been teasing Allan about that. "'Back of the Yards Cinderella to Marry North Shore Prince—Couple Met at University.' Viva the republic of letters! You will be written up in *Vanity Fair* and *Time* magazines. Marry your own kind, Archibald. A serviceable debutante, one of the serious-minded ones who will adore you and always wear pearls over her high-necked sweater on country weekends."

It could be a long engagement, which would absorb the fuss over the announcement. Irena did not want to get married until she had her degree and neither did Allan. "No position to get married" was a stock phrase among graduate students who were scarcely able to pay tuition and eat, and, though Allan knew where his next meal and the one after that were coming from, he wanted to stay in step with his university friends rather than his North Shore ones.

Getting the degree had come to stand for the completion of a rite of passage for Allan. It would signify full adult status, his coming into his majority, his moving into the phase of his life when it is proper to take a wife. It would be a long engagement, but the closer it came to Irena's leaving, the more Allan wanted it. He was certain of her, yet . . . and Brundage was now telling him the men would go crazy over her in Berlin, the brilliant, charming American girl who speaks German so fluently. "Better lock Cinderella up or she will be engaged to some *Freiherr* with a dueling scar by Christmas, Archibald."

The ring was ready the morning of Irena's last day in Chicago. Allan squinted at the inscription, *Love, faithful and forever, from Allan to Irena, October 23, 1931,* before the clerk put the ring in a slit between two plump, plush mounds in the gray velour ring case. This went into Allan's suit-coat pocket as the young man, light of heart for once, swung southward on Michigan Avenue, walking the two miles to the Metropole singing the lyrics to Cole Porter's newest hit:

> Like the beat beat beat of the tom tom
> when the jungle shadows fall
>
> . . . .
>
> Night and day, you are the one.

In the Metropole lobby, Sailor told him, "Ya missed the big show, buddy." He took a drag on his cigarette, holding it so when he moved his fingers the snake coiled around the anchor of the tattoo wiggled. "They got outa here fast, took everything. They were gone in three hours. Joint looks like they were never here."

"Who?"

"Capone, Nitti, all of 'em."

"You mean . . . ? But where?"

"Who the hell knows with those guys? They coulda gone to ground. The government's givin' 'em a rough time, ya know."

160

A depressed, almost lethargic panic told hold of Allan, giving him the impulse to make telephone calls, look people up, run around. But each tick of nervous energy would spark and disappear in morose passivity. Without the Metropole, he had no center, no sense of being able to stay in contact. It was like beginning again. He smoked, looked out the lobby window, and heard the bells and the braking steel of the trolley car wheels on 22nd Street, the thoroughfare that would one day be called Cermak Road.

His hand in his pocket feeling for nickels, he went into the phone booth to spin the dial and re-establish the lost contact. He picked up the receiver, dropped in a coin, and then, hanging up, he continued to sit in the closed booth smoking, indifferent to the foulness of the air in the glass box. The tears in his eyes were not as much from the smoke as from an angry sense of abandonment, from this further recognition that he didn't count, that he was on the outside. His face burned, his stomach felt rotten; he sat in his telephone booth working to repress a tantrum. The sorrow he felt for himself was compounded by knowing nobody would sympathize with his humiliation; nobody understood it. Irena too. She would tell him to count his blessings. Goddamn his blessings.

The phone rang. "Is the phone booth door closed?" Andy asked, telling Allan what Mona wanted. "If it was me, pal," Andy advised, "at two o'clock this afternoon I'd be on line buying a ticket to a talkie."

Allan walked back up Michigan Avenue, but he wasn't singing Cole Porter. Soon he was across the street from the Stevens, the world's largest hotel. So many people coming and going, anonymous people, and Allan became one of them.

Mona, in a Chanel suit and a cloche hat with a flat bow, opened the door to look at Allan for two full beats. When she spoke it was the way you would talk to a puppy or a child. "Come in here, hero." When he did as he was bidden, she pushed him up against the door and kissed him the way Andy had told him "real hot numbers" do, with their tongues. Mona stopped, saying to herself, not Allan, "This better be good, you better be good, hero." As she spoke, like someone giving an order, she slipped her hands past Allan's overcoat and suit jacket and, fingers outspread, smoothed them over his pectoral muscles. "You will be good," Mona said, and she looked at the young symmetries of his face, studying the perfect eyebrows as Irena sometimes did and then tracing them with her hands as Irena never did.

Frenched. Andy called it being frenched. Allan was being frenched by a hot number. Yet the sensations were spoiled for him by the thought of Irena. In a few minutes, if he played his cards right, he would see a female nipple. Count your blessings. That he was here was Irena's doing; if she would let him touch her. . . . French Irena. A man has needs. Andy says if you don't, you'll get sick. His father says no wild oats. No oats, many blessings. Mona was taking his tie off. He would get to touch Mona's nipples, get to see her naked; he was going to get a chance to do it, to do everything. After twenty-two years it was going to happen to him. The other hemisphere of his brain still had things to say; the ring was in his coat pocket. "Mona, let me explain that—"

"Will you shut up, please? Will you please shut up?" And she kissed him and undressed him and when Allan used a hand to help with an uncooperative garment, she softly bit it. When she had him naked, he started to speak. "No. Shut up, please," she told him and then said to herself, but aloud, "Yeah."

No yeah for Allan. He saw himself in the mirror attached to the hotel room dresser. He saw Mona, still fully dressed, kneeling on the bed, his erection in her hand, putting it against her cheek, and he felt shame. No oats for Irena, and his erection softened. Call this a blessing? The desire which had commanded him had receded.

"Drink this," Mona said, giving him a tumbler, perhaps a quarter filled with whiskey. Allan put it to his lips and then said, "Mona, I'm not sure that—"

"You're not sure?" Mona said. *"I'm* not sure. I'm not sure how much a man you are, Allan. First you come up here and now . . . I thought you were a man." She began to undress, taking her blouse off, and Allan, watching her and drinking the whiskey, defied his father and forgot Irena to sow this one oat with Mona.

She watched him drink the whiskey. "I want to loosen you up, Mr. Hero-baby, yes, I do. I want you loose and I want you to do just like I show you to do." Allan's excited hands and lips touched the female nipple for the first time since Ottoline had weaned him. He was so excited he was jumpy and uncontrollable. Mona got him to lie flat on the bed to soothe him and get him in order, but in the process she touched his genitals, the most grazing touch, and he commenced to ejaculate. Mona, expelling voiceless air from her mouth, tried to straddle and get on top of Allan, exhaling. "Oh, no, goddammit!" As she tried to put his penis into her vagina, her knee, barely on the mattress, slid off, pitching her onto the floor. She lay where she landed, listening to him making moans and gasps. When he was quiet, his breathing tapering off, she pulled her leg off the bed and, sitting next to it, looked at his body, eye level to her. White jelly blobs of semen were here and there on his abdomen. One had gotten shot well above the belly button.

Mona took a mischievous pinky finger and touched a jelly blob. Then of an instant she took the palms of both her hands and smeared Allan's semen over his chest and stomach. "Goddamn you, Allan," she shouted. He gave off a confused, whining, what-did-I-do-wrong noise, to which Mona responded by ordering him to "Get me a drink and a cigarette." After taking a sip, Mona lay back on the bed, one knee drawn up, the other leg crossed over it, puffing and considering what next. "I . . . Irena and I . . . uh, I—" Allan told her, lying on one side, face turned away, puffing also.

"Will you please shut up? Don't mention her name, Allan, I don't want to hear that name, get me?" He turned toward her but now she looked away so that Allan, who was still too embarrassed to stare at Mona's body, could look and understand that she was his to touch. He began to do so, his erection returning enough for them to try coupling again. The second time was better.

When they were done, Allan admired the curves of Mona's body as he watched her get out of bed and walk across the room to the toilet. He got to his feet and crossed the room to the telephone, though not without an inebriated stumble into a chest of drawers. "Tight as a tick," he told himself. Still, Allan had the presence to ask the operator to connect him with home—hotels had no dial telephones then—and, he thought, disguise his condition as he asked his mother to bring his dinner jacket to Uncle Fenwick's. He would be late and would dress for dinner there.

"You jerk!" Mona let fly at Allan after he had put down the phone. "You dumb jerk," she repeated as she walked over to him, put her arms through his, stuck her fingernails as deeply as she could in his shoulder blades, and yanked down. "Ya know the hotel operators write down every number they have to call, ya know that? Somebody could trace you through that number, Allan, you know that? You know what'll happen if he finds out?"

"Wha'?" Allan wasn't totally drunk, but the whiskey was beginning to hit him.

"He'll kill you. He'll kill both of us. You cheat with that Mick's wife, Allan, you're stealing his property. You're a jerk."

Allan drank some more whiskey. "I'm a jerk? I'm a thieving jerk. I wanta steal Gunner's property. C'mere, Mona," Allan said, pushing a cooperative Mona back down on the bed. "I want this property," he told her, as he entered Mona, coming in and out, not with violence but with steady purpose, talking to her, posing questions, telling her, "He should see this, he should see us now, he should watch me do this to his property. He should get close to there, right there," Allan said, looking at the point of union between their two bodies.

"He'd go crazy," Mona said, falling in with Allan. "He couldn't stand it." As they reached their climax, Allan fell to one side of Mona, saying, "I wanta tell him. I want him to know. I wanta ask 'im if he thinks this is a joke too. Hey!" Allan said, pushing extra hard into Mona. "Hey, Gunner, is it funny? Big laugh?"

"He could watch," Mona agreed.

"I think I'll call him," Allan said after a few minutes of silence. He began to roll himself off the bed, but Mona, sensing he might be going to do it, pulled him back and bit him on the earlobe until the pain had gotten his attention, until she had bitten through the alcohol and euphoria of Allan's sexual release. "What do I have to do to get it through to you, Allan? He . . . will . . . kill . . . us, if he finds out."

"But you like the idea, you said so yourself."

"There's a lotta ideas I like I don't do, and don't you think about doing any more, Allan. I mean it."

Drinking and wisecracking, Allan was readying himself for more sex, but Mona shrieked that it was five o'clock. She ran around the room reassembling herself, urging Allan to do the same. But he sat on the bed, drunk now, talking to himself, fumbling cigarettes. She could hear him say her name and Irena's. This time Mona paid no mind. She heard him talking about McGurn again and that worried her. When she had dressed and looked the usual Mona, she made an attempt to get Allan on his feet and moving. He had almost passed out, lying half on, half off the bed. He was nude, semi-paralytic, just able to get a cigarette in and out of his mouth. He was the drunkest he'd been in his life.

"Jesus, it serves me right." Mona scolded herself as she stood by the door, looked at his physical beauty, exclaimed "Jesus!" one more time, and let herself out. She was petrified Allan would sober up enough to phone the Gunner at the Edgewater Beach or somewhere.

At a pay station she called the cigar store and got Zep. "After six, lady; we don't take no bets after six, lady," he said.

"I wanta talk to Andy. Is he still there?"

"Hey, lover boy, Andy, there's a broad on the phone for ya," Mona could hear Zep shouting.

Andy told Mona he was not going over there. "Ya gotta!" she shouted into the speaker; Mona promised him another twenty dollars. When Andy let himself into the room, Allan had not moved. "So she got your cherry, you dumb, gold-plated muff diver. Hey," he said out loud to himself, "will you look at the body on this kid. He could be a fighter, an ath-a-lete . . . looks, money wasted on a muff diver." Andy went to the phone and almost picked it up to call room service for coffee when he recollected what he was about.

"Look!" said Elting Archibald in the reedy, half-hysterical voice that had become almost habitual with him in these months of strain. "A whole patch of hair!" They were in the rooms they usually occupied at Fenwick's. Elting had been in the bathroom making the final adjustments before putting on his dinner jacket. Ottoline had been ready, reading a magazine while her maid tidied up the room and made it ready for night. "Your brother! He's deviled me so much about my hair, it's happening. Look! Look! A whole patch. It just fell out."

"Oh, E," Ottoline said in sweet exasperation, coming to him and readying herself to repeat again that he was making something out of nothing. "Oh, dear!" she said. "Oh, E, it is. You have a bald plug on the side of your head. It's the size of a nickel."

"You're not supposed to tell me that!"

Down the corridor in her room, Irena was dressing. She had asked Ottoline for a few suggestions about her hair and had gotten them, even as her prospective mother-in-law told her, "Irena, you are so pretty, it doesn't matter what you do." She had wanted to give Irena a silver and amethyst ring that Elting's mother had given her, but her husband was having none of it. Everyone in the family had picked up that this would be the night that Allan would formally propose, except Elting, who kept saying he meant to have a talk with Allan, a talk about not marrying until one can afford to support a family, and not marrying a Polish Roman Catholic even if he could.

Irena was pleased with how she looked, but she didn't know what undergarments to wear and there was no one to ask. She had pur-

165

chased her copy of *Mrs. Grundy Is Dead,* but, dead or alive, Mrs. Grundy did not say what to wear if you were going to pet on the night you became affianced. She looked at herself in the mirror another time and could see how high her color was. Although she did try to keep her thinking abstract, to think of petting as "behavior," as the psychologists put things, sometimes she would think of Allan touching her and, to her surprise, it was a pleasing thought. If men were beasts, could some women be beastesses? Probably the sisters and the women in her family were correct in general, man's love *is* carnal and woman's love is spiritual, but what of Eloise and Abelard, of Tristan and Iseult? Spiritual love is the purest love, of course, but if it gets too intense it might partake of the carnal, well, call it physical.

What if Allan did not like her breasts? How do you know you'll please a man? Petting isn't wrong if you're sincere. Irena had never looked at her body with an eye to love. This petting, how would they do it? Should she put Allan's hand on her breast? He's tried so often; he may have given up hope. Well, anyhow, there is nothing wrong about an engaged couple petting, people who love each other; that cannot be wrong or a sin, thought Irena, trying to talk away her Catholic training. After they were married, Allan could tell her what she should do.

Without Allan, dinner was slow and terrible. Mr. Archibald would not talk at all and Uncle Fenwick would not stop talking. He talked about how smart he was, he talked about how rich he was and how he was getting richer, he talked about the dangers of Bolshevism, and he talked particularly about Allan and Irena, "two beautiful Greek gods, like Praxiteles' marble incarnated in the flesh of love." It was lush language and he could not be stopped, not even by his friend Miss Isabella, who would whisper, "You're embarrassing everybody," to which he would reply, "But I am the Great Fenwick."

"Yes, you certainly are," Miss Isabella agreed as the many clocks in Fenwick's house struck ten, and an obviously drunk and disarrayed Allan appeared at the dining room door. After waking up in the back of a cab at his parents' house in Winnetka, he had gone inside, drunk half a water glass of whiskey in his shame, directed the cab more miles to Fenwick's, stumbled upstairs to attempt to dress for dinner, stripped to the waist, and put on his dinner jacket, forgetting a shirt customarily goes on first. Now he was at the dining room door.

"Two Greek gods," said Uncle Fenwick. "Aphrodite and Bacchus."

166

"I am a muff diver," Allan intoned. "I have been diving for the immortal muff."

Before Irena put on her nightgown, she stood herself in front of the full-length mirror in the bath and looked at her naked body. Her right hand cupped her breast. She shuddered. Her nipples were so hard she could feel their rigidity without touching them. Then Irena put her hands to her face and bowed her body backward, her elbows high up in the air. Between her compressing hands she forced a sound, half gasp, half sob.

In the morning, Irena waited for the sound of the car bearing Allan's father away before she went down for breakfast. She'd gotten up early to pack before the maid knocked and asked if she could help. It was embarrassing that she did not have enough clothes to fill those capacious suitcases and embarrassing that she was embarrassed by it. How did people like Uncle Fenwick live with maids and waiters looking at them when they were undressed or angry or needed to be alone? Not that the Irishwoman who was called "the guest maid" was intrusive. But Irena considered getting her bath "drawn" more a nuisance than a help. On Marshfield Avenue it would have helped to have a guest maid fill up the washtub when she and Steffy tried to get themselves clean and Granny guarded the window. Oh, Steffy would leave home tomorrow if she could get a job being the guest maid in a house like this. She'd have her own private room, Irena thought.

She had forgiven Allan for last night, though she couldn't decide what to do about it. She was always forgiving Allan, Irena reflected; Aunt Helen was always forgiving the rotten Morton; Ottoline was always forgiving Mr. Archibald. The men are the fighters, the aggressive ones, which makes them unstable, prone to do things the women have to forgive them for. At a lecture Margaret Mead had said women were the real fighters, but perhaps she was joking.

Last night, Irena had decided, was Allan's way of putting his foot down, telling her no Europe. Irena wished he could be blunter, just say no, I forbid it. He's the man, after all. Margaret Mead would not agree with that; Mr. Park would not take her seriously if she gave up her fellowship, which would affect her dissertation. And for what? Allan hadn't proposed. The woman doesn't give up her life except for her husband. But why did he have to wait until her last night to misbehave . . . and in front of everybody?

Ottoline was alone in the breakfast room with coffee and a cigarette. She was poised, as Irena always found her, but not aloof. How could she keep her back straight and her hands so still and yet be sympathetic? It must be something they teach in those girls' schools.

A chime sounded ten. "Allan hasn't been down yet. You know how he can be," his mother said, signaling to Irena that now she too had the duty of sustaining his sullen funks. "I think I'll go up and drag him down," Ottoline added, reclaiming the burden. "You can't leave with him having locked himself up like this." They weren't married yet. He was still his mother's problem.

"I'll get him, Mrs. Archibald," Irena said, indicating her willingness, indeed her insistence that the transfer be made. "If we're going to be—well, I'll talk to him."

"Yes," Ottoline replied, the calm eyes looking at her prospective daughter-in-law.

Allan, in the silk pajama bottoms a valet had buttoned him into the previous night, had taken the eiderdown comforter and slid underneath the Sheraton four-poster. He was a fetal mound, covered and hidden in protective darkness. Allan's brain, swollen by alcohol, pressed against the inside of the cranium. Highly sensitive, fragile brain cells abrading against rough, unfinished, concave calcium walls.

Allan did not feel guilt. Allan felt shame. Guilt had not yet come into its prominence. College-educated Chicagoans did not converse about recognizing guilt, sublimating it, handling it. Guilt was the condition of being guilty, of being the one who had done wrong.

You can handle guilt; shame you suffer. He rolled on his back; he rolled over on his stomach; he stretched his length; he shrimped into a circle so tight his head touched his knees. He could not think, he could only remember; he could hide, he could writhe, and he could force himself to drop back to sleep until he heard Irena's knocking on the door. He could not let Irena look at him.

It was a probing, quiet knock. Her voice was hushed and sweet, as though she would lift him up from this darkly hurtful place and, minute by minute, restore him to brightness. Allan tensed himself under the Sheraton. But Irena did not go away; she knocked again so that he knew she would not go away until he said something, which he could not do because he had no words. He made a slow noise, an elongated tone of pain and negation.

The knock again. Allan heard Irena say "Dear heart" to him. Couldn't she go downstairs? He made his noise but knew that he would have to get over to the door. She knocked again, making him slide out from under and come barefooted to his side of the door.

168

"Your hand's on the knob, isn't it?" she whispered. Allan said nothing. "Isn't it? Isn't it, Allan?" She turned the knob, felt resistance, and stopped. He was holding it. "Please, Allan."

On his side he saw the catch that would throw the lock. It was hurting him to keep her out with the force of his hands. He did not put the catch on. He held the knob, sensing the pressure of her grip on the other side until he made another subverbal request she go away. The pressure on the knob lightened, and Allan, believing he heard Irena sob, slid down onto the inlay of his uncle's floor.

Ottoline found Irena in the solarium. The younger woman was no longer crying, only touching the corners of her eyes with her handkerchief. "He's being rude," Ottoline said. Irena looked up at her. Ottoline could see that, if she said more, her prospective daughter-in-law would recommence crying and she did not want to deal with that. The contusions of young love heal. Turning out of the room, she slipped into the library, where Fenwick was in consultation with a contractor about strengthening the walls and defenses of the estate. "I want a berm—there!" she heard her brother demand of the man.

Irena stayed in the solarium composing herself. She lit a cigarette, thought how much she was smoking, and wondered how angry Allan was with her. Gathering material from Poland was not part of the original work plan; it had emerged talking to Mr. Park and it wouldn't have come to anything if he hadn't arranged the fellowship. Mr. Park would understand. He would be disappointed, but he would understand.

"'The Polish Immigrants'!" he had exclaimed, giving her work a title. "I'm going to show your thesis to one or two editors at publishing houses." Margaret Mead had done that too, had broken out of the circle of academic readers and reached a wider audience with her anthropology. The prospect was thrilling: to describe Polish people, her Polish people, to the same reading public Mead had introduced the Samoan people to.

If she stayed, the thesis would be less than her best and, Irena supposed, it would not be published. Was Margaret Mead married?

The second time Irena left the solarium to tap a light knuckle against Allan's door, she had lost clarity. She had been downstairs, now she was upstairs, worried, urgent, strained, explaining, "My train is leaving in a few hours." No sound, no movement. Another three taps, stubbornly timid sounds. "Allan, please, please don't do this to me." More silence. Irena spoke at fullest voice just short of being a cry, a calling out: "Please, please!" The urgency, the pain, the subjection, made her words carry down the gallery, a wail to penetrate wood and stone.

Below, in the library, they heard it, and its pleading sadness drew brother and sister out of the room. They stood by the library door listening. Irena's "Please, Allan" came to them.

"Ghost," Fenwick said.

"What?"

"That beautiful girl is going to make a bad ghost."

Upstairs, Allan had opened the door a crack. Irena looked at a strip of cheek and a closed eyelid, squeezed against the opening. She touched his face. The door opened a few inches more. She caressed the side of Allan's forehead and tentatively forced her way in.

She had not seen Allan unshaved before, and the beetled and overhung look on his face, the face on which so little was yet written, set Irena back. He seemed more pained than he had on his knees the night Gunner twisted his ears.

She guided him over to the four-poster, helped him down on it, held his head, smelled the alcohol on him, kissed him, ran her hand across his chest, and told him that she was sorry, that she hadn't known, that she did not understand, that it was too late not to go to Europe but that she could cut her trip short, that she was sorry, sorry, sorry. Irena put her cheek against Allan's hair and cried into it. Allan accepted her tears and apologies. Irena kissed him again and told him she was sorry again. Allan kissed her and murmured and said he would write.

Uncle Fenwick supervised the lashing of Irena's steamer trunk to the luggage carrier on the rear of the biggest of his cars. He was taking her to the railroad station. Ottoline had begged him to be nice, the expression she used whenever he was allowed to be alone with someone.

For most of the ride he was uncharacteristically silent, as Irena looked out the window and he looked straight ahead at the little black button on top of the chauffeur's cap on the other side of the glass partition.

"I want you to come back for Christmas. I'll send you the steamship tickets. Chicago for a week and you can return to Europe.

"You have to come back and laugh, be happy, Irena. You may have made a ghost, and if you have, it's damn well going to be a happy one."

"You're superstitious, Uncle Fenwick."

"I'm serious. It's the same as spilling red wine on damask. Emotions. They stain a house."

Chapter 8

You'll find us there before the office opens
Crowding the vestibule before the day begins
The secretary yawns from last night's date
The elevator boy's black face looks out and grins.
We push we crack our bitter jokes we wait
These mornings always find us waiting there
Each one of us has shined his broken shoes
Has brushed his coat and combed his careful hair
Dance hall boys pool parlor kids wise guys
The earnest son of the college grad, all
Each hides the question twitching in his eyes
And smokes and spits and leans against the wall.

—ALFRED HAYES, "In a Coffee Pot"

The winter of 1932 was even colder and poorer than the winter of the year before. A window at Kroch's bookshop on Michigan Avenue was given over to a display of the season's best-seller: *A Fortune to Share* by Vash Young. The door-to-door salesmen were no less desperate. Despite the below-zero days they were trying to sell Bibles and pressure cookers, the new cooking utensil that did not shrink food, thereby making a little go a long way. Every district in the city had its Fuller Brush men except the Negro section on the Near South Side, where the neighbors were preventing Municipal Court bailiffs from evicting tenants for nonpayment of rent. The court officers took the furniture out and the neighbors moved it back. Soon would come the nonpayment of the bailiffs.

The reiterated predictions about prosperity returning by the second or surely the third quarter were petering out in Washington. From everywhere else came explanations of what was coming to be

171

called the Great Depression. The *Tribune* had a story in which a prominent radical asked:

> What is the cause of this starvation, misery and hardship of the millions of workers in the United States? Is it because some great calamity has destroyed the food, clothing and shelter available for the people? No, on the contrary. Millions of workers must go hungry because there is too much wheat. Millions of workers must go without clothes because the warehouses are full to overflowing with everything that is needed. Millions of workers must freeze because there is too much coal.

Others held that the cause was too little money. People were hoarding money instead of spending it. Money should be printed, they argued, with an expiration date on it so people would be forced to spend it before it became worthless. Secretary of the Treasury Mellon, who a year previously understood what needed to be done, told the newspapers, "None of us has any means of knowing when and how we shall emerge from the valley of depression in which the world is traveling." Back in Chicago, Sewell Avery, the president of Montgomery Ward, confessed, "To describe the causes of this situation is rather beyond my capacity. I am unfortunate in having no friends that seem to be able to explain it clearly to me."

The giants of commerce had fallen mute before the mystery, but Fenwick said it didn't matter. "Who cares why or how? Leave that to the astronomers. They can get on that one after they find out how the earth was created. Conditions good or bad, there's always money to be made."

Fenwick wanted to make money, Cermak wanted to find it. He wanted to find the City of Chicago's money. After taking office, the new Mayor could find none of it. The retreating Big Bill had destroyed the records in the treasurer's office. It would take months to reconstruct many of the most important of them, but, regardless, the City's revenues were next to nonexistent. What had not been lost or stolen was not being paid in taxes. Against the deficit, A. J. threw his beefy self. The official limousine was parked in front of the La Salle Street entrance to City Hall before eight o'clock every morning, its master in his office firing, laying off, furloughing, reducing pay, postponing payments, while looking for any money he could get a hand on. Where the hell *had* the city's money gone? If it had been stolen, why the hell didn't the thieves at least spend it? Recirculate it?

Payless pay days for the city employees, workless work days for the ward and precinct captains of the political organization A. J. had labored through two decades of Republican dominance to fit together. He had an imagination. Having worked himself up from the bottom of a coal mine, he knew some exertions had to be made patiently and in the dark. You crashed your pick against the sides of the pit and persevered.

Tax squads of teachers were formed and given lists of delinquent property owners. Collect the money for your salaries yourselves. A passing municipal enthusiasm, tax squads raised little revenue, but they made it appear that somebody was trying to do something. Four public school teachers worked their way from house to house down Marshfield Avenue until they had come to 4508, where Granny opened the door and listened in uncomprehending fear. For sure she would lose the house and Robert had a cold and Steffy had been fired her first day on her first job.

Blandishment and charm, such as the family possessed, had been layered onto Bob Delvecchio, the manager of the F. W. Woolworth's Five and Ten Cent Store on Ashland Avenue, with the result that, after several months, Steffy was taken on as a sales clerk trainee at six dollars a week. The weekend before the Monday Steffy was to start, the family, even Granny, had reminded her more than once how the money was needed, how lucky she was to have a job when nobody else did, how she had never done anything to earn this chance, how big a company Woolworth's was and therefore how steady the employment would be. All these things Steffy had already said to herself, so that when she waited on her first customer, a lady who gave her a quarter for a glass candlestick, price one nickel, she went to the cash register and she froze. The tears came to Steffy's eyes and watered down her cheeks. Who's got the time for this? Bob Delvecchio asked himself after he had sent Steffy home.

Meanwhile A. J. persisted. If the schoolteachers tramping through the slush of March could not locate money, Cermak would find it, if he had to extort it. Which is why he summoned the Enforcer, Frank Nitti, the new chief executive officer of Mr. Capone's corporation.

Scarface Al, dissuaded by no less angry but more prudent business associates from murdering the U.S. District Attorney and the jury and the witnesses against him, had been convicted of income tax evasion. A month before, in a Prussian blue overcoat, gray hat with Prussian blue band, green suit, green spats, and black shoes, Snorky had said adieu to Chicago in the train shed of Dearborn Station. In the company of four federal marshals, Mr. Public Enemy Number One was preparing to board the Chicago and Eastern Illinois Railway's *Dixie Limited* for a fast, first-class run to the Atlanta penitentiary. Allan came as before and, as before, stood at the outer edge of the circle, unrecognized by Snorky, who waxed eloquent to the reporters.

"I'm willing to go to jail," Mr. Capone said in answer to a question. "I can take my stretch if I can come back to my wife and my kid without being hounded by the public, which didn't give me a fair chance 'cause of you sons-o'-bitches. You're the people who made me into Public Enemy Number One. It's impossible for a man my age to have done everything I'm charged with. I'm a spook, an imaginary bogeyman in millions of people's minds so you guys can sell papers. But it ain't the spook who got found guilty; it's me, Al Capone. I'm going to jail when I could be going to the fights or watching a ball game. How do ya like that?"

"Great violin solo, Al. An' we thought the only musical instrument you played was the machine gun."

"Fuck you, Joe."

Turning away from the reporters, the ugly man in the pretty clothes said, "Come on, you guys," to the marshals, who followed him up the Pullman car stairs. As the *Dixie Limited* jolted, its couplings banging, and its wheels began to turn, Mr. Capone made his final farewell appearance in Chicago on the rear platform of the observation car, where, leaning over the illuminated decal of a darky picking cotton against a Stars and Bars sky, he held the index finger of his right hand rigid, pumping it up and down at the group of journalists.

Now Big Bill and Big Al were gone to their retirements and Frank Nitti was leaning back against the leather of the principal guest chair in the Mayor's office looking at A. J. Cermak's big gut. A pig, concluded Nitti, as he watched Cermak take out a chunky cigarette lighter, flip up the top, and crank a light for his cigar. The Mayor's fingernails did not glisten.

Anton Joseph was not a schmoozer politician. He did not lean back in the mayoral chair and ask his guest, "Who'da t'ought I'd be sitting here and you'd be sitting there, eh, Frank?" What he said to Nitti was, "Ya know, Frank, I got elected on a reform ticket."

Nitti pulled his upper lip down over his teeth, the better to check the lower edge of his moustache with the tip of his middle finger. "What am I supposed to make of that, Tony? What does that mean?"

"It means," the Mayor said, "the price is double."

Nitti's eyes stayed where they were as his hand reached for the pillbox. "Ya gotta glass o' water, Tony?"

"Double," Cermak said, pouring one out of the desk carafe. "Double."

The gangster looked closer at what might have been a dust speck on the glass, then he put two pills down with a sip of water. Cermak, not overly given to thinking about other men's characters, wondered how a killer could be so finicky.

Frank Nitti put the used glass back down on the tray next to the carafe, he drew his feet, encased in pointed shoes, so close they touched, he put his hands back on the ends of the leather chair's arms, he composed himself; and when he was neat and straight and symmetrical, he said, "No."

"Then I'm gonna close you down, Frank."

"You're not gonna close us down. You know and I know that if you was to close us down—which is not a possible thing, Tony—Chicago, Illinois, the second largest city in America, in the United States of America, would be outa beer. If the WCTU could not do that, you can't. You're not gonna take this town's beer away."

"This town is not gonna run outa beer. I'm selling the beer franchise to a distributor who'll meet my price."

"Who zat?"

"Roger Touhy."

Mr. Touhy was in the beer business in the northwest suburb of Arlington Heights and thereabouts. He was known to Mr. Nitti, who sold him the beer that he delivered in the six or seven trucks he owned. That he could assemble the distribution system necessary to service three and a half million people was self-evidently impossible to a business executive like the impeccable Enforcer. "He's got no salesmen, he's got no collectors, he don't know the routes, and he's got no trucks. So what's Roger Touhy gonna deliver beer in?"

"City of Chicago Street Department trucks."

"And who's gonna drive 'em?"

"City of Chicago policemen."

"Oh, Jesus," Nitti said, so flatly the expression didn't merit an exclamation point. "I used to think Big Bill Thompson was a crazy man, Tony. . . . An' where you gonna get the beer?"

"We'll get the beer, Frank."

A sign stood on the tarred oblong roof, spelling out in uncertain neon, DINER—EAT. Down the street from the padlocked Ludlow Silk Factory, it had been a true dining car on the Lackawanna Railroad— the Route of Phoebe Snow, the genteel young lady who appeared in the magazine advertisements tucked in a Pullman bunk, asleep, soot-free, and white because, on the Lackawanna line, they used clean-burning anthracite in the steam engines. The D'Amico boy leaned over the counter to get closer to Bettina, the owner's daughter.

"Joe . . . he's got the Lindbergh baby," the young D'Amico said.

"No!"

"Yeah, he's got that baby. He's all the time disappearin'. He's goin' off to feed the kid somewheres."

"Where?" She was thinking of the reward.

"I dunno where. Somewheres. He's got the baby. He knows that territory . . . around Hopewell where the Lindberghs live . . . where he was working before he got laid off, when he didn't get paid that time, when he was muttering about how he was gonna shoot some-body. But he's got money now. I seen it."

He was the kind, they agreed, to kidnap a baby. The pair of them drifted over to the damp cubicle where Joe washed dishes in his rub-berized apron. Its skirt scraped the top of the little man's shoes. Slops slid down the front of the sink, the slick of the apron, the side of the garbage can. "Hey, Joe," the D'Amico youth teased, "you steal the Lindbergh kid?"

"Lucky Lindy, his kid. They gonna steal the bosses' kids. You see. S'gonna be lotsa more . . . these kidnaps."

"So what do ya know about it, Joe? You do it, Joe?"

"Lucky Lindy! Lucky Lindy, not lucky no more. That's what I know."

Later, after the diner closed, Joe got out his tools and finished tiling the toilets. When he was finished, he washed the walls and fix-tures to a gleam, put his tools away, brought a chair up to the case-ment refrigerator, and stood on the seat to look at the shelf above the box where the first-aid medicaments were kept. He stared at the bot-tle of gentian violet. Very blue. Joe reached for the bottle and took it.

He had it in his pocket when he was locked up.

Allan went home to Winnetka and stayed for two days in his bedroom, attempting to alleviate his pain by looking in the New Tes-tament for words that would absolve him. By the morning of the third day, time had done what Scripture could not. The shame and remorse

176

had lessened and Allan went down to face his father over the breakfast table. Hangdog, he waited over two strips of bacon and a triangle of dried toast to hear his father's judgment, welcoming it as the cleansing ritual he could not find in the Bible.

"A man sometimes can get, well—" Elting said, looking at his own two strips of bacon, "a man can do something he doesn't mean to, get into a situation. She's a beautiful girl, Allan, and you're young. And a Roman Catholic. I don't think of them as being so attractive, but, well, you suck in your breath and do it. Break it off. Polish, I never think of them as being an attractive people, so you're right to want to end it, but you just have to do it, Allan. Do it, don't go getting drunk, boy. As you now have reason to know, the courage whiskey gives a man serves him badly. You sit down with her—I hardly suppose that in her heart of hearts she thought it would get *this* far—sit down with her and say it. Give her a present, that's the decent thing to do. Anyhow," he began to conclude as he searched the stock tables to confirm what he already knew, the new lows Insull Utilities had hit before yesterday's final bell, "anyhow, we do things we regret. I have done things I regret," Elting said, placing the "I" as though the statement would come as a surprise to his son. "Deeply regret," he repeated, and this time it was evident he was speaking more to himself.

Allan could not imagine his father in a hotel room with a woman like Mona. He tried shaking the thought off. His father was vain, self-centered, and mean sometimes, but incapable of doing something truly bad, something like what he had done. As he thought about it, all of a sudden Allan was taken by a physical remembrance of Mona's body.

"Thank goodness," Elting said, "no 'Cinderella Marriage' headlines. It would not have been a normal wedding. It would have attracted riffraff. But break it off the right way, Allan. Make your feelings clear to her, as a gentleman would. That's a good boy. I have to go to the counting house."

Allan had now been misunderstood and forgiven by both his fiancée and his father. The conviction of wrongness stayed with him, braiding itself into a confusion of desires and emotions. He loved Irena and he wanted Mona; he wanted Irena and Mona had gotten him; now he wanted Mona again and he blamed Irena because Mona had bonded him physically to her, made him remember her, miss her.

A few days later four fat letters arrived from Irena. She had writ-

177

ten them on the steamer and mailed them from Cherbourg so that they had come across on the return voyage of her own ship.

Irena's letters were loving, thoughtful, and purposeful. One of them was given over to Robert and Helen Lynd, the husband-and-wife sociologists who had written *Middletown,* the study of Muncie, Indiana. Allan thought the Lynds probably did not have children, but he was moved by her trying to see how they might accommodate each other. He was also moved by his memory of Irena holding him on the bed. He could have had her there, possibly. He realized he did love her, and in the fullness of his feeling he began a letter asking Irena to marry him.

He labored at writing, particles of thought ricocheting off each other, splitting into new urges, passing out of his field of consciousness. In the middle of his scribbling, he remembered the engagement ring and went through the pockets of his jacket until he found it. Putting it on the escritoire Ottoline had burdened his room with, he began to settle in, writing less distractedly that he loved her, taking up Irena's game of finding other famous husband-and-wife teams like the Lynds, like the Curies, the Webbs. Didn't Milton have a wife who read to him, or was it his daughter? Or was that John Stuart Mill? Which put him in mind of Frankenstein, though Allan could not think why. He wrote Irena they could work together; he wrote he wanted to have children with her. He saw her on the bed, touching his chest, and he put down his pen. "What's wrong with me?" he said, bewildered. He had an erection.

Walking over to the bed, Allan threw himself on it, his eyes on the electric fixture in the ceiling, the foci of his lust for Irena blurred by the memory of Mona lying next to him in the hotel room. He rolled over, drew his knees up under him, his arms crossed over his head, and withstood successive attacks of sexual demand so strong he shook in his shortness of breath. A few minutes later he was yipping and hissing aloud. "It works! It works!" he breathed, as he jumped up and down under the freezing drops of a high-pressure shower.

The next day he finished his letter to Irena and mailed it. But four days later he was using the upstairs phone in his parents' house to call Mona. The night before he had five tortured hours with the Gunner, who had goosed Allan again as his chosen floozie of the night watched, this time from the front. The man's hand had grabbed his testicles; standing bent over, hands cupped over his crotch, was more demeaning than straight-out servile kneeling. The rest of them had shouted and laughed, and Allan in his angry embarrassment had had a vengeful picture of Mona and himself. Bang her. Andy always used that word, bang. Bang her. Bang Mona and think about that bastard as he banged her.

Mona made a guttural noise and hung up on Allan. Some hours later Andy was on the phone to Allan. "Tomorrow, any time after two P.M. Central Standard Time, and, if you don't mind me asking, do you know what the hell you're doing, pal?"

"It's business," Allan replied. He felt out of control, mixed up, doing things without plan, things foreign to his nature. Lying to Andy, of all people. "Business," he repeated.

"Monkey business."

"You're always going to be a runner for a bookie, Andy."

"Muff diver." Andy hung up. There were days when it seemed to him his life sentence was to do minor chores and errands for others. But it doubly fried him to be setting up dates between Allan and Mona. He thought about himself and Allan. Andy paid for everything, for women with money, for money with labor, or by taking chances, and he would pay for esteem if he had the right coin. Mona paid for hotel rooms to shack up with Allan by living with Gunner; Allan did not have to do anything but let cigarette smoke curl out of his nostrils. Life was a racket. God, Andy knew for sure, was on the take.

Andy did not give up trying. It he could not have it, whatever the *it* of his concupiscence might be, he would settle for making it look as though he had it. Andy toyed with the idea of making it look to Zep as though the magnificent Mona was his. Mona wouldn't have played along, though. For she was aware of Zep, watching from the back room through a crack, imperceptibly shaking his head. "What's that broad doin'? Lemme see the slip. I wanta see what fuckin' nag that dame bet on," Zep demanded, coming out from behind the mirrored wall as soon as the floor tiles stopped echoing to Mona's heels. Andy put a hand in a trouser pocket and shook a few coins. "I gotta collect. It's getting late, Zep," he answered, preparatory to moving through various offices in City Hall, paying off yesterday's winners and taking from the losers.

Allan found himself at the hotel room door. His game with himself was to pretend to be in a trance, waking up in places where he should not be, to say, Where am I, how did I get here? When Mona let him in, she had her hat, coat, and gloves on; her purse was in her hand. "Jerk!" she told him, going into her purse for a cigarette and then waiting for Allan to light it. As he did she slapped at him with her free hand and screamed again, "Jerk! Jerk! Jerk! Calling the hotel. You are a *fool*. Ya got more money than brains. If he finds out about us he *is going to kill us*."

Allan felt his face. It had not been a grace tap. "My ring cut you," Mona said, putting down the cigarette and coming over to Allan to wipe a smidgen of blood off his cheek. They kissed and Allan held her, listening to her tell him, "You can't ever call me, Allan. Not ever, sugar. If you want to get in touch with me, do it through Andy. Gunner thinks he's my bookie. But don't call."

"Sometimes you exaggerate, Mona," replied Allan, taking his most upper-class, young-swell stance. "It's not as though *I* were a gangster. They only do those things to each other, you know that. Look at who *I* am. I don't think Gunner would do anything to me. Do you, really do you?"

By way of answering, Mona pushed her pelvis against Allan's, ran her fingers through his hair, and scratched his scalp with her nails.

He yelped. "That hurt!"

"It hurt? How could it hurt? You said no one would do anything to *you*. Look at who you are. You! You! You rich boy. Well, I'm his goddamn wife and I know what he'd do to me."

"That hurt," Allan repeated, his surprise changing to wounded feelings.

"Not as bad as Gunner'll hurt you," she whispered in his ear and then leaned back away from him, holding one of his hands, inspecting him, his handsomeness, looking at him as if her eyes could pick up his quirky inability to see how the world was put together. She led him to the bed, still holding his hand. They sat. "Didya ever hear about Gunner at the testimonial banquet? Did nobody ever tell you about that time, Allan?" Mona asked, lighting up again, talking as people do when addressing dogs, children, and incapacitated adults. "It was one of those dago things. Like the Sons of Italy. I don't remember which. They gave the banquet in this guy's honor, and they have him up there at the head table and all to present a scroll sayin' what a great guy he is, and then two other guys grab him—that's the way they tell the story, honest to God; they laugh about it—and he beats this guy over the head with a baseball bat."

"Who did? Who beat him over the head?"

"Gunner! Who d'ya think? Gunner does. Kills the guy. There.

On the spot in front of the waiters and everybody. The two other guys hold him up and the way they tell it the guy's still holding his testimonial, his scroll, when he dies. In front of all those people . . . sitting at the tables with coffee and parfaits in front of them.

"When he came home . . . his tux, I threw it out. Blood, spatter marks on the shirt, what looked like bone, bits of bone. I never asked him. An', Allan, not one of all those guys at the banquet, not one of them, squealed on him. You know why, Allan?" She spoke the next words slowly. "Because . . . they . . . were . . . afraid." Mona bit Allan on the earlobe and got up as he jumped in pain.

"Scotch?" Mona wanted to know, pointing to the bottle on the dresser. "It's the good stuff which they don't sell to nobody. This is the stuff they keep for themselves." She hung up her hat and coat, accepted the drink he had poured for her, continuing her monologue. "It don't matter to them, Allan, that you went to Cambridge and Oxford; or that your family owns the stock market and all; they'll kill you if they wanna. They killed that reporter, did ya know that, Allan? Killed that Jake what-was-his-name? Killed him. They'd kill you too; they'd kill the Mayor or the Governor. They'd kill President Hoover. It don't matter to them."

She switched on the radio and, when it had warmed up, fiddled with the dial until she got a rumba she danced to with an imaginary partner. "Come here, sweetie pie," and the two danced till she stopped to take her earrings out of her ears. "Just because you got money," she told him as they resumed dancing. "They got money too, Allan. More'n you."

Standing in one place Mona put her hands behind her head, keeping time to the rumba beat with her body; then, pushing back against Allan, she told him over her shoulder, "Undo me."

"Huh?"

"Undo me, Allan, unbutton me. . . . I could dance for you, only you'd think I'd done it for other men too," Mona said, dancing out of her dress, which she picked up off the floor and hung in the closet, all in time to the music. "But," she continued, putting her hands behind her neck and making a hip-wrenching bump and grind at Allan, "it isn't true."

"I didn't say—"

"Well, would you like me to, Al-lan, would you, Al-la-an?"

"Can I say something, Mona? I wrote Irena that—"

"Will you please shut up about her." Allan began to say something else. "I don't want to know about it. Shut . . . up . . . will you, please. I don't want to hear about it." She was shouting at him, coming with fingernails extended. Allan caught her by the wrists. They did a few taut dance steps around the room, fell on the bed, and mated with the sweat and energy of sexual infatuation. The music ran over them, poured over their interlaced bodies as they grunted, scratched, and slammed against each other. "The South American Rhythm Hour, brought to you for your listening pleasure by radio station WLS, the call letters of Sears, Roebuck and Company, the World's Largest Store." After they had driven themselves into exhaustion and their pulse rates had come down, they lay on the bed, he fingering the mattress ticking, she running a palm over his buttocks, examining the beauty of his body.

They smoked. Mona lay naked but for an ashtray in the vicinity of her belly button. Allan poured whiskey in their glasses. "Don't get soused like the last time, Allan," Mona ordered him as he came back and lay down next to her, this time his head propped up by a pillow at the foot of the bed, the toes of one foot tousling her hair.

"You can get a divorce," he told her.

"Will you shut up?" Mona hadn't raised her voice.

"I mean it," Allan persisted. Having proposed to one woman by mail the day before, Allan was now making an offer to God or propriety to pay for the hours of delight with this woman, to make a show of recompense for his appalling pleasures.

"Yeah, we can have a double casket wedding ceremony," said Mona, who sensed that on this one she did not have to take Allan seriously. "Does this stiff which used to be a stupid rich kid named Allan take this stiff which used to be me, Mona, for his wife? They can skip the till-death-do-us-part—because we'll already be dead."

"The Cook County Coroner performed the service, which was held in the icebox at the city morgue out of consideration for the noses of the guests," Allan added.

"Allan! Disgusting!"

"The bride wore a simple birthday suit adorned with a cardboard tag on her big toe. The couple will honeymoon on a slab in the forensics laboratory before taking up permanent residence at suburban Longwood Cemetery."

"Allan, for chrissake!" With that Mona chucked the contents of her glass at him and, knocking the ashtray on the floor, reared up to launch an attack. As she did, the alcohol in the whiskey, which had

182

landed on Allan's genitals, began to sting, causing him to yip-yap off the bed onto the floor, putting a bare foot on the burning cigarette that had fallen when Mona knocked over the ashtray. Shouting, "God, oh my God!" Allan held his testicles, yelped, and hopped into the bathroom.

Mona put the smoking butt back in the ashtray, extinguished it, lit another cigarette, and smoked, listening to the bathroom water run as Allan went about the task of washing the pain away. When he came out he stood by the bed, readying himself to tell Mona he did not enjoy this kind of treatment, but she reared up, took his genitals in her hands, held them against her cheek, and informed him, "We don't want to hurt these, no, not *these,* Allan."

"What are you doing?" he asked her. She was kissing his testicles. "What are you doing?"

They lay on the palm of her hand as Mona gave them the smallest, pecking kisses. "Meat balls on the platter," she said, more to herself than to him, now taking the tip of Allan's rigidifying penis between her teeth and gently stretching and pulling it toward her. Then Mona dropped it and, looking up at her beautiful young man, told him, "I could have bitten it off."

"Sometimes I don't understand you, Mona. I don't."

"That's 'cause you don't believe anything bad can be done to you, Allan. You think you're armor-plated. You're not, though. One of these days somebody's going to come along and bite it off for you, Allan."

They went after each other again, pulling each other's hair, inflicting bites on each other's shoulders. After they subsided, Mona again tried to make Allan see what kind of men Gunner and his associates were. As she talked, Allan steered the conversation around to Frank Nitti's visit to Tony Cermak's office. She began to tell him about the meeting until she looked out the window and saw Michigan Avenue below penetrated by the oncoming dusk; she shrieked she was going to be late, bit Allan on the ear, and fled into the bathroom to dress. Allan put his clothes on more slowly, turning over the importance of what Mona had begun to impart. He left the Stevens sober this time, perplexed, revenged against the Gunner, excited, grateful. It was wrong, this hotel-room love affair, but Mona gave him so much.

The top of Elting Archibald's desk was in order. Nothing on it but his pen holders, his telephone and office intercom, and his large blotter framed in Moroccan leather. The first edition of the afternoon papers had been placed in the geometric center of the blotter.

HEARTBROKEN APPEAL FROM MOTHER TO
BABY THIEF
Mrs. Lindbergh Begs for Child's Health!

Further down the page the text of Anne Morrow Lindbergh's statement appeared: "The baby has been sick and its recovery may depend on you. You must be careful of his diet." The paper referred to the appeal as "a long-shot attempt to light a spark of humanity even in the cruel heart of a baby-napper." There followed the baby's menu: two tablespoons of cooked cereal night and morning, one yolk of egg, fourteen drops of Viosterol, and on and on. The mothers of America's unkidnapped children pondered the wisdom of the baby Lindbergh's regimen and switched to it. Poor baby Lindbergh! Gentle nappers, more like silky nippers, they would be to make sure he had "½ cup prune juice after afternoon nap."

None of this information was being absorbed by the banker. Elting was drawn up to his desk, sitting, back straight, doing what Ottoline called "grinding": arms on his desk, hands clasped, fingers interlaced, rubbing his palms together; his jaws were locked as he rocked, milling his teeth, fixing his eyes on invisible points.

In his body-rending trance, Elting stared across the room, not seeing his Currier & Ives print, grinding at the insoluble problem of the Insull stocks. To win back what he was losing on the thousands of shares he'd bought with A. J. Cermak's money, Allan's father was playing the game of puts and takes, buying contracts to buy or sell the stock at a set price by a given date in future time. Played right, it enabled a man to make as much money from a drop in the price of a stock as he would from its rise. But the game of puts and takes demands a trader's quick brain, a mind that can keep track of dozens of transactions, their amounts and terms, the hour of their expiration. The slow banker mind, trained to look things over, to mull and delay, had the wrong traits and habits for puts and takes. For what Elting Archibald was doing he had to be on the phone to his broker ten or twelve times a day, buying back in the morning what he had sold the previous afternoon and selling in the afternoon what he bought in the morning. Short-term gains and quick switches. To win at puts and

184

takes a man must have ears which hear rumors and a mouth which starts them; he must mingle with other traders and invent angles, keep telephone numbers in his head and spin them quickly.

A puts-and-takes man gobbles a roast beef sandwich at a counter; he does not lunch in quiet dining rooms in which the occasional clink of silver spoon against Limoges plate is cushioned by monogrammed linens. He must be daring; he must accept the market for what it is; he must not be one of those men who say prices are too high or prices are too low and who grieve at money lost; he does not need to cover sheets of paper with notations, as Mr. Archibald did, to remind himself of what he had done. Sometimes when the door was left open, Nadja Pringle could hear him pulling the handle on the hand-cranked calculator installed incongruously on his mahogany presidential desk. On the grimmest days he would be at it for hours at a time, punching numbers, cranking the machine as the tape sliding out of the glass enclosing the stock ticker rhythmically printed the hieroglyphics of his financial disaster.

McGurn and Andy had taught Allan the normal-man theory, which he was buying. A normal man has to do it at reasonably frequent intervals or it—a different it—will back up in a normal man's system doing what a backed-up septic system will do to a normal house. Ergo, a normal man, his necessities unattended to by wife, girlfriend, or fiancée, was within his rights to save himself from this form of toxicosis by seeking help elsewhere.

The normal-man theory lessened Allan's need for self-recrimination and buffered what he did with Mona from what he felt for Irena. During the separation they wrote freely and often. Irena sent Allan copies of her field notes from her Polish village. They described how, once people had gotten used to her, her position had changed in the eyes of the villagers. When she had first come, they thought of her as a special visitor, a person of rank, but after a time they came to see that she was a young woman from a peasant background, like themselves, not truly American—but not truly Polish because she did not behave as a young woman of her class should. She was a farm girl with ideas above herself, but Irena persisted, boarding in the schoolmaster's home, using a patient tact she had seldom exercised in her homeland.

Irena tried to tell Allan how much she loved him but the words formed by her fountain pen were stilted, conveying nothing of the message of her heart. She did better when writing about her feelings concerning her country.

> I did not know how much of an American I am until I came here. I had been brought up thinking I am a Polish-American, one of Uncle Fenwick's hyphenates with one foot on each side of the ocean. Here I've learned that what I am is an American of Polish background. Poles here aren't like Poles in Chicago.

When she wrote of herself like this, Irena wondered if she could *say* the same things to Allan; she never had, not to him, not to anyone else.

"I'm back from Berlin again," she told him in one of her letters.

> I ought to take my holidays in Warsaw, but most of the people I know are in Berlin. Mr. Park's introductions. I met one man at a party who kept asking me where in Chicago is "the spot." I thought he was crazy, but nobody else thought he was crazy so then I thought *I* was going crazy and then I got it. The spot, as in being put on the spot. They know all the gangster argot in Berlin like that one, but they never get it exactly right.

In another letter, Irena wrote:

> Dearest, if you were here. Sometimes it seems I am too far away. I need an American man. I need you. These people click their heels too much. They kiss the women's fingertips, brush them with their lips actually. I can't get used to their ways. They know less about us than we do about them. A woman asked me if I visited Hollywood often, and when I told her that the distance between Chicago and Hollywood was greater than between Berlin and Rome, she would not believe it.
>
> I went for a walk with a lawyer on the Unter den Linden. Romantic? It was very harmless I can assure you, but I should not. I like it when you are a little bit jealous, Allan. Were you when you read that? He gave me a book by an Austrian novelist, Franz Kafka. It is a nightmare book. I think it has the theme of how Europeans are frightened by the way they are ruled by governments and their civil service. He said this man's work is being translated into English and will be printed in America, but I do not think it will make sense to Americans. Still, the book comes back to me when I am thinking of other things. You are the American I miss. It will be good soon. For us, I mean. I love you.

186

Irena's letters were received with tenderness sometimes, interest always, and occasionally with a powerful sexual longing. Allan discovered he could think about having sex with Irena without feeling guilty if he imagined they were already married. He imagined the first hour of their being alone in the honeymoon suite. He would place Irena in front of a flowery decor in her wedding dress as he explained to her that now she was not a sociologist, now she was not a professional person, now she was a wife, and in that capacity she was required to undress as he watched her. As often as Allan played this movie in his mind, changing details, sometimes masturbating, sometimes not, he did not once step outside the theater to ask what this plot might say about him. He was already accounted for by the normal-man theory. Wasn't it Irena who had gone away, Irena who left him overwrought, running from him always, running, sideways and uncatchable, through the city like one of Uncle Fenwick's misbehaving Irish setters loping across a field eluding the gamekeeper?

When his mind was not out bird-dogging, the retrievers of the mind flushing the chicks of his imagination, he was able to enjoy the greater respect he was gaining at school. With what Mona told him about what was going on, whom to sidle up to, where he should hang out now that the Metropole was gone and Andy had decamped from his observation post in the coffee shop, Allan had been able to fit together a reconstruction of the conversation between Cermak and Nitti and of the oncoming struggle. When he'd spun his story for the seminar the men around the table were astonished, enthralled.

"Afterward," he wrote to Irena,

> even Wirth came over and admitted it was an "outstanding job." Maybe I am going to be able to write the thesis after all, and I'm doing it on my own. Two or three people have asked me if I might be doing the fieldwork seminar next semester . . . if you weren't back, of course. There seems to be curiosity about cultivating confidential fieldwork informants. I guess they think I've had some unusual experience in that regard. Working with this kind of informant takes special skills.

Anyone who knew Mona would have agreed.

CAPONE OFFERS TO FIND BABY LINDY

Al Capone, the overlord of gangsterdom, said today from

his cell in the Atlanta Federal Penitentiary, where he is serving a 20-year term for income tax evasion, that he would find the kidnapped Lindbergh baby within two weeks if the authorities would parole him for that length of time. The nation's top gangster said his brother Ralph "Bottles" Capone would stay hostage of his return or he would offer his own son, provided Mrs. Al Capone agreed. New Jersey State Police have not yet decided what to do about the offer.

Bettina pointed the New Jersey state policemen toward Joe's cubicle. She was scared; something might let Joe know who had turned him in. As soon as she and the D'Amico boy had done it, had finked on him, their contempt for Joe had turned to nervousness. On the wooden stoop outside the diner's back door the boy stamped his boots on the encrusted ice. He did not want to enter until the men had taken Joe away. He stamped and figured out how he could lay claim to the reward.

The troopers had Sam Browne belts, gray-blue uniforms with flat-rimmed drill instructor hats; their buttons were silver; when they stood their leather creaked. They were big men, twice as tall as Joe. One of them undid the metal catch on his holster flap. When he got the gun out he pointed it at Joe. The other trooper grabbed Joe under the arms and lifted him off the floor. He dangled at an angle, the food blobs running off the rubberized apron, and in that manner, the one holding the revolver, the other holding the runt man who swung, shouting, this way and that off the ground, the three left the diner.

They got him in the back seat of their police car, one man on each side of him, the revolver waving, trying to hold him, putting handcuffs on as the driver ground the gears and got the machine moving forward. "Serfs!" Joe shouted. "Tools!" Fools for the bosses who wouldn't pay them. "They don't pay you. You'll see. Goddamn capitalism. Turn on the lights! Make it blue."

They lit the blue police lights on the front fenders, turned on the siren for Joe. "Give ya ride like we give the Governor," they told him.

"I kill the Governor," Joe said.

In an instant he leaned over trying to bite one trooper, thrashing his legs trying to kick the other. He got a crack across the mouth for that. At the police barracks Joe confessed to taking the Lindbergh baby. "Next time I get J. P. Morgan's baby." That made them wary. They had him handcuffed in a chair. Joe tried arching his back and stretching himself to kick at them. They slapped his face a couple of times and, taking him by the short hair growing out of his skull, they bent Joe's neck and head back against the chair. His eyeballs vanished save for two brown half-moons which shone out from under his lids. "I get Rockefeller's baby too. Watch. You see," he whispered. "I'm gonna get all the big shots' babies."

They bent Joe more, bent him till the back of his head was touching his backbone. Looking down at him the cops saw white throat and bulging Adam's apple.

"Fuckin' wop!"

The slush wet Joe's pants; it froze his fingers as he sat on the sidewalk where he landed after he was thrown out the door of the police barracks. His neck hurt; the blue globes flanking the building's entrance had been left on. Even in the daylight Joe could see a faded, animated incandescence coming from behind the azure glass.

The D'Amico kid was in the dishwashing cubicle when Joe returned to the diner. It had been a long cold walk. "I gotta have somebody reliable," Bettina's father said. "You wasn't around for lunchtime. I gotta have somebody I can count on." Joe looked at the other man. "Look, Joe, I don't want trouble. Not with you and not with cops. I'll get your money."

He put money in Joe's hand and said, "Don't forget your coat."

Joe said, "I shoot the King of Italy. Vittorio Emanuele. I get the Lindbergh baby. Rockefeller too. As' the cops. I get the baby."

From behind her father's shoulder Joe heard Bettina say, "You couldn't get fleas, Joe."

Mr. Archibald was reading the *Evening Post.*

FOOTPRINTS FOUND AT KIDNAP SITE
Lindy Looking for Clues

Col. Charles A. Lindbergh has joined New Jersey state troopers in attempting to locate his baby son. Col. Lindbergh was seen by reporters tramping the countryside looking for clues while friends of the world-famous aviator were doing aerial photography of the grounds of the Lindbergh estate in hopes of picking up the trail of the criminals.

"Mayor Cermak's on the phone, sir," Nadja Pringle told him. She was standing in the doorway, for Mr. Archibald's secretary preferred announcing telephone calls from very important people in person rather than on the intercom. Several years ago Vice-President Curtis had called. She had not spoken to him herself but it was a thrill, announcing it.

"No."

"Sir? No?"

"No! Take the message."

He called Sam Insull as soon as Nadja Pringle had left the room. Dialed the phone number himself, although he had to shout at her to find out what it was.

"It can't be. He hasn't found the trail of those deposits yet. . . . I know what Cermak knows because I make it my business to know. If he did find out about those accounts, you wouldn't be getting a phone call from him, mark me. Call him back. . . . You're talking too fast. . . . Don't blame me, it was you; you wanted to make some money. . . . Get hold of yourself. Call him back and find out what he wants, but I tell you when Thompson walked out the door for the last time the city's books were indecipherable. They're having a devil of a time reconstructing them, my friend. Take 'em months."

The lord of the power lines, the platinum parrot with the cockney accent, hung up and looked at the faces of his money advisers. Sam Insull's way was not to tell anyone all of his business. The men in the room had no idea about Elting Archibald, any more than Archibald knew that some of his fellow bank presidents had done the same thing. If the utility trust was going to go down, something Insull did not believe, it was going to take much and many with it. The edges of the Insull empire were raddled into the fabric of Chicagoland. He had wanted his community to share and take pride in what he had done. Now that involvement would protect him; his fall would be everybody's fall. Nevertheless, three or four of Chicago's most important banking figures were about to be caught with corruptly obtained, unethical, City of Chicago non-interest-bearing accounts, which they had broken into and embezzled to buy Insull stock that had lost two thirds of its value. Dear Lord! And with Cermak turning over the foundation stones under City Hall to find the money to pay the teachers and other city employees. Dear Lord!

But I have not profited, Insull told the Methodist divinity he had inherited from his missionary parents, who had given over their lives to preaching Jesus and sobriety to the factory workers of London and Manchester. I have not profited, and that was the topic his advisers were nagging him about. For weeks they had been telling him that

190

Morgan and his Eastern allies could not be stopped from driving Insull Utilities stock through the floor and into the basement; when it was low enough, they would have Insull utility loans called in and, with the stock so cheap, there would be no way to pay them. Reverse bingo—bankruptcy.

The advisers had given up hope of saving the utility trust. The companies were going down to be sold for a nickel on the dollar to whoever would have a nickel when the auction was held. Morgan and Eaton would have bags of nickels at the ready. The advisers were concentrating on saving Insull, and they had come up with a plan. Since they couldn't stop Morgan from driving down the price of the stock, they wanted Insull to save his fortune by shorting his own stock. Puts and takes, ride the price of the stock to the basement, making money on it the way Morgan was. The company would go down, but Insull could preserve his own fortune and, who knows, he might be able to buy back the utility trust after it had gone on the rocks. At least he would have a small bag of nickels. Insull rescued, Morgan foiled!

"Puts, sir. We have to buy puts, Mr. Insull," Harold Stuart, the tycoon's stocks and bonds man, insisted.

"I won't do it," Insull told them again. "Forty years ago this month I came to Chicago—March 1892—the city had just reached a million in population, did you know that? I came, I beat the competition. There were five light companies then. I came here and I became Sam Insull, which may not mean much to you boys, but to me it means my name is a Chicago name. I am the giver of light, and Chicago has almost four million people. Chicago and me, we built together. You fellas are too young to remember those days when the electric company gave its customers five hours of juice on weekdays, three hours on weekends. I made electricity reliable, a friend in the night, a workhorse in the day, always there, always ready. Hephaestus! Me, I did that. Sam Insull, they'll never forget me. When they say the names of our city, they say McCormick, Swift, Marshall Field, and they say Sam Insull. I never sold myself short; I don't sell my city short; I won't sell my company short. I don't sell short. I'm long on Sam Insull, long on Chicago. I'm a bull-market man. We'll hang on."

"Let me buy puts for you for a few months, Mr. Insull, for three months, sir, and you'll beat Morgan." Harold Stuart was begging the boss. He loved him.

"I lit up the night."

They went at him again. They told him he did not own enough to hang on with. There was no money, no credit, nothing left to borrow on, or steal, for that matter. Morgan had won.

"He hasn't won until he knows he's won and he doesn't know that. He thinks he's still got a fight on his hands, so we still have a chance. Sam Insull doesn't sell short. . . . I built the opera house," he added. The men in the room looked down past the points of their shined shoes to the carpet, a special order from Gobelin. These days they watched the old man for signs the pressure was getting to him. King Lear as tycoon. What an imagination he had. Like the opera house, forty stories of art deco, an embodiment of Chicagoland. Viewed from across the river, the west face of the building looked not unlike a severe steel and stone chair. Some people called the place Insull's Throne. "By 1950—you boys are young enough to see it—this city will be as big as New York. They've stopped; our future's still ahead of us."

Some of his boys looked at him with noncommittal straight faces; some of his boys looked away. "I know how many families in Chicago own Insull stock. Do you?" the old bird asked them, moving his head to face first one and then another. "More than thirty-five thousand families have invested in shares in these companies. I keep track of these things. I know that more Chicago families put their money in my stock than in the telephone company. Their retirement money, their children's college money. You know how we marketed our stock. 'Better than the bank and safer,' that was our motto. Cursed Tophet, we sold that stock in chemist shops, in currency exchanges, wherever you could pay your electricity bill. If those people found out I sold short, profited from the destruction of their savings . . . Oh, dear Lord!" Insull moved his head in a peculiar way, like a bird jerking about to find a grain or a grub to peck. His neck muscles were twitching, thinking of the working people he, he himself, had seen in the currency exchanges buying his stock, coming out of the stores, recognizing him, thanking him, telling him they were with him.

"No selling short. No puts, Harold. Find another way," the old man said, his voice dying off, his head cocked to one side as though he had been distracted by the passing flight of an idea. "Remember," he picked up, as though connecting his words with the idea that had flown by, "to win we need but stay alive. Hang on. Invent. Buy time. There's a point, a dollar figure past which not even Morgan can stay in the game."

Elting Archibald called back. He said that Cermak wanted him to put together a group of Chicago bankers who could make an emergency loan to the city, secured by what was called tax anticipation warrants, notes promising the money owed the city by its taxpayers would be used to repay the emergency loans. In normal times it was a routine transaction, but these were abnormal times, with unpaid teachers and firemen going door to door begging the persons who answered their knocks to pay their taxes with money they did not have. Given these shaky foundations of municipal finance, the banker said he did not see how he could be party to making such loans. He had his responsibilities to his stockholders and his depositors to keep in mind.

"My religion forbids uttering oaths and blasphemies," Insull said into the telephone. The reedy quality that tinged Elting's voice irritated Insull, particularly since the other man's words carried with them the implication that the utilities magnate was the cause of the banker's troubles. "Head up the committee, man," Insull told him.

"I can't, considering . . ."

"Considering what, man? What?"

"Considering what you got me into. . . . You don't want me to say it, do you?"

"Don't want you to say it? I'll say it, here and now on the telephone. You don't want to lend the city back the money you've embezzled from it. Too risky. I wonder why." Insull could not stand bankers. None of them. Not Morgan, not this whiner. Over the telephone line to his ear came a sound of strangulation, an *"ahrkd!"*

"Hmmmm!" replied Insull with a subverbal sound of his own. "Charge Cermak interest on his own money. Do that, Archibald. That's what you bankers do, isn't it?"

A few miles north of La Salle Street, the Cardinal was still at his desk. Spread out on its leather top was a catalogue with color pictures of fire engines. "They want that one?" Mundelein asked Monsignor Cavanaugh. The Prince of the Church dabbed at the picture of a noble engine with flashing red paint and brass accoutrements. The ruby in the episcopal ring glinted under the desk light. "That's the most expensive one in the booklet."

"The Mayor says the most expensive one is the most suitable to the town's new dignity, Your Eminence," the Monsignor explained. The Cardinal, suspecting a nuance of derision, looked up at the priest who stood in front of the desk staring down at the brochure. The Mayor in this case was not the Mayor of Chicago but the Mayor of

Area, Illinois, the town close by where the Cardinal had decided to build the archdiocesan seminary and his own country house, a replica of George Washington's Mount Vernon. The Cardinal believed that he and the Father of His Country's sharing the same Christian name had a touch of the providential about it.

From the start the archdiocesan consultors, the Church of Chicago's council of elders, were of the opinion that the name of Area took away from the dignity and meaning of this project, the most costly one ever undertaken by the diocese. It had been gotten across to Area's Mayor and town council that the new residents would not take it amiss if the community saw fit to change its name. Marysville, Madonna, and other names with Catholic associations were proposed to the elders of the solidly Protestant hamlet. These presbyters let it be known they were not happy at seeing so much property taken off the tax rolls, but they would consider a change of name if the archdiocese, in lieu of taxes, made a contribution of a fire engine. The new name would have to be something less Popish than Marysville. One of the consulters, Monsignor Polejiewc, thought Mundelein would make a good compromise name and it was done. The deal was struck several years before, *"melioribus annis"* (in better times).

The Cardinal sighed. But now that the name had been changed, a fire engine was incontestably owing the town. "The most expensive one, Monsignor?"

"The Mayor said that, with its new name, Your Eminence, they look forward to the village having a more important place in Illinois. They think they're going to grow an' all, and they believe they ought to have the biggest and best in modern rescue equipment. They don't call them fire engines any more, Your Eminence."

His Eminence took another glance at his subordinate to assure himself he was not being laughed at. The man had such a poker face. When Cavanaugh doesn't want you to know what he's thinking, you can't know. "Well, Monsignor, *Dominus dedit, Dominus abstulit* . . . God gives and God takes back," the Cardinal said, quoting from the Book of Job. "Blessed be his name. Give them their fire truck."

The last order of business did not appear on the Cardinal's appointment diary. Fast Father Frank had called to tell Cavanaugh, "I gotta see the boss. I gotta this afternoon. I gotta."

"Yeah, well, the boss has a bone to pick with you, Father," Cavanaugh replied. "Come in after the close of business. The back way."

After the little priest had genuflected and been waved to a seat, the Cardinal tossed a glossy photograph at Fast Father Frank, whose acne craters could be seen in the dim light of the office. *"Tolle, lege!"* Mundelein said, the approximate meaning of which might have been intended to be "Read it and weep." "Taken at Holy Guardian Angel Cemetery, Father: consecrated ground," the Cardinal rumbled, in a tone that those who worked with him knew to be one of phony anger. For the week past, the photo had been handed around a hooting, entertained Chancery Office. People came back for second and third looks at the picture of the Rooney family plot, squarely within which was a row of three identical statues of Kerry blue terriers, names chiseled in marble, Princess, Princess II, Princess III.

The priest could see the picture plainly enough, but he fumbled for his glasses and made a small delay for himself by putting them on. "Consecrated ground, is it, Yer Eminence?" Fast Father Frank asked a question whenever he was cornered. "I was given to understand the line ran like, well, about here." He leaned forward, drawing an imaginary line between the sacred and the profane on the photograph. The Cardinal looked at the silly picture and, clasping his hands under his chin, pressed down on the ruby ring to keep from laughing.

"I should not have to catechize a priest who has been ordained more than thirty years, but I will. Animals do not have immortal souls, Father Rooney. While they are capable of giving and feeling a high degree of animal affection, they are, nevertheless, among God's lesser creatures for they lack the gift of free will and the capacity to be in a state of grace and therefore, Father, they may not licitly be buried in consecrated ground."

"Yes, Yer Eminence."

"I want that wolf pack removed from Holy Guardian Angel Cemetery."

"Yes, Yer Eminence."

"Is there a Princess Four?"

"Yes, Yer Eminence."

"When Princess Four comes to the end of what I trust will be a long and happy life, she is to be disposed of in a manner fitting to her nature. What that might be, I leave to your newly enlightened judgment," the Cardinal said. "Now, what brings you here this evening, Father Rooney?"

"Sam Insull had me to his office," Fast Father Frank answered.

The priest had gotten no offer of a drink in that office, but the Methodist tycoon did not throw this pockmarked clergyman. As a lad who had started out making extra pennies as a "Shabbas goy," lighting the Saturday stoves for the Orthodox Jews on the Near West Side, Frank Rooney was accustomed to being in new places for the first time. As for Insull, Sam knew "the gangster priest" by reputation, the Catholic Church's political go-between and all-around fixer, the man you went through to get to the Cardinal.

Their conversation began, as the priest put it to his superior, with Insull "blowing off about how much he had done to help your people." He had always hired Catholics in preference to Jews, he said, omitting to explain that Jews were too smart and too independent for his tastes. He then laid heavy emphasis on how he had let Roman Catholics in on his stock, and how that stock was in danger of becoming worthless. This his guest knew, but then Insull got to the part he did not know, the part having to do with the bankers—no names were mentioned, but none needed to be—having to do with the city's non-interest-bearing accounts and the use thereof to prop up the price of Insull's stock, the destruction of records, and the certainty that Cermak's auditors would reassemble the paper trail and pursue it.

"And?" the Cardinal wanted to know.

"He thinks he can squeak by, save himself an' everybody else, I guess, if he don't get leaned on, if Cermak don't find out about the bank accounts until the stock goes up and they can put the money back. He tol' me, Yer Eminence, even if Cermak finds out, he's gotta leave it alone. He can't do nothing. If he withdraws the deposits the bankers'll have to throw their stock on the market to try to get whatever cash they can, but it'll push the price down to a few cents a share. It'll be over, all of it, for everybody, Yer Eminence."

"And?"

"Well, he said something about would the archdiocese, there being so many Catholics with Insull stock, want to support the price. I didn't care who he was, Yer Eminence, I wasn't gonna let 'im think that about us. I looked right at 'im and I told 'im George Mundelein's mother didn't bring up no dumb babies. I let 'im have it so he'd know the archdiocese wasn't interested. Never had no Insull stock, never will."

"And, Father Rooney, what clse?"

"What he was really hinting around about, Yer Eminence, is he wants us to talk to Cermak, tell 'im not to go after the money in those accounts. But I say, Yer Eminence, if I can offer an opinion, why tell Cermak if he don't know?"

196

"Can you find out as soon as he does, Father?" the Cardinal asked.

"I think so, Yer Eminence."

"Well then, do what needs doing, Father, but be careful."

When the two were alone, Mundelein asked Monsignor Cavanaugh, "Can we go home to dinner now?"

"Sixtieth anniversary of Sister Catherine of Sienna's taking her vows. She's the oldest nun in the diocese, Your Eminence. You told Mother Superior you would lead the community in a rosary."

"Could I send her a card?"

The Lindbergh kidnapping was off the front page, but a banker's daughter in Joplin, Missouri, had been stolen and the wife of a wholesale grocer in Philadelphia had been made off with, though this one turned out to be an elaborate matrimonial hoax. Kidnapping had become the fad.

On the following page was a small item headlined

POLICE RAID

Colosimo's Café, around the corner from the Metropole, had been raided by the Chicago police. Big Jim's place, Big Jim, the man who had brought Scarface Al out from Brooklyn. Big Jim himself had been shot to death years ago; his restaurant, though, had continued to be an important watering hole for the men in his protégé's organization. It was the mother house, the headquarters for fun and memories. Cermak was moving in.

Chapter 9

Rain clouds hung over the lake, taking the last of the bad weather eastward. In the western sky, behind Irena's back, the sun was mopping up the wetness on Archer Avenue's cobblestones, shining on the factories, the gas works, the railroads—makers of soot and smells. Yet the air was sweet, cool and dry for a July afternoon in Chicago.

Archer Avenue was machine shops and warehouses; it was the Lablau Bathroom Fixture Company with a twenty-five-foot flush toilet on the roof. The high-rise crapper had kept up the morale of the neighborhood for years. Even Irena, who did not tell scatological jokes, got a small lift when she glanced up at the Lablau Company's advertisement. It reminded her of Chicago's more famous double-entendre sign, the Hires Root Beer billboard on the Outer Drive, which blinked electrically and asked the city every ten seconds, HAVE YOU HAD IT LATELY?

A motorcycle policeman had stopped traffic and pedestrians from crossing the intersection where Pershing Road and Western Avenue met Archer. From the southwest, police sirens blew their way toward the ears of puzzled pedestrians. "Who is it?" people around Irena were asking as a short motorcade moved toward them. "It's Governor Roosevelt," a know-it-all man said. "He's flown in from Albany, New York, to make his acceptance speech tonight."

"Is he Teddy's son now?" a man with a brogue asked the know-it-all. "We wouldn'a been in a fix like this if he was still around, rest on it."

"Which one is he? Which one?" several asked as the lead touring car came abreast of them and the three men in the back waved.

"The one on the left. See, he looks like Teddy," the know-it-all said, pointing to Raymond Moley, one of the Governor's speechwriters. Chicago and Mayor Cermak had backed Al Smith, the Roman Catholic, for the nomination. Of the Hyde Park squire they knew little save the man was a wet pledged to bring back prosperity by Repeal.

The motorcycle policeman kicked the starter of his machine and did an ice skater's cursive turn, going loudly off down Archer to block another intersection. The trucks awoke with a start and the pedestrians began walking again. She would not wait for the street car, Irena decided. She would save the nickel fare and walk the mile and a half through the freshness of the afternoon to Marshfield Avenue and home.

When Irena returned from Europe she had moved back in with the family. She could contribute more money that way and also the trip had touched her, reigniting her interest in the neighborhood and its people as she finished writing her thesis.

Living at home was also convenient to her job at the branch library, which was supposed to give her an income until October, when she began teaching at the university. It was a library set among factories, a library where there were no books to speak of. Sometimes people came to read the newspapers, but the city could not afford to buy the papers either. The janitor said that in the winter people would come to keep warm until he drained the pipes when the coal gave out.

No books, no one to borrow them, and no income. In the past, when people worked, they were paid for it; now they worked and they weren't. The people from the public school system were marching around with armbands reading UNPAID TEACHERS. Irena thought she should have one that said UNPAID LIBRARIAN. Meanwhile, Irena had to put up with Morton telling her to count her blessings, she had a job.

She could thank the regular Democratic organization for that, particularly her friend Mildred Wajciechowski at the Fourteenth Ward headquarters. They were proud of her at the headquarters, a Polish girl from the neighborhood being made a professor, a doctor. Besides the family, Mildred and several others from the neighborhood had gone to Rockefeller Chapel for the spring convocation to see Robert Maynard Hutchins, the university's president, place the rolled parchment in Irena's hand. After the organ music had played "Gaudeamus Igitur" and the academic procession had moved in robe and fur and velvet hood to the choir, Aunt Helen had whispered the ceremony

200

was as impressive as the Cardinal saying High Mass at Holy Name Cathedral.

Sister Mary William, the nun who had made this possible, had wanted to come, but the pastor of St. Thomas of Canterbury, where she was still stationed, said it would not be proper for a nun to sit in the pews of a church built by heretics and heathens. Monsignor Szymczak had told the women of the family they "deserved the highest commendations. Irena has done a wonderful job, but they read books on the Index there, books not even a monsignor is permitted to read with the permission of the Chancery Office. She should remember her immortal soul." Irena's mother and Granny agreed between them that Irena, her blondness against the black robe and mortar board, looked prettier than she had for her First Communion.

Allan had been there too, reconciled to Irena's getting her doctorate first by telling himself that she was almost two and a half years older. It was on the lawn where the chapel fronts on the Midway Plaisance, the green canal of grass where Allan and Irena had walked together two years before, that he met her family. She had been afraid her family would make over Allan in some embarrassing lower-class way or would bore him with their stories. They hadn't done either. Afterward Irena realized she ought to have known that Aunt Helen, for one, was too prickly, too proud, too aware of appearances to let that happen. Allan did well also. His two years of playing Marco Polo in Gangsterland had taught him to be relaxed among alien peoples.

Granny made the moment though. The old lady, wearing a babushka, looked up at Allan and spoke to him in Polish. As she did, Irena's mother and Helen nodded and laughed. Helen slapped her thigh, she thought what Granny was saying was so good. Steffy and Robert, whose Polish was rudimentary, were confused.

Allan, naturally, did not understand a word; he listened with an attentive and polite expression as though he did and when Granny was finished looked to Irena for a translation. She, however, was so astonished that no words came, until finally she translated, "Granny says it's a pleasure to meet you."

"That's all?" Allan responded, confused that it should take so long in Polish to say so little in English. The old lady, who knew a little English, ordered Irena in Polish to tell him everything she had said.

Laughing and blushing, Irena said, "Oh, I can't," but Granny poked her again, Allan looked as if he wanted to hear more, and Helen and Irena's mother began saying, "You should tell. . . ."

"Oh, God," Irena shrieked in embarrassment. She grabbed Allan and pushed herself against him, hugging him, hiding her face in his shoulder. "Granny said . . . oh, God! And Granny said . . . I can't say it . . . Granny said she hopes you are not like most men. . . ." Steffy was sighing and Robert was giggling. "And that you will not beat me . . . well, that you will be gentle to me and love me and be loyal to me. You will, won't you, Allan?"

Allan blushed and hugged Irena back very tightly and murmured through a fluffiness of tender feeling that he would. Irena's mother and Aunt Helen stopped their happy hooting and switched over to love-dove sounds; Granny had a kind look in her eye, but her mouth trembled, for the old lady knew that rich princes marry peasant girls only in fairy tales.

Since Irena had come back from Europe, she and Allan had had these cameo moments of loving closeness as well as hours of his sexual demands. But relations between them had never been less even, less reliable, less comprehensible for her. Allan did not talk about the letter of proposal, and Irena, her bluntness turned to paste by the fears of love, could not bring it up. Nor was Allan giving off any clues about what he wanted her to do about a job. Irena's was the first doctorate awarded in her field by the university in several years— "That's why all of ours get jobs," Mr. Park said—but for the academic year 1932–33 nobody was hiring. Nobody. The university had given Irena a one-year instructorship until they could arrange a job elsewhere, probably at Wellesley. They did take care of their own, but Irena would have to decide if she was going to Massachusetts or getting married or—she didn't know what.

Allan said nothing, though they went out a lot with his family, their friends from school, and his gangsters. There had been more than a few nights in the speakeasies this summer with the Gunner and Mona, with her shouting to everybody at the table, "Will you shut up please, will you?" Once McGurn hit her. Irena and Allan shared so much, yet she did not think they were building a life together; they were not planning, they were not talking about themselves. Physically she held him at arm's length, and emotionally Allan did the same.

"Roosevelt, you say?" Irena heard an old man question a younger one as she stopped for traffic. "I thought Roosevelt was dead, but I'll vote for 'im again," the old man announced.

"No, this is his son, Franklin, the Governor of New York State."

"I'll vote for him if he's half the man his dad was. I was a Bull Mooser. Twenty years ago, before your time."

"It's his son," the younger repeated.

"So Hoover's not running again, huh? Just as well, I suppose."

Irena scarcely knew more herself, sitting in the empty library listening to polished wood floors give off an occasional crack. She was forgetting what she knew, watching Morton send Robert to the store Sunday afternoons with a dime to buy a pack of Lucky Strikes, the kind with the green circle on the front of the package, so that he would have smokes when three o'clock came and the organ music seeped through the brown cloth of the radio receiver to signal the beginning of "The Golden Hour of the Little Flower . . . brought to you through the facilities of station WJR Detroit and the Radio League of the Little Flower. And now the radio priest himself, Father Charles Coughlin. His text this afternoon: Banksters, Banksterism, and True Financial Democracy." Everybody in the neighborhood listened; Irena was sure the man was becoming a force and once went so far as to mention Father Coughlin to Uncle Fenwick, who gave out a noise that meant Papist tommyrot. "The only thing that will save this country is a dictator."

On this evening some of the people who owned the new, smaller table radios had put them near their porches so they could listen to the last night of the 1932 Democratic Convention in comfort. One or two on the block sat in their cars, the doors open to let the night breeze touch their skins. Car radios were a rarity, and you had to burn gas to listen to them. Irena's family sat in the kitchen.

They heard that there had been a parade a little while before, led by an airplane tugging a white banner across the sky on which was lettered in orange the word PEACE. The announcer said that the plane was piloted by Miss Joan Thomas of Hull House. On the ground, the parade was led by Hull House's founder, Miss Jane Addams, who rode in an open-top LaSalle along with a very large American flag. The next morning the newspapers would report Miss Addams had told the press that "No nation can afford war. War today is a suicide pact in which both sides perish. The new patriotism is peace." Her words were so self-evidently true that no figure in either party disagreed.

While the announcer was saying that tonight's speech would be the first time a candidate had ever accepted his party's nomination at the convention, Irena told the family circle she had seen him on Archer Avenue coming from the airport. Imagine flying! They missed the beginning of Governor Roosevelt's speech because Steffy reached for one of Morton's Lucky Strikes and an argument broke out about whether she was old enough. They heard the part in which he promised a new deal, but it did not register on anyone. The whole affair coming in on the ether, as they liked to say in those days, reminded them of how little they had. Only Helen was actually pulling in cash and not much. The back yard and the front were planted with vegetables like every lot in Chicago, and some s.o.b.'s would steal the produce at night.

"They cut the carmen by nine cents an hour today," Morton said as the speech was ending and "Happy Days Are Here Again" was making its way through the whistle and static of the Giron family radio.

"Shits!"

"Helen! The children!" Irena's mother said.

"Well, they are. First they cut the rate and then they don't pay nobody anyhow." Helen was the family's acknowledged fighter.

"If *she*'d ask her boyfriend for a loan, leastways we wouldn't have to worry," Morton said, pointing at Irena.

"Please, let's not start on that."

"Well, jeez, he *is* a millionaire, Irena," Helen said. "It's not like he'd miss it. Look at your own family. Don't you owe your own family something? Or don't that count after you get a doctor's degree? Your own people. I guess that turns blood back into water, the graduation an' all."

"Please, let's not start that. You're *my* family, but you're *not* Allan's family."

"Well, we will be when ya get married, for God's sake," Helen answered.

"I'm not even engaged, exactly, and I don't think this is anybody's business but mine. If you're all going to start on Allan and his money again, I'm leaving. I'm fed up with it. I didn't move back here to be treated like this."

"Hoity-toity," Helen said. "The duchess does not desire to be disturbed by her family."

Irena went upstairs into the bedroom with the blanket still hung across to divide it, there to seethe in private. But Jerzy, Helen and Morton's kid, followed upstairs, ostensibly to fiddle-faddle in the part of the room he shared with Robert but really to make mean.

The other day he had stuck his naked posterior through the

blanket and mooned her. The bastard, no longer a little one, had his way of attending to detail like pulling his cheeks apart for full effect. The tacit family agreement stipulated that Irena could not holler or that would rile Helen, who would complain to Morton, who would take that as a sign he was free to harass Irena. So she had faced the wall and stood stock still until she thought she heard him leave. He hadn't gone, though, until she agreed to pay him a dime she could not afford. Then she could not make herself forget what he looked like. That was the worst of it.

This time he was dressed when he pushed the curtain aside to say, "My dad says you're stuck-up because you've never had it. He says you need it bad. He says one of these days some guy is going to give it to you real good because you're begging for it. He says he wants to watch when you get it."

Irena put her hands to her ears and pushed against her skull. She stood cemented in tension, attempting to generate an interior pressure strong enough to keep what he was saying out, but the words got into her. When he went away, whooping down the stairs, shouting, "Hey, Pop!" to report to Morton on her reaction, Irena sat down. Jerzy had frightened her. She was twenty-five years old and she had never had it. What would it do to her if she had it? Make her a better person? Was she going to be an old maid? But the man who gave it to her the first time, didn't it make a woman always want to obey him? That's why it should be with your husband. It's not so bad with your husband. She should have had it by now; having it is something you should start before you're too old so you can get used to it. There were one or two men in Europe who wanted to do it to her, but they were polite when she indicated no.

The men all said she should have had it already; the women all said nothing. The men at the university told her she should read Freud—the ones who were not telling her to read Marx—and she would understand. Irena had begun reading Freud and, though she was fascinated, she did not understand. Freud was writing about other people, not her. This was not the time of her life to have children. But it made her decide to write down her dreams.

She awoke, knowing she had dreamed about sex, but she could not piece it together. When she took out her notebook she wrote that on campus they look down on twenty-five-year-old virgins and Back of the Yards they laugh at an eighteen-year-old who still has her cherry. The thought jiggled something loose in Irena's concentration and she thought she remembered that in the dream she was wearing a white robe, like an angel or a hospital patient. She was barefoot, that she was sure of, standing in front of the Hires Root Beer sign. It would blink HAVE YOU HAD IT LATELY? and she would shout at it, "I've never had it, not once." Irena shook her head and giggled; nobody could dream that. As she pondered her dreaming the undreamable, she pictured the Lablau toilet with a Paul Bunyan–sized Jerzy on it. Disgusting. She tore up her notes and made an appointment to see Mr. Park. She could not go on like this.

"Not in my lifetime," Mr. Park said. "I've lived through the depression of the early nineties, and it wasn't this bad. The one in the seventies, from what I remember my parents and older people saying, wasn't like this. The government not paying its employees—well, look, Irena, here is a check, a loan until the city pays you or the university does or somebody does." She had not had to ask. Again, he had come forward to help.

After the thank-yous he wanted to talk about her future, her next research undertaking, something that would be, as Mr. Park phrased it, "Portable to Wellesley or who knows. I'm working on Ohio State. I want them to make you an offer. I don't want you to go to Wellesley."

"No?"

"It's a good school, but it's a women's school and once you're in that league you'll never get out of it. It's like teaching in a Roman Catholic college. They tab you. We can't let that happen to you. And if I may be so bold, I think you should be living over here around campus. And not in that nunnery across the Midway, Irena. You need to be seen, meet more people, mix. . . ." He thought for a moment. "Would you have any objections to renting a room in an older woman's apartment?"

He arranged for Irena to meet the Dean of Women, Salvation Winthrop. "My serious friends call me Sally and my light-minded friends call me Salvation. They love it." Salvation Winthrop took a puff on her cigarette, which was inserted in a carved ivory holder, and then she smiled. She had a big face with features chiseled too sharply to be beautiful. The Dean of Women gave a theatrical sigh before explaining. "This terrible name has been going on for generations in the family because one of our ancestors was burnt as a witch at Salem."

Irena was captivated. More than that, she was captured. Here was a friend.

"Her first name was Salvation, and the story goes that she uttered a curse—they always *uttered* curses, didn't they?—before they put the torch to the fagots. Unless one girl in every generation was named Salvation there would be no more male issue in the family and the name Winthrop would die out. Have you ever heard anything sillier? If they were about to make *me* into a Puritan shishkebab I wouldn't be talking about naming my unborn grandchildren, but I think the men in the family felt guilty about what they'd let happen to that poor woman. They made up the legend by way of expiation. Of course, it was the women who had to pay. Every generation must sacrifice one little girl to that terrible name to propitiate a Calvinist hex so there will be plenty of little boy Winthrops, not one of whom has amounted to anything for three hundred years. . . . I know we're going to be friends, Irena."

They were. They meshed, the dean in her late fifties and Irena beginning her life's explorations. Several times a week the two would have supper together, usually at a tearoom on 55th Street, and often Salvation would tell Irena about the knots and kinks she spent her days trying to undo. One night she told Irena she was helping an undergraduate woman get an abortion, a scandalous thing, which confirmed Irena in her belief that you could safely tell Salvation Winthrop anything.

"Sex."

"Sex?"

"I have some points I need to bring up, Sally."

"So it's Sally tonight. Not Salvation?"

"It's Sally tonight. . . . When he does it to you the first time, it hurts, but then later on you get to like it?"

Several suppers at the tearoom were needed to clear up the misinformation and crazy facts Irena had accumulated by listening to people of two cultures and at least as many religions. Salvation told her how she and her Howard, killed in France in 1918, had come to take up modern ways. In the end Irena agreed with her tutor that she should get a diaphragm, but when it was explained what that involved Irena shouted out, "Oh, Sally, I couldn't! The doctor would have to see me, wouldn't he? I don't know if I could let *Allan* see me. He'd know I wasn't married." But Salvation knew the right doctor, a man of advanced years and beneficence. Sally volunteered to go with Irena, who said absolutely not, she was a woman, and as a grown woman she would do fine, although the idea of a man seeing her that way took getting used to.

Irena went punctually to her appointment. During the examination she wore a smock and a nurse stayed in the room; the doctor was gentle and helpfully clear in his explanations. The only untoward thing was that as he began his measurement of Irena's cervix, the tense young woman in the stirrups blurted out, "Root beer!"

She left the doctor's office with a small leatherette pouch in her handbag. That night for the first time she dared, timidly and not very specifically, to think of Allan touching her. She could do this for the shortest time only; then a confusion of emotions stopped her. But in a few days' time the buds inside her broke open and she felt desire. Simply thinking about it made her breath short like Allan's. Irena was amazed.

Her amazement and her new self-knowledge coincided with Allan's taking her to the Drake Hotel for dinner and giving her the ring. About time, they would have said on Marshfield Avenue; the right time, Irena thought; and when they had finished exchanging the promises of love, Allan's bashful but blunt, not always finely spoken, but never more beautiful fiancée reached her arm across the heavy linen cloth, touched her hand to his, and told her handsome young man, "Now you can pet me."

Well after Joe had gone, Mr. D'Amico came to realize his revolver was gone also, vanished from the back of the closet where it had lain, wrapped in a rag along with several other items he did not want his children to see. He blamed Joe immediately, because it was easier to blame the one who was gone than the children who were still at home.

Joe had left the night of the state troopers, taking with him his toolbox, what clothes he had, and the revolver. He had the bottle of gentian violet, a copy of *La Voce d'Italia,* and a maundering fury. A dwarf man, slipping through streets of frozen slush, he stepped into the puddles and slid on the shiny gray patches of sidewalk until he was back in the region of the railroad yards. He saw men sleeping in the alleys; he saw them in doorways and wrapped in cardboard under the loading platforms of closed factories. Everywhere there was a slow swarm of homeless bodies, bundled gray figures standing in a circle around smoky garbage fires, arms flapping against torsos to keep warm.

The tool chest hit against the risers as Joe climbed the stairway in the three-story clapboard house with the sign: PRIVATE ROOM—FULL

208

24-HOUR OCCUPANCY—20¢. In the private room he took off his shoes, hung his socks on a steam pipe, and cursed: in Italian, in English, in a mixture. The private room contained a cot and turning around space; its walls of wooden planking rose to within feet of the ceiling; the gap between was covered with chicken-coop wire, through which the light from the bulb in the corridor shone.

The anger was strong with him, as was the closeness to the already seen, the already lived, to scenes on the Isonzo, to life lived and closed out on Joe; the blue conviction was strong with Joe also. Half naked he lay on the cot holding the bottle of gentian violet between his eyes and the light of the low-watt sun coming through the octagonal pattern of the chicken-coop wire. Make blue, make clear; with a craftsman's hand he daubed purplish blue from the bottle onto his chest, swabbed himself evenly, no streaking, no patches of white skin. Joe did the same to his stomach, his legs, and, taking off his shorts, to his genitals.

He held the bottle to his eyes again. A blue suffusion took hold of him as always, but the present moment did not drop away from Joe. He was going backward and he was holding on to himself.

A breeze, humid and hot, the last exhalation of summer, came off Lake Michigan, across Grant Park, and into a fifteenth-floor window of the Stevens Hotel. It came across Allan's naked body as he lay crosswise on the bed, reading a newspaper. Mona was floating in the bath, staring at the ceiling, smoking a cigarette, thinking. She had planned this meeting to be long, to be slow, and to be their last. She had had her prince, Mona told herself, she had had him many times, and it had been as sexy and romantic to be made love to by a gentle and handsome young man as she had daydreamed it might be and now she must stop it.

Too dangerous. Even with her precautions something could happen. They were pushing their luck, and Allan could not be made to appreciate the perils. He never would. He was bringing up her getting a divorce again. They had been in the room since midmorning. They would have at each other bruisingly for twenty or thirty minutes and then come floating apart, Mona to bathe, Allan to loaf on the bed, talking sometimes between rooms, sometimes being silent. Allan was reading the early editions of the afternoon papers, which under the headline were largely given over to the affair of Mr. and Mrs. William ("Zep") Moneypenny. Mrs. Moneypenny had identified the kidnappers as Roger ("the Dodger") Touhy and a known confederate of Touhy's, Basil ("the Owl") Banghart. The identification was confirmed by the other couple with the Moneypennys, a Mr. and Mrs. Peter Silverman. The Silvermans' ages and occupations were not given. The most entertaining story was in the *Daily News,* which was going with the revelation that Mrs. Moneypenny was not Mrs. Moneypenny but a stripper who bumped and ground under the name of Lorna Doone. This made little difference to the Cook County State's Attorney, to whom the word of the ecdysiast was bond; he issued warrants for the arrest of the Dodger and his Owl; it did make a difference to Mayor Cermak's Commissioner of Police, who said the kidnapping was fishy as hell. Dodger and Owl were not being "sought" by his policemen; they were out looking for the Silvermans instead. The narratives of what actually happened were fragmentary and contradictory in detail. The story under Thea Epps's byline told how William ("Zep") Moneypenny, reputed to be the busiest bookie and wire room operator in Chicago, had been kidnapped on his way back from the Wisconsin Dells, where he and his wife had spent the evening with friends at Salvatore's, a popular roadhouse. According to Thea Epps, the Moneypenny family was stopped by hoodlums in two cars at three o'clock in the morning. After being ordered out of their car, Mrs. Moneypenny and the Silvermans were left on the empty road as the kidnappers drove off with her husband. A business associate of Moneypenny's, Andrew Mousmoulis, told police he had received a telephone call from a man at seven this morning demanding a $50,000 ransom.

Allan let the paper fall on the bed as he called into the bathroom, "Did you know Andy's got his name in the paper on the kidnapping?"

"What kidnapping?"

"You know," he said, "*the* kidnapping." Mona, tiptoeing and wet from the tub, landed on the bed, kneeling, her legs straddling his face, the damp beard of her pubic hair trickling onto his chin.

"God, Mona! Get off!"

"Al-lan, you're so dumb. You think that was a kidnapping?"

"Mona, you're dripping! . . . You mean it wasn't?" Instead of answering, Mona was brushing slightly back and forth so the hairs grazed Allan's lips, making him spit and sputter. "Stop it, Mona. Tell me. What do you mean? Mona, please. You mean it was a put-up job?" Mona continued her rocking while she made flirty little noises. "Mona, I'm asking you a question. Mona!"

"Kiss first."

"Well, get off so I can."

"Kiss there."

"No! God, Mona, that's disgusting. Your privates?"

"Kissie . . . kissie . . . I just took a bath, Allan."

"No, God, that's . . . well, I'm not a muff diver."

"You are now. Kiss."

"Mona. It's perverted."

"Kiss—kissie—kiss." Allan gave her a peck on the labia. "Kiss again. Longer."

"No. Men don't have sex that way. I won't."

"Will you please shut up, Allan? You don't know anything about men. You're still in school."

"I'm not going to do that, Mona," he informed her, rolling his head to one side, looking up past her belly button and her breasts into her eyes as Mona, with an irritated smirk, looked back into his. Putting his hands on Mona's hips and buttocks, Allan readied his muscles to heave her off, but he didn't. He was smitten with the female torso, its form and kinetics. Allan was feeling in life what his eyes had seen in marble in the museums. Instead of throwing Mona off him, he moved his cheeks against her thighs, let his face rub against her hair. He kissed her.

"French kiss," Mona ordered, looking down at him, thinking Allan was handsome and silly, a real boy, a boy prince.

When they finished Allan did push Mona off him, slowly but off, and as he began to sort out what he had done, he ran into the bathroom to wash his mouth out. One of Mona's hairs was snagged between his teeth.

This panicky washing irked Mona. She could hear him in there, the door open, swishing and spritzing water around his mouth. He was insulting her body. "You didn't put your tongue any place you haven't put your dick a hundred times, Allan, and you never caught nothing," she shouted at him. Her words pinged a cell or two in Allan's brain. Mona had tasted good, he reflected, yet it was demeaning. That she could have gotten him to do such a thing. "I'd let 'em cut my balls off first," Andy had said to Allan once. "Make a broad suck your cock sometimes to show her who's boss, but not too much. I don't think

211

that's good for you neither." As with so much else concerning what he and Mona did with each other, Allan oscillated between shame and excitement. He dried his face and, coming out of the bathroom, studied Mona, decided he could not make her do it to him, that he could not show Mona he was the boss. He understood he would never boss her.

"What did you mean about the kidnapping?" Allan asked the houri shape spread face down on the bed, diddling with her cigarette. "What did you mean," he repeated, walking over to her so that he was standing over Mona looking down at the platinum curls and whirls. Another cigarette diddle before Mona told him, without looking up, "This is our last time, Allan. We can't do this no more."

"What did you mean?" Allan said for the second time, heedless of what she was saying.

"I mean it's over," Mona repeated, rearranging herself so that she was now looking upward, an arm propping her chin. "This has gotta be the last time," Mona said in a low tone, the crooked index finger of her free hand stroking Allan's penis. "We gotta be apart," Mona repeated, rearing up, kissing the penis's tip, giving it a fast swipe with her tongue; she rearranged herself another time, kneeling on the bed, and, somewhat as Allan had done with her before, she put his penis in her mouth and felt the smoothness of his buttocks, the planes of the small of his back, the masculine shape in the marble; taking his genitals in her hands she brushed her face against them. When Mona looked up at him, Allan saw she had tears in her eyes and heard her say to herself, "Prince, baby, prince. . . . Why?"

"What can go wrong? It's foolproof."

"Oh, yeah?" Mona answered. She rose up from her knees, and, as she did so, leaped on him, nails in his back, kissing him. Then she bit Allan on the shoulder, screamed, "We're pushing our goddamn luck. Can't you understand that? Can't you?" The next that Allan was aware of was the bathroom door slamming, sobs, and then sobs drowned out by running water.

So what should he do? Get dressed? Stand there? Pour himself a drink? The buzz was gone from his head. Should he sit down? Mona knew how to get to him. Lie down? Irena frustrated him, but the woman in the bathroom made him frantic. He did not think to go over to the door and knock on it. He lit a cigarette and sat on the bed where Mona had been kneeling. Mona was always saying things, but Allan had not seen her cry before. Tough, cocksure, angry, loud, un-

212

predictable, funny Mona, never-a-dull-moment Mona, but not tearful Mona. Would he ever figure out what she meant?

"Where are my stockings?" she asked. Mona was in what they called the foundation garments. She found her silk stockings and began the careful work of putting them on by rolling them up, inching them on, smoothing, inching some more, twisting to see if the seams in the rear were straight, and, lastly, hooking them to her garters.

"Your eyes are red," Allan said, hurrying to dress himself. He felt embarrassed when she had something on and he didn't.

"I can say I got hay fever, if I have to," Mona answered. They had fallen into a race to dress fastest. They crisscrossed the room, jerking and bumping into each other, getting items of clothes, buttoning, busy handed. Yet when they were both about to cross the finish line, they backed off, slowed down, made small adjustments. They knew that when they declared themselves dressed they would have to talk to each other again.

Mona had her hat on. Allan held his in his hand. Dressed and facing each other. "I don't get it, Mona. The kidnapping."

"Oh, Christ, you're a jerk, Allan. They oughta give you away Wednesday night at the movies. You're a prize. . . . I told ya. It's a put-up job. They're after Roger Touhy, and if you want to know anything more, figure it out for yourself. Figure something out on your own, Allan."

"I don't get it."

"Well, I guess you don't. You didn't know how to say hello when I met you, an' you don't know how to say goodbye." Mona leaned up and kissed Allan, briefly yet sweetly, on the cheek. Her eyes glistened, but Mona was gone.

The goodbye kiss arrested Allan's morality cycle of remorse, resolution, and failure. Allan was the saddest kind of Christian, strong in a superstitious, unthinking faith in sin, yet rational, skeptical, and agnostic as to the promise of redemption and the hope of forgiveness: the burdens of faith without its strengths. No God in the inner sanctum; when Allan turned to that holy place, he felt nothing but the consciousness of his wrongdoings, for he was the opposite of the religious optimists who filled the pulpits of his time or the complacent idiots who said they didn't go to church of a Sunday morning because they reverenced God on the golf course.

But when it reached him that no more Mona meant no more Mona, he felt the sadness of a love cut short and that surprised him.

As long as he had thought of Mona as the temptress of his lusty daydreams, he continued to understand himself in the familiar language of his despoiled Calvinism. But there was a part of Allan which insisted on being glad of Mona. In those moments of reflection when he reconciled himself to there being no one to forgive him, Allan had diagnosed himself as having a morally split personality. The good Allan loved the good Irena and the bad Allan could spend hours naked with this woman, drinking, having sex, and gossiping about gangsters, politicians, and other crooks. Joking and carrying on. God, Mona Jupiter could carry on. Irena, earnestly affectionate Irena, discussed social theory; Mona was social fact, and Allan now knew that besides needing her, he wanted her, and he would miss her.

The State of Maine, which in those days preceded the rest of the country by voting in September, had been carried by Governor Roosevelt. As Maine goes to hell so does the nation, Uncle Fenwick shouted. A Democrat in the White House! Won't people ever learn? Allan had been twelve when the last Democrat had left the White House; he had been more concerned about the Black Sox baseball scandal than in which party the famous politicians took up their place of abode. Even so, Allan had been raised on the home truth that the Democrats were an aberration; if not the party of Rum, Romanism, and Rebellion, then of immigrants, humbuggery, lynching, and populism. America was great because America was Republican. The party of Lincoln, the party of Roosevelt: Theodore, that is.

But the party of Hoover was struggling. So many municipal workers had been laid off that Chicago was in a visible state of disrepair and filth and, far away, men in the highest places embraced crackpot schemes like those the graduate students argued over in the lounge of the Social Science building. In the East, across the mountains that Midwesterners thought protected them from the insanities wafted over from Europe, the President appointed Col. Frank Knox to head a committee to bring money back into circulation. The Depression, which should have been over by now, was being prolonged by people hoarding their wealth.

In Chicago, the newspapers were happy to turn their attention from the economic crisis to the kidnapping. Reporters had crowded into the cigar store, where Andy was holding forth. From Mr. Capone's soup kitchen of two years before, his position and Allan's had been exchanged. Allan was at the fringe on tiptoes, looking over

214

heads and shoulders to see Andy, to whom the questions were directed and whose answers were making news. Thea Epps was taking notes as fast as Andy was talking, for it was through Andy that the kidnappers were sending their ransom messages. The reporters treated Andy's story with good-humored incredulity. Allan waited out the journalists and in due course went down the street for coffee with Andy, who paid and left a quarter tip.

Allan wanted to ask Andy how much they were paying him to read those ridiculous lines. "This kidnapping, is it true? Is it a set-up?" Allan asked. Andy could tell that this time Allan was impressed, that he understood that it was to Andy that Frank Nitti had turned for help. He could see that Allan needed what he knew and saw for the first time a rough parity in their relationship. Hands across class lines.

"What if I was to tell you I know where Zep is?"

"They couldn't have kidnapped him, could they, Andy? He's too fat."

"You want to know where Zep is? I know where. I gotta take care of the sonofabitch, as well as run the cigar store, and the wire room, and make the collections." Andy wanted Allan to know that Andy had become an important man. "So I'll see ya around, Allan."

"Hey, where is he?"

"He's right under your feet."

"Under my feet?"

"Yeah, I'll show 'im to ya. You can help me. Come back to the store 'bout eight, when I finish with the books. I'll be makin' a food run, but if you ever say anything, it's my ass, boy."

That evening Allan picked Andy up in his car. The two drove over to Hannah's, a back-alley restaurant much favored by the gourmets in Mr. Capone's business group. Andy gave Hannah several empty pots in return for the same number of full ones. "He says—" Andy began to tell Hannah, who cut him short.

"I don't want to know, I'm not interested, I couldn't care less about the private lives of my customers, so whatever your names—and I don't want to know—you gimme the empties every day. I'll give you the full ones." This done, Andy and Allan opened the kitchen door, to hear Hannah shout, "Hey! You boys take care of yourselves. You're nice-lookin' boys."

"How much are they paying you?" Allan wanted to know as they drove back across the Chicago River on the Harrison Street bridge.

"They're not paying me."

"You're not getting anything?" Allan couldn't believe it.

"Zep said he'd take care of me. . . . Zep didn't want to do it much, but they got a squeeze on everybody. They're tight for cash. So who isn't? An' they wanted a bigger percentage of Zep's handle, but Zep—the sonofabitch has got the first dollar he ever saw—he asked them to let him work it off. So it's this an' I'm luggin' the buckets."

"Moola-moo-la, moola-moo-la," Allan sang to the melody of the Yale college song. "Where are we going?" he asked when Andy directed him to drive back to the cigar store.

"I thought you knew all the answers, Al. . . . Someday soon I'm gonna *give* shit instead of taking it. Be nice to me, pal. You're friends with a guy on his way up."

The two young men carried the food out of the rumble seat of Allan's roadster and made for the back of the building in which the cigar store was located. There was a watchman inside to whom Andy gave a quarter, saying as he did, "Fifteen minutes."

They descended the freight elevators to the sub-basement, where Andy led Allan past barrels of trash to another elevator. Putting the tip of an index finger to his mouth for silence, from here on Andy spoke with gestures in the illumination of his flashlight. This last elevator cranked and ratcheted downward into a tunnel of blackness and the caked dust of disuse where narrow-gauge railroad tracks were laid. Thirty years before, at the turn of the century, the congestion of horses, trolleys, and pedestrians had congealed to such stiffness that an electric railroad for freight had been built under the center of the city, connecting the major buildings with the railroad depots. Along with everything else the Chicago Tunnel Company had gone broke; the little trains ran no more. Even when they did, few people knew about them; now the deserted tunnels were inky rodent runs, eerie night spaces.

Zep was in a room once used by a dispatcher. He had electricity, a chair, a cot, a toilet, and nothing else. His weight had broken the cot so he slept on the floor or sat in the chair reading the papers Andy brought him twice a day. From the spot in the tunnel where Andy had left him hidden, Allan could hear Zep cussing out Andy and grousing.

"Muff diver! Fuck head!" Andy said as they regained the street. "He wants a radio. The asshole can't get it through his fat head a radio won't work down there. He's bored, the muff diver."

"Why are they hiding him down there?"

"'Cause they can't truck a three-hundred-and-seventy-five-pound fat man around the city of Chicago without risking somebody seeing you got the world's largest bookie in the back seat. This way for sure he can disappear without no slip-ups, see?"

"They could have put him in the back of a beer truck."

"They coulda, but this is safer, wise guy. You don't think they know what they're doing?"

"Sounds ridiculous to me."

"Well, you're wrong as usual, Allan, 'cause you don't know what you're talking about. It's a perfect plan. They get Touhy off the streets without shooting him, which would cause a lot of heat. *And* they deliver their message to Hizzoner, Anton J. Cermak."

"Rather risky, don't you think?" Allan had learned the less he sounded impressed, the more he could goad Andy into bragging and telling him things.

"Rather not risky, don't you think? *I'm* the only one who knows where Zep is. Even they only know he's down there in the tunnels somewhere. Zep can't even get out. You can't call the elevator down from above if you're in the tunnel, and the fat man can't fit up the emergency stairway. The muff diver would have to try to walk out with no light through all those miles down there. So it's not risky 'cause it depends on me, an' I'm reliable. I'm the only one who knows exactly."

"Not the only one now," Allan said and gave Andy a smirk.

"Oh, fuck! You don't count, Allan."

Allan did count at the university. It fell out that it was his turn to make a presentation before the Social Conflict seminar, and its members were looking forward to Allan, the student of organized crime. In the corridors of the neo-Gothic Social Science building the fascination with gangsters extended to those who studied them. Word that Bob Park at Chicago had a student who was "getting some remarkable stuff on organized crime and politics" had even begun to spread to the universities in the East.

Allan did not disappoint. Without being self-dramatizing he was dramatic, giving the people around the table a full and coherent account of the chaotic events they were reading about in the newspapers. Speaking with an insider's authority, he told them what they would not have guessed—that the Mayor's recent police reorganization, or shake-up, as Allan preferred to call it, had nothing to do with reform and efficiency but rather with destroying the network of communication and assistance set up by Mr. Frank Nitti's agents in the department. "It wasn't a reform move; it was a war move," he said.

When the seminar had reached the end of its scheduled hour, it was agreed to extend it another thirty minutes. Unheard of. And Allan, feeling his moment, talked on and on until, finally, he told his round-eyed auditors that he knew where Zep, the world's largest bookie, was being hidden. The air bubbles of egotism making his brain light and nimble, he improvised on the difficulties of staging an apparent kidnapping of a 375-pound mass of slow-moving flesh. Allan was funny, Allan was hypnotic, but just as he was on the point of telling them where Zep was secreted, he was interrupted by Louis Wirth, the brilliant, aggravating rival doing it to Allan again.

"A couple of questions, please. You and one other are the only two who know where Zep Moneypenny is? Then aren't you putting yourself in danger saying you know? Wouldn't you be putting people in this room in danger if you tell them?"

"This is probably as good a place as any to adjourn. We've run almost an hour and forty minutes," Mr. Park put in. "A remarkable presentation. I think we all agree." Three or four agreed so much they gave a few claps. But Allan could not appreciate his success. Wirth had smudged his moment. It put him in a funk. When Irena took him off to dinner, he was still saying, "As if I was going to say where Zep is. He said all that to make me look bad. What kind of a fool does he think I am? If anybody knows how dangerous this kind of knowledge is, wouldn't it be me?"

They were joined by Salvation Winthrop, and halfway through supper the two women had Allan believing again that he was the fine fellow everyone knew he was, save when he occasionally went astray or was attacked by envious colleagues. Allan's charm re-emerged from behind dark vapors. He told them amusing stories, he sang them ditties of his own composition, and proved to the two women that it is worth the expenditure of self to release the man hidden in the boy.

Allan got home after eleven that night. His father was up lecturing his mother about the Knox Committee. The committee was enlisting volunteers to go door to door to beg money hoarders to take their gold out of their sugar pots and their mattresses and return it to the banks. The mystery was where the money had gone, billions upon billions, hidden or blown away or dried up. If the money could be found, the gold hoarders coaxed to open their pots and spend, there

218

was still time to save the country. That went for Uncle Fenwick, whom his brother-in-law suspected of sending millions out of the country to safe and profitable repository in Great Britain. Elting Archibald repeated the speech he had given his wife to his son, after which Ottoline Archibald told Allan a woman had called, the same woman, every half hour. The name she gave was Mona Jupiter. Would that be a stage name? Ottoline asked.

When Mona called again, she addressed Allan as Al and spoke in such nervously voluble language that Allan supposed she was not alone. "Well, the reason for which I was trying to get ahold of you, Al, is that a mutual friend and acquaintance of yours and mine, both of ours, Andrew Mousmoulis, has been arrested by the police. It was suggested by certain other acquaintances, mutual friends like Mr. Jack McGurn, that you might want to assist in this situation by getting Andrew Mousmoulis out of jail."

This un-Mona-like Mona no more aroused a premonition of danger in Allan than Wirth's words had. He did not imagine a husband might be on the extension arranging to punish him for his adulteries. Allan's sins were egocentrically his alone. Mona's fears and misgivings were beyond his conceiving.

She told him he was to go to the nineteenth floor of an office building at La Salle and Wacker, and, telling his parents he had an emergency, he was on his way. He was surprised that he was alarmed about Andy, but mostly he was glad to be called, glad to be useful to these men.

The building was one of the last to be completed before the Depression stopped everything, but it was in bankruptcy, unrented, its floors uncovered cement, its spaces without partitions, a place of darkness and dangling light bulbs. The suite to which Mona sent Allan, however, was completed and decorated in gangster lush-lavish. No Gunner, although Allan did know several of the men in the waiting room.

One of them gave him a playful shot in the arm; another told him he was a champ, a real pal; then they took him in to see Nitti. Natty Nitti, Allan thought, seeing the chairman of the board again. He wondered if this would be the right time, the best opportunity to get closer, to arrange that one conversation in which Nitti would give Allan all he would need.

One o'clock in the morning, and the clothes on the Enforcer looked fresh from the closet. But the face was tired as the body rose from the chair; the arms elbowed out a bit to adjust to the way the suit coat hung, and a hand came forward to shake Allan's. The same hand then gestured toward a chair. These were marks not shown Allan before.

Nitti was gracious but speedy. Problems in the great corporation. A pal of yours, Andy Mousmoulis, arrested, too bad. There is more to it than that, but the nut of it is he is in a jam and for certain reasons his friends can't get to him to help him, if you catch the meaning.

Nitti's professional reticence kept him from telling Allan why he needed the lowly Andy, and Allan did not understand the situation because he had not believed Andy's bragging. Something so important would not have been left to Andy to take care of. Andy was permanent low status, and, as Allan believed, gangsters were more punctilious respecters of class distinctions than the Junior League. Andy was born to stay put socially; he was not a riser; he was a fetcher, a doer of errands, a bringer of coffee and doughnuts. He tried too hard and he showed it.

Nitti reminded Allan that Allan had once done him and his business associates a favor. The Thanksgiving soup kitchen. For which again thanks and the hope that in return Allan was getting whatever it was he needed. But now a new favor was being requested; help to get Andy out of jail. This was the chance to ask for the interview, but that would be an admission from Allan that he was helping them so that they would, in turn, help him. He could not do it, not out front.

When Allan said he would help if he could, one of the men in the room was introduced to him. Pete Bavas was a lawyer and a Greek like Andy, Nitti explained. He and Allan would go together to get Andy. A young friend, obviously a college man, clean-cut, influential family, and a Greek, but a Greek who is a lawyer: two people unconnected to Mr. Nitti's business endeavors. They stood the best chance of getting Andy out without giving the police the idea they might have a more valuable prisoner than they knew.

"Let's think this out. I'm a believer in reason. We Greeks are," Pete Bavas said, as they stood on the empty sidewalk. Across Wacker Drive to the east Allan could see the drawbridges at Michigan and Wabash rapidly swinging airward. The bells on the bridges closer to where the two stood had begun to warn traffic off, preparatory to going up. A fog made the cobblestones wet and the trolley rails glisten. A freighter coming off the lake could be seen moving past Streeterville toward the Michigan Avenue drawbridge, the black prow coming toward them. "The Greeks were the ones who made a science out of thinking."

"Go ahead and think," Allan replied, but Pete Bavas either did not get it or let it pass. Thinking was in order, however. Pete had a writ of habeas corpus in his pocket, but they had to figure out in which jail Andy might be held. The Chicago Police Department operated under the seventy-two-hour rule: a person could be held without being booked for three days. For three days there would be no record in any station-house desk of the prisoner. There was another catch. In the seventy-first hour the prisoner could be moved to another lockup in another station house for another three days, thereby making it impossible for the prisoner's friends to find him.

The Police Department shake-up had displaced the gangsters' spies, informants, and protectors, rolling them out of their accustomed places. Last week it would have been impossible to hide anyone more than a day from Mr. Nitti; this week, with new people in old places and the network torn, Andy Mousmoulis was gone. As of that hour the Silvermans were gone also, the only witness left to attest to the kidnapping being the discreditable Lorna Doone. Below the city in the tunnels, the 375-pound fat man had been put on a diet. He could die, he could begin wandering through those midnight tubes, he could find his way out into the accidental arms of a copper. The State's Attorney would have to release the Dodger to return to the beer business.

"What would Pythagoras do?" Pete Bavas asked Allan. "He'd play a hunch. He'd say not enough is known to employ reason so let's go to the Humboldt Park Station and try luck. I got a friend there that I don't think got transferred."

Nothing doing at Humboldt Park, or at the Chicago Lawn station, or Belmont, or at a succession of smutty tan brick buildings of Romanesque design or red brick structures with Italian Renaissance ornamental dib-dabs. They had blue police lights on either side of their front doors. Within, the floors creaked, the paint on the radiators was chipped, and there was never any place for friends and relatives to sit down. By late morning they had gone everywhere and gotten nowhere. Pete Bavas was imperturbably the same, still speaking evenly, still extolling the ancients, but Allan, indifferent to the classical mind, was cranky, tired, and confused. Would it help Andy if he told someone—who? Pete?—of Zep's whereabouts. He did not want to continue the tour of the branch offices of the Chicago constabulary. Wouldn't they let Andy out anyway?

Pete was in a phone booth in the Austin station. As a bailbondsman as well as a lawyer, he knew people up and down the line and was using several dollars' worth of nickels. Allan watched Pete through the glass of the booth's folding door, his fedora pushed back on his head, shouting into the speaking tube, the black Bakelite receiver wedged between shoulder and ear, leaving his hands free to make notes.

Pete came out of the telephone booth on the run. Another bondsman had got it from a prisoner he had bailed out that Andy was in the Grand Crossing lockup on the other side of town, halfway to the steel mills. Definitely Andy Mousmoulis, but he's being worked over by the watch commander, a prize shit by the name of O'Connor. And we don't go in asking if he's there. Smack the writ down on the table like you know he is or you won't get him.

"You did it, Bavas!" Allan exclaimed as he aimed the roadster toward Grand Crossing. It was going on noon; he had been without sleep for a day and a half, but he felt fine; Pythagoras was OK and he, Allan, was OK, charged up with a part to play. He wheeled the roadster around trucks, he passed streetcars, frightening disembarking passengers; he weaved in and out between iron pillars holding up elevated tracks and, turning onto South Chicago Avenue, kept pace with a steam engine pulling a train parallel until the tracks of the New York Central transected the main line of the Illinois Central in a soot and cindered late-nineteenth-century complex of iron and stone, tunnel and overpass, steel rail and flanged wheel—the Grand Crossing. Near it was the police station, its parking lot covered by the clinker residue from coal-fired railroad boilers.

Habeas corpus: You may have the body. A judge had said so, the Honorable George Washington Maneschewitz. The desk sergeant turned the writ over, inspecting its outer skin, as though the document might have been dipped in poison ivy juice.

"My understanding of the law," Allan announced with upperclass finality, "is that you can't trump a writ of habeas corpus. You are obliged to deliver the prisoner into our custody *instanter.*" The sound of his voice and the high-toned manner of command pleased Allan. It had gotten him what he wanted most of his life. Now, after his long sojourn among those not to the manor born, he was beginning to know when to play at being imperiously well born and rich and when it was less than the best idea.

The sergeant looked into the face of one and then the other: a greasy Greek lawyer and a society snot. "You're gonna have to see the lieutenant on this."

They did see the lieutenant. He did not consider the writ too toxic to read. Coming out of his office, where it had been brought in to him, he studied it as he walked toward the desk. "Got yourselves a sheeny judge for your writ, did ya?"

"It's a valid writ," Allan instructed him.

"Don't tell me my business, sonny. . . . What would you be wanting a piece of garbage like that for?" He motioned backward with his head toward the lockup. He looked at the paper again, inspecting it for technical flaws, and, apparently finding none, shrugged his shoulders and told the sergeant, "Give 'em that guy . . . Moomoolis . . . Andrew, the Greek bookie."

Allan was puzzling why Lieutenant O'Connor did not deny Andy was there, sneak him out the back door, and take him to another station. Were there, after all, rules this struggle was conducted by? Or did O'Connor presume that he was nailed and that he risked too much trouble violating a court order? If Cermak lost, George Washington Maneschewitz could hang O'Connor by the thumbs, or so Allan's tired, racing mind was speculating when the lieutenant picked up a nightstick from a shelf and pointed it at him. A heavy, hurtful club. Allan imagined the concussive wood on his skull. "We're on to you, sonny. We know your type. Society boy. Gets his thrills hanging out with mobsters. You watch your step, Mr. Stage-Door Johnny." Two patrolmen came up to the desk to ask the sergeant if they were facing another payless payday. "What's the skinny, mac?" one of them asked, but before the sergeant could answer, a hobo came up behind them. He smelled as bad as he looked.

"Ptooee!" one of them said, moving away.

"I wanta give myself up," the hobo said.

"Well, you can't do it here. We wouldn't even let ya if you'd had a bath. There's a soup kitchen over on Cottage Grove. And when ya get a meal in your belly, take yerself over to the municipal bathhouse, fer God's sake."

"No. I wanta give myself up."

"Ya gotta commit a crime first, fella. We haven't been paid in weeks ourselves. We can't be feeding the unemployed, you know. Go rob a bank, then we'll give you a sandwich, which is probably more'n you'll find in the bank vault."

"I did commit a crime. I'm an army deserter."

"An army deserter, are you? You're not shittin' me?"

"No, sarge. I am. AWOL for two months from Fort Leonard Wood. Twenty-third Cavalry."

"Then step right this way, my good man. Haynes!" The sergeant shouted. "Incarcerate this gentleman, give 'im a sandwich, and get me the telephone of the Department of War downtown. It's me lucky day! . . . See, fellas," the sergeant said, turning back to the patrolmen, "there's always money quietly making its way toward you, if you only take it easy. The army pays fifty bucks for each deserter you arrest."

Habeas corpus, you may have the body, but the condition the body arrives in does not run with the writ. Andy was conscious when two jailers brought him in, but he was in bad shape. He could not see out of his eyes, which were just lines in swollen tissue; his nose was broken; he had a cut in his scalp, dried blood in his hair, and spots and blotches on his shirt; he had been hit so hard around the mouth that his lips had pulled away from his teeth and gums. He was next to unrecognizable, and Allan, unmindful of the prudent or the politic, put one of Andy's arms around his own shoulder to steady him and, as he did so, turned to let the Grand Crossing detail of the Chicago Police Department know what his opinions were.

"Shut up! Fer chrissake, shut up!" Pete Bavas hissed. Allan was ready to tell Pete a thing or two, but thinking he saw O'Connor move toward them out of the corner of an eye, it finally got through to him this was not the place. "Let's get the hell outa here before they do the same thing to us," Pete Bavas pressed him.

They got across the field of clinkers. The three of them would not fit in the front seat of the roadster, so they had to hoist and pull Andy into the rumble seat, Pete panting, "Let's go, let's go, let's go." They went east on 79th Street, Allan driving as fast as he could but in no particular direction. The plan had not foreseen that Andy would be returned as a hospital case. Pete, in the rumble seat with Andy, banged on the roof of the coupe to stop.

While he went to phone, Allan got out and stood by Andy, telling him he would be OK. Allan had never seen a human face so disfigured. He patted Andy on the shoulder; he was afraid to touch him. Andy made a gurgling noise that sounded like bloody foam coming out of his mouth. Andy was trying to form Zep's name, to tell Allan to go to Zep. Allan could not understand. He told Andy they were getting him to a doctor, that it would be OK, that he should not try to talk. The more he gave Andy the comfort he did not want, the more Andy tried to talk. Then he went silent, a red bubble of saliva on the fleshy hole of his mouth. Allan looked at Andy.

Pete Bavas came out of the phone booth running, motioning Allan away from Andy. "Nitti's been shot . . . it just happened. . . . Screamin' an' shoutin', ya can't hardly hear on the phone."

"Is he dead? Who did it?"

"I dunno. The guy I talked to said to be careful with Andy. He thinks we got lucky gettin' him out. He thinks the coppers are looking for him still."

"He needs a hospital, Pete."

"We check him into a hospital and he'll be back in Grand Crossing before a doctor gets to look at him . . . I called Jerry Kyros, but I couldn't get him. He's gone to ground. Everybody's hiding, I guess. Kyros has a setup for situations like this."

Kyros was the boss of Greek gambling on the Near West Side. The main thought in Allan's head was Nitti could not be shot. If you shot Nitti, you'd have to get blood on his suit jacket, you'd have to muss his hair, you'd have to perturb the imperturbable. Nitti could not be shot. "You got an idea? Some place for an hour or two till I can get ahold of Jerry Kyros?" Allan drove north on Stony Island, two Greeks in the rumble seat, going as fast as he could toward Salvation Winthrop's apartment on Madison Park, a private, closed-off street of sycamores and elms near the university.

Both women were there but they were not helpful. Irena was good for nothing but saying, "Oh, my God! Poor Andy! Oh, his poor face. I can't look." Allan steered her into her bedroom, where, out of sight of those misshapen features, she clung to him and repeated, "How awful!" until she had calmed down enough to remind him Wirth had warned him. Allan snapped at her: Wirth had not warned anyone about *Andy*. Where had he gotten the idea women had an inborn aptitude for nursing?

Lightheaded from lack of sleep, Allan felt swashbuckling. He saw himself on display as a man of action. Irena had never seen him rise to the occasion, never watched the boy who would have gone Over There in 1917 had he been old enough. He told her, using the terse phrasing of self-importance, that Nitti had been shot. "We could have been spotted. We had to get Andy off the streets as fast as we could. Don't worry, we'll get him out of here as soon as it's safe." Irena understood none of it, barely heard it. She was looking at Andy's mutilated face.

"Allan, this is dangerous! And it's not doing sociology. It's going too far. Do you want them to do that to your face?" It was the wrong approach. A beautiful young woman who begged him not to risk his handsome face was inadvertently egging him on. You got Allan to stop by telling him that he was making himself look ridiculous, that he was acting stupidly. If you said he was not doing sociology, what he took in was that he was doing the kind of sociology a woman or a Wirth couldn't do, and that was fine with him.

He told Irena not to worry, left her in the bedroom, and went into the living room, where Salvation Winthrop was saying, "This man needs immediate attention, Allan, and whoever did this should be reported to the police."

"The police did it."

"Well, then, this man is a criminal," Salvation pronounced.

Allan shrugged and turned away. Yes, Andy is a criminal. He makes his living providing an illegal service for the people who work in City Hall and the Cook County Building. They give him their bet money. Andy is a lawbreaker, Frank Nitti is a lawbreaker, Mayor Cermak is a lawbreaker. Allan had stories of insurance-agent lawbreakers, landlord lawbreakers, contractor lawbreakers, lawyer lawbreakers. At this preposterous minute, with Irena cringing in the bedroom and his friend Andy swaying, bloody bubbles on his mouth, and Salvation Winthrop worried he might stain the tapestry covering her antique chairs, it struck Allan that non-lawbreakers can be divided into two categories: those who don't need to break the law and those who don't have a chance to. To Salvation Winthrop he said, "The man is a bloody criminal and we'll get him out of here." The Dean of Women never thought as much of Allan after that. Cheeky and a touch fatuous, too, that one.

Allan and Pete Bavas dragged Andy back into the rumble seat and went northward to the other end of the city along the littoral of the lake, up the service elevator at the Edgewater Beach, to bang on the back door of Mona's suite, there to be admitted by an Irish maid who looked at Andy and cried out for all three persons of the Holy Trinity to render immediate assistance.

Mona was unfazed. After exclaiming, "Hamburger meat!" she went off into another room to telephone. "Mr. Bavas," she said, returning, "they say for you to take him down on the loading dock and you'll get picked up in a few minutes."

"I think I should go too . . . after all."

"They said Mr. Bavas. Not you, Allan. You go home."

She made him feel like a little kid, but besides helping the two to the back elevator and saying goodbye to Pythagoras, there was nothing more for Allan to busy himself with. The adventure was over.

"I don't want you to talk to me that way again. Never!" Allan said to Mona when he came back from getting the two other men on the elevator. The first time Allan felt like a fully enfranchised man out in the world, Mona publicly kissed him off as a useless juvenile. He'd had all of that from Mona he could take. "Never talk to me that way again."

"I'm not gonna talk to you any kind of way again, Allan. I'm never gonna see you again." Mona could see that Allan had found a man's part to play; she knew those lines but she did not like to hear him recite them. Allan was her Allan so long as he was handsome and tender; she cherished looking at his body because it was so unscarred, unmarked, unused. He was smooth, and his cock was the only cock which had never hurt her. She loved him as a pretend prince; if Allan was working on becoming one of the guys, she had no further interest in him.

They upped their misunderstanding. Allan took Mona roughly by the shoulders; Mona slapped Allan and kicked him in the shins. He flopped down on the overstuffed chintz chair to look at her in injured dejection. Now he looked like Mona's Allan again and she came to him, pressed his head against her stomach and her breasts. "We'll do it one more time, baby, one more time. But not now. It's getting too dangerous. Allan, Allan, you are a little boy."

He did not want to hear that but he nuzzled against her. The curves and flesh of her body gave him a comfort that was at once motherly and erotic. The battle for Chicago departed his mind.

Elsewhere in that city a famished fat man, down to 373 pounds, the mainspring of his bioclock busted by abandonment in his room under the earth, took a disoriented step into the darkness of the tunnels. Zep did not know where he was going, but he would have Andy killed for this.

Chapter **10**

Ottoline heard her husband making an awful noise in his sleep. The spirit in Elting was dying. She was convinced of it. She knew he had been wounded, but he would not tell her how. The sound coming from his room traversed the bathroom they shared and struck Ottoline's ear. She put down *Lady Chatterley's Lover* and thought of the heroine and her crippled husband.

She was in her third reading of the banned novel since her friend Josephina had smuggled it through customs. She had hidden it in a box of chocolate bonbons, brought it to Chicago, and snuck it to Ottoline, saying, "You will be *bouleversée,* Ottoline. I was. It has changed my life. I am serious."

Josephina inclined toward French literature, Ottoline toward Bloomsbury. They were not silly women but underused women, unable to spend enough of themselves shopping and attending to charity. There was so much of them left over that they lived semi-secret, second lives of vicarious, vivid intensity through the arts.

Ottoline had taken up the book with some small misgivings. Josephina occasionally moved across the line separating brilliant boldness from bad taste, and *Lady Chatterley's Lover* had been dismissed by critics of the stature of H. L. Mencken as scarcely more than flowery pornography. After the first reading Ottoline had concluded that Mencken would have approved of the book if he could have been sure only men would be allowed to read it. She had a suspicion men were frightened that this odd Englishman betrayed his gender when he put such powerful emotional information in the hands of women. Naturally, the customs agents—men, you might be sure— seized the book.

Ottoline repeatedly read certain of the passages, forgiving them their exuberance; she read them in anger, in wonder, in confusion, in passion, demanding to know why she had not been told:

> Then as he began to move, in the sudden helpless orgasm, there awoke in her new strange thrills rippling inside her. Rippling, rippling, rippling, like a flapping overlapping of soft flames, soft as feathers, running to points of brilliance, exquisite, exquisite and melting her all molten inside. It was like bells rippling up and up to a culmination. She lay unconscious of the wild little cries she uttered at the last. . . . She turned and looked at him. "We came off together that time," he said.

If Connie had been a heroine of Zola's sociological fiction, Ottoline would have looked down on her. But D. H. Lawrence's lady was an upper-class Englishwoman, the sort of person Ottoline knew, the sort of person Ottoline saw herself as, though American and Midwestern. If that person could experience carnal knowledge firsthand, if she could think about her own orgasm, have her own orgasm, if that person could have those words spoken in front of her, to her, those words whose definitions Ottoline was not positive she knew . . .

"Sex is really only touch, the closest of all touch. And it's touch we're afraid of. We're only half conscious, and half alive. We've got to come alive and aware." She reread that also, and it confirmed a half-formed romantic and emotional doctrine that she had brought on her wedding night. Touching, loving, was the life elixir; it had the power to bring a husband back from the dead. This book proved it. She was like Mellors, the hero, able by the sensuous touch and breath of love to renew her husband, deadened by the conflict he drove off to engage in every weekday morning. She would *make* feeling. She could not form the words . . . what Mellors said to Connie:

> "Yes, I do believe in something. I believe in being warm-hearted. I believe especially in being warm-hearted in love, in fucking [that word!] with a warm heart. . . . It's all this cold-hearted fucking that is death and idiocy."

Ottoline put the book down on the blanket, sat up, slipped into her mules, and crossed over through the bathroom into her husband's bedroom. His pillows were on the floor, his lamp was on. Elting was sleeping on his stomach, flat, his face square in the mattress; his arms were extended to the headboard, his hands holding onto the bedposts. She thought she heard him make the pained sound he made before, but softer, an almost inaudible echo of his earlier cry. Ottoline sat next to him on the bed. She touched his shoulders; his teeth ground against each other, making a grist of his worry and tension. They had had little sex since Calvin Coolidge, since the last time Elting had gotten tiddly and they had come home, cranked the gramophone, and done the tango.

Being warm-hearted in love: the phrase returned to Ottoline, who spoke her emotions with such difficulty. "It's touch we're afraid of," the novel had told her. She let her hands glide over her husband's shoulder muscles. They seemed to relax and Ottoline bent over, laying her cheek against the back of Elting's neck, her flattened hands moving slowly over his shoulders. For a minute Ottoline stayed bent over Elting; then she rose, dropped her nightgown, and got in beside him. As she did, one of Ottoline's hands found the end of Elting's pajama top and insinuated itself under and up toward his chest. She pictured the scene in the novel which had first shocked and then enchanted her, in which Mellors puts forget-me-nots in Connie's pubic hair. Lady Chatterley and her lover fused the sentimental style of Ottoline's girlhood days with modern ways, and she wanted so much to do the same.

Ottoline rested her head against Elting's back, listening to her husband's heartbeat. After a while she began caressing him with the thought of lifting him softly into quiet intimate consciousness. Elting's hands unclenched around the spindles of the headboard. He made a noise that might have been interpreted as responsive until he jolted over and sat up and asked her in a rasping, startled shout, "What are you doing? What *are* you doing? What are you *doing?*"

"Elting, E—" Ottoline was going to call him dear but she was cut off.

"You don't have any clothes on!"

"I—"

"You're naked! Naked! Nude!" He moved away from Ottoline as he rattled his voice at her, his words forcing her off the bed. "Nude! Look at you! Starkers! It's two A.M. and you're in your birthday suit!" She stood by the side of the bed, now wide-eyed, staring at this man in striped pajamas screaming at her in whispered shouts, making her aware of her nudity in shamed embarrassment. "Look at you, look at you!" Elting continued in his hysteria, and Ottoline crouched over to conceal her pudendum, one arm trying to cover her breasts as the other hand felt for her discarded nightgown. "Running around nude in the middle of the night! Like a madwoman!" Ottoline could not find the thing. She gave up. With tears in her eyes, whimpering little "oh!"s she ran stooping from her husband's bed.

Sleep did not give Elting rest; his dreams were a reprise of the humiliating telephone call, the Mayor's voice, slow, low, sardonic, insulting. The only words Elting had been able to get off from his end of the telephone line had been, "You should understand—I did it for the colored, the colored people." Cermak was used to thieves who, confronted with the evidence, said, "So you caught me. So what?" Rationalizations like Archibald's were novel to him, but he had not called to have a conversation; he had called to tell the banker that he was "a cocksucker!"

When his people had told Tony Cermak about the hundreds of thousands of dollars—it could add up to a couple of million—in interest-free checking accounts, he had said, "Nah, I don't believe it." Then his people showed him the work sheets and Cermak said, "I believe it." But Ten Percent Tony, the nickname stuck on him by his fellow pols years ago in recognition of the standard Cermak cut, could not bring himself to believe it. For weeks he had been negotiating with Archibald and his committee of bankers for a loan to keep the city running and these cocksuckers had stalled the whole time, trying to make Chicago pay interest for withdrawing its own money from deposit.

Ten Percent Tony did not want to believe it of Elting Archibald, Newbold Clayton, Ben Croaker, or Ralph Van Derveter. He thought of them as being like the McCormicks, the Armours, the Blairs, the Cudahys, and the Swifts, people rich enough to be honest; these were the family names of the Anglo-Saxon aristocracy chiseled on museums and hospitals. If his people had told him that Cardinal Mundelein had screwed the city, it would have given Cermak a chuckle. Before he was a cardinal he was another Brooklyn Dutchman; what Anton Joseph Cermak did not understand was that John Jacob Astor was too.

The anger of outrage put the telephone in Cermak's hands. If you can't count on the best, who can you count on? How could he run the city if *everybody* was going to steal from it?

Insull had told Archibald that, if Cermak did find out, the banker would not learn it from the Mayor, but Insull had been wrong. When Archibald collected himself, he called the utilities tycoon to croak, "He knows. He called me. He called me a terrible name, Sam."

"We've all been called terrible names, Elting."

"It was a disgusting name he called me."

"For heaven's sake, man! Make a deal with him. You boys will have to work out some kind of payment schedule. Give the city its money gradually. A bit at a time."

"I'll have to start liquidating, Sam. Sell everything."

That was what Insull did not want to hear. Selling everything meant throwing large blocks of Insull stock on the market, destroying what little value it had left and thereby pulling Insull so much further into debt that his situation would be irretrievable.

But if the largest banks in Chicago were to tell Cermak that if he pulled out the city's deposits, they would have to close their doors, that they would not be able to cover their smaller depositors' withdrawals, Cermak would have to back off. The plan was plausible but Insull failed to see that the hysterical, piping, gasping man talking to him on the telephone could not bring it off.

The man who could was Cardinal Mundelein, the Prince of the Church. When he heard of Cermak's discovery from Fast Father Frank, he called the Mayor to speak in lordly generalities about "the grave situation on La Salle Street . . . the need to avoid doing anything which might disturb the present fragile balance obtaining in our financial institutions . . . a time for caution, would you not say so, Mr. Mayor?" Less lordly specifics about the archdiocese's Insull stock went unuttered. Although Holy Mother Church did not assert infallibility in its investment decisions, the Cardinal did not want others knowing of any mistakes or inadvertencies; it was not conducive to the grandeur of the institution.

Mr. Mayor had been getting his own palpitations. Banks up and down the Mississippi Valley were quivering. There had been stories and rumors about bank panics forestalled only at the last minute in Little Rock, St. Louis, Memphis, and now, as Cermak was discovering the hidden no-interest deposits in the big Chicago banks, the papers were carrying stories of a crisis at a major bank in New Orleans.

Tony Cermak did not need Mundelein to tell him the banks, even Chicago's banks, second only to New York's in wealth, could go down. "Yes, Your Eminence, this is not the time to be doing anything too quick, you're right there, Your Eminence," he had told the Cardinal, while telling himself that it gave him a royal pain in the ass to think of those rich society cocksuckers getting away with it. They had millions of the city's money, and they would pay it back when they were good and ready, pay it back without interest, and nothing would be said.

If Elting Archibald had gone about his business like the others, daring the Mayor to pull the money out, he would have gone on riding in the back of his limousine. Instead, he was dumping his Insull stock, dumping every asset of his and his bank's at ruinous discount prices to get the cash to cover the city's deposits. He had lived with the fear of what he had done so long, had been so fixed on his guilt, that he had lost his understanding of the levers and pulleys of his business.

As soon as the money to cover the withdrawal was securely on the books, he called Cermak to tell him. "The account, your account, the account of the City of Chicago is in order, Your Honor. . . . You may send a messenger over to get the money, in cash if you would like." Now came the part that was the most difficult but the most necessary for Elting Archibald to speak: "I do not appreciate being spoken to, being . . . having . . . well, that kind of language. . . . I—"

"I'll send a messenger over for the money," Cermak said and hung up. When money is proffered, take it.

When the money was gone, when the fear was over, when a sense of proportion returned to him, Elting saw what he had done, saw that he might have put himself out of business. He had sold everything he owned; he had even mortgaged his house; he had illegally mortgaged his mother's farm; he had illegally sold Ottoline's assets; he had stripped the bank of all its ready cash so that, unless money was transfused from somewhere, Great Lakes National was not going to open Monday morning.

No one would find out that he had taken sinful favors from Big Bill, but he was still bankrupt and an embezzler. The first day the bank examiners and the auditors looked at the books, they would see what he had done. He had to get money, a lot of it.

Even in his panic Elting recognized that if he made an approach to Fenwick, his cash-rotten brother-in-law, he would get scorn and no money. It would come out that he had embezzled the part of Ottoline's wealth he had been given to administer, the money she had demanded from Fenwick to be a sign of trust in her young husband.

There was another way. Elting asked Nadja Pringle to bring him a list of the bank's largest stockholders. There were many, many names, too many for one person to telephone and convince before Monday morning. These would not be happy stockholders; they would need a lot of talking to, a lot of persuading after it was broken to them that the bank was in danger of closing its doors and making their stock worthless unless . . . The unless was that the stockholders would have to put up money to cover the emergency. If they did, the bank would be saved and their stock would hold its value. The rub was that each shareholder would have to come up with three dollars for every share he owned and do it fast enough for Great Lakes National to have it in the vault Monday morning.

To make his plan work, Elting would have to recruit Nick Luckhurst and several other of the senior men. He would have to tell them what he had done. He would have to bear that humiliation—oh, sweet goodness, all his hair was going to fall out. He would have to act quickly before Luckhurst left the building and he would have to decide how much to tell Luckhurst, who would never respect him again, who would go to the board after this was over and force him out. He could not let himself think about that yet. They would need to work all weekend, into the night; he was almost as low on time as he was on money. Elting had to put aside his shame, brazen it out. Simply tell Nick Luckhurst fast and hard—no apologies, no explanations, tell him what the situation was and what had to be done, tell him and the others that if they couldn't do it, no one would have a position by Monday afternoon. As for the board, save the bank, then save the job.

The meeting did not go as Elting had feared. Archibald's senior vice-president listened with complete calm, smoking his banker's fifty-cent cigar as his boss lurched through the recital of the story of Moncrief Borders and the Insull stock. He had to tell the whole of it because he had to keep saying, "I didn't do it for myself, as you can see, Nick, I did it for the colored people."

At the end, Luckhurst observed, "Well, you lost your shirt and so did the niggers; so what, Elting? You're not telling me anything new. Hell, what do you think? You think you can run a deal like that without the other officers in the bank knowing about it? You're not telling me anything we didn't know."

Then Luckhurst told Elting Archibald something that *he* did not know. Luckhurst told him that he and several of the other major vice-presidents had been doing the same thing, borrowing money from the bank to buy stock to use as collateral for the loan—stock which was now essentially worthless. The bank's position was worse than Elting had thought. Then Elting told Luckhurst about telling the Mayor he could pick his money up any time he wanted and how the Mayor had taken it away.

"But that was our vault cash!" Luckhurst shouted. "That's what we have to have to stay open, to keep things going until we can cover our losses. For Christ's sake, Elting, we can't open Monday, you dumb jerk! You've busted the bank, you goddamn fool! You stupid sonofabitch, you've destroyed Great Lakes so you can have the satisfaction of telling the Bohunk over in City Hall to stuff his money up his ass! You proud moron! You've ruined us!"

Elting's hands were clamping on the desk edge, his eyes fixing on Luckhurst, his back muscles grinding the disks between the ox tails of his spine.

Elting's catatonia silenced Luckhurst. The boss could have a heart attack on the spot. So, as Elting began to relax and come back to himself, his vice-president suggested Elting's own plan as the only hope. "We gotta ask the stockholders for more capital an' we gotta do it over the weekend." The bank president pushed the file cards containing the names of the stockholders across the desk in Luckhurst's direction, and he took charge of recruiting three or four other bank officers. The boiler room operation would start after the close of business and would go on around the clock until Monday morning or until they knew the plan had failed or succeeded.

Elting could hear Nadja Pringle typing in the outer office. He wondered if she knew. In a few minutes she came to his door to ask if he wanted her to spend the weekend working.

But telephoning Ottoline was on Elting's mind.

"What kind of trouble at the bank?" she asked him. "You've never worked all night before. What is it? What's wrong?"

"Things have come up. I have to go. I'll call you later or tomorrow. I have to go now." He rang off, but his hand did not let go of the telephone. He had nothing to do. Luckhurst and the other men had taken over; he wondered whether Luckhurst had taken over months or years ago.

At home Ottoline called her brother. Fenwick would know what was going on. "That husband of yours is in the final stages of destroying Great Lakes. That would be my guess. It's taken him years, Ottoline. That was a strong bank, but you can't keep a good man down or a poor man up. Incapacity will out every time. Ha!"

"Please find out for me, Fenwick."

"You won't like it, Elizabeth."

"Please don't devil me. Not now, Fenwick."

"As you please, Ottoline."

"Find out for me . . . please, for me."

"For you, dearest sister."

"'Did I notice anything unusual about him?'" Bettina said, repeating the detective's question. "Sure I did. Didn't we put the state troopers onto 'im?"

"We know that. That was good. But what tipped you off to him? We have to find out if he acted alone." He and another G-man were seated with Bettina in a booth. The D'Amico boy, wearing the rubberized apron Joe had worn, leaned over the back of the next booth, wanting recognition also. Weeks and weeks after Joe had gone, after the excitement had abated, they had traced Joe back to the diner. "So what made you suspect he was a criminal type?" the G-man elaborated.

"He was all the time talkin' about how he took a shot at the king of Italy. Can ya imagine? He liked to brag about that. He was all the time talkin' about shooting, the squirt. He was against the bosses. I heard 'im say that a lotta times. He had the moxie to take a shot against the king of Italy or somebody. He was a tough little s.o.b., but how could you know if he was bragging about the king of Italy? You couldn't for sure."

"He did."

"He really did? The king too, huh?"

"Yup," the detective said.

"It don't surprise me none," Bettina told him.

"Me neither," the D'Amico boy said, leaning farther over the back of the booth.

Having failed to connect with the father, Ottoline began to look for the son, but Allan was off playing tag-along with the gangsters.

The swelling in Andy's face had gone down, the aurora borealis of bruises was gone, and he was back at work at the cigar store. Zep had also returned; the bookie had bumped and stumbled his way through the maze of tunnels until he had emerged into the daylight of a railroad freight yard. The picture he presented on his return from the depths was as disgusting to others as it was embarrassing to himself. Zep, who, to compensate for his size, was customarily neat to the point of daintiness in his person, appeared out of the bottom of the city unshaven, wrinkled, smirched with dust and cinders. He had soiled himself and he stank. When he told his story of kidnapping and abuse by the Dodger and the Owl to the reporters, there had been no time to clean him up. Thea Epps said it was the smelliest yarn in her twelve years of newspapering.

Zep blamed his crucifixion on Andy. He had it in his head, despite the stitches and the wounds on Andy's face, that his runner had abandoned him there, had told no one where he was, hoping Zep would die and he could take over the business. Zep knew he was a punk. "Like the way he was carrying on with Machine Gun McGurn's wife. He don't know it, but I seen 'em from the first. The broad walks into the store, gets the hotel room key off of 'im." He had recognized Mona Jupiter; he had watched but had not spoken. Information like that is valuable; it is not to be gossiped away but traded for significant considerations; it is to be used to get something or someone. Andy. The punk who had wormed a job off Zep was no longer disdained. Now he was hated, but the fat man, always conscious that his flesh made him helpless against the least physical force, took care to organize his retaliations. Andy was looking forward to thanks and a reward. That's what he told Allan. He got nothing from Zep, who picked up bookmaking where he had left it. The payoff, Andy explained to Allan, would come from the Capone organization. They had reason to be grateful. Andy had kept his mouth shut through the questioning; it was he, more than anybody else, who made the kidnap story stand up enough so that Cermak's people could not shake it and the State's Attorney's police could chase Touhy around Cook County, hampering the setting up of the new beer distribution monopoly. He saw himself as one who had done important services for rich and powerful friends.

For once Allan, who was doing his hanging out in the lobby of Stella Urbis hospital on the West Side, had a more realistic picture than Andy of what was going on. The Enforcer, Mr. Nitti, was upstairs being guarded and doctored back to health from a bullet that came within less than an inch of killing him. Allan understood the organization was in a state of war with the Mayor, and it would be a long time before it got around to thinking about Andy. Listening to the men who stood in front of the Virgin Mary statue, Allan had learned how the protected and cautious Frank Nitti had been gotten to and by whom. The act was simple, audacious, and unstoppable unless one had been forewarned.

The night Allan and Pete Bavas were sifting through police stations looking for Andy, Detective Sergeant George Breed and officer Jack Novack had come off the elevator on the nineteenth floor of the La Salle–Wacker building. Both of them were on the Mayor's personal police detail. They said they had a warrant for Nitti. What's the charge? The charge is driving a vehicular automobile without a driver's license. Since Frank Nitti drove men, not cars, and since Illinois would not require driver's licenses until next July, it was concluded that Breed was there to talk in private. Cermak was ready to deal.

Sergeant Breed, ushered into the inner office, walked up to the desk where Nitti was seated, looked at the Enforcer over the gooseneck lamp, took out his heater, and let Nitti have it. Louis Campagna— Louis Little New York to newspaper readers—grabbed Breed. Officer Novack threw up his hands and said, "Hey, don't look at me!" So they didn't look at him and let him go. In the next few minutes, while the ambulance was on its way and the fallen chairman of the board was being ministered to by his associates as best they knew how, Detective Sergeant Breed was shot in the left pinky finger by a person or persons. The wounded pinky was to figure in the trials and investigations of the affair that would linger well into the mid-1930s. Why a more vital part of the detective sergeant was not shot was open to conjecture.

The shooting of Nitti was a breach, even a permanent breakdown, of the rules by which business had been done. When he admitted Breed, Nitti was going by the old customs, and he thought the Mayor was too, although looking back at the train of events Allan was puzzled as to why he would. Cermak had told Nitti, right in the Mayor's office, he was going to use the cops to deliver beer. That should have been a sign he was making up new rules. New rules for a new time. Possibly the Mayor thought Nitti was doing the same with his attempt to get rid of the Dodger, not by putting the blast on Touhy but by using the police, the law, and the courts. If Nitti could use the government to knock over the Mayor's friends, why shouldn't the Mayor use the police like gangsters? Allan would love to have a talk with Cermak, too.

Mr. Park was as excited by what was happening as Allan was. In their conferences Mr. Park's language was spotted with geologic metaphors about the end of eras, the beginnings of a new age. He told Allan that the social sciences perforce must study how things are, but this was one of the rare chances to watch death and rebirth. His excitement made Allan see himself as standing at the edge, looking down at the boiling.

"The interrelatedness of everything!" Mr. Park exclaimed. "The collapse of business and the failure of prosperity have created a political crisis. The political machine can't pay for itself, can't generate enough money to cover expenses, so it reaches out to put pressure on the one industry that seems to us, anyhow, to be pressure proof— organized crime. And what does that do? It disorganizes crime. Breaks the rules. Fascinating, Allan. But now you have to follow this to the end. What's going to happen? Will new rules be made? How? Will they have to go back to the old rules? And how might that happen? Allan, Allan, you've got something here."

"They'll go back to the old rules, Mr. Park, the peacetime rules, but not until the war is over. It's a war now and anything goes, I guess. When the Mayor got Touhy to go into the beer business, he was going after the foundation, the biggest moneymaker of Nitti's organization. The Mayor, as I see it, sir, is after more than a bigger cut; the Mayor is after a big piece of Nitti's territory, and he's breaking the rules to grab it. He had the police try to assassinate Nitti."

"Where does that take us?"

"Oh, I know what's going to happen next, Mr. Park. Even the underlings are talking about it."

"What?"

"They're going to kill the Mayor."

The leader of the bindlestiffs gave Joe approbation and protection. Joe could keep Mr. D'Amico's revolver in his blanket roll. "That sonofabitching Joe, he's crazy. He can cook, though. He's a good 'bo."

There were six or seven in the band camped beside the railroad tracks in the Baltimore & Ohio's freight yards outside of Wilmington, Delaware. They were moving south in front of winter, but everywhere that the freight trains slowed, at the tops of ravines and on the curving embankments where empty cars rattled and compressed air brakes gripped, men were jumping on and off, trying to get to California, trying to get out of California, moving on, making their way to Memphis, catching rides to Roanoke, pushing on.

After the night in the boardinghouse, Joe had thrown away the gentian violet bottle. He had seen through the blue; his past and present were continuous, the parts of his life were joined in purposeful intention.

As Joe stirred the tasty stew he had made from an onion, half a rotten green pepper, and cow tallow, the lead hobo was saying, "Me and J. P. Morgan!" He walked back to the men clustered around the fire, tying, cinching, pinning, and buttoning himself into his ragged cold-weather gear after taking his dump. "J. P. Morgan and me! We both go south for the winter." He sat on a rock, leaned back, and knocked the ash off an imaginary cigar. "I'm spending the cold weather at my Miami Beach cottage. It's a little fifty-room shack but I like roughing it. My yacht has a hole in the bottom so I'll have to borrow Vanderbilt's or Astor's. Joseph, or should I say Giuseppe, how do you plan to break up the tedium of warm days and sunshine?"

"Why do you act like one of the big shots? Like a boss?" Joe remembered the indignities, being cheated out of his pay, but he remembered the sergeant too, the Milan cathedral. The confusions had blown away. "I'm gonna shoot the bosses. This Astor. This J. P. Morgan maybe." He had read about Morgan in *La Voce d'Italia,* a boss of the bosses, that one. "When we get there, you show me his house. You do that."

"You talk like an anarchist, my good man, or my not-so-good man."

"You betcha. I shoot the king of Italy."

"And well done too, I say."

They all laughed. Giuseppe Zangara, Joe, he laughed also.

Fenwick was filled with an emotion he mistook for magnanimity. That's why he did not call his sister Elizabeth when he telephoned her Sunday afternoon. "Your husband is going to jail, Ottoline. He has stolen your money; he has stolen everybody's money—not mine, though; he has sold your house out from under you. That house does not belong to you; you are temporarily in your home thanks to the Mount Olympus Finance Corporation. You do not even own your automobile, and that facsimile of a man you married cannot pay the chauffeur's wages. I have gotten the car back for you."

He told Ottoline what had been going on down at the bank over the weekend, a time of helplessness and worry for her. "Death thrashings," he called them. "Not one chance in a hundred thousand he can make it work. Pack your bags, Ottoline, and move over here. He's lost his good looks. He has nothing to offer you any more." Ottoline hung up on her brother and sat at the telephone table, her head bowed. She picked up the telephone to dial the bank and then hung up, picked it up again to call Fenwick back to ask him to save the bank and thought better of that too. She called Irena. Irena would know where Allan was. Could she find him? There was trouble at the bank. Ottoline was not talking in complete sentences but Irena deciphered enough to know that warm bodies were wanted.

Irena thought that Allan was at Stella Urbis, but the Italian sister on the other end of the line whom she was shouting at was not equal to finding and bringing A-l-l-a-n-A-r-c-h-i-b-a-l-d to the telephone. "You call tomorra in da morning." Before starting out on the long El and trolley car ride to Stella Urbis, Irena considered the four languages she was fluent in and sympathized with the Esperanto movement, just then gaining adherents as a possible way out of the worldwide depression. While she was waiting in the Loop for the car to take her to the West Side, Irena saw the headline on the bulldog edition of Monday's *Tribune* and lined up with everybody else who had three cents to spare to buy her copy.

INSULL BANKRUPTCY!!! UTILITIES EMPIRE IN RUINS!! TYCOON FLEES!
Suicide Feared

The main story told how the holding companies and the utilities in thirty states had been "looted"—that verb was frequently used—in a three-year losing effort to keep the price of the stock up and out of the hands of "eastern banking interests." There were many other stories. One was a biography of Insull, written like an obituary. Another was about the thousands of Chicagoland families whose savings had been in Insull securities. There were people on Marshfield Avenue who owned some. Irena imagined a low keening coming from the bankrupt and pauperized city.

The most affecting story was about the shooting of the animals at Insull's farm near Libertyville. It was where he bred his Suffolk horses, the milk-wagon animals of his London boyhood. They had all been shot, the dogs too, even the cat had been killed, the farm foreman had told the newspaper reporter, on instructions from Mr. Insull, because he said there was no money to feed them. Inside the newspaper Irena studied a picture of this rural abattoir but, thankfully, it was smudgy and indistinct.

On campus some people talked about capitalism and some people talked about socialism and communism. Some people talked about the selfishness of the rich, but Irena was coming to think of what was happening to her country and to Chicago as more like a plague. It was taking off every class of person. The rich were being destroyed with the poor. It was even killing the animals; the vegetation was dying in the parks from want of gardeners. It was carrying away everything, but what was it? The libraries were closed half the time; would the university be next? The hospitals? Was the world going to stop? Were the same people and factories and cities that were rich and enthusiastic and making and doing four years before going to petrify, to stop dead in the midst of living, like Pompeii? But in ancient Italy there had been an explosion, a volcano; in modern Chicago, everybody was stopping for no visible reason. The farmers weren't growing, the factories weren't making, the offices weren't officing; one by one, as though responding to an inaudible command, like a radio wave, it seemed to Irena that the work and the pleasure of the world were ending.

The nuns had moved the lounging hoods from one end of the hospital lobby to the other, shifting their smoking area from in front of the Holy Mother in sky-blue robes to where the I-Am-the-Light-of-the-World Jesus stood in a brown robe with a hand and finger up and extended in the teaching position. At first Allan was annoyed that Irena had come; he often gave her the impression that her presence in certain situations diminished him, although how this could be she had not puzzled out. Then confusion took over. He understood even less than she did about what might be transpiring at the bank. His father never, ever had worked on a Sunday. And a Sunday evening? Sometimes he came down to the Loop to go to the prayer service held in Symphony Hall, but to the office?

Great Lakes had the emptiness of office buildings on Sunday nights. No charwomen even, only clicks and echoes, chills from the heating system running on low; on the corridor ceilings, one brass and glass flower in four was illuminated. Shadows and dead air. But light shone behind the opaque glass in the doors opening to the executive offices, where Nick Luckhurst and his team were going over the lists, toting up columns on the adding machine as Nadja Pringle and several other secretaries poured coffee and managed the trays on which room service from the Bismarck Hotel was brought over.

In the outer office, seated like a customer, was Allan's mother. Ottoline had draped her fur coat on the rear of the chair. Her posture was straight and more ladylike than her usual ladylike self. Her purse was in her lap; her hands were on top of each other; she held her gloves: a woman of breeding in command of herself, but she had little to say except that the bank was in trouble, that Elting "and the other men" were working to save it, that it was proper to "be here and show your father." What was to be shown—love, loyalty, support—she did not say.

"The bank could . . . go *under,* Mother? How? Father would have mentioned it, don't you think?" It seemed to Irena that Allan had an irritated, superior tone in his voice as though Ottoline were not able to get the story straight. Walking out of the reception room through the door to the working areas of the executive suite, Allan blundered into a room where a tired, unshaven, and barely-in-control vice-president told him his father was in the boardroom.

The boardroom of wood, leather, and brass was scarcely lighted. Two green-shaded lamps gave off more gloom than illumination. Allan's father was seated at the great table, but not at its head. Elting had gone more or less rigid again. He was wearing a frock coat and a detachable winged collar and cravat. The ensemble was one only elderly gentlemen of great means and politicians at their inaugurations wore. But Elting's look was not that of a well-to-do gentleman frozen in the past. He had not shaved since Friday and one of the wings of his collar had sprung, so he looked disturbed and disheveled too.

The contrast between the empty boardroom and the work debris in the office of the vice-president registered on Allan. There were no papers in front of his father, no papers on the polished surface of that huge table. He had no telephone. There was no food tray. The man was locked up in mind and in body.

"Father, what's going on around here?"

"I'm busy."

"If you'll pardon me for saying so, you don't look busy."

"You should call your father 'sir.' Show some respect."

"Father, what's happening?" This time Allan's voice was softer. He was frightened. He did not know of what, but this was not like any other encounter he had had with his father. "Is there something . . . something wrong?"

"I told you, I'm busy."

"But—"

"I'm busy. I am busy. I am bizz-*eee!* Bizzy! *BIZZY!*" After Allan had backed out of the door he could hear his father shout one or two more *busy*s before the purple rigidities reclaimed him. The son stood for a second looking at the double doors to the boardroom before

244

returning to the reception room to march up to his mother and demand of her, in a voice almost as loud as the one his father had used against him, "Mother! Mother! What the *hell* is going on here?"

"Leave your mother alone!" Now it was Irena shouting at him.

"I want to know what is going on here?"

"For God's sake, Allan." Irena had him by the sleeve and was yanking at him, and when Irena yanked, even a strong young man could feel it. "You know what's going on here. You know perfectly well."

"I do not. I want to know what's happening."

"What's happening is what's happening all over, Allan. Face it. Look at the newspapers. You know what's happening, you know it, you know it."

"Mother, is that true? I do not believe it. Not Great Lakes."

"Yes," Ottoline said.

"I refuse to believe it. Not *my* father's bank. Well, what does that mean for us, Mother? What about us? How could that happen? How could that be?"

"Allan, be quiet. Shhh! I'll take him out of here for a while, Mrs. Archibald."

"No, it's all right, Irena. You are a dear. And Allan," his mother said, lifting her face to him so her neck looked long and supple, "Allan, it's going to be the same. There's nothing to worry about. Not exactly the same"—she sighed—"but for you, the same." Ottoline rose, the finishing-school posture as much a part of her as before, and, walking out of the room, told the two young ones she would not be long. She did not want them to hear. She did not want them to see the tears or the defeat she felt for her life and for her life's love.

Ottoline went into a vacant office and called Fenwick, who told her he was listening to Rudy Vallee on the radio.

"Save him," Ottoline asked.

"He's weak and he's egotistical."

"Please, Fenwick. Use my money."

"No."

"Please. For Allan."

"If I save him it will be on my terms, Elizabeth."

"You've got to, you've got to do it."

"On my terms?"

Ottoline sighed. "On your terms, Fenwick."

245

"Take Nick Luckhurst aside. Let him know he's the new president of Great Lakes and—"

"No! No, Fenwick."

"My terms, Ottoline, I said *my* terms. Tell Luckhurst if he tries to steal from that bank again, so much as a three-cent postage stamp, I will put him in the penitentiary. Did you hear, Elizabeth?"

"I will not say such things to anyone."

"I suppose you won't. Put him on the phone. *I'll* tell him."

A half hour went by before Ottoline, alone with her husband in the boardroom, was back on the line with Fenwick. Elting took the phone and said almost nothing. There was no fighting. Elting said yes several times and goodbye once. Then he looked into his wife's eyes and told Ottoline—his voice was froggy—"You are going to live at, with, yes, with him from now on."

"I am? . . . I am not."

"You have to. He said you agreed."

"And where are you going to live?"

"In the gardener's cottage for a while." Elting got up, looked at her, and said, "You never supported me. You never supported me."

Ottoline melted into the chair, crying slowly. "Never supported you? I always supported you . . . when you let me."

"I'm leaving this office now." Elting was as stiff as ever. "The car is yours, of course. Everything is yours, Ottoline. I will take public transportation to the house . . . to pack." He was remaining straight, but Ottoline had broken. Her head was down on the glossy wood table and she was crying.

In the reception room, where Allan and Irena saw Elting in better light, he looked mangy, a man of incipient sores, squamous. "I don't know where one transfers from the Elevated to the suburban line to go home. You must know that, Irena," the father said.

"Allan will drive you, Mr. Archibald." She gave her young man a look and Allan took his father off. Irena found Ottoline in the boardroom. While Allan drove his father north and out of the city, neither of them speaking, Irena and his mother held each other and cried. Allan was crafting his resentment at his father and Irena was fighting off bleakness. Nothing was staying stuck together, not empires, not banks, not families. So how would it come out for lovers?

Chapter 11

Joe got to Miami the morning of February thirteenth in an empty box car of the Seaboard Air Line Railway freight train number 41. Shoot the faces, blow up the places. "Where is Rockefeller? Where the big shots?" Joe asked one of the other hoboes.

"Miami, Palm Beach—around here, but the cops are unfriendly, Joe. Three days here, you'll be in jail."

"Maybe." Joe remembered the scenes of the battle, of falling back in front of the Edelweiss Division, lines of men trudging in long coats in the cold; Joe saw lines of men in America waiting for soup. Joe could call up to mind today or yesterday, merge the two, remember what he wanted. He could remember the sergeant. Shoot the faces.

"Hey, stay with me, Joe. We'll hitch over to the other side, to Naples. That's Naples, Florida, greaseball. Heard of it? We'll go over there and you can take another shot at the king of Italy. Hey, Joe. Ya get it? *Naples* an' the king of Italy."

"I shoot the President."

"He's in Washington, Joe. You're in the wrong town. Come on with me."

"I get him."

Chicagoans were looking eastward off their lakefront toward Michigan where, to prevent the lines of depositors at the tellers' windows, the Governor had closed the banks. Where had the money gone? Businessmen in the Loop were hearing stories about localities issuing their own scrip, the national currency having vanished. What had happened to the money? Indiana was trying to save its banking system by forbidding withdrawals of more than 10 percent of any account.

On Lawrence Avenue, not far from Mona's apartment in the Edgewater Beach Hotel, the North Side Union Bank had posted a sign on the doors. Standing tiptoe at the rear of the small crowd at the entrance, Allan read it over the head of a woman banging her gloved fists on the plate glass.

We Regret to Announce That the Board of Directors Has Been Forced to Close the North Side Union Bank for the Protection of Its Depositors and Stockholders. It has been impossible to liquidate our mortgages and other investments rapidly enough to meet the unusual demands made upon us resulting from false and unfounded rumors circulated by irresponsible persons. We hope this action will not cause undue inconvenience.

Banks get saved. Allan knew that last Sunday night Fenwick had caused armored trucks to move; by Monday morning money was piled up on the counters of the tellers' cages for the hysterical and the skeptical to make note of; every check, every draft and withdrawal slip was honored with a smile and a flourish, so that by noon the rumors Great Lakes was going under had broken up and blown away. But there were enough other banks in trouble to divert the anxious attention of the dwindling number of solvent Americans.

"You'll break the glass if you hit it like that, lady," a man next to the inconsolable woman told her. "You wouldn't want to hurt yourself," he said.

Allan looked at the woman, a small thing with a beret for a hat, her hair pulled into a chignon on the back of her head, mother-of-pearl comb holding it in place. She would not leave her position by the door. The great Sam Insull had had to flee—the papers said he was living a royal life in Istanbul because Turkey did not have an extradition treaty with the United States. The commercially failed, the economically dishonored were all around them. Allan's father was not the only ex-millionaire in Winnetka living in his gardener's cottage.

The woman banged on the glass again. On the other side, a man, his suit coat off, his waistcoat unbuttoned, appeared in the glare and the gloom. "There're people in there!" someone behind Allan called out. "Form a line," someone else ordered, but instead the crowd pushed inward.

"Careful now!"

"Hey, watch out!" The people lurched in convulsive disorder; the woman, her beret squashed out of place, was shoved in front of Allan, who grabbed her and kept her from going down. He tried to guide her away from the crowd. "No, I'll lose my place in the line," she said, but there was no line, there was no place, there was no money.

Allan and the woman were free of the crowd. The people in front of the bank had quieted, compacting themselves against the barrier, scared, hoping, hopeless. "Money in the bank! Good as money in the bank! Safe as money in the bank! Oh, dear lord, that's what they used to say."

Allan saw his father in his new life too, learning how to drive an automobile, how to garden. Elting talked about gardening, his "civic work." In happy tones he told Allan, "Regardless of what happened I have not given up on the colored people . . . as a race."

"I had my husband's insurance in that bank. Twenty-eight hundred dollars and the nine hundred I'd saved myself. That's what I thought I had, but I don't have enough to buy my groceries. I can't go to the grocery store."

"Take this," Allan said to the woman, finding a ten-dollar bill.

She looked at it, shook her head no. "I don't want *your* money. I want *my* money. What have they done with us?" She moved away. Now she was crying. She moved toward Allan again. "I'll pay you back." She took the money, walked away, stood still; Allan watched her going down the street, stopping strangers, throwing her arms out, moving on, stopping someone else.

Allan was on Lawrence Avenue stalking Mona in the cold winter morning, hoping to catch her when she went out. She had promised him a last time.

"Look, pal," Andy said after Allan had gotten him to phone Mona the second time, "she don't want to talk to ya, and you don't want to be with her 'cause that husband of hers is gonna kill ya. Can't you get that straight?"

Allan could not get that straight. Mona had promised one more time and she owed him as much. Mona had gotten him into the hotel; she had set up their complicated system of deception. She had. She starts it, she stops it, he comes when she wants and goes when she doesn't. She owed him one more time. Allan remembered her body. She owed him. He remembered their lovemaking and their idle hours on the bed, drinking, smoking, talking, and felt hurt and hungry.

Also Mona had information he could not get from anyone else. He wanted to know how Crime Incorporated was going to kill Anton Cermak. He wanted the information not for his thesis but for his prestige, so he could drop it to the admiring astonishment of the seminar. He wanted them to believe that he had penetrated the innermost chambers of power.

Allan knew a score of lesser hoods, but the lesser hoods knew no more than what was the talk of the bookie joints and taverns. They knew the Mayor had bought several bulletproof vests; they knew he had moved out of the Congress Hotel to a penthouse on top of the Morrison. It was accessible only by one private elevator, which was guarded by the Mayor's police detail. That was the unit to which Detective Sergeant George Breed, who had drilled Mr. Nitti, was assigned, a unit where it would be hard to place a traitor. The fraternity of wise guys and inside dopesters could not imagine how the retaliation could be accomplished. No man could get close to the Mayor, and a long-range assassination, a distant rifleman with a telescopic sight on a hunting piece, was not the way of Mr. Nitti and his associates. Artistic but complicated, too many elements to be timed to pull off such a tour de force. The organization killed close up, point-blank; it left powder burns; it preferred firepower to finesse; it was bloody, brutal, and tight-in. It did not execute; it destroyed.

Allan had tried to get through to Mona by phone, but she had told the hotel switchboard not to put through any calls from him. She did call Andy, though, to order him to tell Allan he was never to do that again. Stamping in the February cold, red-faced and purposeless, he decided he would have to make Andy make Mona talk to him.

Andy was not feeling compliant. He had his own problems. The reward for his services had not been forthcoming. His body had not completely healed; he had a tooth that would have to be replaced, and there was Chip. "Show 'im the ropes," Zep had said when Andy had arrived at the cigar store of a morning set for work. "This here's Chip. I want you to show 'im how the operation works. Ya know I'm gonna lose ya, Andy. They're gonna give ya a real good job. Gonna get what's comin' to ya."

But it didn't feel right, Zep acting like a regular guy. Since the kidnapping he had been acting like a shit. What was with this guy? It was of Zep and Chip that Andy wanted to talk as they sat in the Clark Street speakeasy trying to drink the terrible beer. It was non-organization, Roger the Dodger beer, with flakes in it and a funny taste.

"So what am I supposed to do about it?" the man behind the bar asked, arms akimbo. "I buy the beer they sell me. I'm gonna tell the lieutenant I'm not buying no more Police Department beer? Tell Ten

Percent Tony to shut me down if he don't like it? Drink the flakes, 'cause it's the only beer you're gonna get around this town till things change, if ya know what I mean."

They knew what he meant. Everybody was waiting.

The *Nourmahal,* Vincent Astor's 263-foot ocean liner, turned its bow northeastward as it moved through the warm swordfish and marlin water of the Caribbean, pointing for Miami. His principal guest was a sun-tanned and happily fished-out President-elect. On the bounding blue catching his fish, eating and drinking with some of his Harvard chums, he had escaped from the men asking for patronage and favors.

He had been seen off at the dock in Jacksonville by Ed Flynn, Democratic boss of the Bronx. Flynn had stood at dockside, waving goodbye to this man he had worked and strained to elect, and wondered if the others had been right. Franklin Roosevelt might be a fatheaded squire from Dutchess County. A gentleman in a blinding striped blazer, with the moniker of George St. George, was by the Hyde Park farmer's side. Ed Flynn thought of what was happening in the country; news was reaching them that Maryland had closed its banks and ten more states were planning to do the same in the next twenty-four hours. And lo, off into tropical southeastern seas sails the Hudson Valley patroon on Astor's yacht with that idiot in stripes. The boss of the Bronx allowed himself to mutter, "Lord have mercy! The Hasty Pudding Club puts out to sea!"

In Chicago, Illinois Central train number 5, the *Floridan,* all-Pullman service to Miami, moved out of Central Station with Anton J. Cermak occupying the bedroom suite in car 9. He had four detectives from his special detail in compartments on either side of him. The Mayor was one of the importuners, going south to beg the President for jobs, for money to pay the cops, the teachers, and the street sweepers.

The *Floridan* made a stop in the city to pick up South Side passengers at the 53rd Street station, where four more men from the Mayor's detail got on the train at either end and walked through, rudely opening the doors of occupied bedrooms, searching for murderous riffraff. In compartment B, car 11, they rousted Louis ("Little New York") Campagna, he who had been with Frank Nitti the night of the shooting, he who, it was said, had been brought in from the East to do the job on the man in the bedroom suite of car 9.

Little Louis had his constitutional rights violated when he and his baggage were taken off the train. A Railway Express Agency wagon handler on the platform, looking up into the window of car 9, could see a man—he did not know he was a detective—enter the Mayor's suite; he saw him tell the Mayor something and saw the Mayor slap him on the back and laugh; then he could see the Mayor talking to someone out of sight as he took his suit coat off and began unlacing a bulletproof vest.

A brakeman, one foot on the steps of the club car at the end of the train, one foot swinging free, held a handrail and, leaning out over the platform, waved a signal flag as he called out his last "All aboard!" The engine gave a volcanic hiccup; the car couplings banged into each other and pulled taut. The wagon handler saw the Mayor tilt slightly off balance from the jarring of the locomotive as someone handed him a highball.

The wagon handler did not see two men jump on board car 7 as the *Floridan* began to accelerate for the run twelve hundred miles southeast to Miami.

"OK, you muff diver," Andy said to Allan with a tincture of affection. "In five minutes you walk over to the phone booth, close it, and wait for it to ring. When it does . . . don't ever say I didn't do nothing for you." It was several days later, and the two young men were in the same Clark Street speakeasy.

Andy's morale had improved. Zep had told him that his reward was coming through; a guy had died and the organization was going to let him take over a small betting parlor around Milwaukee Avenue and Halsted Street. "It's all Polacks and quarter bets, but it's my chance. I'm on my way, pal. This time next year the suit on my back is gonna be just as good as yours, Al. What do you think of that?"

Allan didn't think anything of that. His mind was on Mona.

When the phone rang, Allan was in the booth. "You said once more . . . we were going to see each other one more time."

"You can't understand it's too dangerous, can you?"

"I guess not." Allan was disappearing in his cigarette haze, but Andy knew what they were saying.

"All right. Tomorrow afternoon, same time, same station, like they say on the radio. Gunner's outa town."

"Well, where did he go?" Allan was demanding.

"That's for me to know and for you to find out, Allan. I know when I'm being pumped, ya know."

"Where did he go, Mona?"

"You're a shit, Allan. For your information he and Sam Hunt have gone south. Sam brought his golf clubs and Jack took his violin. I guess they went on a vacation." Mona laughed. "It sounds like a vacation to me."

"What are you talking about, Mona?"

"You're so dumb, Allan. I'm not telling you anything else."

"I don't get it. Tell me, Mona. Please."

"'I-don't-get-it.' That's your middle name, Allan." She told him about their using Little New York as a decoy. "And I guess you don't get that too, huh? . . . Don't answer. See ya tomorrow. Tell Andy I'll come by for my key around noon."

But Allan did get it. He knew Sam Hunt was called Golf Bag in recognition of his keeping a sawed-off shotgun in one; he knew violin was slang for machine gun. If they couldn't get Cermak in Chicago, they would bag him out in the open in Miami. He could not be protected on a golf course or someplace like that. They needed only to stalk him till they could take a good shot. The Mayor was going to die in Miami.

"They're going to rub out Cermak in Miami," Allan told Andy.

"Everybody knows that," Andy replied. "Nitti's people have got one of the Mayor's bodyguards on the payroll."

"Everybody knows that," Allan said.

"Who told ya?" Andy wanted to know. "Mona?"

"I have a lot of sources of information."

"You do, do you? Who shot Jake Lingle, if you know so much."

Instead of answering, Allan looked down into the beer mug to determine if the flakes had sunk to the bottom. It was too dark to tell. "Jake Lingle . . ." Allan said in a dreamy way. "I saw Jake Lingle get shot." He told the story of the Randolph Street underpass and ended by saying, "I had a lot to learn back then."

Andy gave him a look.

"I didn't know how anything worked." For that Allan got a second look. "Now I know, but I can't tell anybody."

"You better not," Andy said, but Allan was contemplating tomorrow afternoon with Mona and then tomorrow evening with Irena. He did not like to see them close together. The tricks he had taught himself to skip around his disloyalty failed him when he saw them back to back; and Mona exhausted him.

"Can you swing by the Stevens and get the hotel key before you go to work? Mona wants to pick it up around noon."

"Oh, Christ!"

"It's the last time. It really is."

"Last time you said it was the last time."

Allan bent over to examine a large beer spill on the bar before it got cleaned up. "The last time. I mean it this time."

The *Floridan* was taking on water and a fresh crew in Carbondale. In a compartment of car 7 Sam Hunt and the Gunner had taken their suit coats off; their waistcoats were unbuttoned; they both wore suspenders. Sam was looking in the lavatory mirror while, outside on the platform below, the station crews were checking the cars for hot journal boxes, loading on ice and provisions. The Gunner had a joke book in his hand and was saying, "Hey, Sam, lemme read ya this one."

"Don't start with that shit, Gunner."

"One more. The last time."

Golf Bag leaned into the mirror and pulled down his lower eyelid. "I got a fuckin' cinder in my eye," he said.

The diaphragm had stayed in Irena's dresser drawer where she had put it the day she got it. As her life with Allan had patterned itself, she would have to make some specific indication that she had changed her mind about making love, and Irena did not know how to do that. He did not talk about the subject with her. The night of the engagement ring in the Drake Hotel dining room remained with Irena. She remembered his discomfort after she had said, "Now you can pet me."

Irena brought up the impasse with Salvation Winthrop, who said spontaneity was important for some lovers. Unplanned, secret, misty and sudden. She began thinking how to manage an arranged surprise. She thought of whispering in his ear at the end of an evening at Uncle Fenwick's that Allan could visit her in her bedroom after the house had fallen asleep, but she was not sure she wanted to have it, as the sign said, the first time under Fenwick's roof. He would know what they had done when he looked at them the next morning and it would be like him to say something embarrassing. Irena wanted the first time, above all, to be romantic.

She did not want to be whispering to Allan, "Shhh! Somebody'll hear." She might be noisy herself. When at last they had petted—on the street in Allan's car, with Irena sure a cop would rap his nightstick

254

on the window to tell them to stop—she had heard her own breath gasping out of her mouth, had felt a power, physical and emotional, that made her more sympathetic to Allan. Irena had almost allowed him to undress the top part of her in the car; she knew she had used up the last of her Please, no, Allans, so what must it be like for the man, whose force and feelings were so much stronger than the woman's?

Irena began to think of Allan as the gentlest of lovers. It was a sign of his love for her that he had made so few demands, that he had not tried to force himself on her. She remembered the foreman at Swift's and wondered if she had understood the word passion. Irena began to ask herself if she had been considerate of Allan, and she also began, for the first time, to imagine Allan's hands on her body. Talking circumspectly of her imaginings and sensations to Salvation Winthrop, she stopped, looked at the older woman, and said on a rising note, "I guess there is a female animal too."

Salvation laughed and replied, "You're ready."

Salvation's way was to make a sour face when saying something sweet.

"I'm not going to be here next weekend. Why don't you and Allan make it your lovers' bower?" On Monday she made her offer of the apartment; on Tuesday she was talking about candlelight; on Wednesday she was saying, "Why don't you kids use my bedroom? My grandmother spent her wedding night in that bed, and her marriage lasted fifty years." Thursday the two of them decided on a dinner menu too simple to spoil. Salvation would make the salad dressing and leave it in the Kelvinator refrigerator; Salvation appeared with a set of lace-trimmed sheets for the bed. "I never had a chance to use them," she said.

Irena thought how lucky she was. For that minute the Depression outside vanished. She was happy the sheets would be used as they were intended, for Friday night, whatever formal ceremonies might come later, would be her wedding night. "Thank you," she said to Salvation Winthrop, who looked at Irena's face, appreciating the light in it.

"I hope this works for you, Irena dear."

For twenty cents a night, the last of Joe's money from the diner, Mrs. Molina provided a clean and tidy private room and, on this day, a misdelivered copy of the *Miami News*. Joe made out from it that the yacht *Nourmahal* would be docking in the evening and around nine o'clock the President-elect would ride up the palm-lined boulevard to Bay Front Park, where he would make a short talk to the two or three thousand people expected to be there. It was to be more of a reception than a rally; there would be other dignitaries such as Mayor Anton J. Cermak of Chicago. Mr. Roosevelt's time in the city would be short; after the reception he would take his private railroad car to Washington, D.C., for his inauguration.

Joe tore the article out of the paper. He undid the cords of his bundle roll and found Mr. D'Amico's revolver; he looked at it closely, rotated the chambers. In each cylinder he saw a bullet.

"Chip!" It was Zep's voice, wheezing and squeezing through the glass and chrome door behind the cigar counter, "I wantcha ta take this over to Mike Hanlon's in the Recorder of Deeds office." When Chip and his envelope were gone, Zep addressed a man studying the array of cigar boxes displayed in the cases. "OK, Sylvester, he's all yours. He's in there alone. Like I said, she was in to get the key half an hour ago. Jus' like they always do, those two."

Sylvester and his companion, both in double-breasted overcoats and fedoras, came around back of the counter and went into the room where Andy was talking on the phone to the customers and writing down their bets in his bookie's shorthand code. The companion took the receiver out of Andy's hand and reached over his shoulder to hang up the phone. "Up!" Sylvester said.

"Hey, pal, whatever this is, you got the wrong guy," Andy said, his words carried on frightened breath.

"Empty your pockets," Sylvester said.

"I work for Zep. Ask 'im."

Andy put the contents of his pockets on the table: penknife, three one-dollar bills, one silver quarter, three copper pennies, a rabbit's foot, and Allan's key to room 711 of the Stevens Hotel. Sylvester shook his head slowly from one side to the other and picked up the key by the point, so that the paddle with the room number and hotel's name embossed on it dangled at Andy's eye level.

"You got more balls than a bandit," Sylvester told him, "bangin' Jack McGurn's wife." The three stood looking at each other. Then Sylvester said, "Come on, dead meat," but he did not speak the words harshly. He said them with affection, like a lover conducting his mate into the bedroom.

Allan got to the Stevens late. The crime had come and gone, discovered by a maid entering 711 to bring towels and put two gold-wrapped chocolates on the pillows. The woman had come out screaming, holding her wounded eyes. The house detective, the one who had called the police, said he had not seen anything so awful in the trenches in France during the Great War.

When Allan came out of the elevator, the same mixture of officialdom and journalism he had seen after Jake Lingle's murder had reassembled itself in the corridor. Puzzled, Allan made his way through the men and their cigars; he thought there must have been a fire in one of the rooms; these men shouting and running around would spoil it for him and Mona. Their last time together canceled. Maybe it was better; Allan's libido was in remission.

"I wouldn't even take no picture of it," a photographer said, holding his Speed Graphic with the big flash reflector on top of it. "They ain't gonna use no pictures of what's in that room."

The words were going into Allan's ears but he wasn't hearing them. As he made his way down the hall, Allan could see that the center of the excitement was near where he supposed room 711 was. It was going to be impossible for him and Mona. End it. Never again going to Irena with a touch of Mona's perfume about him. Have a drink, say goodbye, but he could see the center of the comings and goings was not near room 711; it was 711. Allan made a fast move forward, bumping into a young policeman who looked doubtfully at him.

"You gonna go in there?"

"I thought so."

"Jaysus! I wouldn't. They haven't taken her head down yet. It's still where those bastards left it hanging." Allan took in the star on the policeman's uniform. His badge number was 711. "Not me. I wouldn't go in there. They say the guy's nuts are in her mouth. What kind of an animal would do a thing like that?" The numbers on the star were raised. The badge must have been die cast, not engraved. "How could somebody do that to another person? They say she was a beautiful woman. Young. Built," the 711th cop said. How many policemen does Chicago have, anyhow? "I wouldn't go in there 'less the sergeant ordered me. Hey, what paper are you with, buddy?"

"The *Tribune.*"

"They sent a lot of you guys out on this one, didn't they?"

"It sells papers," Allan said, backing away.

"Don't that beat it all to hell? The public wanting to read about an awful thing like this?"

"It beats it all to hell," Allan agreed.

"Changed your mind . . . not goin' in, huh?" star number 711 asked.

"Not going in there," Allan answered, pushing his way back through the men and their cigars and cameras toward the elevators.

Dialing Andy's number downstairs in a lobby phone booth, Allan had finger tremors; a great fear was growing up in him. He needed Andy. He needed this explained, but Chip answered the phone. "Mousmoulis ain't here no more. . . . Nah, I don't know where the guy went. He quit. You wanta bet on a horse?"

Seven'll get ya eleven. He quit? Andy wouldn't quit. The hand on the telephone receiver was jerking. Allan could see the tips of two fingers being jumped by a fearful and horrified nerve. "Heebie-jeebies, I've got the heebie-jeebies. The jitters!" Allan said aloud. His finger tremors were turning into shakes. He sucked air and rigidified himself in the booth, tensed his body to bring his limbs back under control.

Another nickel in the slot; he dialed the cigar store again. "Zep, please. . . . He's there, let me talk to him. . . . Then gimme Mousmoulis' phone number. . . . Well, fuck you too!" They weren't giving out Andy's phone number because he had gone to Milwaukee Avenue and they didn't want him taking any of their customers.

Allan drove the coupe off to the world of Milwaukee Avenue, of butcher shops with whole dripping chickens hanging in the windows, bakeries displaying cakes and pastries of exotically Eastern European shape and coloring. Babushka-land, Polish and Ukrainian and Serbian women with string bags and packages, and baroque basilicas, high bell towers of scalloped cornice. No Andy that he could see from these crowded winter sidewalks.

The car was parked on Noble Street. Allan got in it, started the motor, and wiped the inside front window clear of fog so that he could see his way to drive out of this place. As he released the brake, he screamed, *"Who was the man?"* The shakes returned. If the other man was not Andy, where was Andy? If it was Andy, why was he in the room? Oh, my God, Mona. Think about Andy. Who could do that to her? Think about Andy. Her head? Star 711 had said her head. But McGurn was in Florida.

He got the car out into the stream of traffic splashing on slushy streets. Had they mentioned *his* name before they died? What did the killer know? He drove north toward Winnetka, forgetting he did not live there any more, rubbing the mist off the inside of the front window with a coat sleeve, hearing car wheels swish through the slush, braking, shifting gears, executing the mechanical tasks until he came to the gates and saw the gardener's cottage, a light within. A picture of Sunday evening prayer services presented itself, baritone-voiced lions of the pulpit. What the hell did they know? He swung the car away. Allan wasn't going to do *that*, he told himself. Ribbons of words, meaningless to Allan, were moving in his mind.

He walked into the main drawing room at Uncle Fenwick's and demanded money from his mother. Immediately. A lot of it. Special reasons, special purposes and urgencies. She got him a wallet full of Fenwick's money and gave it to him when he stood in front of her with a suitcase.

"There's a sock sticking out. Why don't you let me repack that case?"

Allan kissed her on the cheek.

"Irena telephoned. Twice."

"Call her and tell her I'm on my way."

"You're acting like you're escaping from an insane asylum."

"Eloping!"

"If you're going to the tropics, you may not want woolies."

"Who said anything about the tropics?"

He was hours late at Irena's. He had no flowers in hand when she, bathed and perfumed, admitted him. He looked awful but she could not see it, taking a hand and leading him into the living room. Irena kissed Allan, first on the cheek and then on the lips. He put down his suitcase.

Irena yanked at his overcoat while he grabbed for the afternoon newspaper.

POLICE BAFFLED
Mutilated Couple Found in Hotel Room

Chicago police had no clues tonight in the grisly slayings of a young man and woman found in a Loop hotel room. "This is a mixture of a crime of passion with gangland methods," said Lt. Edwin Hurlihy of the Homicide Squad. Police have not been able to learn the names of the victims, evidently

tortured to death, since it appears the killer removed every
identifying clue.

Slay, slaying, slew. They do it in the Bible and they do it in Chicago.
Allan asked Irena for a drink. He had to get out of town. She offered
wine but Allan said no, he needed a drink drink, he would go out to a
bootlegger's and get whiskey. She got him some whiskey from the
cabinet. "Allan, I don't want you to drink a lot. This is"—Irena softened her bossy line—"a special night."

"I guess so," Allan replied.

"It *is*. You'll see." But it was not going as Irena had imagined the
evening. It was after nine, the baked potatoes were rocks, the lettuce
had wilted under a premature application of the salad dressing Salvation had made up, and she was daunted by the two steaks lying raw
under the broiler. She had pictured them as the couple in the *Saturday
Evening Post* advertisements for Waterford crystal. She lit the can-
dles, but she could see from looking at Allan they were not going to
whisper their love to each other. It was not going to be that kind of a
night, not at first, but later on . . . afterward . . . they would speak
their hearts.

Allan could tell the whiskey was having no effect on him; he was
not going to be able to get drunk. He had to get out of Chicago.

"I want to run away—elope," he told her as they embraced,
cradling her head by his cheek. "Now . . . in Indiana . . . tonight.
We'll go on to New York and we'll go to Europe. We can fly to New
York. I've never done it—flying—and neither have you." He spoke,
caressing Irena in frantic circular rubs.

"Allan, dearest Allan, I do love you. I'll elope, but not tonight.
Not to Europe." Irena gave him little kisses over his face.

"Tonight," Allan repeated.

No, she had classes to teach, he had a thesis to write, they had
responsibilities.

"Will you shut up, will you please shut up, please, and let me do
the talking?"

Mona's phrase. Irena recognized its familiarity but not whose it
was. Allan did and it made him pause. He shut up and, frightened by
the clue he might have given, kissed Irena with a simulated passion to
which she gave an unsimulated response. Her ardor transferred to
him. Allan lost himself grabbing her, clutching, jerking, snatching.
His clutchiness was not the gentle loving she wanted of him, but she
could hear her breath answering his gasps with hers.

260

"No, Allan, not here, not with the lights on." Irena thought of the bed, a flower in a bud vase beside, left by Salvation Winthrop. "Shhhh," she hushed, "hold me for a minute."

Irena had dressed without a brassiere. He stood behind her, Irena's head twisting around to put her mouth on his, Allan's arms hooked under hers, his fingers squeezing her. She felt so different under his touch than Mona. Mona! His desire deflated in a groan Irena misunderstood.

"Come with me, Mr. Allan," she said, taking him by the hand and starting them in the direction of the bedroom. Then she stopped and hugged him and whispered, "Please, be patient with me. I don't know how." Allan kissed her hair and Irena, struck by a thought, leaped a little way from him and said laughingly, "You must be very experienced, Mr. Allan, aren't you?" He leaned toward her and kissed her hair again. "What does that mean? Oh, Mr. Allan, you have to tell me if you've been with other women. . . . Have you?"

"Have I what?"

"What I said."

"One."

"Tell me about her. Did you do it just once with her? Or more? Who was she? Do I know her? Is she very pretty? Is she older? What's she like?"

"Stop it, Irena, will you stop it. Stop it, *stop it!*" He was shouting, shrieking.

"What's wrong with you, Allan? Ever since you got here—" Irena did not finish her sentence. She walked into the bedroom, slammed the door, sat on the bed, and began to cry.

Allan found the whiskey bottle, poured himself another drink, looked at it and did not drink it, but opened the bedroom door, slipping in and over to Irena. With his arms around her he drew her back against his chest so that he could whisper, "I'm sorry."

"Allan, what is it? You can tell me. You're so unhappy. What's happened to you? I want to make you happy." She turned in his arms, kissed him fully on his lips, his eyelids, his cheeks, frank, enfevered kisses. "Tell me. I don't care what it is. Tell me. I love you."

"They're going to kill Mayor Cermak. I know who."

"Is *that* what's bothering you? Allan, it's rumors, street gossip."

"No, Gunner and Sam Hunt, they're on the way. Maybe they're in Miami already."

"Phone! Now! Phone!"

"Phone who? Who phone? Andy said—" Allan stopped in mid-flight. "He said," he went on, speaking slowly, "that Nitti has a man on the police bodyguard detail."

"You have to warn him, Allan."

"Can't, unless we can get to the Mayor himself."

"Then we'll go!" Irena ordered him. "We've got to." She packed while Allan on the telephone discovered passenger airplanes did not fly at night, and as for trains, the fast ones south had left. For passengers wishing to depart Chicago at midnight, it was a milk train.

The ticket agent leaned close to the brass wicket to let them know the State of Florida had closed the banks. He sold them two two-foot-long tickets for the run to Indianapolis, where they would change trains for Louisville, where they would change trains for Atlanta, where they could board the Southern Railway's *Royal Palm,* travel in a fine private compartment, bathe, and order food.

"We could be married there," Irena said as they jounced shoulders through Indiana and talked of how they might find a justice of the peace, which, given their Protestant-Catholic problem, might be for the best. They bounced on woven straw seats and Allan put what he was fleeing from his mind; Irena decided she did love him though he had wrecked tonight as he had wrecked every single romantic evening she had counted on.

The train out of Indianapolis was late and uncomfortable. It dated from forty years earlier, was made of wood, and was heated by a little stove into which the conductor fed a scoop of coal from time to time. He told them the company had rationed him to three pounds of coal for the distance to Louisville. "Can't blame 'em hardly. You two are the only revenue we're carrying tonight . . . the banks an' all; what's it coming to?"

Allan and Irena did not know.

"When are folks going to wake up?"

Allan and Irena could not say.

They jolted next to each other, taking what sleep they could. The morning paper in Louisville had the headline:

HEINOUS CRIME IN CHICAGO!

Allan did not read underneath, falling into a drowsing sleep of memory. Oh, God; oh, Mona and Andy too.

In the dawn Allan woke with a startlement that Irena could feel

262

through the violently rocking railroad car. She opened her eyes to see Allan, a look of facial paralysis holding his features. She reached up and over to touch him.

In their compartment on the *Royal Palm* Irena fell asleep in the upholstered armchair even before the train had left the station in Atlanta. Allan smoked, collecting himself to think through what he was doing. The train was now running through the flat citrus country of central Florida; in Jacksonville the state editions of the Miami papers had been thrown aboard, telling of President-elect Roosevelt's visit. Since they did not know where Cermak was staying, the Bay Front Park ceremony was the one place they could go to find him.

Mrs. Molina gave Joe one of her dead husband's ties. She smiled and Joe smiled back. She sewed a button on his shirt and helped him tie it before he went out with the revolver in his pocket. He shoved and wiggled his way to the front of the crowd, close in to the reviewing stand. People were telling each other who the bigwigs were. "There's a revolution coming in this country," a woman in gloves and floppy straw hat said to her companion, who nodded and asked, "Is that man, the portly one, isn't he the Mayor of Chicago?"

The *Nourmahal* had docked and Governor Roosevelt in a white suit was riding in the lead car for the trip down the dark sea-girt boulevard to Bay Front Park. The automobile was an open touring car. Behind him was another filled with Secret Service men; then came the one in which Mr. Astor and other friends rode.

An ocean breeze stirred the palms in greeny blackness. Vincent Astor said he did not like this drive. It was too easy a stretch for assassination. He would feel better when they got to the lights and the people waiting for them in the park.

"Will Gunner be at this park? The park where the Mayor's going? . . . Turn around so I can fix myself, please," Irena said.

What had Mona and Andy said before they died? If they had named him to the man who had done the murders, if he had phoned Gunner, then God! he was running straight into Gunner's sights, going to the place where Gunner would be. He was going to his own killing, to his slaying . . . gangland style. Slay, slaying, slew. They slew them by the hundreds in Chi town, one by one in Miami under the palms.

"He'll recognize me!" Forgetting he had been told to look the other way, he turned toward her and saw her naked to the waist and lovely. Irena gave a little shriek and twisted her back to him. "Allan! I told you not to look. I'm blushing."

"He'll recognize me! He'll see me! He'll know who I am!"

"What are you saying?" she asked, swaying as the train rolled through the steel frogs of a set of switches.

"I said I can't go. I can't go to Bay Front Park. He'll recognize me!" Allan was shouting in his fear. Holding her dress against her chest, Irena turned toward him, shouting in her own anger. "You can. You will, Allan!"

The *Royal Palm* was grinding steel, rattling chain, slowing down. The fear Allan had never had and that Mona had tried to put in him, the knowledge that he could be hurt, had now taken hold of him. Standing face to face, he shouted room 711 to her. His voice bursting, he told Irena the story with incoherent speed, his words driving her down to her knees, her face in a chair seat, her fists pushing into her eyes. When he finished, standing over her, swaying with the Pullman car, Irena was crying. Not a sob, not a gulp, a sustained calling cry, a beseeching cry of sorrow.

Allan moved to comfort her; he told her as gently as he could, "Will you please shut up, Irena, will you, please?" She remembered the phrase, whose it was, and getting to her feet, went into the little lavatory. She leaned her face against a steel-riveted wall and cried harder and told herself in a hoarse voice, "I hate him."

When she came out of the lavatory, Irena was composed. She took out her compact and worked at getting the red out of her eyes and off the end of her nose. She said nothing to Allan, and Allan, in the thrall of his new fear and knowledge, said nothing to her.

The affair at Bay Front Park would be starting momentarily. Irena quickly assembled her things and, suitcase in hand, was ready to leave as the *Royal Palm* came to a stop at its Miami terminal.

"Your friend," Irena said at the compartment door, "and the woman you love have been murdered, Allan. I'm going to warn Mayor Cermak so it doesn't happen to him. You can come or not as you please."

Allan said nothing.

"Two is enough," she told him and, heaving up her suitcase, she walked out the door. He began to follow her but changed his mind, too ashamed to pursue.

When he changed his mind again and arrived at the taxi line there was no sight of her. He told himself he loved her, that he would tell the police about Mona and Andy, that he would be better. Against his fear, Allan ordered his taxi driver to hurry.

Irena's cab reached Bay Front Park while Roosevelt was speaking. She was on the edge of the mob, trying to get through it with her suitcase. Her beauty came to her aid. A policeman saw her struggling and, taking the suitcase, helped her to a place off to the side but in front of the crowd, where "Y'all be able to see the whole historic moment, miss."

Joe saw clearly. He could see past and future, armies climbing down the Alps, he could see cruelty and disfigurement, he could see humiliation and hunger, the lines of men in overcoats. He was composed.

Joe saw, but the people listening to the speaker did not see him. Joe took the revolver out of his pocket. Irena had not been able to locate the Mayor. When she did, she abandoned her suitcase and ran toward him. She ran out of Joe's line of fire and almost into another one.

Allan, who had followed, had seen Gunner in the crowd and had seen him grasp the lucky chance, watched him take out his piece the instant Joe gave him covering fire.

Allan saw Irena dancing across the floodlit grass, dancing through the blue smoke of cigarettes and revolvers, of shrieks and of falling people. He saw her go down as he saw Cermak go down. He ran to Irena and threw himself on her to protect her. But the need to do so had passed. Joe had been disarmed and the Gunner was gone.

Irena rolled over, and only after pushing Allan away did she recognize him. Her face was contorted. She looked at the Mayor, his shirt soaked with blood, wounded to the death. She saw the President-elect's touring car back up and heard his voice, the one that came through the cloth speakers of the radios, directing the Secret Service men to bring the Mayor to him. She saw Franklin Roosevelt lean out the door and help drag Cermak in. The car moved off, whipped forward by the shouts and orders of the bodyguard, Roosevelt holding the dying Mayor in his arms.

"I love you, Irena. I do. I do."

"Oh, go to hell, Allan, go to hell."

EPILOGUE ———————————————————————

As she climbed down the high steps of the *Lake Shore Limited,* all-Pullman service from Boston, onto the platform of the La Salle Street Station, Irena watched a crowd of a hundred or so women besieging and beseeching the door to one of the cars of the *Twentieth Century Limited,* soon to depart for New York. Their shouts echoed off the cast iron and glass tracery of the train shed; Irena noted there were newspaper photographers among the women and a large motion picture camera from Movietone News.

"Robert Taylor, miss, the movie star," Irena's redcap explained. "They been here since six o'clock this morning."

"Oh!" Irena said. "I want to watch."

Irena remembered that women had done the same with Rudolph Valentino back in the twenties. The twenties. In a few days they would be eight years away, not so long a time in the short recounting of a human life and yet so much a part of a lost America that Irena read articles about the Roaring Twenties as though she were discovering the world of her grandmother's childhood. Years of honest graft and wonderful nonsense. That small mob of women jumping up and down around the movie star, pleading for what?—autographs, kisses, locks of his slicked-down hair? Could they be the vanguard of fun returning?

Irena inhaled. Mixed with the air of the train shed, the exciting flavor of travel, Irena thought she smelled the zest of Chicago. This was her first time back since the spring of 1933, when she had said thank you and goodbye to Mr. Park and Salvation Winthrop and her other friends to move to Wellesley. Chicago was connected to Allan in her mind, and she liked New England. She had brought Steffy to visit several times but Steffy hadn't liked it; Robert, who did, came every

267

year, sometimes twice a year. After her grandmother died, Irena would have liked to have Robert live with her; several times she tried, but no. He was a burden on them, they made him unhappy, but no. They knew she wanted him and they united, even Steffy, against her getting him. Irena had been given too much; she wasn't getting any more, not from them. Irena had accepted living with no one to love and make over. She thought about a kitten, but the substitution of animals for the affection of people was a confession of hopelessness to her.

A woman who has Armand doesn't need a kitten. Armand Du-Plessis-Wigglesworth. Salvation Winthrop, who had gone to school with DuPlessis girls and to tea dances with Wigglesworth boys, had written, when Irena had told her friend that she was dating this professor of French and Italian literature, "Both families died out a generation before Armand was born. He's not a person, he's a family memory, a friendly flesh-and-blood ghost. I remember him when he was a little boy, an amiable, good-looking epicene wraith." To Irena he was also sweet, tirelessly helpful, attentive, intelligent, and perfect in his deportment; above all, he was loyal, which sometimes made her think of Allan.

Since leaving Chicago she had done another study, this time of the immigrant population of Haverhill. A university press had published it. Irena now wanted to immerse herself in an American subject: Hollywood.

No book by Allan Archibald, as far as she knew, on Chicago crime or anything else had been published. Looking out the cab window onto Van Buren Street, Irena was disappointed to find that the city looked as it had when she left it. She had imagined she was traveling back to the dynamo of the heartland but she could tell from the grayness of the people on the streets that last year's boomlet, the false spring of 1936, had been blasted here too. The name of the Mayor of Chicago, Irena taught herself, was now Edward Kelly. He was a Big Ed in the newspapers, but weren't they all?

It was the way that Armand DuPlessis-Wigglesworth had proposed that made her tell UCLA she was interested. UCLA, my dear, do they teach anything but cheerleading and automobile mechanics? You have a hope of making it from Wellesley to Williams or Amherst and then, another book or two, something spectacular, why not Columbia? No one who leaves for UCLA returns. Armand's proposal might have been entertainable if he had not made it so specific. To come with two dozen roses, to get down on your knees, and then to offer a "platonic" marriage. "After a few years, 'those things,'" he had said, "lose their appeal even with the most, well, 'active' couples."

She and Allan would have been an active couple. A Victorian etching. She had not seen Allan on his knees, except, except, in the compartment going to Miami, trying to explain, when he used Mona's expression. Ahead on Van Buren Street, Irena saw the patterns of sunlight coming through elevated tracks on the cobblestones. Allan had not been platonic. The cab turned left onto State Street, and Irena saw that she had doubled the index finger of one hand and was biting its joint.

Upstairs in her room at the Palmer House she lit a cigarette, lifted a grain of tobacco off her tongue, reminding herself that she had known coming back would give force to the emotions she had struggled to muffle. The girls she had gone to college with were married. Most of the men in the sociology department when she had been there were married. Allan had not been as attentive as Armand. There's not a wiggle's worth in him, a voice in Irena's head, an unfamiliar authoritative echo-chamber voice, told her. She got up from the chair and, cigarette between her lips, exhumed the accusation she had taken to making against herself. If they had made love, if she had understood how important it was . . . to her too, then Allan wouldn't have gone to Mona. They get their way or go away. The voice of finality interrupted: "Or they're faithful because they don't want anyone." Irena had spoken aloud, to her surprise.

Irena wrestled back into her galoshes, put on her coat; she walked into the winter morning, the wind blowing off the lake, across Michigan Boulevard, past the Art Institute in Grant Park, fields of off-white snow and gray ice. Off to the north she could see the Hires Root Beer sign, unilluminated in the daylight but its question still gigantically legible: HAVE YOU HAD IT LATELY?

At Wellesley they had been proud of the American Sociological Society's invitation to Irena to be a featured speaker at the convention. She would speak in the main ballroom of the Palmer House. Around the lobbies were small placards with her picture advertising her paper. "'Red-Brick Romanesque!'" she heard one of the sociologists say to his colleague. "'Ethnicity in a Yankee Mill Town.' Ha! I'd listen to a girl who looks like that read Dialogues with Donald Duck."

She went back up to her room trying to remember what Donald Duck's wife's name was. Minnie Duck? Daphne Duck? Darling Duck? Could Donald Duck be a bachelor? She felt the old anger against Allan. Armand DuPlessis-Wigglesworth-Duck! She would get through this reading, then down to Salvation's for dinner . . . and Allan would be there! It came on Irena as a certainty that Allan would be there. Salvation would have arranged it some way. "There is one person, one man, one woman, who is the love of our lives," Irena remembered Salvation saying. They were on the lake in Massachusetts with that impossible name: Chaubunagungamaugmaugagungachau-bungamungachaug. It had taken Salvation three days to teach it to Irena, laughing in the sailboat, talking in the summer vacation sun. Salvation had told Irena it was Chicopee for I-fish-on-my-side-you-fish-on-yours-and-we-both-fish-in-the-middle. "There is one person, one man, one woman, who is the love of our lives. We may lose him; he may die; we may leave him or he may leave us; we may marry someone else, we may not marry; but we're bonded to that one for-ever. Our heart's secret." So romantically unlike Salvation to talk that way, but it had put a tear in Irena's eye. We may lose him; he may die, but can we forgive him?

Irena went over the excerpts she would read; if Granny were still alive she would have invited the family, for it was a proud moment. They had not told Irena until after the funeral. Allan would be at Salvation's apartment, at the piano:

> You're the top!
> You're Mahatma Gandhi.
> You're the top!
> You're the National Gall'ry
> You're Garbo's sal'ry,
> You're cellophane.

Cellophane? Cole Porter was falling behind the times. Soon, Irena had read, silk stockings will be made from an artificial material. No more worms. You have forgiven him? the loud inner voice asked. He's not the top! Not the National Gall'ry, but she wanted to see him. What had Allan been doing? How was he? Irena knew he had dropped out of school, not much more. When Uncle Fenwick wrote he seldom mentioned Allan, and when he did it was to say he was "well." For five years Allan had been vaguely well. Five years! Had she punished Allan or herself? Salvation's apartment in Madison Park

would be as it was the weekend she had left it to Irena and Allan, and he would be there. He hadn't gotten married, Irena was sure. Salvation would have written. He would be there. He would be playing Cole Porter.

He was not seated at the piano. Allan was not there. Salvation had as many people as she could think of from Irena's time on campus, but not him. They toasted her, the book, her accomplishments, and they talked about where old friends were. Teaching at Michigan, gone to work for a government agency in Washington, young advisers to the New Deal, on leave of absence with a union organizing committee, two with the Loyalists in Spain. "You're not my generation," Salvation said, "but you're marvelous. We had the war and it was terrible. It made us cripples, but, my God, the Depression has been worse and you all are getting through it, you are doing things, all of you." And they were. They were as ardent as the times were drab. Even Irena had been caught up in politics to the extent that she had been invited to Washington to serve a summer in the Secretary of the Interior's office. She had become "that woman, you know, the one in Massachusetts, the one who knows all about foreign language groups."

The last to leave, Irena said her thanks, hugged her hostess, and said, "Oh, Sally, where is he?"

He was where he had been, more or less, since they had seen each other last. He was in the gardener's cottage playing cribbage with his father. They had come together in mute misunderstanding, young man and old man joined in an exile they did not discuss. Allan came over from Fenwick's to play cards or board games, bringing Alice. "She's somebody's cousin," he explained, somebody's poor cousin, cheerful in tedium, attentive in affection, hopeful in the awareness of the moneys coming to Allan some day. With Alice in the back seat, Allan drove Elting down to the Sunday Evening Club, where conservative Christianity forgathered to lift its voice and lend an ear to the homiletics of Calvinism.

While his father prayed, Allan and Alice went to the movies, usually to the Trans-Lux, the all-newsreel theater. "I don't want the world to pass me by," Allan said. At night, in the quiet of his uncle's mansion, Allan stayed up late. Some days Ottoline would dare ask if he had plans. "I have plans. I had them, but I wasn't prepared. I wasn't ready. I didn't know!" he would shout. Other nights he read

his fieldwork notes, his diaries, and his private journals. He had three sets of books on his life of that period; he had kept records on himself like a dishonest banker. The notes could be read by Mr. Park or anyone, the diaries had been for Irena, and the journal Allan had kept for himself alone. Some nights he took a day or an entry in one and compared what he had written in the others. He went back and forth over these ledgers of life, but they would not balance out.

August 27, 1932, he could trace the outer Allan, the one having coffee with Andy, interviewing the driver of a beer truck; he could trace the middle Allan showing off for Irena; and, for the same day, he could trace the inner Allan, the one who lay with Mona and who made his friend die in his place. The last half of the journal was blank pages, containing newspaper clippings of the murders. On the nights when he did these accounts he was up late, sometimes until dawn, and fell asleep taking the blame.

"Leave him alone," Fenwick told his sister. "He was hit by a meteor. He has been struck by a force from outside . . . nothing we know about."

Ottoline got Allan to a psychoanalyst. The second visit ended in shouting. The doctor had been trained in Vienna and was unused to being told by a patient that he did not know the difference between right and wrong. To Ottoline and Fenwick he explained the distinction between psychosis (untreatable) and neurosis (treatable). "I don't know what the hell that man is talking about," said Fenwick.

Allan made the first of his clandestine visits to the Paulist Order's instructional chapel in the dingy interstitial edge of the south end of the Loop. "The sacrament of penance," Allan said, when the priest asked what had interested him in the Catholic Church.

"I can't absolve you until after I baptize you," the priest whispered. But the creed would not come out of Allan's mouth. Too Presbyterian to utter *incarnatus est de Spiritu Sancto, ex Maria Virgine,* too despairing to say *exspecto resurrectionem mortuorum. Et vitam venturi saeculi* (I look forward to resurrection of the dead. And the life of the world to come)—too despairing for that.

"'Mr. and Mrs. Ely Culbertson,'" Allan read to his father and Alice from the *Chicago Daily News,* "'have decided to dissolve their marriage partnership, but will continue to play bridge from opposite sides of the table, they announced last night.' Oh, how the old order doth change." Allan's sardonic words hung in the room while Elting Archibald's fingers worked to fix the clacker on a cheap windup alarm

clock. "I think I can, Mr. Archibald," Alice said, and he gave it over to her in amiable gratitude for not having to fuss with it longer. The bald patches in his whitened hair had grown back; the fight and the anger had gone out of him last year when the papers carried the story of Sam Insull being found dead in a Paris subway with two dollars in his pocket. He told Allan not to ruin his life as he had; he was touched with an appealing, regretful feebleness; he had run all the audits he had had to run. Elting Archibald was reconciled.

The lawns outside the gardener's cottage were gray slush. Blades of grass came up through the thawing silvered confection. "The *Föhn*," Allan said to himself, surprised he could remember any German words. He fished in his pocket to see if he had his car keys when Alice came out with both their coats. "Stay there, I'll have them send a car over for you."

"Allan!"

"I'll phone you, Alice."

"If you leave me here, you needn't trouble."

"Then I won't phone you."

"Allan!" They stared at one another. "Say goodbye to your father, at least." He remembered the night she began to take off her clothes in the front seat of the car when he asked if she would sleep with him. He had not meant it and did not know why he had done it. Alice had had to reassemble herself untouched. "I'm sorry," Allan said now.

"I was telling Alice," Mr. Archibald explained, "that Franklin Roosevelt is the same as Woodrow Wilson. He won't fight. The Japs sink an American naval vessel and Roosevelt says he'll take money and apologies. That's the way Wilson was. Too proud to fight. Ha!" The U.S.S. *Panay*, an American gunboat, had been sunk on the Yangtze River in China a few days previously. "But there'll be a war anyway, and it'll be your chance."

"I've had my chance," his son told him and walked out the door again. Alice came after him, trying to put her coat on as she walked. "Alice, leave me alone. I'll send a car. Can't you see I can't be . . . I'm sorry, I can't be—leave me alone, please." He went off through the slush, got into his car, slammed the door, and could not think of where to go. A movie? Back to his room? To the ballroom at the Palmer House? He would be just in time to hear her. But he didn't go.

Allan did not hear her voice until the following morning. He was sitting very stiffly in the graduate student lounge, on the same sofa he had been lounging on the day of their walk. He was waiting for Irena to pass by the open door when she had finished her visit with Mr. Park. Salvation had phoned him.

There was no Cole Porter left in him, she saw that at once. The charming young man at the piano had been leached out of him.

"Come on," Irena said quietly. They walked the damp sidewalks cleaned of ice and snow by the *Föhn*. They did not speak; yet they walked arm in arm going down the Midway in the direction of Lorado Taft's statue of Time. A dank west wind, with a whiff of the stockyards, slapped their faces, blew hair in their eyes. At the base of the statue they came together, cheeks touched.

"No!" Irena said. She remembered seven years ago when they had taken this same walk together. Now look at him, she thought, how dried out, how overtaken. Now look at me. She grew angry again.

Allan also remembered the walk. Vas you dere, Cholly? Yes, Cholly, I went there. No, damn Cholly, I didn't *get* there, I didn't. I only got to look. I hurt people, Cholly, people get hurt. And I got hurt too, Cholly.

Allan reached into his pocket and gave her the journal, the sole accounting he had, his only explanation. "Read this," he said. "I want you to. . . ."

"I can't understand. I never will, Allan."

The statue dripped melting ice. "Please, just read it."

"Sometime . . . maybe . . ."

"Please. Take it with you."

"All right."

She looked in his face again, studied the lines around his eyes. "You have cobwebs, Allan."

"Crow's feet," Allan said.

Irena touched the lines with her finger. "Crow's feet," she said.